A Blues for
Shindig

A Blues for Shindig

MO FOSTER

PaperBooks

First published 2006 by PaperBooks
PaperBooks Ltd, Neville House, Station Approach
Wendens Ambo, Essex CB11 4LB
www.paperbooks.co.uk

ISBN 0 9551094 2 6
ISBN 978 0 9551094 2 3

1 3 5 7 9 8 6 4 2

A CIP catalogue record for this book is available from
the British Library.

Cover design by Chris Gooch – Bene Imprimatur Ltd

Typeset by SetSystems Ltd, Saffron Walden, Essex
Printed and bound in Great Britain by
Cox & Wyman, Reading

For the pox doctor's clerk
– and his overcoat.

1 Blues After Hours

Soho, the sexual apparatus of London, throbs away at all times. The London genitalia. We fester moistly in her midst, a rather smelly dump. It is 1956 and we are one of the dozens of clubs that exist to defeat the insane licensing laws.

'The Rendezvous Club' is a squalid little gaff off a slippery courtyard, decaying happily into itself. It will be vigorously revamped soon, but for now, having put all its effort into avoiding the bombing it is relaxing. Inside, when the dim red lights are in operation and the punters fill it with temporary warmth and the juke is going full blast, then it seems cosy. And Soho has far worse dives, clip joints where you can find yourself buying fizzy water for ungrateful girls who will lift your wallet as soon as look at you.

So, a little light robbery in the shape of high prices for low liquor really shouldn't be a cause for complaint. In fact it fulfils its function, which is to supply booze in the bleak desert of the afternoon when the pubs shut their doors, very tightly. The glasses are clean and the prices are within reason, just. You might be asked to sign in as it is supposed to be a private club, and a dog eared book full of Mickey Mouse names lives under the counter near to the door. Every now and then the law come round by previous arrangement and examine this book for a laugh. They also come round on a more regular basis to receive their bung, but I know nothing about this. I keep my head down when it comes to the law, I know how they can wantonly upset a girl's life and throw it into disarray.

When daylight filters and creeps its way through from the courtyard and hits the ancient seats and the bar, the dust that lives in every crease and crevice forms a grey, greasy skin and the walls look like potato blight in action. The cellar which is now used for storing booze and for rehearsal by a bunch of jazz musos, is particularly creepy. It throws up the slightly peppery stench of dry rot combined with yellow soap and

meths along with older, nastier smells that overlay the scent of
dope and resin. I reckon it was once a plague pit myself, and
the air has a way of moving around you when you're down
there.

Tiger, the governor, knows I am spooked by the place and will
milk it with graphic tales of suicides, dead babies, bodies found
bricked up in the walls. He is perfectly suited to this role. Built
like a wishbone, angular, with a face as sharp as a cut-throat
razor, stupendous stained ochre teeth and a spiv moustache, he
has the look of an elderly horse with a sense of humour. Tiger
had his eye on me for months before I worked there, but it was
a badly focused, slightly bleary eye. He'd oil up to me whenever
I went to his emporium to flog him dodgy liquor from the
American bases. I think he was attempting to captivate me with
his charm. His dedication to love was spasmodic and his chat-
up original.

'You're a good-looking bird, fantastic gams, bit lippy, but I
like that. Do yourself a favour, darling, I'll see you right. Do
the books for us. Come over to Le Mans with us if you want,
no need for the old woman to know. Think about it, doll.'

'No offence, Tiger, I'll give that one a miss.'

'Fair enough, gel!' So I feel his passion lacked urgency, and
once he realised that captivation wasn't a goer he gave me a
job in his club as barmaid.

'Wave yer legs about, dolly, keep the beer coming. You'll be
laughing,' he says.

In his favour, Tiger gives off a nice aroma of Lifebuoy and
his hands are scrupulously clean, which is a mercy.

At three or thereabouts the club jerks into vibrant sudden life
as the pubs close. Our clientele transfer its attentions from one
drinking hole to another with minor changes in personnel.
Most of our regulars are small time crooks; men in their middle
years, of a villainous mien, who don't take a lot of notice of
me. They talk in hushed voices and stop if I come into range,
so ear wigging is difficult. One or two made a half-hearted
attempt at a chat-up when I first worked here but I knew in my

bones they only did it because they felt it was expected of them, it lacked any serious commitment.

Occasionally, a bird will come in with them and perch on a stool and chirp and preen, but nobody takes much notice. These are men's men. They are mostly called one-syllable names; Vic, Stan or Reg, and are not my idea of what gangsters should look like. No Sydney Greenstreets here, or Bogarts; this lot are scruffy, with dandruff, lank hair, paunches, bad breath. I don't think I'm altogether their idea of a perfect barmaid either. I try asking intelligent questions about the penal system and capital punishment, appealing to their area of expertise, but they don't respond well. *The Sporting Life* features heavily with Tiger and his friends, a quasi religion for them along with motor racing and boxing. They are fervently patriotic when drunk and 'Land of Hope and Glory' rings out. I hum 'The Internationale' very softly at these times and collect glasses.

I never expected the job to last; I don't see myself as one of the workers of the world. I expect I would have got the order of the boot if it hadn't been for me flattening the geezer. It happened like this:

One very usual day, I am bored but no more than usual. I look at the sheen on the carpet, which features a sort of pattern on the patina. I smile to myself the same time a solitary stranger plants his arse on the stool the other side of the bar. Close enough to breathe on me.

'That's what I like to see, a happy girl.' He beams drunkenly at me, elbows on the bar.

'Give us a light ale, darling.'

I give him his drink and he buries his snout in it. His face has relaxed into that state where the bones appear to have melted under the onslaught of drink and eyes and mouth are only loosely aligned to his face. Some of the regular team are sitting over by the door muttering away, and a crew of strangers comes in. This happens sometimes, a conference or motor show, hundreds of males of the species on the loose. Drawn to trawl Soho by the irresistible instinct of the hick.

Like spawning salmon they thrust to penetrate Soho, brave together, coming up the river, they egg each other on. Then, tragically; mid stream, the pubs shut. Wild with frustration, looking for more booze, the poor bastards find us. They creep into the dingy dump with the scent of beer in their nostrils and theoretical lust in their loins and I'm the female in the front line, ripe for the odd jest, bit of baiting a pleasure.

'All right, my girl?'

'Afternoon, gentlemen! And what can I do for you?' I grin lewdly – encourage them to get all their ribaldry out at once. They snigger and shift their feet about. I can feel a snarl building up on my face; it travels up from my stomach like bile. I check it, convert it into a grin.

'No draught beer, I'm afraid, chaps.' I crack the word 'chaps' to make us all smile, and they order nice as ninepence, carry their beer into the corner by the bog and whisper about me. One time I wish my nasty leery friend Frantic would show; she'd assist them on their quest to corruption, no danger. Not a sign of her, naturally.

Meanwhile, the loner by the bar guzzles his beer and waggles the empty glass at me.

'Another beer, sir?' The 'sir' weighing in at half a stone of sarcastic intent.

'Yes, my darling.'

He leans over, reaching towards me, I take his hand firmly, return it to the top of the bar.

'Aw, come on.' But his hands stay in place. 'Have one yourself, darling.'

'Thanks, but no thanks.' I take his money, ring it up, turn back to him with his change and as I put it on the bar he reaches out, grabs my entire left tit, and tweaks it.

I don't think at all, I just see his pale face with the whiskers starting up on his chops, the little grin pasted on his mouth and the knowing look in the eye. My fist comes up and he's off his stool and headed backwards for the deck.

It's one of those moments when time goes into free fall and I watch as he arcs quite gracefully. I slow motion my eyes to the guys in the bar and see all their faces dead still and silent, then time comes back to its usual bustle and they return to life. He is flat out on the slippery carpet, his foot still hooked in the metal stool rung. I feel my face, white and cold. Their eyes are all focused on me. A great cheer goes up and Tiger and his mates are lifting my arm in the air like a champ, calling me Rocky, buying me drinks. The offender lies in a heap in the courtyard. Sharks will discover him soon.

My reputation with the middle aged boys of Soho is made that day. I am an asset to old Tiger.

The salmon crowd have melted into the Soho afternoon.

First I was dubbed Rocky, but as there was an excessive number of Rockys about Soho at that time, Tiger changed it to Shindig. I liked it immediately; I was due a name change.

That was my first week working at the Rendezvous, a defining event, and I've been here ever since.

Late afternoon Tiger often sends me off for a break.

'Get yerself a roll, darling, no hurry,' he says, bunging me a quid. 'Hang about a sec, dolly,' and he shoves a bulky envelope into my hand. 'Stick that in yer bin, gel. Rathbone Street.' He winks.

This mostly happens just when the club is filling with more than the usual quantity of nefarious gits, and is looking moderately interesting. I never know until I'm at the door if my duties as gopher are to be called upon. These are a mystery to me and I have every intention of keeping it that way. I schlep round with envelopes to a few regular addresses in the West End with my curiosity turned off like a faucet. First time he sent me I asked Tiger what it was about; 'Hope you aren't involving me in nefarious activities, my son?' His old eye went dead like some spent mackerel on a fishmongers slab;

'You don't want to know, darling,' said with quiet emphasis. I never asked again. His face extinguishes all curiosity.

There seems to be no pattern to my trips. Today, as usual, I am pleased to go, I love Soho. He slaps my bum as I pass, for the audience. I can feel all their heads coming together for a brief resumé of my charms as I leave. They will be back to the important stuff of who's running in the four thirty or working out an accumulator within seconds.

I walk through Soho and the smells slide up to my face into my nose and through my brain. I am numb with salami, pastrami, herrings, garlic, French bread, the piquant green scent of olives. Well past the deli doorway and a sneaky tendril of parmesan catches up, trickles into my nostril. The patisserie and my eyes slither over the brittle pastries, by Isows and my own private vision of chopped liver, salt beef, latkes, rye bread. Berwick Street market, fruit exults in its own sharp colour, peaches pastel softly. I nick one and the juice runs down my chops.

Up, over Oxford Street, another world. Straights rushing for bargains at the scruffy end of the street, all speedy bustle, all tat. My mate, Ace, with his empty camera, taking photos of happy families, lovers, kids. All the better for not being immortalised. Men with cases of foul furry toys, or nylons with no feet, three card tricksters. All doing their own sweet thing. All ready to run at the first sign of a copper.

I hand the envelope to some old bird but she sends me in to speak to a very fly young geezer in a nasty cheap sharp suit who oozes over me from behind a desk:

'So, you Tiger's new bird are you?'

'No, I'm not. I work for him.'

'Must be losing his touch. All right, darling, thanks very much.' His eyes slide down over me and I can feel them linger on the backs of my ankles like a couple of bluebottles; I reach the door. I see by the brass plate outside that it is a firm of accountants.

I take my time on my way back, stop at the record place and flirt with the governor who knows more about jazz than anybody I know. I play myself some sounds in the cubicle, which leaves me feeling so cool I practically bebop my way along the pavement and back to the club. Soon as I come in, Tiger joins his mates at the table and I do my stuff collecting glasses, washing up and serving the punters as they amble up to the bar. I am reading *Down and Out in Paris and London* and usually manage to fit that in around my bar duties by clearing the decks, wiping the top of the bar and yelling 'Any more for any more?' I can get away with this sometimes, but today the nefarious gits appear to have reproduced themselves and keep on coming.

The day I whacked the geezer is the first time Sid speaks to me.

'Hear you administered a bit of the old GBH today. That right, is it?'

I put down my book and see him looming gently the other side of the bar. He is vast and gives the impression of softness from his immaculate hands to his subtle cologne.

'I certainly did but I don't expect to add it to my official duties.'

'No, that would be a bad idea.' He moves off like he's on casters and stands near the table, observing. Tiger offers him his chair, but Sid shakes his head, a no. I get back to the kitchen in Paris, the juke plays Pat Boone and Vic Damone. I am tempted to put on some Elvis but I resist, then just after eight Tiger closes the door from inside;

'Get an early night, gel. Leave those glasses,' he says as he brings out the brand new packs of cards. That's me dismissed. I get out before he changes his mind.

I retrace my steps of earlier in the day.

2 Don't Sell It, Give It Away

It's night, Soho has changed her underwear and got her slap on ready. She sparkles now and smiles down in the warm, thick dusk. This time I continue northward and, as always, I make for the Roebuck in Tottenham Court Road, see what's happening. I've been fascinated by black culture since I first heard Billie wailing her dark blue songs of love lost, men gone and suffering womankind. I think I wanted to lose a man before I ever had one of my own.

Round the back doubles. I approach The Roebuck sneakily from the rear. Crowds outside. High haired African men with pegged pants, West Indians, Yanks with nice new suits from Alexander's. The occasional Zoot suit. Hep cats and heroes along with the usual bunch of crooks. Johnny-just-come with old timers, a few whites. The sweet smell of tampi and after-shave floats high above the heads. Through the door and the ancient reek of stale beer and fag smoke takes over. Packed as ever, nobody I know, knots of men parting, looking me over coldly, boldly. My face is frozen into a rigid smile under this icy appraisal.

I move through the mass of gently, slyly shifting humanity towards the bar. They move just enough so I can pass, never quite enough for me to pass with any ease. It is like swimming through a shoal of fish, with bodies touching, sliding softly along me. I know that if I lose my footing I will disappear and it will close above me. I will sink without trace, lost to sharks in the Tottenham Court Road, and I feel cold sweat trickle down the centre of my back. Then I see my cohort Rooster, and it's all change. I strut out from the crowd towards him and a drink has appeared like magic. I mingle, with enthusiasm.

'Wha' 'appen, darling? You looking fat so, must be a man you have found, sweet you up good.' Rooster, into his greeting routine.

'Nuttin happen as yet, buoy!' I respond.

'Make I make it happen now!'

And after these pleasantries we can both talk sensibly about our concerns involving whisky and gin from the base; tampi to the base. The American Airforce might have been sent, a gift, for the likes of Rooster and me.

'A sweet lickle number y'hear buoy' is how Rooster thinks of it and he isn't far wrong.

We go outside for a draw and stand discussing business, other people's for the most part. Then he does one of the speedy exits that are an integral part of the dope dealer's repertoire.

'Soon come y'ear.' And he's away.

I want some action so I move myself down to the Corner House, see if I can't catch up with BB. I need some halfway decent conversation after my day. I enjoy the great benefits that Joe Lyons has brought to the West End. The Coventry Street Corner House is startling in the way it fits in and complements deviant life.

It is a centre for mysteries and petty criminals. All classes and sexes trawl here from time to time. Ponces home in on likely fodder, old lecherous men after young boys and young boys from the meat rack in Piccadilly in search of rich men. Prostitutes are officially barred, but who knows what a girl is doing with her bits? Gamblers will drop in on their way home and bevvy merchants take a breather between the club and the next watering hole at Covent Garden or Spitalfields. There is never a time when you can't drink in London, but it requires a bit of ingenuity. The Corner House is a coffee shop in the morning, Palm Court in the afternoon, restaurant in the evening and then an all night cafe of a superior kind. People gird their loins, ready for the next alcoholic foray or the next bit of villainy.

It is buzzing as usual. A few hyenas and jackals lurk, with larceny in their hearts and cups of tea in their hands. They give a nice frisson of excitement to the atmosphere. I know most of them at least by sight and nod a greeting, give out a mutter from the side of my mouth, an affinity of the bent. Now and then a copper will come in but he sticks out like a sore thumb. Grasses, however, abound.

I see Billy straight away. I watch him for a few moments. He is also called BB. A Bengal Lancer of style and one to be watched. He is thin, wiry, yet not skinny; his face is in motion all the time. Eyes watching out for angles and boys, mouth ready to spurt scalding sarcasm and sharp wit, chin set hard against the world. One tough little fucker. I like his smartness, his sexiness, his style. We two reckon we're a cut above the rest. We're right too. There is some old geezer talking to him so I go and get myself a tea and I hover. BB is my favourite working boy and we share an enthusiasm for books, republicanism and idleness. We are artists manqué and are convinced of our talents, which we have yet to identify fully. Meanwhile, we keep our bodies and souls together best way we can. We are also preoccupied with the Suez crisis – BB has a crush on Nasser. For my part, I am quite ecstatic about Nasser's nose, but it's a chaste affair. And of course his politics appeal to us, what we know of them. Mostly we are driven by a sense of the unfairness of the whole business into our usual violent anti British stance.

He spots me and his face lights up briefly, he dowses it fast. Cool is our watchword.

I bring my tea to his table and sit.

'How's my fave palone? What were you waiting for, girl?'

'Thought that geezer might have been a punter, BB,' I say as I join him.

'No, sweetie. I can't face that tonight. Did one earlier and that's enough for me.' He shrugs a languid movement. He nods over towards Victoria who is trolling in at speed. Otherwise known as the purple queen, he rackets along, more femme than most females with unique hip movements and swinging gait.

'Victoria has brought six men to fruition in slightly over an hour. Makes me tired just to watch her,' says BB. 'Must be stashing her bread in here the way she trots in to punctuate every trick.'

'It's her calling. I think hustlers are born not made, don't you?' I say.

'You're probably right, sweetie but I think the purple hearts have a lot to do with it in her case.'

Sure enough Victoria steams up to the table, all scathing anger at our laziness all virtue at his industry.

'Don't know what you two are doing sitting on your arses, there's money to be made out there.'

He gestures with his head in the direction of Piccadilly. It's nearly impossible to call Victoria 'he' but that's what he is, officially.

'Get her, duckie,' says Billy, to Victoria's back as he swans off at a rate of knots. 'Killer whore.'

'Yeah, I think it's her creative outlet.'

'Creative inlet, more like.'

We laugh.

'Mind you, I can't stand it myself,' says BB. 'But that's the men, they're grotesque.'

I nod.

'Yeah, I'd sue Zola for misrepresentation. If he was still around. It was never like that for Nana.'

'Well, to be fair he never went into details, did he?'

'But he made it sound exciting, glamorous.'

'Exciting? Hardly. Still, it beats working doesn't it?'

I agree. I'm in favour of whoring on principle and I say so now to BB.

'That's because you never had to do it, sweetie. Be an amateur darling like the rest of womankind. I prefer to give it away myself.'

'Vadar the amount of straights in here tonight, man!' I say.

'It's early, sweetie. The deviant faction will increase when the boozers shut. Do you fancy some speed?'

'Why? You got some?'

'Soon get some, must be a lot about, I've been offered three lots this evening.'

I must have looked dubious.

'I've got enough handbag to go halves,' he says. 'We could go down the Harmony and watch people. Might score a new homme each, I'm rampant.'

'Not sure I wouldn't rather have some blow.'

'I fancy speed, girl, had a hard day.'

I bung him a quid and he shoots off.

Some of the African students come in and sit in a huddle. They are like a separate species from the African guys I know, who are mostly ex seamen who came here on spec and drive around in their sharp suits with criminal intent. These students lack romance with their side parted hair and stuffy clothes. But I love their ideas, which I plunder and claim as my own. They greet me and I join them. It's all talk of the Gold Coast and independence. These guys listen to what I have to say with patience and answer my questions. They never flatten me with their superior knowledge or sink me with my own foolishness. I would like to have a lover among them and they regularly chat me up with courtesy and some enthusiasm, but I like ruffians.

Must be an hour at least before I look at the clock. When I realise that BB isn't coming back I am not worried, more annoyed. I guess he's scored himself a boy. Least he could have done is come and tell me.

Next morning, well before nine, there is a frantic clamour at the door and when I open it, Victoria whisks in like some joyous avenging angel on speed and imparts the news that Billy got nicked last night, is up in court and I'd better get my arse into gear pronto. He looks happier than I've ever seen him and far younger without all his slap on.

'Bow Street it is. And you'd best get along there in double quick time. He might need bail.'

'What was he done for?'

'Who knows? But you'd better get your arse down there if you want to see him.'

He vanishes in a cloud of fag smoke and I bustle down to the court. Can't find BB's name on the board. Most people have an array of names and change them like their underclothes; so this is not surprising. I retreat home to bed.

Later that day I hear from Vic that Billy got three months for importuning.

'Be out before you know it, a shit and shave sentence,' says Victoria. 'Anyway, he only uses you because you've always got handbag.' Has more than his fair share of malice does Victoria. Having put the poison in he scampers off, but when I wait for a letter with a visiting order and none comes, I suspect Vic might be right. I tell myself that such disappearances are not unusual. But it niggles. I remember our conversations about the future and what we both want:

'Well, sweetie, what I think is; we want it all don't we? Money, fame . . .'

'I don't want fame BB, all I want is to have enough bread so I can sit and watch people and listen to them and never have to worry about the rent again.'

He gives me a scathing look, so I add.

'And enough dope and a good screw now and again and . . .'

'Oh no, don't you want to be a success?'

'A success at what? No. I don't want to be part of a capitalistic bourgeois society, I want to be an outsider looking in.' I sound pious to myself and BB laughs.

'Bless you, my daughter!' and he crosses me. 'I want it all, everything, but I want the poor and oppressed to have some too, which is why I'm a socialist,' says BB. 'As long as I'm first in the queue, eh?'

'You sound like any other greedy cunt to me, BB,' and he laughs and we link small fingers in a collusion of some sort.

'Solid,' I say.

And now that he's gone I have nobody to have conversations with and no place for my dreams to hang. So I take up with Nifty who's a drummer and has been sniffing around me for some time, and I cultivate Tiger or he cultivates me because I enjoy his company more than enough. So, altogether it was a good thing I took on the little number down the club, or I'd have missed BB even more.

3 Don't Get Messy Bessie,
Keep Your Whiskey Cool,

'Friday night is Amami night' goes the advert. 'Cover your head in blue gloop, stay at home with your hair for company.' No chance.

At home, Friday night had been a grisly affair of boiling coppers, filling baths and generally malodorous nastiness.

In fact my entire family could win prizes for nastiness. Look at my gran: she sits, wheezing, in her crossover pinny and steel curlers, glowering at me.

'That girl was born to be hung!' She's always saying this and she will glare across at me as she coughs a phlegm-sodden cough that comes up from her entrails. It hits the room like a soggy bag and splashes into my ears. She intensifies the glare like she knows that I punctured her gas mask with a hot needle and spent the last year of the war waiting for an attack so I could watch her splutter out her finale.

I smile a Mona Lisa job.

The entire family is involved in a permanent primping of the house; dad is seldom seen without a paint brush or palette knife in his hand. He fills the tiniest hole with meticulous precision, the family live on the periphery of the house, viewers, not participants, worshiping at the altar of home improvement, making yearly pilgrimages to the Ideal Home exhibition, the local hardware shop, a shrine. Evenings, we would stare eagerly into the bright lights of the shop that sells fireplaces in all colours of grey and fawn, gleaming back at us like bad teeth as we compare the merits of the grey and fawn over the fawn and grey. They were the bland tombstones to my life. I could have spent my whole life there without being hip to anything if I hadn't read *Germinal* and heard Billie Holiday.

Now, I get wasted every Friday to celebrate my liberation. Nearest thing I've got to a religion.

I've been speeding for two since BB got nicked and I've been moving alone.

Tonight it's the Sunset Club in Carnaby Street. The only place to be. Half the black population of London fetches up here weekends, along with hookers and hustlers of every kind you've ever seen, and some you haven't.

The singer performs with lewd and languid energy. Slow, but emphatic.

> Please mister don't you touch me tomato
> Please don't you to touch me tomato touch me hair me
>   pumpkin potato goodness sake don't touch me
>   tomato.

Her mouth is close to the mic, suggestive. The last line is a camp screech and she performs a brief, lewd grind. I laugh, clap. She walks out of the spotlight, raises her hand, grins at me, goes into the gloom. First set over.

The Afro-Cuban band blasts into the light with discordant vigour. Nobody dances this early. Before midnight and the club's half empty. It's dark enough to stumble, dark enough to pour hard liquor into soft drinks with ease. So dark that people are invisible round the edges of the room, outside the dance floor light. The smell is of Dixie Peach, Old Spice, clean flesh and inflammable hair lacquer from back combed confections. Several conflicting perfumes fight it out for supremacy and the whole is topped off with a dense fug of cigarette smoke shot through with pungent dope. Friday night aroma.

Waitresses tray it around with soft drinks, a photographer flashes his red eye trade into corners, and into groups of grinning, preening girls, bashful boys, flashlight bright for a second, then back into giggling, snogging gloom. My sometime lover on the conga drum lifts his shades, gives a wicked wink, and grins a big tooth grin at me. I lift my Coke to him, a puny salute. He mouths something, I nod and he gives an affinity rap on the drum, a double de-clutch. Banga booma bang.

BB's face gleams through the gloom, fish belly white prison pallor. Even with my shades on he is phosphorescent and with his shades he resembles a luminous panda. There aren't that many white faces in the club; certainly none so white as Billy's. He lifts his own shades to peer at me from five feet away. I am delighted to see him.

'How you doing, man?' he asks, comes to my table, joins me. We are going to play it cool.

I want to say something about him languishing in the slammer but my voice mechanism is not up to it, I limit my words:

'Solid,' I say, although that scarcely describes it. 'When you get out, Billy?' jerks out staccato.

'This morning, at eight on the button, I hauled my poor benighted carcass out of the dreadful Brixton.'

He raises his eyes, a sanctified Madonna.

'How was it?'

'Dire! Ghastly and profoundly depressing,' he gives a shudder. It involves his whole body including his hair.

'What you doing down here, man?' I ask.

'Where else would I find you, sweetie? Know your carnal habits of old, dirty little trollop. Out the house on the pull every night if you can afford it or not.' I am so pleased to see him I almost say so, but I resist.

Earlier in the evening I had ingested the cotton from an entire Benzedrine inhaler, and swallowed some mysterious brown caps. Now, I am chewing gum with such ferocity that speech is practically out of the question. My mind leaps, whizzes. My thoughts, buzz-saw fragments, shoot into my brain. I recognise their brilliance as I watch them slither out the other end, leaving odd, small blanks.

'Vadar that homme with the bona lallies?'

'How can you tell he's got bona lallies?' The voice is coming into its own.

'Poof's instinct,' he says, and preens. 'Watch the way he moves.'

Yes, I had missed Billy more than enough.

Now that he's clocked this young geezer, he is engrossed in long distance flirtation, yet he still rabbits on to me.

'Who is he? Do you know him?' I shake the nut.

'Any amours in Brixton?' I ask, wringing the words out.

BB shrugs, his face goes tight. I don't follow it through.

At the stage of speeding when I have ceased to want to move, a plateau has been reached. Now my mind is astounding in its lucidity, my breath coruscates up my throat in a gush, removing plaque and enamel with indiscriminate zeal. I certainly don't want to talk.

'You speeding?' Astute Billy.

I nod. Feels like a small, pleasant earthquake.

'I know what you need, daughter!'

He takes my glass under the table and pours from a small bottle. I swallow the lot in one gulp.

'Don't go mad, girl. Seen Victoria?'

I shake my head a 'no'.

'Not for weeks, B. Why?'

'Owes me, doesn't she?'

He replenishes my drink, hesitates, he must want a favour. He looks at me carefully through the gloom, reaches over and lifts my shades. I grab them back.

'Pupils like prunes,' he says, and nods.

Now all the hairs in my nostrils have ganged up to pierce and preen noisily, together and separately.

'All your teeth will fall out you know.' I nod. Wish he hadn't said that. I can feel my choppers melting down, disintegrating. I slosh more bevvy into my mouth. So dry I feel desiccated. Watch his lips, can't read a thing. Thoughts puncture the edge of my brain, cut wavy lines like a pie crust, crisp. I insert another stick of gum, chew to the drum while Billy's lips still move and his words slip by harmlessly.

I drink another soft drink stiffened with Billy's bottle.

'So what do you think I should do?' His voice has become peevish. His face is straining on a leash of pink fury.

'You're impossible, now get that down your screech and come and dance. That gorgeous boy's been vadaring me something rotten. Who *is* he?' I tell him about the American show that has come to town. My words ejaculate in short blocks of noise and whack into BB. He never notices.

We dance some hip wriggling thing and I feel my bones separate from my muscles and flesh, a sort of fillet job. All move in intricate, slightly different motions. Billy clasps me with his tight strong arms; a sinewy strait jacket. I breathe in his face; he takes a fast step back and jives. My body re-assembles. He's still talking and edging us both toward his quarry. The beautiful boy sits with several mates but is definitely giving Billy the eye. Must like whey-faced gits, I suppose.

I step back out of my body and watch myself. See girl dancing going nowhere. I look at Billy; he's put his shades in his top pocket and he smiles, pulls me towards himself, careful to avoid my breath.

'Can I crash by you, man?'

I nod. 'That's cool, man,' I say. I am delighted, but cool is still, apparently, our watchword.

He's off. I'm abandoned. Dance myself back to my table, where I sit, twitching, enjoying more mind romping. I watch Billy in the distance through my shades, so it's a vague apparition. He is making progress with the boy. When these dancing guys had first come to town they had caused a great sensation: twitching and spasms of parts had been rife, until we realised that most of them were Marthas. Now old BB had got himself in there. For the first time that night somebody is listening to him. He looks happy as he unburdens himself. The boy probably doesn't speak much English, but is clearly fascinated: lucky old BB.

The singer sashays back expertly on to the dais, giving us the benefit of her fine rump as she adjusts the mic. The audience hasn't a lot of interest in the floor show. This club is about meeting and mating and, to be fair, the singer doesn't see this as the apex of her career. She sings:

> Got a letter from a boyfriend Joe, went to Africa not long
> ago won a prize in a market show for his lovely water
> melon. He's got the biggest and the best in Africa it
> really is a lovely sight and when I go to Africa I'm
> going to have a little bite each night.

All accompanied by lewd movements and profane gestures.

Just a little bite of lovely water melon.

She sings with great gusto, her brown skin moist with sweat, hair straightened, tarry with oil gleam. She stands, legs apart, knees slightly bent, and I see her freshly oiled calves tense as she moves. I can almost smell the salt on her. She turns away from me and I look at the back of her neck, with circles of hair flat against her damp skin. She turns in my direction, sings over my table into the gloom, loudly, gives off an energetic disdain.

Back to her Tomato again:

Mister, take advice from me, the more you look, the less you see.

Set over, sparse clapping. I yell: 'Encore' and she sucks her teeth:

Kiss me bloodclart!

The band is back. My body is part of the rhythm section and thrums happily. BB has left his bottle and I down it in Coke. Feeling mellow now, in a twitchy way. I watch old BB operating. His sharp cheekbones catch the light: a gaunt preview of an older lantern jawed BB.

'Hello, gorgeous, how's yer quim?'

Great laugh resounds, bounces echoes in my brain. 'Christ, doll, you look wasted.' Frantic's voice in my earhole, foetid breath makes its way round to my nostrils. I gag.

''Ere, I hope you're not going to be Uncle Dick. You want to watch it, gel, drinking too much and taking them bleeding drugs like you do.'

'What you been eating, Frannie?'

'Pickled egg and onions . . .' She laughs a gust of poison fumes that scratches my nasal follicles on its way past.

'. . . and jellied eels earlier on.' She leans over, drinks from my glass. 'Seen BB at it, have you? Little bastard queer. He'll get filled in if he don't watch it, chasing that lovely young boy.'

'Looks happy enough, the boy.'

'Don't understand, do he? Probably thinks that's what

normal English blokes do.' Takes one of my fags, lights it, blows hefty gusts of smoke out. Pockets my matches.

'Just come out the nick hasn't he, dirty bleeder.'

'Yes came out today, didn't he. Why dirty bleeder? You only come out yourself a few weeks ago. You going to put those matches back?'

'Oh, they yourn, are they?'

She puts them back on the table, grabs my chin and looks into my face. Shakes her head.

'You want to get out in the bog and get some slap on, gel, you look diabolical.'

Frantic fidgets and waves at the band. This woman never needs speed. She runs on spit and venom and brings an aggravating energy with her, always jagged, always on the move. Always sober. No sex appeal at all that I can tell, her skinny self insinuates itself in all kinds of unlikely places. She doesn't like blacks yet here she is at the Sunset. A woman with a mission, I think, but no idea what it is. Now, she leaps off her chair.

'I'm going to put the mix in, see if I can't snatch that young geezer away.'

She nods over at Billy and shoots off before I can get my mouth to consider the idea of speech. I can't hear the words but the movements ratchet up fast. Frantic speaks to BB, pushes him out the way and grabs the boy's hand, pulls him on to the dance floor. The boy laughs and it could all have been cool, with BB protesting in camp outrage, hand on hip, laughing.

Then one of the guys who works in the club is yelling at BB and next thing you know he's being called a batty man and is out the door. I move over the floor and protest, I grab a guy to speak to him, he turns round and head butts me, so I've got a gob full of wiry hair laced with Dixie Peach and my mouth has gone soggy and bloody inside. Frannie and the boy come back. Frannie gives the guy a mouthful, and next thing you know we are all outside in the night being shoved around by Big Charlie, the doorman, who is vast, nasty, far too dangerous to mess with.

We mill around a bit, mourning the loss of our drinks and fags. BB and the boy are happy enough.

'I'm not bleeding walking away, I paid me entrance money. Anyway it's got nothing to do with me,' says Frannie.

'That's outrageous! You started it,' says BB.

I say nothing. The fresh air has had an odd effect on my brain, which seems to require peace above all. F/2039801.

My fat lip vibrates.

'No, I never. Anyway, you can't go. Your bloke's in there,' she says to me. And then she's off, performing her unique negotiation techniques on Charlie.

'Ere, Chas, you know me, you'll let me back in won't you, darling? Me and me mate.'

'Frantic's struck again, you've got a fat lip, I've got a ripped jacket, we're all barred and that one will trot back in, cunt!' says BB. The boy is laughing now and BB joins in. Frantic is draped around Charlie, grovelling.

'You've got to let her back in, she's with Nifty the drummer, and you know you can't bar me, Chas.'

'Why that? Me n'want them nasty batty men in the club.'

'I'm nothing to do with him, don't even know him, dolly, and if you bar me you'll never get me knickers off!'

She stands looking at him, tits to the fore, grin glued on her face, eyelashing it. He scowls, then grins, gives her a squeeze that includes her carnal parts and relents.

My mouth tastes of oily iron filings and all I want is my bed, a couple of Seconal and a nice, long collapse.

'I'm not coming back, Frannie, got to take these guys home and my face hurts.'

'Looks ghastly, darling,' says BB.

'Won't notice in there, will it, too bleeding dark? Besides, who's looking at you?' from Frantic. She moves from leg to leg, blows smoke, a ferocious dragon.

'What about Nifty? You can't expect him to lig about on his own on a Friday night, against nature that is. He'll be off with somebody else he will, you watch.'

'Tell him "later" eh?' I say.

BB has gone to the corner of Carnaby Street, past the bomb site that smells of damp earth and buddleia, he is hailing a taxi. The boy hovers between BB and me. Frannie is disap[pearing] into the bowels of the earth along with a crowd of Yan[ks]

firmness of step and sudden spurt of speed might mean she has
remembered, at the same time as I do, that my handbag is still
on the seat in the club.

Not for long. I can nearly see her swift fingers plunging into
its interior.

4   Good Morning Blues,
Blues How Do You Do?

Morning clangs in like a geriatric tramcar on a cobbled street. Sounds rasp and reverberate inside my hollow skull. I'm aware of my mouth first. I look in the mirror and see the entire edifice marching out, independent, an inch ahead of the rest of my face. Each lip strutting, but not to the same beat, the upper striking southward, the lower travelling east. My two front teeth wobble dangerously around the first fag of the day, my hands alarm with a tumultuous tremor as I strike a match. I think of a cancellation of the whole day, then I hear the boys shifting softly and I know that the morning must go on.

I bang into the kitchen;

'Right, who's making the tea? Rise and shine!' I yell. I slam out satisfied I've demolished any morning loving plans. I put on Bessie while I smoke a tiny draw, a one skinner to put my brain into synch. 'You gotta give me some.' she husks, sexily, inappropriately. I turn her down as BB enters with tea, looks at my face and shrieks, a cross between a giggle and the alarm call of a peahen, way too high a sound for that time of morning.

'State of your eek, dolly!' He turns to the boy who looks seriously appalled. The boy holds my face while he examines my mouth.

'Ice?' I shake my head a 'no' but BB says he'll get ice from downstairs.

'Or your poor eek will be destroyed!'

He faffs effectively and I liberate a bottle of Burton's gin from my stock and they both get into full flamboyant fussing. He gets ice, opens the gin.

'Mother's ruin, darling, get it down yer!'

And he swallows a vast one himself, giving a theatrical

shudder, while I gingerly sip, first one side of my mouth, then the other. I drool like a geriatric on downers.

'Need a straw, my sweet,' BB giggles. 'Get a good belt down yer screech, anaesthetise your gob,' and he tips the glass so I swallow a good whack of the gin while more drenches my front.

'Nourish your jubes, sweetie!' BB says. 'Perhaps they'll grow.'

'You going to be able to work today?' BB asks.

'Course I will,' I mumble round some highly suspect ice that gives off the faintest fishy whiff.

'Where'd you get the ice, BB?'

'Downstairs, sweetie, your landlady. Seems charming.'

Unctuous git been schmoozing her.

'Was thinking,' says BB.

'Watch it, duckie, you'll wear yourself out before your time,' I riposte. He smiles.

'Could me and the boy stay a couple of days? The landlady says she might have a room at the end of the week. Be nice, having a lattie in the same house?' He looks down modestly. The boy is dusting the tops of furniture.

'Does the boy have a name?' I hedge. I can see the advantages of having BB about, especially if the boy takes up residence. We lived together before when we were between men and it had been fun.

'Yes, he's called Angelo. Isn't that just *too* adorable?' Angelo looks up at the sound of his name and smiles tenderly at BB.

'I would, of course, be the very soul of discretion. Wouldn't we?' To Angelo, who hardly has a word of English. He gives another adorable smile.

'And Marmalade, Carlotta and myself are hardly speaking, so you won't have to put up with them. 'And I cook and stuff . . .' He finishes vaguely.

'Where's your gear?' I know when I'm beaten.

'Paddington station, take me half an hour at the most.' Briskly.

'You're on.'

'Oh, lovely one! Precious treasure, I *knew* we could rely on you for compassion and understanding. And Angelo is working in the show so that's the rent paid, and free tickets, and I'm soon going to get my own act together. Oh, blissypoos!'

'Well, quite,' I say and wonder if I've made the right decision.

'Have to get a key cut,' I say.

'Got one from your charming landlady.' He holds a front door key aloft.

'Cheeky cunt!' I remark.

He blows me a kiss. I got this kind of edgy feeling all mixed up with pleasurable anticipation. They walk me to Bayswater to stretch Angelo's legs and sober me up.

'Try to come home nice and early and put your feet up,' says BB. They both kiss my cheek very carefully as I get in the taxi.

'Don't move your face, sweetie, think "donna immobile".'

The driver moves off far too swiftly muttering about poofters. I hold my tongue, save my lips. I close the glass between us.

Soho seethes as usual but the door of the club is locked, which is a first. I bang on it and yell.

'Come on, my son! One o'clock it is! Hope you haven't been shagging some old boiler all night, you dirty old git!'

The door opened while I was concentrating on getting the words through my misshapen gob. A middle-aged woman looks down at me from the step. Her eyebrows are plucked to a two hair width all along and emphasised with pencil of a unique brown that goes off at a tangent towards her hair line. Max Factor American Tan pancake make-up is a mask on her face. Orange sherbet lipstick, navy mascara and blue frost eye shadow make up her maquillage ensemble. The perfume is Blue Grass and the attitude hostile. Don't take a genius to realise this is Tiger's old woman. She has all the dreadful authority that goes with legit wives.

'Oh, hi there, I work for Tiger, he here is he?' I try to walk past her but she blocks me. She examines the visage closely.

'You been giving a jack hammer a blow job have you?' She laughs long and shrill at her joke and I get a nasty view of a complete set of metal fillings. She moves aside to let me through. The scent of Harpic overlays the Blue Grass. You can tell she's one of the world's natural cleaners.

'No, it's all right, if he's not there I'll shove off.'

She puts out a big, bony hand, almost touches me, withdraws.

'No, hang about. So you the bird that knocked the geezer out? Don't look up to much to me. Come well unstuck this time din'cha? Hear you knock about with Shwartzers too. That right, is it?'

She speaks in short sharp sentences like quick body punches. I want out. From behind her, big sleek Sid comes to the door.

'It's all right, Renee, she's only the barmaid.' He speaks to me: 'Tiger's gone away for a few days, my dear. He's got your address so when . . .'

Renee snorts: 'If.'

Sid continues:

'. . . when he comes back I'll let you know. If there's money owing I'll get it to you. Now, Renee.'

And he turns away with Renee reluctantly in tow. She takes the time to give me a venomous look over her shoulder.

So that's me unemployed again.

The rest of the day is empty in front of me. I kick the idea of home around inside my brain as a thought enhancing device but the brain has slipped into free fall. I walk, and even Berwick Street market doesn't rouse any enthusiasm for life.

I see Marmalade trolling on the other side of the road and I yell his name, causing all kinds of damage to both lips and head. He bustles towards me, we meet in the middle of the road. His hand flies to his mouth and his eyebrows reach for the sky, never one for understatement he is in full shock horror.

'Hello, daughter!' He bends to plant a kiss on my cheek, I smell his Rose Geranium perfume and feel a rudimentary whisker or two. 'Whatever's happened to the eek, my sweet?

Marmalade is well over six feet of willowy effeminacy topped off with natural deep auburn rhia, the word glamour could have been invented for him.

'Is this a new style of lip decoration or did you fall out with somebody?'

He doesn't wait for an answer.

'Hear your governor got busted for receiving last night, five clubs got done.'

'Is it a purge do you reckon? Are they going to bust everybody?' Don't know why I'm asking really. He shrugs a fancy movement, doesn't utter. I continue, 'What do you reckon?'

'Don't ask me, darling, these things are quite beyond me. Did you hear that Carlotta met this Count?'

'No, did she?' Marmalade turns to me giving me the benefit of his hazel orbs complete with Eyelure nylon pointed lashes. Carlotta, an almost completely evil bitch, is the love of his life. They have been together for what seems like forever.

'Yes, at the Ritz it was.'

Like the Ritz is part of their regular beat. I say nothing. He looks at my face.

'Want to get something done about that fat lip, darling.'

'Not a lot to be done, Marmalade. BB and Angelo put ice on it. I'm not bothered.' He gives a hurrumph noise which could mean anything but which I interpret as: Wouldn't catch me going out in that state.

'Anyway, Carlotta was in the Ritz with one of her showbiz friends and this funny little man came along and it turns out he's a Count and it was love at first sight.'

'And don't you mind?'

'Don't push your luck, daughter! The Count fell for Carlotta. You know perfectly well that Carlotta is devoted to me.'

'And you to her,' I say sweetly.

'So what kind of a Count is he? A no count motherfucker, or a count me out the next round or what?'

'You are so coarse!'

'I know. It's a gift.'

'So where is this Count from?'

'Basingstoke.'

I crack up, my lip hurts. He looks at my face and amends quickly.

'He doesn't come from Basingstoke, he's Italian, he lives there.'

'Not a lot of Counts in Basingstoke. Could count them on the fingers of one hand,' I chortle.

'It's only temporary, he's based there for work. And he has the most gorgeous accent.' His eyes go quite misty until he sees I am stifling giggles.

I shape up to sobriety.

'Be able to do a lot for Carlotta's career.'

Afraid I giggle again and Marmalade retaliates with a spiteful tweak of my arm. He has hold of me too tightly for retaliation.

'You going to behave?' he asks, and I nod, resist asking if it is Carlotta's career as a street hustler and importunist or amateur drag artist that is going to be aided.

'Her career?'

'Her theatrical career, as you know perfectly well.'

'In stasis far as I know, isn't it?'

'Don't be rude,' he tweaks lightly.

'Means it's stuck, in limbo like. When did she last work?'

'The panto, of course.'

'But she was only third rabbit, wasn't she?'

'Second actually, but she shone. The director said she shone.'

'Oh right. That's some achievement really, shining through pink fake fur.'

I nearly snigger but his strong hand has tightened a tiny bit on my arm.

'Next thing is to get her an equity card and introductions to the right people; the Count has connections.' This last given huge gravity.

'Fruit, is he?'

'Don't think so. Camp as a row of tents but not one of us, no.'

A short plump man approaches. He has a Liberty bag in his hand which he waves at us.

'And here he is!' Marmalade's voice sounds like he's announcing the winner of some contest. 'Gio! This is our friend Shindig, please excuse the lip she doesn't usually look quite so rough.' We shake hands and he gives a really sweet smile. I do hope Carlotta doesn't rip him off too badly.

'We're off to meet Carlotta in the pub, want to come with? She's performing,' says Marmalade. When isn't she? I think.

And I'm not up to it. The days events suddenly hit me like a sledgehammer. I need my bed.

At home Angelo and BB are established like they've been in residence for weeks.

The gaff already looks more civilised and I am glad to see them.

I hear nothing from the club for days and languish, my fat lip and me, enjoying the company of the boys and their civilising influence, they cook. Finally, I am driven by poverty and lust and succumb to Rooster's urging me to shift my rarsclot and I make a meet with him at the jazz club up west.

5 Double Crossing Mama

Off Leicester Square on another Saturday night. Chad and Lucky earning a living, the sounds of the dice rattle, a counterpoint to the music and the Yankee voices: 'Baby needs some new shoes'. 'Snake eyed motherfucking cocksucking bastard.' 'Sheet man how you get there?'

Laughter and curses swing above their heads in the damp air.

Chad's face, hooded eyes observing. Another Yankee man ups the ante, Chad raises his hand, the dice hits against the wall. Dark faces animated, eager, greedy. Laughing swearing voices. A whistle shrieks out and the boys scatter away. Blue black Chad lifts money and dice from the ground. Lucky scurries along the alley. Both gone away into the night.

The players, lost, nothing to do with their hands or minds, money gone, stand looking. Looking out for the law that never comes.

'Those cocksucking motherfuckers!'

Had taken moments to sink in, the boys were gone.

But Rooster is waiting and I have a meet to make, I slide past the drinking, smoking dudes. 'Where you going, baby girl?' 'Hi, sweet pea, how ya doing?' 'Come here and have a drink, girl, you know what's good for you!' 'Hey, baby, get yourself a drag of this sweet weed.' 'Where your brain at, girl? You can't see this handsome face of mine, shining in your eyes?' The last from very close by me. I looked up to see the sweetest reddish golden copper face, mean small mouth, eyelashes unbelievable. I'll definitely have him away.

'You going to let me pay you in, girl?' I bypass the queue and smile at the geezer on the door.

'No thanks, I get in free, don't I, Stan?'

'Yeah, come in, gel, yer mate's inside waiting.' I don't ask which mate – got to be Frantic, she's been tracking me for weeks now. Has taken to coming into Tiger's, sniffing around. He's told me to get shot of her, reckons she's hitting on his mates for tips or drinks. I don't want her hanging round either, Tiger has the impression we are big time spars. In fact all over the place people said 'Yer mate's waiting for you.' She's moving into my life. I don't know what she's after, and I don't like it.

Inside, this club is seriously devoted to jazz, among other things.

In the centre of the floor are many chairs set out in totally straight lines and occupied by the jazz cognoscenti: serious characters who make not a sound neither do they move. They sit and they watch. Every move of every musician is given attention, and they give silent small nods of approval and quiet applause at a spectacular achievement of finesse. Bass solos are greeted with a degree of concentration that could split the atom, drum solos accompanied by tiny movements of parts of bodies in synch.

Self-congratulatory grins slide from face to face in this elite audience.

'See that? Yeah me too! Are we not clever fuckers? *Yeah*, man, cool. Nice. Solid.'

I walk softly past them, stand at the back. I am a woman of little discrimination and less expertise about jazz, an obvious person. Love it all: sexy sax, strident trumpet, cool clarinet.

But the blues are my thing. Along with a million other birds I want to *BE* Billie. Meanwhile at the edges of the dance floor quiet hubbub rules as the crew waits for between-sets music so they can dance along, show off, feel up and make out.

Knocking shop meets salon here at the Mapleton.

The girl singer, envy of us all:

> Well all right, OK, you win, I'm in love with you
> Well all right, OK, you win, baby what can I do?
> Anything you do or say
> Just got to be that way.

Didn't realise I was singing along. My voice screeches to a halt as some female glares at me, she moves off. The musicians play on, and they are some of England's finest. A sharp bunch of wise guys with their egos in their instruments and their minds caught up in the glamour and responsibility of being musicians and adored by dopey females who glare at people who sing out of tune. I know these guys, they use the basement where I work to rehearse, but now, they have their mystique wrapped around them: I am intimidated.

The club breathes in smoke, breathes out jazz, flourishes on the mixture. Dark walls, softened with a nicotine patina, give off a dank brick stench. The carpet on the edge clings to the feet, tenacious as a limpet, both slippery and sticky on the soles. Jazz has sunk into the walls. Early morning when the music has stopped and the players long gone, I am convinced it breathes out the sounds like some old harmonium, bronchitic lungs relaxing, until the walls settle into sonorous silence that sighs on to a blue beat.

Frantic's voice hits on my ear, an oil drum smacked with a light hammer, high ping.

'Ere, dolly, just been talking about you, haven't I?' She has in tow copper face and a short arsed geezer. It's hate at first sight.

'Hi there, baby, how you doing? I'm Lefty.' He makes a feature of his height and reckons he's well amusing.

'Heyee, baby, I just love a tall woman.'

'Hope you find one some day.' Unoriginal, eh?

He cracks up, but his eyes, almost squeezed shut with laughter, are full of hate.

'I was telling these geezers that you know all the musicians, Shindig and they want to meet them,' says Frantic.

'No chance,' I say.

'Sheet, girl, I'd rather meet you anyway,' from copper face.

'That's very wise of you!' I look at him closely, those eyelashes.

'My name's Berry and I just know we are going to have a sweet association, you and me baby.'

'You reckon do you?'

'I'm certain of it, and once you taste this sweet berry, you will thank your sweet lord for tonight and for meeting me.'

Puts his hand on his heart like some preacher man. I laugh. He reappears all night. When I dance he's there, dancing. When I'm listening he buys me drinks, offers me foul Lucky Strikes. I feel uncomfortably, dangerously, cherished. I smell his skin as he leans to whisper in my ear, the warmth from his flesh in my face. Can very nearly see the blood moving under his skin. I pull away a bit sharpish, plus Frantic is tugging at my arm.

It is at least a half hour since she first pulled me. Thought she'd gone.

'Look, gel, I promised them didn't I? I told them you knew all the musicians, you do.'

'Terrible thing! Why the fuck would I want to introduce you to anybody?'

'So happens I won't need an intro to your Nifty.' Her face alight with malice, then fear.

'What the fuck do you mean?'

'Had him away, didn't I?'

'That's no trick.'

'You don't mind then? I said you wouldn't. He told me not to tell you but I knew you wouldn't care. Bit of all right, innee?'

I got this vision of the two of them discussing me in post coital bliss. The blood leaves my head, slips down to my belly, I want badly to belt her one in her face. Blood zips back up again. I have an almost overwhelming desire to put my boot six inches up her arse and twist it.

I smile and it feels like very hard work.

'Got to go now, man about a dog, know what I mean?'

I see Rooster moving like a cobra through the crowd. I greet him

'Wha' 'appen, Rooster?'

'Come make I talk to you.' Pulling me into his orbit.

'Me 'a search for you, you know, we have a deal with one new Yankee man.'

'Great!' I make to move off.

'Him here you know, in a' this club.'

So I linger with Rooster while we wait upon this guy to finish his heavy-weight listening. Rooster and me make a good team. Neither trusts the other an inch: we're on par.

'Gonna let me drive your car?' He chucks the keys at me.

'Well catch, sah!' he laughs.

Nifty is playing the next set and he comes on stage, grins at me, greets me with his drum. I blank him and just then Rooster gives me the word, we're ready to split.

'You coming back later are you?' Frantic, outside on the pavement, smoking some draw with Lefty.

I whack her one so hard I feel her neck crack back on its bone and she disappears from view.

Swear to god I had no idea I was going to do that.

Rooster and the guy don't miss a beat. We all get in the car and I drive off.

'What happen to your spar?' And Rooster laughs this deep sound, the Yankee boy gives one of those high range giggles. I join in with my own paean to humour.

'You don't know that woman mess with Nifty this long time?'

'She know now, man. She know now!'

We all laugh. My knuckles are swelling by the second.

6 Triflin' Woman Blues

We all agree that it's bona. Living in the same house works well. So well that two of the original tenants have left in protest after Victoria moved in upstairs. The house is looking gorgeous with many embellishments of a very camp nature and so far the landlady, Vera, is charmed. I worry slightly about how she'll feel if she finds out that Victoria is using her room as a knocking shop, but no matter. Frantic has ingratiated herself with Victoria and visits regularly, her new sideline career of receiver fits well with her personality and gives full reign to her meanness of spirit, knocking down the price to the seller and beefing up the price to the buyer. But it is well handy, and we are glad to take advantage of the fringe benefits.

'That's what capitalism's all about, sweetie,' says BB. 'Our Frantic would make an admirable Chancellor of the Exchequer.'

'Perhaps we could guide her into government, get her to stand in the election. What would be her platform?'

'Oh, free enterprise for hustlers of all kinds across the board,' says BB.

'Thieves charter.'

'They've got that now sweetie, remember the taxman?'

We sit on the roof getting a tan while Angelo makes our lunch and does his dance routine. He dances everywhere, incorporating it into all his work round the house. He is tidying me up a lot. BB has blagged a bookshelf for me from Vera and I can see the carpet in my room for the first time. A TV had appeared in BB's room via Frantic and it was while we fixed the aerial that we discovered the charms of the roof. There is a valley up there, ideal for sunbathing, and if we go to the edge we can peer into the houses opposite. We both get slightly vertiginous but Angelo will terrify and thrill us by dancing on the ridge, entrancing the people over the road.

BB hasn't been working Piccadilly since he came out of Brixton. There is one copper who has it in for him and told Victoria that he'd have Billy – at least, that's what Victoria told us and it suits us well enough to believe it. BB has the confidence to take on anything on offer. From bar work to decorating, shop lifting to a bit of kiting. I get him in to Tiger's to do odd jobs when I can and he's a fair old hustler, better not ask really. BB is not called 'Born to blag' for nothing.

Tiger has returned from the nick or Le Mans depending on who you listen to and I am ensconced again in spite of Renee. I am almost tempted by malice to take up Tiger on his offer for the post of his bit on the side but can't face it. Anyway, since I flattened the geezer in the club, my job is secure.

When I see Berry in The Roebuck, I realise that he is the reason I came here on this particular night. My voice raises itself an octave without my permission so I squeak a 'Hi, Man' at him and sound like a castrato on uppers. Soon as he comes into range, my body pulsates with no input from my brain which has taken an unscheduled break from duty. We stand touching while I drink my beer. Again, I get the impression I can see the blood moving beneath his skin. Now, I breath with him and when his leg moves close enough to touch my thigh, I flinch away then lean into him and feel my temperature shoot up to fever pitch. He pulls me, very gently, outside and I see Rooster saying something to me that I neither hear nor care about.

'Where can I buy you coffee?' Berry says and grabs a taxi. I tell the driver the Corner House instead of telling him my address, which would be the sensible thing to do. I don't do first dates, my normal process is one of horizontal interview. Then, maybe, I date. In the taxi he kisses me tenderly, I nuzzle his neck and beneath the Old Spice I can just catch a faint feral scent that I breath in as he pulls my face back to his mouth. The driver coughs loudly, moves his bulk. Farts. 'Ooh pardon me! Where you from then?' he says. Berry has pulled away from me.

'Kent.' I say.

'Him! Your black boy, where's he from?'

'Ask him.'

'No, you just tell him, no offence like, we got enough coons in Britain and if I'd known he was with one of our girls, I wouldn't have stopped.'

'I'm not one of your girls, wouldn't touch you with a barge pole! We'll get out here.'

He drives off before we can pay him and I give him the two finger salute. Berry looks scared. 'Don't worry about him, he's just your average racist git.' I laugh to lighten the atmosphere but Berry looks gloomy as we walk the last few hundred yards. I feel tender towards him and link him. I can feel his warm arm through his jacket.

I don't indulge in love. Lust is my driving force. I understand lust, it's simple and cool. Love stings, in my experience. It has a person acting like an idiot and splashing bits of themselves all over the place in an embarrassing way. I try to joke Berry back into good humour but he is freaked by the taxi driver, so when Vic arrives at the Corner House in all his glory, I'm not as peeved as I might be.

Victoria makes BB look like an homme. His take on feminine behaviour and gear is well beyond camp and has slipped into the stratospheric. His arrival is greeted by a nervous wave from me. Vic habitually wears the nearest thing to drag without getting nicked and on this particular night themed lavender is the motif. A mauve felt hat with a small lavender veil and seed pearls tops off a very tight navy jacket and pants and high-heeled boots. He shrieks across at me: 'Darling flower, my sister.' We had met briefly on the stairs this morning, he ignored me.

He veers on the side of emaciation with a sharp-featured face and big beaky nose. With such unpromising material he makes a fair queen, all attitude, all style, so you hardly notice how his sad little body minces and jerks into excess by speed.

'Hmm, who's this gorgeous boy?'

He bends over me, gives me a kiss on both cheeks, then he hangs over Berry, who cowers slightly then shoots off at speed to get coffee.

'Glad he's gone, darling. Marmalade and Carlotta have got nicked and they want you to go and bail them out. I'll come with, but I can't bail them.'

'What were they nicked for?'

'An affray.' I must have looked blank.

'They had one of their up and downers outside the Rolls Royce show room in the Dilly,' Vic says crossly. 'Makes it bad for us all.'

He purses his painted lips emphatically, peering at his empty fag packet.

'Bleeding coppers must be having a slow night,' I say.

'Well, I can't bail them, I owe a fine. They'll probably let them out anyway later, if you're too busy. I told them I'd tell you, and I have.'

Followed by a moody look of disapproval. He does an extensive vadar of the entire place, narrowed eyes not missing a thing.

'Who's the homme?'

'A friend.'

Vic raises his finger and lays it by his nose as though the idea of our friendship is the most obscene idea in the world. Just then Berry comes back with a cup of something for Vic who feels it necessary to leap up and kiss him on his cheek.

'Dear boy! How sweet.' His voice has taken on the upper register of a piccolo and Berry looks both alarmed and appalled as people turn to discover the source of the aural damage. Berry freezes for a moment then lifts my coat and holds it out for me to go.

'Gotta go, honey! Dances to do, people to see.'

His eyes reach for the sky then slither sideways, escape.

'Sorry, Berry, I have to,' I say feebly.

'Oh, don't mind me! The girls can just rot in jail while you enjoy your new homme!' Vic turns to Berry; Berry turns to me.

'Now if you want to come along with me, fine! I'm leaving now.'

'Get you, ducky! Masterful or what?'

Berry kind of raises his hand to lift my coat, but Vic winces back and looks so scared and little that I know I can't leave him. I wave Berry away and he turns wordlessly and leaves.

'Oh dear, he's got the hump. You're well out of that, darling, nasty bit of work if you ask me!'

A strand of mousy hair has fallen in front of his left ear and wrecked the whole image. I lean forward and Vic winces. I push his hair behind his ear and smile at him.

'Come on you venomous old tart,' I say and he laughs.

At the nick they are unhelpful. They keep us waiting so I sit with Vic on the only two scruffy chairs in the joint and get more pissed off by the minute.

'State of the décor in here is vile. They still got distemper. They do it on purpose to demoralise the punters,' I say.

'Only just got rid of the posters saying "Careless Talk Costs Lives".'

'Yeah, they positively encourage careless talk now. Grassing a speciality.'

'The ones with "Kitchener Your Country Needs You" were up until a couple of months ago, then somebody fell in that they were antiques and flogged them,' jokes Vic. 'You'd think some of them would have a sense of style wouldn't you?' We mutter critically.

Then Jack from the drug squad, whom everybody who's been within a hundred yards of a spliff knows, happens along with this dish, Dixie. I don't know who she is, an unnatural blonde, on the voluptuous side, with eyes all over the place and the ring on her small finger.

'Hi, Victoria, what are you doing here?' Eyeing me up.

'Oh, Sergeant Dixon, some friends of ours were nicked in the 'Dilly and Shindig and I came to see what's happened to them.'

'And you're Shindig, are you? I've heard about you from Jack. I think we've got friends in common.' She turns, but Jack is away.

'Do you want me to ask the desk sergeant about them for you?'

She goes off to the desk, exchanges a joke, laughs loudly. Looks over her shoulder at us.

'Wow, she's gorgeous, Vic. Bet she looks divine in uniform.'

'Didn't think you approved of uniform.'

'I don't, don't approve of coppers either, but she's a bit of all right, isn't she?'

'I prefer Jack, but she seems taken with you, duckie!'

She comes back towards us; her eyes locked on to mine.

'They've gone, Shindig. They let them go half an hour after they were arrested, on their own bail.'

She stands in front of me, looking into my eyes and I forget what I'm here for. Her lower lip is fuller than the top one, and I focus on that.

'So you've had a wasted journey, girls.'

'We have,' Vic chips in.

'Oh, I don't feel it's been a waste, Sergeant Dixon, not at all. I met you, didn't I?'

'You certainly did, Shindig.'

She looks amused and I realise I haven't taken my eyes off her for minutes.

'Any chance of a lift, Sarg?' says Vic, and he grabs my hand in his, very tightly.

She shakes her head.

'Can't be done, girls. I'm on duty, I'm afraid. Reports to write.' Makes a writing gesture. 'All paperwork my job. Everybody thinks it's just the fun bit of nicking people and harassing them, but it's not,' she laughs.

'Anyway, I suppose you can't mix with the likes of us.' Vic again.

'Oh, I wouldn't say that.' She looks me straight in the eye again but any knee collapse on my part is curtailed by Vic's tight grip. He pulls sharply and we are at the door and down the front steps at breakneck speed.

'What's the matter with you, Vic?'

'Just seen some geezer I clipped, didn't I? Anyway I didn't want to watch you mooning over some blowsy copper, do I?'

He bustles me along quickly, skinny fingers tight, painful on my arm.

'What's the bleeding hurry, Victoria?' I'm out of breath while his skinny legs are going like dynamite pistons.

'Told you, didn't I? A punter I clipped was in there. I want to get as far away as I can.'

'Shit! You mean you clipped him tonight?'

'Yes, round Half Moon Street.'

'You're joking, I never thought you did that, Vic!'

'Oh yes, they're usually far too embarrassed to go to the bill,' he says serenely. Or as serenely as you can say anything when trotting on high heels at thirty miles an hour.

My ecaf must have taken a turn for the worse. He sounds defensive now:

'A girl's got to make a living and you've no room to talk, flogging drugs and booze.'

He looks like a stick insect now, all angular resentment.

'But Vic, it's fucking dangerous apart from anything else.'

'You think what you're doing isn't? All those dangerous bastards you mix with? They're all gangsters in that club. And that Rooster you knock around with shot a copper in Jamaica.'

I'm impressed. Even though I don't know whether to believe it or not.

'How stylish, how do you know that?'

'Oh, somebody told me. Now do hurry, I don't want that great lump catching me, could crush me with the sheer weight of his body.'

I look at him, imagining his skinny bones breaking like matchsticks. Wouldn't stand a chance.

'Can you run in those high heels, Vic?'

'I'm sure I can run faster than you can anyway!' Which I feel is missing the point.

We practically gallop our way to Piccadilly and I am puffing and blowing while Vic smokes a cigarette and keeps rabbiting away without losing a beat.

'I don't know about you but I'm going to get the all night bus.'

He huffs off into the darkness and light of Bond Street.

I watch as his frail form goes from light to darkness then into the light of a window again. I think of catching him up, but he's whisking along with such fury that I can't face either babying him back to good humour or rucking with him.

I let him go.

So I am alone when the car draws up beside me by Green Street Station and Dixie calls me over to ask if I want a lift.

'Bit dicey picking up strange birds this time of night isn't it, sergeant?' I slip into her Alpine, feel the leather seat communing with the flesh on the back of my legs. Nice.

'Certainly is, taking my life in my hands I am.' She turns her head my way as she changes gear and grins. Puts her foot down. 'Especially a bird with your form.'

'All youthful folly, sergeant.'

I am flattered she looked up my record.

We have arrived at the Serpentine. She puts the hand brake on and leans back in her seat, stretches her arms high in a great phoney yawn, catches my shoulder on the way down.

I light up and lean against her

'What did you do with Victoria?'

'He went to get the all night bus.'

'And where were you making for? All on your own.'

She has her hand on my thigh; it feels warm, large, strong and entirely nice.

She tastes of tobacco and mint and her tongue moves nicely on mine. It's rough like a cat's and seems to cleave to mine, waking up all kinds of nerves that I never knew I had. We lean away from each other and look into each other's eyes. Can't see too well. I put my hand on her collar, tug gently until her lips are in range. We start kind of nibbling at each other's lips. I touch the back of her neck then push my face into her throat, tongue the salt. She pushes me backwards in my seat.

'So what did you say you were doing?'

'Was wending my way home, Sergeant Dixon, but this is better.'

We kiss, gently, then firmly, then passionately. Her delicious tongue comes into play again and I wonder how she got it like that.

She pushes me away.

'And what are you doing now, pet?'

I look at her face, not sure what to say.

'Well, I think I'm making love.'

'You certainly are but who are you making love to, pet?'

'You . . .'

Shakes her head.

'Sergeant Dixon?'

She squeezes me, undoes my shirt.

'And who are you?'

Takes my breast in her mouth. Which kind of inspires me.

'I'm your pick up.' Her head nods and her hands are at my crotch. I try to touch her breast. She pushes my hand away.

'Talk!'

'I'm some girl you just picked up. I got in your car, and you ravished me.'

She nods.

'And I'm going to come right now.'

She stops what she's doing.

'Not yet, you're not.' She pulls my skirt up high, investigative fingers probe and blinding torchlight shines through the back window.

We straighten up and when Dixie opens the window the young constable apologises profusely while snuffling giggles.

A slightly older cop comes up beside the car and grins at Dixie.

'Thought you'd have known better than this, sergeant.'

He has such a good look at me I feel he might sketch me later, a mug shot.

I put my tits away, pull my skirt down. She looks furious but laughs with them like a good sport. The bill are still standing together highly amused when she hits the gas pedal and scatters the gravel from the path. I rock back in my seat as we fly along the Bayswater Road. I take her hand on the gear stick and laugh.

She drops me off at the end of my road, kisses me crisply and does her bat out of hell trick again.

'Very bold!' says BB when I tell him.

I don't know how I coped before BB moved in, he is my confidante. He is also permanently skint so when he gets a day's work at Tiger's we are both delighted.

7 Here Come the Blues

Frantic hasn't been around for a week or two and I miss her but then as BB says: 'You miss a boil on the bum when it goes.' Anyway, the day he comes in to work, she turns up too.

Tiger seems to be branching out with his cohorts. Geezers of unaccustomed couth have been coming in of late, they have the look of Bond Street rather than Hoxton. Still well dodgy but better-class dodgy if you know what I mean. The accents not quite so wide, the chat a little bit broader ranging than the horses and the dogs. Now pictures have appeared down in the cellar among the beers and old drum kits. I discover this when Tiger gets me to go and sort out some glasses. I hate jobs like this and will flirt almost to distraction to avoid them. Course Tiger's on to me, and won't wear it. So, finally, I grizzle and whinge my way down the stairs.

'Just shoot down there for half an hour, darling, there's about a million half pint glasses and boxes of wine goblets. Sort out a box or two, gel. It's either that or clean all the shelves.' I opt for the cellar and once I'm over my initial resentment my natural curiosity kicks in. So I poke about among Christmas decorations, an old mangle that I might be able to find a home for, a pile of old photos that could have been of the people who used to live here. I think I'll see if we can stick them up in the bar as a feature. Make a change for the better from Tiger's array of boxers and horses. The light's lousy and it's creepy down there, I poke in a corner by an old copper and a washing board and it's suddenly clean. The part of the cellar the jazz guys never use. I wouldn't know about the pictures, but it smells different. Sort of a let up in the density of the dust so I follow my hooter and find a little group of parcels done up with old curtains and string. I poke at them, lift them up and suss they are paintings but can't look at them.

They are wrapped up so thoroughly it would take a special kind of person to have the bottle to investigate thoroughly. Tiger gives the impression he's Mr Nice Guy but I think it would be foolish to mess him about.

Now he opens the door and yells down:

'All right, my darling? The bogeyman hasn't got you has he?'

He starts down the stairs and I move over swiftly to the boxes of glasses.

'Christ, mate! You need to get down here for a few hours, gawd knows what you might find. Right, gel, give 'em up here.'

He lifts the boxes up and puts them behind the bar. 'That'll keep you busy, my darling. You can wash that lot.'

I try to pump him about the paintings. I attempt to make it casual. 'I see you've got a lot of parcels down there, Tiger, they new are they?'

He looks at me shrewdly 'I'm storing them for somebody, gel, so keep yer thieving little fingers off, eh?' He also pinches my nose quite hard.

'Nose ointment,' he says, which is cryptic but pointed and he gives me one of his winks and changes the subject.

'Haven't seen yer mate for a while, Shindig.' He looks over at me. I look brightly at him.

'Who's that?'

'Old tight arse Fran, the girl who's never bin known to put her hand in her own pocket.'

'Hear she's knocking about with scarface Jimmy.' I heard this from one of Tiger's mates.

'That right, is it? She's living dangerously with his old woman, Queenie, in the offing isn't she?' He shakes his nut carefully. But I'm sure he knew all about this before I told him. Often with Tiger I don't know who's telling who what, if anything.

'What you up to, dolly? I can always tell when you're up to something.'

He laughs the laugh of a man secure in his power as boss and shakes his head, certain in the knowledge that he will find out the innermost working of my mind.

He goes to greet one of the nefarious ones, just as BB comes through the door.

'Hello, Billy, you're in time to help your mate with a bit of cleaning,' says Tiger, and BB has his jacket off and is behind the bar taking over in two seconds flat.

Tiger goes out then so I use the time to tell BB about the paintings.

'I always thought Tiger must be involved in something well illicit,' says BB looking wise and nodding, like he thought of it all by himself.

We get to work, BB takes the role of governor and I follow his instructions. I tell him that Frantic is in love. And after we finish with the ribaldry I tell him who the object of her passion is. Everybody knows Jimmy, he's one of the larger fish in the Soho pond. His face was cut to ribbons years before and it looks as if the stitch up man hadn't been fully concentrating on his job when he repaired him. He is left with lumpy pink and silver scars that twinkle down and across his face, and run wild among his whiskers. This does not detract from his charisma in the least, it might be animal magnetism but I think it's sheer awe that makes him attractive. Like anybody who can withstand that amount of carving and come out the other side has got to be taken seriously, plus what the fuck did he *do* to inspire such ornate tracery? Course, he wears his scars with pride. Being a villain, they give him a certain cachet. Also, he moves like a boxer, light on his feet and graceful.

I hold him in awe, so does BB but he doesn't let on. 'Tiger was talking about Queenie today. Reckons she'll kill Frantic.'

'Too true,' says BB, 'what fun!'

But then Frantic likes a bit of drama and I hope fervently that she'll get a surfeit soon. While I would never be crass enough to push it along, I wait for the shit to hit the fan with a tense eagerness

We take a fag break after an hour or so and both sit down.

'So what did the bold Nifty say about having Frantic away? I expect he used the same script as he does for his wife.' He puts his fag down delicately, using twenty muscles where I would have used two. Raises his neat, plucked eyebrow, wriggles it and puckers his lips into a smile.

'Lot of old fanny,' I tell him. 'Said it wasn't important, a one off, never happen again, all the usual sad excuses.'

'So that you and him off, is it? I mean you know all that guff by heart, it's making you look a cunt that matters, isn't it?' I agree fervently, a lot of my life is spent avoiding looking a cunt, a pity because I have a natural talent for it.

'Not to worry, my darling, you're well out of that. Besides we can watch avidly as Queenie the dragon removes Frantic's minge from her body! Can't see *her* being full of forbearance, can you?'

'Wasn't that brilliant, anyway he's a slippery sod.'

'Nifty?'

'Yes, anyway I got my eye on something else.'

'Good, who? Or shouldn't I ask?'

He looks over slyly. I begin drying glasses again.

'What do you reckon it is about Jimmy that's got old Frantic going?' I enquire.

'Well, sweetie, one thing about him, everybody gives you a wide berth.'

'Yeah, like if you're driving a rough old motor with bits off it, people think you've got nothing to lose.'

'Some people actually like scars, don't they? Scarification and all that.'

I don't actually know what he's on about so I stay shtoum and just then in comes Frantic. I've seen her a couple of times since the night I'd whacked her and either she bears no malice, realises she deserved it, or she can see a use for me, because she is still well matey. The idea that she is holding a festering grudge is far too alarming to contemplate.

'All right, you old sluts?'

She sits down at the bar, nicks a fag, lights it, leans back and peers through the smoke at us both in turn.

'I know, she's doing an Ava Gardner!'

'Either that or she's working out how to hit us for a few bob.'

'You talking about me?' She looks at us both in turn, laughs. 'Don't need your money, mate.' She opens her handbag.

'Watch those moths!' says BB.

She holds her bag open so we can see a roll of notes.

'I know, you've taken up bank robbery,' says BB.

'And what's more she's going to buy us all a bevvy, what's yours, BB? I'll have . . .'

'Leave it out, I'm only looking after it, int I?'

'Should have guessed, you've still got the sixpences the tooth fairy gave you, haven't you?' says BB and we all laugh.

'Be different now, gel, won't it? Now you've got a rich boyfriend? What you doing with old scarface then Frannie?' says BB.

'He's lovely to me, treats me like a princess he do,' sighs, and assumes this really maudlin look.

'Nothing to what old Queenie will treat you like when she gets her hands on you!' I say.

'Yes, better watch that queen mum, my sweet,' says BB.

'Oh he's leaving her! Loves me, he do.'

'Oh yes, and she'll let him, after seeing him through twenty years worth of sentences, visiting him up and down the country, from Dartmoor to Barlinnie, keeping the happy home together with thieving,' says BB.

'Yeah, you can see that can't you?' I add. 'That marriage isn't fucking optional, gel.'

'Oh, you're just jealous!'

''Cos there aren't enough scarfaces to go around?' BB, as always, quick off the mark.

We giggle and Frantic gets the dead needle.

'Least he's not a goolie!'

'That's racism, Frannie?' I say.

'Nah, wouldn't say that, just they're different aren't they?'

We both stare. She takes two swift draws from her fag.

'Yids, shwarzers? Same as ferrets intit? Put a rabbit in with a load of ferrets and see what happens, don't hear the ferrets arsting questions do yer? No you don't, just, wallop!' She makes a gesture of finality, one dead rabbit.

'Well, Frannie, that's race summed up very nicely, and what am I? A rabbit or a ferret?' BB says.

'And what are you? I didn't notice you being backward in coming forward around Nifty!' I add.

But Frantic has seen Sid who's made a place for himself at one of the tables and she's away.

'Looks like a big tom-cat we used to have when I was a kid. Doctored, of course,' says BB. We both watch her shift herself across the floor, all angles, then she gathers herself together when she reaches him and becomes almost appealing as she looks up at him with her frantic smile.

'She's *gamin*,' I say.

'Meaning? Like Audrey Hepburn? No, she's just young and ungainly.'

'Got something though, hasn't she?'

'Got some bleeding dodgy ideas on race she has, don't dare even ask about what she thinks about queers!'

'Must be quoting old Jimmy. All those villains are right wing bastards – ought to hear them in here, like a fascist convention it is.'

'Well, quite. Same as bits of rough, the awareness of peewits most of them.'

BB and me used to fancy ourselves as the communist faction of the petty criminal class; but we got discouraged by the stubborn lack of political awareness among our mates, and the failure of the working classes to shape up. Then, of course, Stalin was exposed as some kind of murderous monster, which shook me rigid, he was held up as a paragon for a while there.

'They must have known he was a bastard,' I say to BB.

'I'm sure they did,' says BB and gives me a pitying look. 'He was a useful bastard, sweetie. Now our esteemed leaders want to distance themselves from commies of all kinds . . .' He lets the sentence hang there so that I have time to realise just how naïve I am. He pulls rank like this sometimes, BB.

Now, I am leaning toward anarchy while BB is becoming liberal. We spend hours in mutual mind preening and sharing our despair about the likes of Frantic and her tribe. Of course, I'd discovered my own political awareness through Zola when I was fourteen and found no reason to change my mind since. But it's all a bit academic and I find the *Daily Worker* hard going but as BB says:

'Well, Sweetie, one could scarcely describe us as workers.'

'But we should still read it occasionally. Perhaps we should try to get a 'Daily Shirker' going eh?'

Sid has turned and he waves over at me, and lifts his hand to his mouth, a drinking gesture, points to BB. I thank him, take the money for the drinks and leave him to the mercies of Frantic who is half way into her seduction technique. Poor man.

'One of us, darling, he's a poof.' BB.

'I know, I only just sussed it though. That'll be a treat for the poor fucker won't it? Lumbered with Frantic on heat!'

'Who is he?' asked BB; I shrug.

'Sid? Think he's a fence. Loaded anyway, all the time. Comes in most weeks, talks to the governor, always nice to me. No lip.'

'Probably in the protection racket, sweetie. Oh look.'

I do, and see that scarface Jimmy has come in with two henchmen.

They all look out of place and I wonder what they are doing here.

All grey they are. Grey gear. Grey flesh. Grey thoughts. The last is conjecture. The juke box sounds loud, with Jim Reeves warbling about losing his mind. He's been doing it for months now. Frantic looks like a petrified rabbit caught in headlights, only for a few seconds, but noticeable. The three grey men move and the tension is broken as they greet Sid, and Frantic snuggles up to Jimmy, who looks well embarrassed. She is almost clinging to him and he's creeping away without actually moving.

'Can't see that lasting, can you?' says BB 'No way, looks like his flesh is crawling.'

'Yeah, crawling in the opposite direction. Sensible chap.'

Jimmy looks over and waves at me.

'All right, darling?' His mouth moves a particular scar which pulls half his face sideways.

'Yes thanks, Jimmy!' I feel my personality squirm, ingratiating, as I speak to him and I hate myself as I smile a big cheesy. Even cool BB wears an alarmed grin.

I rush to the bar to serve him and one of the henchmen gets the drinks in. 'Tiger about is he?' he asks and I tell him no. Sid joins him at the bar and pays for the round. 'Take for you and your mate out of that, darling,' he says and BB and me sit twitching with nerves at the bar.

It is a relief when Scarface leaves, really. Frantic sort of follows at three paces with one of the henchmen's ears in bondage.

'Those geezers don't knock around with birds do they?' I say to BB. 'Not as mates.'

'No, darling, their women are kept in a kind of purdah, where they all go out doing ladylike crimes, like shop-lifting and fraud.'

'Or retired completely out in dreadful Sunningdale, with the stockbrokers.'

We shudder.

'Get taken out on special occasions . . .'

'Like the best china, weddings and funerals.'

'Do hope that's what happens to Frantic, don't you?' I say.

'Oh, yes,' says BB, 'We wouldn't want her dead or anything, but it would be gorgeous if she just disappeared for a while.'

'A few years would be good,' I say.

Then I tell him about Berry, about meeting him and fancying him and the more I talk about him the more I know that I have to see him again.

'Vic said something about you being with a new man, didn't rate him did she? But frankly, sweetie, I'd worry if she did!' says BB.

'Quite,' I say.

'Sounds like love to me, girl. I had no idea you did lurv, sweetie.' I frown and BB says 'Good for you, it's time you met somebody who loves you. Somebody of your own.'

I nearly pull him for being a sentimental twat, but I don't. I feel scared. 'Fuck that for a game of soldiers! I'll have him away,' I say.

Three days later, Frantic is back round the club on her tod again. Says she's blown old Jimmy out but we don't believe her. BB says it's best not to delve too deeply, but we spend many a happy hour speculating.

8 Grindin' Man Blues

Early evening and I got nothing specific on. The world is mine. Who will I see, hear, fuck? I still got Berry on my mind and I smile as I anticipate him.

'Don't know what you've got to smile about.'

Victoria has come upon me, with venomous intent as I sit in the pub. I've got a pint in front of me, a fag in my hand and twenty quid in my snatch. For me, things don't get any better. Now I dredge up a frown to wear.

'Why's that then, Vic?'

'Scandal says BB's been slagging you off something rotten. Reckons he can't stand living with you no more.'

Same feeling you get in school when your best mate changes allegiance, I remember I'm not eight any more.

It's a few days since we were out together and Vic appears to have forgotten our sojourn at the nick. Though he's lived upstairs from us for weeks, I can't warm to him like I do to the other gay boys. He can't resist putting the poison in.

'Doesn't live with me any more than you do, Victoria. Him and Angelo got their own lattie. Anyway, darling, if he's pissed off I'll wait for him to tell me.' Vic shrugs an elaborate move that involves most of his body.

'Says you don't pay your way.'

'This is bollocks, Vic.' I get up and leave but the gloss is taken off the evening. Kind of gloom slips into my mind. So I go up the Roebuck see what I can see. Soon as I go in the door I clock Berry and give him the nod; inevitable it seems. Like the interval in the Corner House had never happened.

We go straight to his mate's in Cleveland Street. A nasty little room with a single bed a straight chair and an enamel bowl, all the furniture. As soon as we get in the door we pull off each other's clothes and fuck a fast emphatic violent number that's over in minutes and leaves me rocking on my heels. I fall on the bed and look over at him as he slouches on the chair and rolls a joint. He is coppery most places darkening to black on his arse and dick. His body bends sweetly into collapse and his curved belly reminds me of a woman. I stare at him.

'Hey, that's some nice dick you got there.'

'Ain't that the truth,' he laughs, looks slyly at me from under the lashes. 'What that they say, girl: it ain't the meat it's the motion?'

'They lie.' And I go and kiss his cock as it rests half soft on his thigh. He runs his hand over me, down my back.

'You are one skinny woman.' I move back to the bed to look at him.

'Shit, man, I'm slender.' And I take the bomb shaped six from his hand. He laughs and sings;

> Got a little girl so doggone thin
> No meat, no bone, just all skin
> One thing about her I can understand
> She wraps all around me like a rubber band.
> It ain't the meat it's the motion
> Makes your daddy want to rock
> It ain't the meat it's the motion
> It's the movement that gives it the sock.

He finishes with a flourish and I applaud.

'That you serenading me?'

'Certainly is, ma'am.' And he laughs again like he's taking the piss, he has a fast line in snide this geezer.

'You got a crap voice, Berry.'

'But a sweet dick.' It's nearly hard again now and he tenses it so it waves at me.

'Come here and sit on this.' I smoke the joint with my chin on his shoulder and we hardly move at all but each tiny move gets to the core of us. I inhale his scent that becomes part of the sex. I could sniff this guy out like a bloodhound if I was blindfold.

The dope brings our nerves to the surface of our skin and the next fuck is a slow, languorous affair where the last thing on our minds is orgasm. Finally we can't help it and we come sweetly softly but we don't stop. Our mouths move on each other and every touch feels like nerves being raked by finger-nails, but softly.

Finally we disentangle and we sleep, but I'm aware of his body touching me and we fit each other perfectly.

Later, I have no idea how much later, he gets up for the bathroom, stands and looks down at me. I look up into the golden eyes, and reach out for him.

'Come back fast, baby.' He puts his finger on my lips, a hushing move. I lick his salty finger. I sleep again and when I next open my eyes, he is sitting on the chair, but this time he is braced, muscles tight as he fixes up with a tourney in his teeth and a needle in his arm. The claret in the syringe is like rubies. He releases, leans back, closes his eyes and his body gives a relaxed, joyful move and he looks over at me. I am leaning on my elbow watching him now.

'You want some of this, girl?' I shake my head a 'no'. I never fixed up before but I'm not about to say so to this cool dude. 'Not now, maybe later, huh?' I say as he puts down the works and I make room in bed for him. I am impressed.

We smoke a fag together and I want to ask about how it feels with hard drugs buzzing round you. He says: 'Nice buzz, come here, baby.' And we go into reverse and eat each other and I never tasted a sweeter man in my life. He falls asleep with his head on my belly. I wake busting for a pee. I extricate myself, escape.

In the bathroom I peer into a mottled triangular piece of glass that is stuck behind the pipe from the cistern to the bog. My lips are swollen, eyes half closed. I smile to beguile and see greenish teeth, close my lips fast and stagger back to the room. We've been here all night and half the day and I am hungry like I never was before, ever. I look down at his face – exquisite eyelashes, handsome cheekbones – and all I feel is hungry; hungry and cuntsore. His eyes are shut but his hand comes out to grab me back to bed. I succumb with fractured concen-tration. I sit on top of him while he moves, he looks up at me and laughs.

'You are one sweet piece of tail, girl, the closer the bone the sweeter the meat. Come here, fast.'

And he waves his hard dick at me.

'Listen, Berry, if I don't eat I'm going to die.'

'Bullshit, baby, come and do it one more time.' I look at his chest hair as we grind on, I think of lokshen. The sweet smell of sex fills my nose; food fills my brain. I close my eyes tight and dream of food.

An egg looks up at me with a liquid yellow eye surrounded by a shimmering skirt of white with just the slightest touch of brown at the extreme edge where it puckers just a little, a tiny bubbling curl.

'Hey, baby, where you at?' He speaks but doesn't break the spell.

I return briefly to smile at him, give an enjoyable wiggle or two. He closes his eyes; I close mine.

The egg is joined by a piece of bacon, pinkish brown with a marbling on its surface. The rind and fat cringe towards me, almost dry. Deep brown, so crisp that at the merest touch of a knife it will splinter into salty fragments. I lick my lips and smile.

'Good, huh?' Him again. He jerks effusive.

'Good,' I murmur.

Now a couple of pork sausages have appeared alongside the bacon and egg; they are fat and glossy bronze with the ends issuing from them, crusty, hard, dark. I add a tomato with its glistening orange face full of contrasting white seeds, a tracery of brown lacing its surface, skin going from red to ebony at the edges. The whole is arranged on a blue plate with bread; fresh, crisp, white. Dark burned crust, light lemony butter. Bread absorbing fat from the plate. With the black crust I poke at the orange yellow egg yolk. Before the membrane ruptures it creases into tiny yellow ruches then the yolk erupts and I climax quietly.

Later in a Chinese I hardly think about the taste of the food. I think about sex, but I eat and eat. Berry does not find the idea of war a hideous affront to humanity. Indeed, he likes being in the Air Force and does as he's told. How else could he get this much pussy? Conversation is never going to be our thing. I just want to rip his gear off and lick him all over, hump him to death. Not sure if I like him, his technique is not the best but he does it for me. I do it for him, too. I look at his lovely coppery face from time to time, give him a grope and eat. He gets restive and we part soon as we get through eating. Him to the base, me to the house. We say we'll meet tomorrow at the Roebuck. I don't know if we will.

'Dirty little cow, on the nest for two days!' BB is given to exaggeration. 'Get this down your screech, girl.' He gives me nice strong brown tea with sterilised milk and sugar.

'What's that for, BB?'

'Shock of the cock sweetie. So who was it or need I ask? Tell auntie, what was it like?' He crouches beside me, avid for details. I begin:

'Brain in his cock, BB.'

'Best place for it, sweetie.'

'But nice, eh?' I say. 'Men with brains always seem unnatural to me.' BB nods as I edit and weave the tale.

I don't mention Berry fixing up.

9 Junkie Blues

Heroin kind of slinks into my life while I am transfixed by Berry's dick. Heroin has always been around, but Berry, with his ready-made habit, brings it into fast track focus. His main spar, Diego, is a highly hip New York stud. A junkie from way back. Like molecules, Colette and him are attracted and they cling. Colette is a feely I know from around, we've had a drink and a laugh together. She was a Soho hustler for a while. Those are the girls about whom all the jokes about sore feet originate. Could call it the volume end of the whoring market. She seems to have found her thrill on heroin hill.

'Cool as ice, twice as nice,' says Colette and I don't know if she is on about Diego or H. Both, I guess. Yeah, cool like all the jazzmen and the blues legends. Hip as hell. Diego just so cool, man. Has tales of vast sophistication in New York. That H can be your lover and main man there is no doubt, it can close over you and absorb all your grief and joy. It can fill your life with a different emphasis, drive all your blues away and replace them with nice, simple, cold, hard, uncomplicated addiction. Like all your troubles in the one container, all the better to focus upon. But it's hip, all right.

Hip is not the word that would come to mind when you go to Joe Lyons at the Gate; meeting and gathering spot for serious junk heads. Characters I don't know or want to know are now my eager mates. Junkies give friendship on the end of a needle, share a spoon with a nodding acquaintance, welcome you into their midst like no other group in the world. They clasp you to their foetid bosom with joy. The more the merrier, leave nobody outside their circle. Colette has appeared among us and stayed on when the studs got a pad round Pembridge Gardens. First week I watch the other three as they crank up, vomit, gouch out. Next week I try it for myself and I can see the fascination. But not as my only love, eh? As a part time amour maybe.

Besides, I am busy with the fringe benefits that Berry brought along. More booze and fags appear so I am working harder, making more bread. More wraps of dope and fifths of liquor are buzzing into and out of the base. Packs of Pall Mall and Lucky Strike are flying up and down from West Drayton to West End, with the occasional skirmish up to East Anglia. There is a popular view that crime is easy money, this is not necessarily so. It's just more fun and gives the average punter a chance at the action. 'Last bastion of capitalism open to us,' says BB.

BB doesn't take kindly to my adventures into H, dire warnings and nags a speciality.

'Don't know why you'd rather knock about with those junkies . . .' He fluffs a cushion with too much vigour.

'We've got it nice here now, thought you'd be here in the evenings when you're not working.'

'You sound like my mum.'

'Nonsense! Your mum's common.'

'True, and brittle. And you'd have to dye your hair.'

He goes into an extended hair check in the glass over the fireplace.

'Don't think I haven't thought about it.' His face has taken on its 'worried about my age' look and that can last for a long time. I join him to aggravate.

'Are those smile lines round your eyes?'

'No, my sweet, they're worry lines. And quite new and all down to you!'

'You *are* my fucking mother, you've transmogrified!'

'Bollocks!' he says into my face. Then he backs off and says:

'I miss you, you've withdrawn into a bloody boring junkie. I can see you getting mouldy round the edges, sort of greyness invading your soul.' I didn't think we believed in souls. He puts a hand on each shoulder, looks well serious, peers into my eyes. I'm spooked and laugh my way out of his reach. Angelo has a softer line, more disturbing. He looks at me, gives sad head shakes with a look of desolation on his eek.

'You starve your spirit too much is most sad.' And he pats me gently like I'm some old Labrador in terminal decline, retreats shaking his nut very gently and making conciliatory noises.

But I'm only dabbling to be cool, aren't I? In Joe Lyons on a very ordinary morning, Tony the dealer comes back to speak on his way out. An honour for me. He squats on the edge of a chair like a buzzard, his hands filthy claws. I've been buying stuff for us all from him. He must see a future in me.

'Bell me.' Gives me the number on a fag packet. Looks at me out of his rheumy young eyes, no interest, no expression at all.

'Bell me and we'll make a meet.' He stands up from the littered table full of empty tea cups, ash trays, dead match-sticks. Moving like some kind of mendicant as he makes his slow way to the door. Like he's giving blessings instead of refusing credit. He hangs on his bones, grey flesh, slightly jaundiced round the eyes, his teeth blackened stumps, curiously pointed. Eyes, pupil-tiny near colourless, red rimmed. Ageless, like some ghastly pixie. I've just scored and fixed up, feeling well happy. Contentment nowhere near describes it.

'You're in there, girl, that's your supply sorted for perma-nent.' Trudy looks expectant so I give her a jack for her trouble and she shoots off to the khazi nicking my box of matches as she goes.

Must be the worst Joe Lyons in the universe this one. Hell's waiting room. You got all the junkies hanging out, tight packed bowels giving out unique farts. Throats retching gently, wait-ing to score. Keeping the tone consistent, the whiskery bevvy merchants looking like seven kinds of bone shaking death waiting for the boozer to open. One or two rancid scrubbers left over from the night before, tea leaves and wannabe ponces dotted among the legit housewives with scruffy pushchairs and smelly brats noising up the place. Trudy back at the table chucks the matches down, scratches her nose with the back of her hand. Rummages on the table.

'Got a snout?' She leans her chin on her arm on the table, looks up at me, smiles revealing greenish coated teeth, scratches frantically at her hooter, reaches her hand out for the fag. Never seen so much movement all at once in her. She lights up, looks at the burning end as she inhales mightily.

''Ave a cup of tea case you're uncle dick, eh?'

'Do what?' I said.

'Get a cup of tea down yer man, so if you're sick it gives you something to bring up, something nice and sweet.'

'Go and get them then.' I hand over the bread for two teas and she goes up to the counter. The nippies here scarcely nip at all, they stand giving out dispirited glares at us lot. Their grey damp cloths hang on their trolleys caught up in the general flaccidity. I wonder is this the punishment block of the Joe Lyons empire? Are the nippies sent down for misbehaviour, six months in the Gate? Trudy comes back with the tea and we each grab the sugar container in turn, upend it four times into our tea. Trudy comes over fastidious, lifts her hand with black rimmed nails 'Sticky!' She pulls a face and I laugh. This nice buzz in my mind making me feel so good.

'Want me to come back to your gaff?' The day stretches ahead pleasantly and Trudy doesn't feature. I shake my head a 'no'.

'Got to do a bit, haven't I?' I say. She shrugs. My nose itches nicely and I enjoy rubbing it gently; no sign of sickness this time. I look round and see that a group of party going characters have come in; I know a couple of them. Trudy has seen them too and her brain can be observed shifting gears. She looks sly and I think she's going to hit me for another Jack but it's not that.

'You still with that Yank? 'Cos Tone don't do the best deal for bulk. If you're selling on, then Roony's yer man . . . Tone's reliable but . . .'

'No, doll, I've no plans to make a regular thing of this game, you know me, crank up weekends.' She raises a brow; this is Tuesday. Lyn is waving over, part of the Linden Gardens team. I wave back.

'It's better when you're hooked.'

'How you make that out, Trudy?' She shrugs, changes tack.

'They'd all do it if they knew about it. Cleaner, neater, smarter.'

'Trick is to do it without getting hooked.'

'Like you?'

'Like me.' Gives this shrewd old look, doesn't she? But I'm not bothered.

'You can flog it for double to that Yank of yourn, in fact you better. We been giving him two for a quid.' I take this in but I don't want to think just now, I'm lost in this deep sweet warmth, any aggravation locked in a chrysalis for the duration.

Over to Lyn, she makes room for me, kisses me on the lips quickly so I know she's drunk.

'Never knew you were taking that route, baby. You ever look at those people? That cat Tony, you know him?' I nod.

'Went to school with him, he's twenty-seven – looks about fifty.' She goes on.

'And a bad fifty at that,' I say.

'Yeah, well, read it and weep man.' She smiles this radiant gleamer at me.

'I'm having one of my parties soon, darling, would you like to come along? They're the most enormous fun.' The whole team look at me and laugh.

'Love to.' I know a chat-up when I meet one, I think.

'Hey, don't go. We're thinking of killing the day on the Serpentine, want to come?' She reaches up and strokes my collar, just touching my neck at the very end of each stroke. She smells pleasantly boozy and the crew with her are tasty but I want to be with my buzz alone. One of the guys smiles into my eyes.

'Aw come on, honey, let the good times roll. We going to take our drums with us and play up a storm on the water. You got the rest of your life to work.'

'Yeah, baby, come with auntie Lyn and smoke some healthy weed, drink some nice booze, spend time with some good people.'

'Yeah, let us take you away from all this,' says the guy. The crowd all laugh as they stand and the guy has my hand in his, pulling. I press the centre of my chest to feel my jacks are still there, check my works, realise I've left my matches on the table, go back to get them. Trudy is gouching out with a fine line of dribble running from the corner of her mouth down her chin.

A rivulet in grime.

I split out the door after the crew.

Days later at home BB has thoughts on Lyn: 'High class whore, sweetie, got to be and those parties are orgies. Bet she won't ask you, anyway.' And he lights up and blows a damaged smoke ring. 'She only gets posh birds to her dos.'

'So that leaves me out, eh?' He does a cynical grunt.

When the invite arrives I am delighted. BB is scathing.

'Up to you, darling, but I expect you'll get ravished by capitalist lackies,' says BB.

'Be a change for the better; been well fucked by the proletariat haven't I?' I laugh.

'That's right, scramble your way up through the hierarchy, forget your socialist roots, do!'

'The whole point is that I didn't have socialist roots. My family were fascist plebs, BB, as you know,' I bleat. Angelo joins in:

'Try to get fucked by not the lackeys but the rich, eh?' We giggle.

'Wouldn't catch me consorting with that lot anyway,' says BB. Angelo lifts the invite to look at it.

'You can bring guests, darling, I will come to be ravished, too!' BB lifts himself from his pose with the well-thumbed T S Eliot on the sofa, grabs the invite, peers intently at it. I grab it back. Look at it again, it does indeed say 'to Shindig and guest'.

'Great, Angelo you can come with me.'

'You'll be working, it's a Saturday. I'll have to go,' raps BB.

'Billy, you have changed your song!'

'No, take the night off, Angelo, they must owe you time off,' I say.

'I shall, it will be for fascination, darling! I will be ill if they say it is not possible.' He gives his beautiful smile. His English is coming on apace.

'I shall drag up! And you too? In drag? So bona, darling,' says Angelo.

BB is pink with chagrin:

'You're not borrowing any of my gear, sweetie!'

'I will wear weird exotic clothes of ambiguous sexuality.'

'Get you, ducky!'

'Quite! Pity you feel so strongly, BB, we could all have gone.'

'Yes, Billy, such pity,' Angelo says.

'I can't possibly let you two go without me, no knowing what would happen to you, I'll have to come too. I'll infiltrate.'

'Says a guest on the invite, BB, and Angelo doesn't mind hobnobbing with the rich.'

'Well, they'll hardly have a doorman will they?' We all know that BB will not only come to the party but will insist on taking over the whole project. And he's welcome.

10   Everybody Wants to GO to Heaven

You meet a better class of addict at Tony's phone box. Twice a day he does his stuff and a small group of nose dripping, twitchy characters make their tremulous way just off the Edgeware Road to score their gear. The form is always the same. We bell him at various times of the day and get fielded by his mum. Finally, a heart lifting moment, we hear his weedy voice and he will arrange to see us at a certain time.

Thing with junkies, they're mostly well punctual. Thing with dealers, they're not. So you get small clumps of characters who would not usually meet socially, scuffling their feet, and pretending to be invisible round this red phone box. I get a taxi but can't afford to keep it waiting, not if I'm going to show a profit on scoring for the others. I find the whole process exciting, like a tourist.

Everybody is morose. Morose and twitchy with the built-in ineptness that comes with being strung out. Musicians with their instruments attempt that casual look and straight looking guys and chicks hover, watching, and getting increasingly tense, increasingly sweaty, panic welling nicely. Add to this mix Junkie Johnny and you got action.

'All right, Dave, how's it going, got a fag? Saw you playing with Ronnie Scott, how is Ronnie? Tell him Johnny Mason was arsting about him, cheers for the fag. Got a light?'

Dave retreats into himself for safety; cutting it fine, and his face gleams wetly, must be playing any time now, desperate.

'What you reckon's happened?' Dave's talking to me. Johnny is accosting, with friendship, a woman in a car.

'Might have crashed out,' I speculate. See Dave's face contort, like he's got stomach cramps. I continue:

'Once or twice he hasn't turned up at all I heard, and

they've all had to go to John Bell and Croydon at midnight.'
Wind him up a little.

'I'm playing ten minutes ago!' He does a shuffle *dance
macabre*. Tony shoots round the corner jerkily, an erratic
scarecrow.

'Had to have a shit, didn't I? First one for two weeks,
priorities mate.' Looks round his fan club. Grins. He speaks to
me

'All right, gel, you first are yer?'

'Let Dave go, eh?'

'Oh Dave, never seen yer did I mate?' He lies. They both go
into the phone box while I worry about why I'm in favour;
disturbing that is. Dave dives away, jerkily, guitar case in hand.
I go in the phone box that has a unique stench; mostly Tony,
partly old piss, with a touch of Dave's aftershave. I feel my gut
go into reverse. Gag.

'You all right, gel?' He laughs, a gust of unbelievable breath,
up into my face.

'You having it off with one of the DS, I hear. Could be
handy, gel. Who you having away? Jack is it? Nah, course not,
you couldn't say, could yer?'

Slyly. News travels. I score and get out of there. He follows
me out, breathing into my face.

'Always in the market for charlie, darling.' A hefty wink.
I nod sharply. Where the fuck does he think I can get charlie?

Johnny beetles up beside me.

'Hang on mate, you going up west are yer?' I'm not and
I don't fancy going anywhere with Johnny.

'Hold on, I'll be wiv yer.' He goes to the motor for a
moment and is beside me.

'You never seen Tone!' I say.

'Nah, gel, registered now meself aren't I? You could deal
with me if you like.'

He looks like Rasputin, long black hair, wicked cheekbones,
fast black eyes. Not as far along the line as Tony. Used to be
called Handsome Johnny before he was called Junkie Johnny.
Also Johnny the Harp I remember. Seen him about everywhere
for years; don't fit in, which is in his favour.

'I'll give you a hit if you want.' Now I'm interested.

'Where?'

'My drum, Maida Vale. Your virtue's safe wiv me, dolly.'

'Fuck me virtue, it's me drugs I worry about.'

His gaff is startling clean and smart. Neat except for the blackened spoons on the draining board and you expect that. Brilliant collages, montages, paintings round the walls.

'You do these?' He nods, turns on music, modern jazz, sleek music.

'Solid man. I'm well impressed, J. This is a nice drum, man.'

'I'm in the music business, gel, got to have a half decent gaff, darling. Anyway, can't stand squalor. No need for it, is there?'

I shrug: 'Thought it might've been compulsory.'

'Nah it's optional.' I take my coat off. 'Tell you what darling, I've got a quack I want yer to go and see, what yer reckon?'

'Wait 'til you've got that hit.'

I cook up and use his belt as tourniquet. I smell the heroin along with the matches. He breathes in and catches my vein on his second exhalation, first time with his eyedropper. It is sexual in a weird way but a lot nicer, a lot longer lasting, more permanent, a mind fuck. One of the best sights in the world; blood plumes into the dropper a deep red atomic explosion into the pure clear dope. A brief tiny moment of delicious anticipation, then it smacks into the brain, the body, the everywhere. Flush back lesser sensation, and again. Blitz time for the brain, the spirit in coalescent transient wallow that leaves in its wake long, clear peace.

I must have gone green because Johnny has the bowl beside me. As I vomit, the warm peaceful tranquillity soaks into me. Every pore of my skin, each lobe of my brain, is absorbed into joy. No jagged edges now, all smooth, no jangling painful needs. This is the up side of high.

'Finished, gel?' I smile up at him, wipe my face with his towel.

He gives me a lighted fag and the smoke joins the dope to cloud round my veins.

'That was the best hit ever, J.'

'Know where to come then, mate? Finished wiv this have yer?' He removes the bowl, sits, gives himself a hit.

'Can crash here tonight, Shindig.'

'Nah, got to get back haven't I?'

'Got somebody waiting for you, have you?'

'Got a small crowd waiting for me, be going spare, they got to get back to base.'

'Yanks?'

'Yeah, but they aren't hooked like so it don't matter a lot.' We laugh.

'You got to stop doing people so many favours, darling!'

Dark sarcasm. He cleans the eyedroppers in a tumbler of water, absently removes their collars, flushes them carefully.

'About this quack, what do you think?'

'What's it about, Johnny?'

'New geezer, likes the birds he do.'

'Right,' I say. 'So what you want me to do, pull him?'

'Up to you mate, don't 'ave to spell it out do I? Be worth a big script of charlie.'

'Who's been there?'

'You don't need to know that. Here's the address, bell him for an appointment. See if you can't weigh yerself in there permanent. Put him in promise land be favourite.'

'Right. I'll see what I can do.'

And you bring the script back to me, OK?'

'Suppose he won't play?'

'You come back and tell me, but he'll play all right, he's a randy cunt. Bird with your looks – no problem.'

'Might not go tomorrow, Johnny.'

'Fair enough, give you me phone number, keep ringing 'til you get me then come here. Never come here without belling me first and I won't be chasing you up. I know you won't let me down.'

We touch hands.

'And if you lose your bottle, tell me 'cos I can always find another bird to do it. I'll walk you down the road.'

He gives me his number on a card.

'Don't give that to nobody, don't schlep it round in yer handbag case you get nicked.'

'Don't worry Johnny. If they nick me I'll eat it before I let it fall into their hands.'

'I like a chick with a sense of humour.'

He leans over and gives me a dry peck on my nose and all he smells of is soap and tobacco; the junkie reek is hardly evident at all.

11 Stoned to the Bone

Back at the flat in Pembridge Gardens the hostility fairly crackles at me as I creep in, oiled joints moving meticulous, feeling a nice kind of buzzing where the brain usually frets. Mellow and full of fizzing static. Sometimes I get ratty on heroin, tonight I'm benign as a bath bun.

'Where you been, baby?' From Berry, vast duffel bag at the ready. Diego strips for action soon as I'm in the door, works at the ready, hand out for jacks.

'Two a quid, OK?' He nods and Colette tourneys him up.

'What kept you, hen?' From Colette. 'You meet somebody did you?' I give her a jack.

'Seen Johnny, didn't I?'

'Oh aye?' She cranks up. 'You'll need to watch him.' Her voice slows, she shuts her eyes.

'Aye, he's tricky so he is.' Her voice is disappearing on the high. She leans back on the cushion, empty of air. I light a fag for us both. She smiles up at me, her huge eyes almost completely iris now. Diego has fixed up. Sighs, shakes his head.

'Gotta go man.' Shakes his head again, emphatically. 'Not doing the thing, Berry?'

Berry drags himself from the mirror where he's been admiring himself, searching for imperfections, finding none, preening.

'No time, this cat's got to make that train, boy. Move it, my man, move it.'

'You away are you, youse two?' Colette grins at Diego.

'Yeah, man, when you gotta go,' Berry answers. He's fretting at the door. 'Come on, man, we gotta train to catch. Leave you ofay ladies to sit on your idle butts and cool it.'

Comes to me, gives me a kiss. His touch still does it for me every time.

'Later for you, babe.' He backs away from me pretending he can't let go, smiling.

'That right, Diego? Leave these ladies at rest on their big fat rusty dusties?'

Beautiful in his sharp four button suit, skin glowing, teeth shining. 'Ready for dead' in this no man's army. The words in my mind, I grab him, hold him tight.

'Hey, hey, babee, you just going to have to hold on to all that nice stuff 'til I bring my sweet black ass back, you hear what I say, girl?'

Diego struggles into his coat, kisses Colette, grabs his bag and they are off.

I look at Colette, at how small she is in her Audrey Hepburn skirt and flatties. Thin as a rail like she always was. Can't believe she was always this grubby. Her hair is claggy with grease, her hands mucky.

We are both gouching for a while there, then we begin to talk. We talk about our philosophy of life. A topic that often gets neglected in junkie circles. Both high so it's a protracted business. Gaps between our thoughts, and gaps between our thoughts and our words.

Colette speaks first:

'Was like a revelation so it was.'

A few beats pass while my mellowed brain receives and understands. A couple more, while my gob catches the drift of my mind.

'How's that, Colette?'

She breathes out fag smoke from her nose, a great satisfied exhalation. More beats.

'Ach, you know what I mean, you've fixed up.' She slides further down on the sofa. The smoke engulfs her. She is diminishing in size, growing in pungency and well being.

Beats.

I turn to look at her, slowly. Everything is nice, and slow.

'I just knew, when I had my first fix that that's what my life has been leading up to.'

I take this in and cogitate.

'You serious? That's it, the revelation?'

Threads of thoughts elude me, swing away, return. Beats.

'Aye, it's my messiah so it is.' She laughs a deep dry sound.

I laugh and even my laugh is thoughtful.

'That it then. Your ambition satisfied?'

She lights another fag from the lighted one.

'Not at all. I want to be like the rich bastards are, coming for their scripts in chauffeur driven motors, so I do.'

I think. What is surprising about this process is that we both think before we speak, and while our brains might not be at their best, this is still exceptional in my experience.

'Better get back to work then, gel, get some bread.'

From class hustler and hurry up merchant in Soho to languid junkie in one easy step. Not a bad move. She takes a few draws on her fag.

'Ach no, I'll attack it from the other direction, get stuck in, then get registered and flog my surplus to the rich and I've still a few punters who'll keep me in fags and tea. That's me.'

'That all you want is it?'

'Aye, unless I can find a rich junkie who wants a companion. Plus Diego, he comes as an added extra.'

We both take time out to be, then she comes back.

'What do you want?' This is the kind of conversation that BB and me have, but we never reach conclusions, and I don't now.

'Fucked if I know, gel.'

My brain scratches round the walls of my mind, like a tongue searching round the teeth for scraps. Nothing is forthcoming.

'Travel?' A suggestion from me.

Billy and me had always said we wanted to die before we were twenty but I don't mention this, our birthdays are getting close now. Colette continues: 'Aye, discover the delights of dope in several different languages. Did you see that syringe that Bobby brought back from Paris? Marvellous it was, all the measurements in foreign.'

'Sounds good, man,' I say.

'What else?' says Colette. Many beats while my brain and mind combine to work, but slowly.

All I really want is Berry, but that sounds feeble so I don't say it.

We have spoken about 'the future', Berry and me. Among his chat about how superior Stateside is we hardly cover racism. I read Ebony and Tan, see all the adverts for skin lightening creams, hair straightening lotions. 'Don't mean a thing! How that racist? Those women choose to do that stuff. Now come here and share your honey.' I read Langston Hughes to him. He won't wear it. 'Some Jim Crow mother-fucker!' he says. To Berry the States is nirvana. He has nothing in common with the Africans. 'Sheet, man, those mothers live in trees! I could take you home no sweat, my mummy would love you.' I try him with Richard Wright and James Baldwin. 'That mother's a homo!' he comes back to me after a couple of days. Strangely, he likes BB, who says I bring a missionary zeal to the project of improving Berry's mind. I feel arrogant and try to stop. BB also says I'm running scared of 'love: the real thing'. But none of this really figures, his body is the sweetest and the sex is the best. Sod the principles. Future? What future?

I come back to Colette now.

What else do you want?' Beats go on.

'I want to stay with Diego. He's not going back Stateside you know.' Think I knew this.

'No?'

'No. We're away to Morocco soon as we get the bread.' Now, the beats are taking more time.

Sounds good to me.

'Aye, he's got a passport from Johnny Mason. Going to do a runner so he is.'

'Sounds brilliant, Colette.'

I use the next few minutes to imagine how good that would be. Hot weather, all conceivable kinds of drugs. Beautiful women. Gorgeous men. Drugs.

'Come, why don't you?' A beat or two while I see the spectacular good sense of this idea. The whole vision slips into my mind and my brain examines it critically. Only a junkie dream, it says. But if it weren't . . .

'Get Berry to come.'

I hold on to the dream and look at it from all angles.

I'm still examining it when I notice she has begun to get her works ready for another fix. I chuck her a jack.

'I'll not ask you if you want a hit,' she says. Colette's hits are haphazard affairs of digging in her recalcitrant veins, very nearly as bad as my own. Anyway, I need to get home. I smell the sweet heroin boiling in the blackened spoon, watch her get a straight away hit. I've no veins to speak of, they conceal themselves deep in my arms.

'You got brilliant veins for a girl.'

'Aye, ain't that the truth, give us a ciggy.' I light it for her and she is in her own special heaven. She blurs the words and it occurs to me she is perfectly suited to being a junkie. Now she is collapsed in total tranquillity, she wears the eye dropper, a crimson leech in her arm.

She takes a few draws on her fag. It drops in the saucer full of butts.

I want to go home tonight, see BB, Angelo. Get my stuff together. Got to pull her about bread but it would destroy the buzz. I leave her alone, softened into liquid high. Got to go. I light a fag, sit down and next thing the door is being shaken vigorously and the fag has burnt to a singe on the carpet.

'Come on you slattern, up you get, auntie's on the rampage.' I open the door to BB. 'Come on Shindig, we're out on the town. I've got plenty of handbag and I'm going to meet Angelo and I'm not going on my own to sit and wait like a Mary while he performs. So get yer knickers on.'

He sees Collette. Looks at the dropper.

'Very tasty. Now I can see why you left home!' I laugh, then notice his tight angry face. He pulls me up close to him, looks hard in my face, shakes his head.

'You been on that fucking muck again haven't you? It doesn't do you any favours you know, your brain goes AWOL.' He lights two fags, shoves one at me. 'Are you fit to come out?'

'Course I am.'

'Hear yourself? Your voice is dead as mutton. That's what it does to you, blanks out your fucking mind you dozy cunt!'

Colette comes to with a snuffle and BB gets straight in her face:

'Leave her alone, you poisonous cow. You and your rotten stinking drugs. Keep them to yourself, she's my mate.'

'Aye, and she's the one bringing the drugs in to us, at a fucking profit so you just fucking watch it, you old queen.'

BB has the air taken out of him so I let her have it:

'You owe me bread, Colette. Don't tell me "see Diego", he owes me too,' I say.

'Ach away on with you, what is it? Three poxy quid? For the love of God don't be tight. I'll fix you up later.'

Colette turns over, covers herself with her coat. Back to the womb.

In the taxi BB begins his usual twenty questions conversation and I reveal all sorts of stuff I'd sworn to myself not to tell him.

He is especially scathing about Johnny's script business.

'Do you know him?' I ask.

'Enough to know he's vile,' he retorts. 'How much would the script be worth if you cashed it? Bet he's making a fortune out of you. Don't you care?'

'I wouldn't even know how to go about it. He's organising it; that's cool.' His face is a picture of concern and it doesn't suit him. 'Just watch he doesn't drop you in it!'

'Why would he?' I say.

Then he looks at me gloomily.

'I expect you're right, sweetie. I want to ask you something, about Angelo.'

'He's the best thing that ever happened to you, BB.'

'I know, that's what worries me.' We light up and I get this uneasy feeling. BB never gets crises of confidence: that's what I like about him. I try to slither out the way.

'Hear Marmalade and Victoria had a right ruck in the pub.'

'Shindig, do you think he loves me?'

The words plummet to the floor of the taxi and settle in a heap among the old vomit stains on the rubber surface. I ignore them. My brain goes off on a tangent: how the fuck do I know? What is this thing called love? And several other remarks slide into and vacate my brain. But I don't utter them. Feel the effects of my recent fix disappearing in a gust of embarrassment. This is why I don't knock about with birds. I wish to avoid conversations like this.

'Course he does.' My voice is all bravura, he doesn't notice.

'Yes?' Eager.

'Adores you, doesn't he? What brought this on?'

'Been thinking, haven't I?'

'Well stop it. It's always fatal, too much thinking, especially about love. Accept it, enjoy it. For as long as it lasts, dig it.'

'What have you heard?' Voice gone high.

'Nothing!'

'You must have heard something, or you'd never have said "as long as it lasts".'

'That was a fucking philosophical comment, you daft cunt!'

Thank God we arrive outside the Maribu club just then; he's bringing me down.

Angelo is his usual sunny self, face lights up to see us, kisses us both on both cheeks. Swans off to perform small rituals with the rest of the cast who are all here at the invite of some rich fucker who's into black art, or black meat. We are here under slightly false pretences. BB fixed it with the lady artistic director who swoops down on us now.

'Billy? Shindig? That right is it? Such a camp sobriquet! So glad you could come, looking even lovelier than I expected.' She has a middle European accent overlaid with American, is so confident as to turn me into instant resentful blancmange. She is also large in every department, with muscles.

She moves off in a flurry of busyness.

'Seems like a nice girl. Reminds me of a probation officer I once knew,' I say.

'She wants to go to 'Gateways' with us.'

'Hope you haven't put her in promise land, BB.' He grins cryptically. Angelo blows him a kiss and he smiles back.

'See, it's OK, isn't it?

'I'm not sure. Victoria said something.'

'Victoria is a malicious old bitch. Start listening to what she says and you'll be fucked! 'But you know that, BB!' and I go to dance with one of Angelo's mates and when I come back I see Tiger has arrived, though what's he got to do with art?

'What you doing here, gel?' He'd come in with big Sid and another geezer but they'd gone to get drinks.

'BB asked me didn't he? His boyfriend Angelo is in the dancing troupe.'

'Oh right. I'm here for the culture meself, aren't I, doll.' And his face crimps into its separate parts of pencil moustache and horse teeth that make up his evil grin. Meanwhile his eyes are extremely shrewd and humorous. The yellows of his eyes match his teeth to near perfection.

Sid and his mate return from the drinks table. The mate is camel hair smooth and creams over me until Tiger introduces me.

'Yeah, Shindig's my barmaid, at the club.' The smooth guy cools noticeably and takes Tiger's arm.

'Excuse me,' he says and they huddle.

'How ya doing?' I ask Sid.

'Oh fine. Here to see some paintings aren't I? What's a nice girl like you doing here?' he laughs. 'You got an interest in art, eh?'

The crowd here are made up of all types, from the really rough to the ultra posh. It 's a weird mix. I think I see somebody from Lyn's crew but can't be sure. Sid and me melt into the crowd and watch.

'What kind of paintings, Sid?'

'Old ones.' His mouth shuts tight, like a trap door.

'Oh! Seen Jimmy lately?' But he's off into the crowd and I make my way back to BB.

We do a sort of review of the people we can see, class, job, marital status. We go through them all. Choosing either the most likely or the most bizarre we can think of.

'Tiger's obviously a gynaecologist,' says BB.

'He wishes!'

'And Celeste is a ballet dancer,' I say. 'Big Sid is an abortionist, I think.'

We are working our way through the crowd very happily, when BB gives me an emphatic jab in the ribs. Totally unnecessary because I'm well in whispering range. A very posh looking geezer has come in. He removes his gloves carefully, looking round as if he's expecting a butler to manifest from the paintwork.

Celeste hurries to his side, all due care and attention. They touch cheeks and do one of those formal grins that disclose choppers and gums, very briefly. No eye crinkles are apparent.

BB looks thoughtful. Like he's scheming. There is something familiar about the guy. Then I recall. I saw him once with Victoria.

'Is he one of Vic's punters?' BB nods.

'Used to take us all out. Marmalade and Carlotta hijacked him, greedy bitches. Like a one man benevolent society for all the bum boys he was. All went back to place in Park Street for parties. Of course Victoria nicked some gear from him, according to Marmalade and Carlotta. Who knows? I got blamed and went down for it. I didn't expect Vic to confess and, to be fair, I did flog the gear. But Marmalade and Carlotta could have got me off, no trouble, but they thought that was them set up for life. In fact he stopped seeing the lot of us so that was us all snookered.' BB laughs, waves at the guy. He smiles over but it's a frosty number that doesn't encourage intimacy and he turns away fast. Celeste and the guy make a huddle with big Sid.

'So why did you let Vic move into our house?'

'Vic got in with Vera before I noticed, sweetie. Anyway, you can't hold anything against Vic. She's so wired up, I put it all down to neurosis, whereas bloody Marmalade and Carlotta have their wits about them. They'd buy and sell you for a tanner, sweetie.' Doesn't sound like the Marmalade I know, or even Carlotta, who I reckon is a hard bitch. I don't share my thoughts.

'So you fell out with them permanent like?'

'Quite! It's all for one in the face of the law, don't you think?' He sounds a bit arch but he's right. Angelo has come back into our orbit and Tiger comes over to me just then so I leave BB to it.

I would love to know what Tiger's up to but he gives nothing away. Like pulling teeth, getting info out of Tiger; teeth would be easier. We talk about me, my specialist subject. Knows how to make a bird happy does Tiger. It all goes on without us, the hubbub and the grinning faces.

'Want a lift, gel? Expect you'll be wanting to get back on the nest soon won't you, been a few hours now hasn't it.' He laughs as I whack him one. I tell BB I'm shooting and he smiles from over Angelo's shoulder. A happy omiepalone.

I still don't know what I am going to wear for Lyn's party and when I get home I rummage among my own and BB's gear and get into a fever of trying stuff on and parading in front of the mirror. I really want to make the right impression at Lyn's.

12 It's a Mighty Poor Rat that Ain't Got But One Hole

We are a good hour late for the party, we've changed gear several times from our skins out. Slap has been carefully applied and then removed. We have overdone the speed and are in a creative frenzy of critical artistry that strives for perfection and fails. Finally we make it out and after a drink we arrive at Lyn's, exquisitely presented.

Shouldn't have bothered, it is well under way towards mayhem when we arrive there. Limbs thresh, mouths mewl, lewd bits are evident, tongues and twats, a vast tumble of twitching flesh. We take our drinks, keep to the edges where we cruise quietly round: a stately promenade of non-participants, watching. Two large women are locked in unholy embrace on an armchair, mouth to mouth, bosom to bosom, immersed. Their flesh hangs over the edge like uncooked dough. BB digs me in the ribs, points to a group of men licking and sucking at their protuberances. One of them, in the process of being buggered vigorously is a top-notch government minister, a leading voice on family values. Now his face is a mask of concentration. Glazed eyes bulge, mouth gapes. Breath enters and leaves his lungs like some old harmonica on heat. We shudder.

'I'll never trust the parliamentary system again,' I say.

'That's the least of it, sweetie,' BB says. 'Corrupt!' BB is vindicated.

'Come on, darlings, join in.' Lyn has come upon us forcefully. She is wearing black leather from her feet up with a half mask over her eyes like the lone Ranger. The bottom of her face looks very cross and I remark to BB that it's surprising what an amount of expression can be fitted round the mouth. Then she brings up a leather riding crop, waves it at me with menace. I giggle with nerves and she gives me a sharp whack.

'Nobody likes a peeping Tom, do they?' She shoves a joint in my hand. Some old dyke grabs me and we dance to the slow music. Has her tongue in my earhole before we've been introduced, menaces me round the floor like an errant tea trolley.

'Come on, my little sausage, let's go to bed.' I can be curiously formal at times and get the dead needle at her presumption. Angelo is being groped by some foul fat American who is forcing his gross leg between Angelo's own and pushing him back on to a sofa.

'I don't give a damn what you are, I want you, baby.' BB, looking twice his normal size in a dress, has struck lucky and got a horn-rimmed, sincere type of geezer bending his ear. I envy him. My own ear is ragged, and when she takes her gob away long enough it feels chilly and damp under her fevered whispers.

It takes me that long to realise we are on the menu.

I recognise my dyke about the same time she starts getting nasty and asks me if I know who she is.

'No, mate. Do you know who I am?' I respond.

'No.' She leans back to look at me and I escape her clutch long enough to see Angelo lift his handbag and whack the Yank over the nut. The fat bloke staggers back but isn't put off and continues to plight his troth, takes out his flaccid dick and waves it at Angelo who says something in Portuguese, bends to the dick, and bites. Hard, by the sound of the geezer's yelp. Angelo snatches me away and we dance and giggle our relief. We've escaped. Lyn advances on us with her riding crop at the ready and one of her henchmen. We twirl off, knocking into huddles and heaps of characters, accidentally to begin with. Then, shrieking with laughter, we aim at busy bodies, belt at tables and chairs.

BB has joined our destructive process and chucks a vast purple dildo into the mêlée. He runs with a strap-on on his head like a unicorn. Hysterical now, the gaff is pandemonium. An inspector from the drug squad has come out of a side room. He looks me in the eye and shoots back again. I spot big Sid in a doorway. I wave but he doesn't wave back. The two old girls with the floury bottoms look up from their event, casually at first, then alarmed, but they return to their unique action. I realise I have seen one of them on the silver screen and point her out to BB but she looks up and moves, swiftly for a big woman, she misses me but clobbers BB before she remembers she's starkers. Her bulbous bits flap and flounder as she makes an energetic grab at him. Angelo scratches her as he brings up the handbag again. Lyn whacks me one so I bring my knee up, then it's all over and we three are out in Linden Gardens. We run as quickly as the high heels and sheaths allow and don't stop laughing until we get to the all night café in Notting Hill when we realise that BB and me have lost our handbags. 'No matter,' says BB, and brings out money from his nether regions. I dig out a few quid from my bras.

Angelo is still swearing in Portuguese, clutching his handbag tightly.

I give him a cuddle:

'You're a bit tasty in a bundle, Angelo.' BB looks proud and gives him a kiss on his chops.

'We'll have none of that in here, thank you!' From the filthy git who runs the joint and regularly panders birds, flogs drugs and grasses people up.

'That you getting judgmental, darling?' I say. Been trying to get in my knickers for ever, creep.

'Yeah, don't like bleeding pooftars in 'ere.'

'Not what I heard,' I quip and we're given the order of the boot for the second time in an hour.

On the pavement we reflect.

'I'm hungry. Thought they'd have had some food at Lyn's.'

'Nothing I would eat,' says Angelo: 'Shower of cunts,' he adds. BB and me laugh, still hysterical.

'Better not lig about in the street too long or we'll get nicked for impersonation.' We stop the first taxi, go down to West-bourne Grove.

'Malibu, cabby.'

'Right you are, gels.' He gives the regulation lewd wink. Then: 'Never guess who I had in here earlier on.' BB wrecks his night by naming the cabinet minister at the party. 'How'd you know that?' The cabby's voice highly aggrieved.

'A wild guess,' says BB and you could almost see the news on the grapevine flying.

The club is jumping, the music meets us half way, slips into our bones and we start to gyrate to Elvis. Girls and boys in drag, femmes, butches, everything in between, some like me who don't know if we're Arthur or Martha.

All cavort. I dance with Angelo while BB goes for a soft drink. Look around the gloomy floor, see a girl I know. Moving towards her when I feel a familiar touch on my shoulder, smell familiar skin and my lovely Sergeant Dixon kisses me gently on my neck and as we dance I kiss her back. I consider telling her I saw her governor at the party but stay shtoum.

Dixie looks gorgeous tonight in DJ and exotic scarlet cummerbund. I dance in tight to her body, feel her breasts inside their crêpe bandages flattened, spread over her ribs. Her hands are hard on my back, slide down over my arse, hold me in tight as we dance. Her leg between my thighs, riding hard in close melting fusion. I take her hand as the music stops, we go out the fire exit, lean against the wall, touching with lips, tongues, flesh on flesh.

'I've my car round the corner, pet.' Just holding hands tenderly, creeping away, when the door bounces open.

'Dixie? That you is it? And who exactly is this little floozy? You simply can't be left, can you?'

Shakes her head in regret. Her voice is humorous. She is small, slender but emphatically butch. Dixie has shrunk, guilt all over her face.

'Come on, darling.' The woman's voice is quite firm. They've been here before. Dixie obediently lets go my hand.

'Sorry, my love, afraid she lacks any vestige of self control this one.' The woman grins at me and they leave together, back into the music.

'Don't worry, you'll find somebody of your own easily. You look charming and as you clearly have a complete lack of moral probity you'll do well. Just what we need on the scene, another slut.'

She leans back to give me a kiss on my cheek, ending with a tiny nip.

'Get her,' laughs BB and we dance together giggling.

13 Doctor Blues

Nice looking bloke the quack, got skin that looks well nourished, with an extra smooth patina from robust country pursuits in early youth. Flesh put down by a childhood of the best of food will become fat as soon as he stops the rugger. His hands are twitching to follow his shifty eyes as they slither over me.

Piece of piss. Time I've told him the tragic, highly erotic, carefully fabricated tale of my young life, he's putty, rampant putty. I manage to nick a few blank scripts as well as the one he writes for me. Tell him I'll be back next week; with an edge to my voice so he gives a sort of joyful wince. Mission accomplished.

BB came along and now he trolls up the road. 'How'd it go, duckie? Bona?' He answers himself. 'Can tell by the ecaf, jubilant you look, what you do to the poor man? No, don't tell me, I'm too naïve!' He links me and we make our way down New Cavendish Street.

'Made him very happy then threatened him with more of the same, captured he is.'

'Clever girl, now get the script to Johnny and get out. He's vile.'

'He's all right, his house is great, full of art works, brilliant.'

'He's dangerous, and all this fixing is dangerous. We all dabble, sweetie, but it's getting beyond a joke since you teamed up with that Yank. Think you're so smart don't you? The only girl in town to make a few bob out of drugs? Crap!'

'Oh bollocks, BB, fuck's sake don't nag.'

'It's not nagging, I knew Trudy three years ago and she was gorgeous, look at the state of her now!'

'You're turning into a boring bastard, BB.' I flounce into a boozer and BB follows in full ruck mode. We are sniping at each other like an old married couple when we realise the pub's gone totally silent. Like we've invaded some old girl's front

room and affronted relations glare at us. I put on a smile of
great ingratiation, assume my vamp stance, ask for a drink and
then I notice scarface Jimmy in a corner with a group of pug-
uglies. Behind the bar a scowling geezer glowers at us.

'All right, gel?' says Jimmy, coldly. The smile dies on my
face. 'And Billy, eh? Strange territory for you two int it? Serve
the lady and gentleman, Freddy.'

He turns back to his mates. We won't stay long here. The
barman dredges up a marginally less ferocious look, gives us
our bevvies and demands, very nearly with menaces, payment
from BB. He ignores me.

'Handbag, BB. I'll straighten you up don't worry.'

We sit as far from the bar as we can. BB's knees are rigid
and tight together, near his chest. I am a coiled spring. BB's
eyes are excited and scared.

'Why did you get a pint? We want to get out of here.'

'Sorry, never thought, did I?'

I look round, try a smile but it comes back untouched. 'Bit
menacing isn't it?' I notice a pain in my legs, realise they are
wound tight round each other. I give a giggle, sounds high
terror. BB has polished off his G and T, frets with the glass.
Points at my pint. 'Get it down yer screech, gel.'

I try, and the beer does that trick where it sloshes round the
gob, reaches the throat and washes out again like the tide.

'Don't use it as a mouthwash, drink it. And why did you
bring me in here anyway?' He follows this with a slight tooth
suck.

'Didn't know it was going to be a den of bleeding iniquity
did I, you daft cunt?' I look over at Jimmy and crew. 'Why are
they all so ugly?' I muse.

'Don't look at them.' He shrieks softly. 'It's the boss!'

I am awe-struck. This geezer's reputation flies ahead of him
and scares.

'Let's go.' I stand up and we start to leave. A small bantam
of a man gets up, comes over.

'Summink wrong with the beer is there, darling?'

I shake my head emphatically.

'Then get it down yer, gel. Another drink for the . . .' He
pauses, '. . . gentleman, Fred.' Moves his head back over his
shoulder. The barman obeys.

BB's visage shines pale as an old bone and I feel my own face starching up whitely. I look over towards Jimmy but he blanks me. My bladder has received diuretic messages from my brain but I can't leave BB. The man brings back a bevvy for him and pulls out a chair with his foot, turns it, sits backwards and leans his chin on the chair back.

'Hear you're a mate of Johnny Mason? That right is it?'

BB, even in profound terror, can't resist a 'told you so' look and a tiny lip pucker.

'I know him a bit, not a lot,' I say and give a slight movement to show how tiny is my knowledge of Johnny.

'Yeah?' He draws on his fag, lifts his brows quizzical. 'That right is it?'

He looks at BB, who opens then shuts his mouth silently. He lifts the drink. 'Cheers!' His voice is a parody of squeak. I have another go at my pint and this time it glides down my screech slowly but surely, at this rate it will take me a mere twenty minutes to get shot of it. I feel my eyes bulge a bit as if they're floating on the beer. In the background the men's voices murmur as I wait for the next thing. The bantam offers us both fags that we accept frantic fast. The sweat on BB's upper lip shines in the flame of the match. My hand has such a tremble on that I can hardly align my mouth with the fag, then I light the wrong end and during the coughing conflagration I feel my bladder give up the ghost and wee myself. I do a fast pelvic floor tug and it stops but it can only be a matter of time. Time and terror will work their inevitable fluid work.

'Yeah, used to play the harmonica din't 'e.' He demonstrates the playing. 'Used to play a bit myself din't I?'

I raise my brows and hang on to my pelvic floor for dear life. 'Really?'

'Yeah, used to be good he did.'

'And you? What did you play?'

'The 'arp same as 'im. Wasn't as good though.'

'Good as what?' says BB, can't bear to be left out of anything. Fervently hope he doesn't decide to take the piss. His face is still livid but he's obviously dying to chat. I wait.

'Good as what Johnny is, never practised did I?'

'Oh, you'd have to practise,' says BB, nodding wisely.

I think they're away into a conversation so I ask where the

bog is to decant my bulging bladder while the going's good.
The innards of the boozer are pink and sort of ruched, like a
vaginal wall, pelmets and curtains abound. Evidence of a very
feminine hand. The lavatory is scrupulously clean and quite
astoundingly pink with tiny fluffy towels, crinoline lady, towel-
ling bog cover, mat, the lot. It looks like a birth canal with the
startling white bog, the baby.

While I have a blissful slash, I ream the crinoline lady for
hidden drugs. Silly really, a conditioned response. I idly lift the
cistern top to have a butchers when I've pulled up my damp
pants, it slips, clanks back into place noisily. A voice I know
issues from outside.

'What you up to, my girl?' A distinctive clear voice, Tiger's
missis. I bustle out. She stands, a sentry.

'Hope you washed your hands.'

'I did, lovely towel.'

'What were you doing with the cistern?'

'Cistern? Nothing.'

'Do I have "cunt" carved on my forehead?'

My mouth has gone dry with fear. There is no answer but
the temptation is too fierce:

'Course not, you'd have noticed.' Why the fuck did I say
that?

She grabs hold of me by the front of my jacket until she is
breathing her spearmint up my nose.

'Listen cocker, I don't like you, I don't want you in my pub
but before I kick your scruffy carcass out I want to know what
the fuck you were doing in my bog.' She is in my face and
while I could definitely outrun her, I'm trapped, looking at the
muscles on her arms.

'Having a slash! I never touched your cistern, must have
knocked it or something.' My voice is high C and just then BB
comes through from the bar.

'What's keeping you? You know we've got to meet the
girls. Oh, hello, Renee! You're looking bona, darling. Isn't
she looking bona? Mind you she always does, don't you, my
sweet?'

He advances, lips pursed, kisses the air by her face. Renee
has almost melted into a smile. Lets go of my coat. I nearly fall
backwards into the barman who catches me, giving a swift

grope. 'Think it's time you left, gel. Stay for a drink Billy but I don't want 'er in my pub, she's trouble.'

'I know, Renee, it's her personality dear, I keep telling her don't I? But does she listen? No! Come on Shindig, let's get you home.'

'What kind of bleeding name's that?'

'Oh I think it suits her, Renee.'

'Shitcunt would suit 'er even better!'

They both hoot and snigger extensively.

'What's Shindig mean then?'

'Noisy party.'

'She's that all right!'

They guffaw, loud and long. 'Yeah, Billy, get her out of it for us mate. And I don't want to see you nowhere, you got that, gel?'

'Say "yes" to the nice lady, Shindig.'

I do and Renee is jubilant. We leave.

I get back to Johnny the next day, bell him, he says come over. He looks well smart.

'Fuck me gently, J, you look gorgeous,' I say.

'Yeah, got business to do haven't I?' He passes me a joint. 'You're looking choice too, gel.' He takes the script.

'Nice!' He hisses, kisses the script. 'How'd it go? You fit for another whack at him?'

'Yes, I think so.' He looks sharply at me.

'Not thinking of going independent are you?' Shakes his nut. 'Already so soon!'

'I just thought I might make more on my own.'

'You might but it's a lot more risky. You gotta schlep it round all over the place. That's the dangerous bit. Then getting the bread for it. See it's not like knocking out a few Jacks. That's a captured market.' He's getting into it now. 'Got to duck and dive, meet people, be sociable, be nice.' His voice has gone high on the 'nice'.

'Yes, I might find that hard,' I joke. He ignores me. His face goes crafty.

'But then, my dear, you got to extract the money off these people.' Now he sounds like Fagin. 'It's social skills, see.'

I'm clearly not up to this.

'And, of course, it's a universal truth that the richer the cunts are, the harder it is to get the money out of them. Cheeky bastards want to give you cheques! Bleeding cheques! Plus, of course, there's stiff competition. Nasty people out there.' Shakes his head solemnly, eliciting dangers too awful to contemplate, his face a picture of duplicity.

'See, gel, the only part of the process I can't do is the quacks but there are always birds who can.' Looks me in the eye. 'Never any shortage of useful birds, darling, so I think we should both stick to what we know, don't you?' I look at him, say nothing. He speaks:

'Trouble with crooks they always distrust each other.'

'That's natural enough isn't it?' I say. He huffs into the draw, looks up at my face. No idea what he's on about now.

'You told anybody about our little deal?'

I hesitate. He looks well solemn. He sighs. I speak, 'Didn't go into details, did I?'

'If we decide to go ahead on a permanent basis, then don't rabbit about it, not to nobody. Think you can manage that do yer?' My brain flicks Dixie in and out of my mind in glorious Technicolor.

'Yeah, you're right, Johnny. I'll keep shtoum.'

'Do yer best, gel. Still working for Tiger are yer?'

He nods, like he's agreeing with himself.

'See, gel, you're in a perfect place there. That Tiger don't touch drugs, one of the old school he is. Straight as a dye.'

He pays me what we agreed and gives me a wrap of charlie bonus. I am well touched and nearly tell him about the blank scripts I nicked, but I hesitate, then decide against.

I make my way to the club and Tiger shoots off straight away. I get my book, *Cannery Row*, and settle behind the bar on a stool, I hope fervently for a quiet day. Frantic arrives within half an hour. I give her a lemonade.

'Hear you got a deal wiv Johnny Mason. That right is it?'

She looks at me with her forty-year-old eyes in her twenty-year-old-face and once again I feel impelled to tell the truth, although there is no reason.

'What if I am?' I hedge.

'Nuffing,' she says in a way that means 'everything'.

'No, what do you mean?' Her eyes triumph as I ask.

'He's well dodgy, gel, well dodgy.'

Some geezer comes to the bar at that moment and as I serve him and exchange the regulation badinage I can see Frantic poncing around with Tiger's gallery, moving pictures according to some arcane scheme of her own. Now, she has put a heroic greyhound among the welterweight and featherweight boxers. The heavyweights are up by the men's bog, too high for her skinny little claw-like hands to reach. Several motor racing pictures have been demoted or promoted to the part of the wall with the race horses.

She lifts a picture of Tiger in the embrace of a boxer whose spread nose face looks familiar and puts it among a clutch of his favourite dogs going back to Ajax the Airedale circa nineteen thirty something by the look of the gear.

'Reckon that's Tiger as a cub, do yer?' Pointing at a boy clutching a dog. She hurrumphs.

'Yeah, mate, he's well dodgy, Johnny. Gives me the horrors he do. The Malts had a contract on him one time. Don't know what happened about that but they reckon he's got a direct line to Saville Row – and not for his suits neither.'

She gives her hurrumph that passes for a laugh, second one today that is. We are spared her hyena job; that, she saves for special occasions. She comes back to her fizzy pop, drinks, nicks a fag.

'But you'd know all about that, wouldn't you? Wiv your contacts like?' I feel my cheeks cherry up.

'You've gone all red, doll,' she says flatly. 'So what's that about then?'

'What?'

'You know, Johnny being a grass? Your contacts?'

'I don't believe it.' I hear my voice, it doesn't convince. She looks hard at me.

'They say that about everybody, don't they?' I say. She shrugs. 'He's all right, a bit dodgy but harmless,' I say.

'You sure about that, are you?' She peers at me from up close.

Plants her arse on the stool nearest me.

'See, you still think like a straight don't you? Got a strictly amateur attitude you have.'

Nods wisely to herself.

'Don't work things out do you? You've got to fink fings frew.'

She stabs at her nut with her forefinger, then she leans on the bar looking over at me.

'For instance: when it's foggy what do you think?' She pauses but doesn't wait for me to speak. 'I'll tell yer what you think: delays of transport, nasty coughs, bad chests, black snot in yer hankie – am I right?'

She nods before I utter.

'Getting lost,' I say.

'There yer go, getting lost the lady says.' As if she's addressing punters from a barrow, flogging fruit.

'But, my dear, fog is all about finding, finding marvellous things.' She sounds quite lyrical.

'It means Bond Street opened up to the poor, smash and grabs, heists of unaccustomed size in unexpected quarters. It means large scale nickage and petty thievery, bottles of booze, fur coats and lovely jewels. Fog is definitely a fucking equalising factor, my dear.'

Does an emphatic final draw on her fag, her entire face collapsed like a bellows to get the full essence out of it.

'Even galleries, picture galleries in Bond Street been known to give up their booty to the liberating tea leaf, in a really good pea souper. One like we had last winter for instance.'

'Never heard you so loquacious, Frannie.' She gives one of her creaky winks in which she moves her lid so slow you can almost hear it. Takes a sip from her lemonade, looks at me so I get the feeling this is what the whole pantomime has been about.

'Hear Tiger's got a collection of real pictures downstairs.' Her voice is less flat now, a jerk of interest in there.

'Do what?'

'That's what I hear, gel.' Lights another fag, blows smoke over me. 'Could always have a look, mate, couldn't we?'

'Where'd you hear that, Frannie?'

She looks at the cellar door.

Then Tiger comes in, sees Frantic, glares at us both.

'You been changing my pictures around have you?' He looks round the walls. Frantic has her head almost on her chest, giggling silently. He leans back, nods his head.

'Oh very good, very witty, a comment on man's relationship with dogs, violence and mobility! Nice!' And he buys us both a drink, doesn't he?

14 In the Jailhouse Now

Then Victoria gets nicked, which shouldn't have surprised us, was on the cards after all. But we are dumbstruck, appalled. Brings all our own sins into focus and has me reaming drawers, poking into cupboards looking for illegal substances; tearing labels off stolen gear in a kind of guilt frenzy.

Of course, it's some geezer he turned over round a corner one fine night. Inevitable says BB: I agree. We'd told him, we say. Yes, he'd been warned, and we make ourselves feel better with blame until Angelo asks us what we're going to do, so then we stop. Get tobacco and papers organised and magazines to take a trip to the nick at West End Central where he is being held. Without bail, says the copper who comes to tell us. I don't want to go because I've got this abiding picture of Dixie in sexual mode in my mind, which upsets my concentration something rotten. Angelo definitely can't go. Being a foreign national, going to visit a convicted Victoria in her guise as male prostitute and tea leaf could be the icing on the cake that gets him deported.

So BB is the elected member and he doesn't like it a bit.
'They've got fuck all on you, BB.'
'They've got nothing on you either but you won't go.' He is petulant, threatening full moody.
'I've told you why I don't want to go; I don't want to see Dixon. I've had her away, haven't I?' He huffs and puffs his resentment.
'Well, come with me and wait in the taxi. I'll feel safer if I've got somebody waiting for me.' I know what old BB means. There's always the feeling that you might be lurking and get nicked for something the police just happen to have outstanding. So I bury my face in the newspaper outside the nick and

wait tensely with the fractious taxi driver nagging about his clock.

'Look, miss, I can't sit here losing money, you better pay me off now.'

'My friend's got the money.'

'Well, go in and get it.'

'Can't be done mate, he's helping the law with their enquiries and if I go in they'll connect me to his nefarious activities.'

Now the driver holds the door, inviting me emphatically to exit. I'm concentrating on his bulbous nose with its broken veins so don't spot Dixie coming down the steps looking clever with herself.

'I thought so! I asked Billy if he'd seen you and he looked so edgy I knew you'd got to be out here. Why didn't you come in and see me?' I shrug nonchalantly. Like it never occurred to me, was the last thing on my mind, I give her a grin. The cabby is still thrashing about in his skin working himself up into frenzy. Dixon turns to him.

'Is there a problem here?'

'No, no problem,' I say, but the cabby got to put his two pen'orth in didn't he?

'Yes there bleeding is. I've been waiting here with my clock on stationary for twenty minutes and this cheeky little . . .' He pauses searching for the right word, gives up. '. . . has been giving me lip.'

'Well, Billy's only been here for ten. And she's a paying customer isn't she?'

And she asks for his documents. His overstuffed face goes into three degrees of fracture.

'You better put the clock up,' I say.

'And you'd better get your money ready,' says he, as he brings out a sheaf of papers and they get engrossed. I go in to see BB. He is leaning on the counter, talking to the desk sergeant. He greets me effusive:

'Darling flower!' He turns to the desk sergeant, 'Here's my friend, so perhaps you can explain to her why Mr Connolly can't have bail.' He very nearly stamps his foot and it crosses my mind that this is probably not the best way to handle the situation. Odd, because BB is shrewd as fuck and gauges these things to perfection normally. I put in my own two pen'orth.

'See nobody's taken up my suggestion of smartening up this place. Ought to get some of that nice wallpaper. It's like going back to wartime. I'm surprised you haven't got an Anderson shelter, for the atmosphere like.'

They both ignore me.

'I've told you why Mr Connolly can't have bail.'

The cop's voice slows and distinguishes itself by its clarity.

'Victor Connolly has a record as long as all our arms put together.'

'What, mine too? Six arms?' I join in. The sergeant leans on the counter, a patient man.

'Twelve arms would hardly cover it. Add to that the fact that he has never, since we first encountered him many moons ago, turned up at court without a warrant and some poor officers going out to bring him in; always a nasty and protracted process.'

He looks deep into my eyes doing a kind copper act.

'And think of the cost! I'm sure that you, as tax payers, can see that the cost is exorbitant and unnecessary.' Sarcastic bastard. He goes on:

'So I'm sure you will understand why this time I've decided to cut out the middle man and keep him here with us. We will take every care of him and now you've brought him some snout and something to read I think he'll be a very happy boy.' He rests his arms on the counter waiting for BB to utter.

'When's he up?' I ask.

'Not 'til Monday which is why I'm so worried, what with his claustrophobia and everything,' BB bleats.

The sergeant shrugs and suddenly gives a beam at me and I'm rather pleased, even though he's quite old and a bill, then I realise that Dixon has come up behind us. He greets her then looks BB in the eye, speaks:

'And he causes pandemonium if we send him to Brixton as you know very well, Billy. And as for the claustrophobia, he should have thought of that when he was clipping some unfortunate bloke who had the lack of taste and, indeed, the sheer lunacy, to join him off Half Moon Street.'

'Yeah, well you've only got his word for that haven't you?'

'No!' says the sergeant. He goes on:

'We have the wallet, driver's licence and cheque book all

found in Mr Connolly's possession but I don't have to explain any of this to you, do I? Unless you're his next of kin and you don't look like his mother.'

'I'm his lover,' says BB. 'That must count for something.'

'It doesn't and you know it, Billy.'

'So can I go and see him in the cells?' I ask.

'Yes, she could be his common law wife, couldn't she?' From BB.

'But she isn't, is she?' says Dixon. 'Unless you've got an unholy threesome on the go.' Dixon and he both laugh at the idea and I join in but also wonder why BB is so keen to get in to see Victoria. BB gives me a sly look that I don't begin to understand. Then Dixon intervenes:

'I could take them down if you like, Sarge, if that's OK? It's only a matter of getting somebody to accompany them isn't it?' He looks well dubious but agrees.

'Yes, all right, off you go then.' I tag along and we go into the bowels of the earth where the cells are and I have a good look round. Last time I came here I was under the spell of a large copper and didn't get the full benefit. Even now, I find it unsettling, what with a drunk making appeals for immediate freedom and the stink of rubber, piss and stale bodies. A female officer lifts her bulky arse to let us in and we both bend down and peer through the aperture you put food through.

Vic shrieks alarm at the sight of our two eeks squashed up so Dixon says:

'I think we can have the door open don't you, Stubbs?'

Stubbs opens the door, gives a shrug and turns away. As Dixie stands back. BB rushes forward to hug Vic, which is very unusual. In fact Vic looks seriously alarmed but I'm engrossed flirting with Dixie, standing really close so I can smell her lovely scent of fresh sweat all mixed up with Coal Tar soap. I'm getting off on the idea of a shag in the cells: can almost feel the nasty rough grey blankets as I push her back onto the rubber mattress, pulling her gear off, fumbling with her buttons, biting her neck. I am completely engrossed so that Victoria's plaintive voice is unwelcome:

'They won't let me have a mirror or hairbrush or slap! Isn't that barbaric? And another thing, I'm sure it's illegal to keep me here rather than Brixton.'

'The rhia looks rough, Vic. They didn't beat you up did they, sweetie?' All cosset from BB who is sitting on the bench next to Vic. He takes his comb out and Vic combs his rhia, but his face is in disarray like he doesn't know which emotion to bring up for our edification.

'Can't he get a shower, Dixie?' I ask, knowing the answer. She turns to me and from the edge of my eyes I see BB bung something to Vic. I touch Dixie's shoulder:

'You got a hair, a long blonde one.' I smile into her eyes while I lift the imaginary hair. Then old Stubbs comes forward:

'I can't have this, Sergeant Dixon, can't have special treatment can we?'

'No, you're quite right, we can't. We'll have to lock you up again, Connolly.'

'What did you bring me?' His voice is high stressed and squeaks but he looks relieved.

'Baccy and something to read,' I say as we back out.

'The desk sergeant will bring you your stuff soon,' says Dixie, who's now got me captured in all kinds of superb pervie fantasies so I can hardly even think. I'm not concentrating at all. We walk along a corridor and I'm away in full frontal lewd while I look at her chunky butt move along in front of me.

'Put your tongue away, you dirty little cow!' hisses BB, and Dixie turns and gives this big, soft, slow, creamy smile that has me enveloped and soaks me in glory and reaches to my toes with pure loving warmth.

Dixie touches me gently on the back of my upper arm. It feels like all the awareness in my entire body goes to that one spot, a gorgeous sexual assault. I turn and know my gob is half open with lust while I look into her eyes.

'When you coming off duty?' I laugh.

'Why wait?' she laughs. 'Give me half an hour. I'll meet you in the pub, OK?'

She brings up her fist and rubs her knuckles on my chin. I poke out my tongue and lick her hand just as the sergeant looks over. He does a throat clearing.

'Right, Billy, and you Shindig, if you want to see Mr Connolly again you can come back tomorrow.'

'How much was the taxi?' are BB's first words. Mine are:
'What were you bunging Victoria?'

We hurry away from the nick as if it might reach out and suck us back in. I didn't pay the taxi and he's gone, so I guess Dixie had something to do with it.

'You seeing her are you? Carnally like?'

'Hope so, seeing her in half an hour. What were you bunging Victoria?'

'Drugs. What do you think.'

'I thought you were anti drugs. You're always having goes at me about them.'

'I am, in principle, but Tony came round and gave me all these pills for her, so I brought them.'

'You never told me that, did you? We could both have got nicked.'

'Well we never, did we? So don't rabbit on about it. Anyway, I think you should watch it with Dixon.'

'Why? I thought you rated the idea of me having it off with one of the drug squad.'

He gives a small shrug. 'I think you're pushing your luck, sweetie. She's got a very nasty reputation. So what happened with the taxi?'

'Not sure. Dixie was talking to him when I come in the nick's all I know. Want to come for a quick bevvy while I wait for her gorgeousness?'

He looks at me a bit doubtfully but grabs my arm anyway and comes along.

The boozer is almost empty. I get a pint for me and a gin for BB. We sit in an alcove. I take my first long draught from the pint, feel it round my lips, a moustache. Drink again, feel the Guinness spread round my throat covering, lubricating. Finally, I lick my lips,

'So tell me.'

'Been working for Tone, haven't I?'

'Thought you couldn't stand him.'

'I can't. I owe him money.'

'You been doing drugs?' He gives a fastidious negative movement.

'Certainly not, the whole idea of sticking needles into myself on a regular basis is revolting.' He shudders.

'He asked me one day if I wanted to make a few bob and I'm sick of being skint, living off you and Angelo. So I said yes. Mostly it's been driving for him and I don't actually touch any dope. But he gave me a sub.'

'How come you never told me. I didn't know he'd got a motor.'

'It's his mum's and he made me promise not to tell you.'

'Devious cunt!' He drinks primly from his gin.

'Anyway, you've been busy with that Yank.' Sounds sulky now.

'Fuck off, BB, we see each other every day.'

'I never know what you're up to any more, what with ghastly Johnnie and the bloody fruit of the forest of yours.' BB has taken to calling Berry blackberry.

'I feel neglected.'

I look at him to see if he's gen but can't be sure. Anyway, a lovely young creature of uncertain sex flounces in so we go into intense speculation, not knowing if we should fancy it or not, and which one of us is appropriate.

'Can't we just fancy it anyway?' I ask, so we do.

Dixie enters like a blond vision bringing a fresh showered fragrance of sweet plump flesh. BB exits swiftly, huffily, in a strop.

15 Stormy Weather

The night begins well with Dixie. It gets increasingly weird. She asks me back and her pad is great, the food is good, even the music is fair. Elvis, Nat King Cole, Patsy Cline. We dance close and do a kind of strip dancing where she removes a piece of my gear then I pull off a piece of hers until we are both in the buff. Fine while we are dancing together, but then she wants me to dance for her. I giggle. She gets the hump and that makes me giggle more, and then she whacks me round the chops. Not hard, not even frightening but insulting.

'You were hysterical, darling,' she says and begins with the weird: 'Who am I who are you?' routine. A variation on me Tarzan you Jane. Me butch you slut. Me control you none. Won't let me touch her while she swarms all over me like some delightful virulent rash. Heartbreak Hotel is playing and last time I heard it I was with Berry and now he kind of inserts himself between me and Dixon and all the danger of sleeping with the enemy, the excitement and naughtiness of it is pointless and silly. I've gone off the whole idea. I don't even fancy her any more, I push her away, walk round the room, pick up my clothes and start to get dressed.

'Come here, darling, I've got things I'm going to do to you,' she coos at me. I ignore her and her face looks like she's masticating on a wasp. I carry on getting dressed.

'Where do you think you're going? You can't just walk out. Who do you think you are?'

'Sorry mate, I don't want to play your games so I'm off, find some other mug.'

She comes at me and I try to get away but she grabs me so I push her violently she falls backwards, I leg it down the stairs with her voice in my ear. 'You nasty little piece of shit. If you think you'll get away with this . . .' I try hard not to take it personally but it sets up a very nasty foreboding in my gut. I shoot down the stairs and out the door, half my gear in my

hand, popped like a cork from a bottle into darkest Battersea.
Which I have no knowledge of or wish to become acquainted
with. I grab the first taxi and put my shoes on when I get
inside.

'You doing a runner, darling?' The driver showing the usual
originality of his breed.

'No, mate, just had this urge to go up west. Sudden it was.'
He laughs.

'Where's it to be, darling?'

'The Dilly and I'll tell you when we get there, OK, sweetheart?' And I start giggling. The driver joins in and I figure that
any pleasure I can get from recent events might well be paid
for in spades so I'll enjoy it, now.

I make it the Sunset first, then on to the Jungle where I can
hang out indefinitely, and I do. In fact I stay until morning
then I lurk in a greasy spoon until the rush hour is over.
Usually I love the rush hour, I look at all the workers on their
way to be wage slaves for the day and me off to my bed and I
am jubilant. Today this doesn't work for me, I still got Dixie's
warning doing a repeat in my head.

Soon as I hit the house I know it. The shit has hit the fan. With
emphasis. I open the door to my room and a cloud of feathers
flies at me, the draught from the door gets under them and
they float and carouse in the air then settle back down ready
for the next air current to show off again. They waft around
me to the floor as I walk past. I can see nothing except torn
bedding, clothes in heaps with make-up oozing its beige colour
on to books, letters, magazines.

Turmoil, and feathers. The curtains have been pulled down
and are tangled with bed clothes that have shoes poking out,
making patterns along with coat hangers at broken angles. A
plastic bowl sets a vibrant red assault on the eye from one
corner and some flowers that Angelo had made from silk and
wire are languishing under a half empty bottle of Burton's gin
that has been opened. The smell, like a distillery.

Only people in the world I know that can make a mess like
this are the drug squad. They get degrees in vagrancy and

destructive practises before they're unleashed on the public. But I'd just spent half the night with one of their finest, so surely it can't be them? Surely even sergeant Dixon couldn't lay on something like this, impromptu like?

I hear a gentle tapping at the front door and I freeze. Angelo's voice peeves itself through the letter box : 'Sheendeeg! Open please.' He has just recently mastered the name. I let him in, he slithers along the wall, pulls me into the bog to talk. His face is pure terror, eyes black glazed fear, his hair nappy where he's not combed it and he is filthy with soot and grime, broken fingernails. He looks about twelve.

They had come at six in the morning and fortunately for Angelo they made such an unholy racket that he slipped upstairs and climbed out of a window. He had been hiding on the roof as he saw BB ushered vigorously out. The other tenants up from their beds staying out of it, while getting their noses fully involved, or not, according to their preference. He had been afraid to come back through the house so had climbed down the back wall and been lurking in the garden 'til he saw me arrive.

'There were very many of them men, large.' He indicated and shuddered. 'They hold Billy by arms and he has only shirt on and shorts. You must take clotheses for him quickly.'

'Come on, Angelo, we'll make some coffee. I'll put the bolt on the front door and if they come back we'll hear them in time for you to do a runner. Get yourself cleaned up and we'll think of somewhere for you to go for a few days.' I am surprised at my organisational skills.

'But why? Why they do all this?' His voice desolate, despairing. He gives a vast Latin shrug that involves his body from his crown to his toe. He might well ask, I answer:

'They do it for badness don't they? There's no need for all this bleeding destruction, showing their power aren't they? It's called taking the piss.'

Angelo shakes his head elegantly at the barbarity and retires to the bathroom. The real Angelo is on his way back and after a few minutes he emerges looking subdued, but as lovely as ever. He found a black shirt and dark pants and he's added an orange scarf which flatters his golden brown face. He smiles gravely. Sits, tastes my Camp coffee and grimaces.

'I cannot stay to live here no more, they will send me off if they find.'

'Then we must make certain they don't find, mustn't we?'

'But where?'

We both light up fags to aid our thinking process.

'You think Victoria tell them of me?'

I'd forgotten about Vic. 'No, why would she?'

'She hate me, I think.'

'If Vic got everybody she hates nicked the jails would be packed.'

'You must go to police, find Billy.'

I'm not at all keen on this idea. 'First we must find a place for you to stay until things cool down.' He comes over to me on his way to the sink to dump the coffee, kisses my forehead.

'Bona palone you are, Sheendeeg!''

I look in the gas meter and find my stash of bread, intact. They're not even any good at their job these bastards. I dress carefully, not taking time for a bath. I put on my most sensible shoes with a long full skirt and peasant blouse. My nearest approximation to what I think of as 'respectable' office girl gear. Angelo shakes his head at the shoes and turfs out from under feathers a pair of black suede pumps. He approves. We split.

We use the back roads for no logical reason apart from general furtiveness and assume the body language of the bad guys in all the French films we watch at the Isolde. I look over at Angelo. He seems tiny, elegant, and dreadfully young.

We arrive at Lyons at the Gate. The usually near moribund crowd is buzzing like so many bluebottles, the excitement is palpable. Soon as we get through the door it all goes quiet. A hundred distorted pupils peer at us in various stages of dilation. Some from behind shades. Some in full, wincing, daylight. Trudy lifts her skeletal frame and jerks towards us.

'So, you been up the nick to see him have you?' Freda joins her; the old guard united for once. Both scrutinise our faces intently. I can feel Angelo tremble.

'They don't know, dolly,' says Freda. They look at each other like they're deciding who should have the joy of enlightening us. Trudy wins the toss.

'They've topped Victoria.'

'What they say, Sheendeg?' Angelo claws at my arm, I take his hand, firmly, squeeze him quiet.

'Do what?' I can't take this in.

'Died in the cells,' says Freda with gloomy relish. Both of them watch our faces with keen interest. I can smell their dry stale stench and it adds to my sudden urgent need to vomit. My mind has paralysed. Angelo clutches my hand, looks into my face. I notice he is wearing navy blue mascara and gold eye shadow. I wonder would it suit me.

'You heard, have yer?' says Trudy.

'No, we've just left home.' I am tempted to trump with news of the bust. But no. My brain is locked yet slippery.

'Died in the cells, dear,' says Freda again. Victoria dead? I can't take this in.

'Victoria is dead? Oh, no, not possible,' from Angelo.

'But we went up to see her, took tobacco and something to read. We got to see her, she was OK,' I say.

Tony arrives then so the attention shifts away. Angelo is stiff as a board and I can't decide if we should go or stay. I

look at his face and decide we need sweet tea for shock. I put
Angelo on a chair.

'You OK, Angelo? Vic's dead.' He nods, looks desolate. I'm
scared to leave him in case he breaks down weeping and shows
us up.

'Don't talk to anybody,' I say. I ask him what he wants.

'Coffee, black,' he says, perhaps he's OK. Within the sliding
of my brain, outcrops appear like wrecks in a sea. The largest
and most alarming is the fact that Billy gave Vic gear in the
cell, and that the cops could have found it. I get the drinks and
put them on the table, squeeze Angelo's shoulder, light a fag
for him and search for Trudy or Freda. I need to find out what
had killed Vic. They have both disappeared down the khazi for
their morning constitutional fix. Priorities. I can't face that, so
go up to Tony.

'All right, gel?' he greets me. 'Dixon's got suspended then?'
Tone knows things very nearly before they happen. He looks
shrewdly at me and I badly want to ask if he knows about BB
getting lifted, but I don't. He asks do I want to score, I say I
don't and he grins at me and nods.

'Don't want to be carrying anything if yer get nicked, eh?'
He looks so knowing I want to either whack him one or
interrogate him fully, with thumbscrews to his nuts. He looks
at me and grins; 'Poor old Victoria, eh?' he says. Then he
shifts off to service another importunate punter. As he goes he
runs his scaly hand along my arm and I've this urge to scrub
myself all over, with carbolic. He's been dealing since time
began, never been known to get nicked, so his contacts are
profound. I hesitate, then notice that Angelo is being hassled
by one of the nastier freaks that hang out here. The guy is
baiting him:

'Cor you look gorgeous doncha?' He turns to his mate:
'Dunney look gorgeous, Del mate?'

He is holding an ashtray over Angelo's head and laughing,
while he tips it up. Most of the people around are copping a
deaf'un but two or three are enjoying the spectacle. He doesn't
let anything fall on Angelo this time. I belt over. 'Fuck's sake,
Peter, what's your bleeding game?' He looks at me and backs
off.

'All right, Shindig? You seen our Frannie, have yer?'

'No I haven't.' One of the Frantic tribe. 'What's your bleeding game, Pete?'

'Just having a giggle aren't I? What's a matter with your sense of humour, gel?'

Angelo finishes his coffee and stands:

'Cocksucking motherfucker you are!'

He jerks his head like a matador, looks them both in the eye in turn. Twists sharply on his heel, begins to walk away. And Del joins in, ''Ere, you're a cheeky little cunt, aren't yer?'

He comes close and pushes at Angelo so Peter goes into the ever popular:

'Leave it mate it's not worth it.' speech and we escape on our toes.

'Don't worry, darling, all you lot of nignogs and nigger lovers will get chased out of Notting Hill. You'll be all right, gel, you know our Frannie.'

'Yeah, mate, no offence like, but we don't want you lot here.'

'Yeah, Teds rule, OK?'

Angelo takes my arm, protectively.

'And you can fuck off!'

He's learned the basics of English well. I do hope Angelo is not going to turn out to be brave. We bustle out leaving the two of them doing limp wrist signs and muttering something about queers. Frantic's tribe is vast and hideous.

Where to go is the problem. We get the tube to Waterloo and shoot in the Pathe News while we think. Angelo was supposed to go to rehearsal at midday but I'm scared the law will be waiting for him. He phones in sick and now we sit in a fug of terror watching the world in monochrome. Tanks churn across the screen and gorgeous Nasser holds forth. He has nationalised the Suez canal. My first thought is how pleased BB will be, not to mention a few million Egyptians. The thought is followed by a sinking of the gut as I remember BB's been busted.

The cinema is half full. There are liggers like us, with time to kill. Sleazy men trying to score women, and beside them bright, jaunty, pristine travellers waiting for their trains; to carry them to the south coast clean sea or to neat, safe, suburbs. It is smoky enough to kipper a lung in an hour, and has a damp warmth redolent of a cooling tower. It smells of old mackintoshes, feet and semen. The cartoons jerk bright colours into our eyes. Raucous animals leap and cavort their murderous antics. Loud hideous music scrapes our brains inside like the defurring of a kettle. How can Vic be dead? It's not possible. I've known him for ever, since just after I met Marmalade and Carlotta in the pub that first time, when I was on the trot. They'd put me up until I got sorted. Victoria had always been around, a bitter older sister of uncertain temper. Angelo is crying, I can feel small sobs.

'Don't cry, Angelo, you'll fuck up your eye make up.' I squeeze his hand and try a laugh but I want to cry too. I feel as if we're babes in the wood. I realise that I'm really scared. Scared for BB and Angelo, and scared for myself. I almost join him weeping.

Poor Victoria never really fitted in. Too plain and lacking in good humour. Yet he could pull men like nobody else. He was older too, and had seemed to come from nowhere, except we knew he was from up north somewhere. He arrived on to the scene a full blown hooker full of the killer instinct. I've known girls like Vic, plain, but more attractive to men than their prettier sisters. Never enough for these ones to take the money, they must miss no opportunity to rob. Sort of an unholy mission, driven by anger or hatred. Or just commerce?

Angelo's head has lolled asleep. I put my spare arm round his shoulder and light another fag. I'm tired too. I think back to last night and realise I hadn't had any kip. I had taken some bombers that Dixie had given me but the effect is long gone. That brings up Dixie and I haven't thought about her, yet. My brain can only handle so much grief at any one time. Now, I think about her getting suspended, and why. Think I might have been involved, this thought scares. Yet, instead of stiffening with terror I am suddenly dog tired and I must have slept there for a few minutes.

I wake to find my fag has burned down to the tip and to the realisation that someone has moved into the seat beside me. I can feel his hand sliding along my leg as he tries to edge my skirt up, I look over at his hand, moving, in the light of Mickey Mouse, to his fly. I watch while he fumbles his dick out, and Minnie's voice pierces, her body cavorts, I wait until his dick nestles in his lap. I put my burning fag out on it, twisting the butt down hard. He gives one almighty scream that brings the entire cinema to attention, frightens Angelo into fits and has the usherette bustling along with her torch.

We light out on to the afternoon sunny pavement, blink and flounder in the petrol air. Angelo vomits neatly in the gutter, he holds his dick while he does it.

The evening paper stand has a crayoned headline: 'Father of two dies in custody.' The paper beside it has a picture of Victoria with a Ducks Arse hair style and collar and tie, almost, but not quite, unrecognisable.

He peers out with a woman and two small children, in tier. They squint against the sun.

We go to the pub under the arches and see a similar variety of people to the ones in the cinema, except the men mostly keep their dicks in their trousers here. We read the paper avidly, watched by a crew of young boozers who send over hot looks and cool drinks. We give them a blank. The news story tells little apart from the fact that Victor Connolly had died in custody while being held for robbery. He had been thirty-three, which is shocking. Not that he looked younger or older, it's just that over thirty is a watershed. Doesn't say how he died but then they'd hardly say 'died from police brutality' would they? Angelo clacks on about him having two kids, which is indeed amazing, but Angelo appears to find the fact emotionally moving. I find it bizarre. I try to imagine Victoria getting married but come up with a vision in mauve lace, which is funereal. We used to call her the purple queen because she favoured all the mauves. Plus her predilection for purple hearts.

I try to see what the wife and kids look like, but they are a post war monochrome blur, faceless.

'So, what do we do, Angelo?'

'You or I must to go to police. I can't bear . . .' and he begins to weep. He does it fairly quietly but the team of guys notice.

'What's wrong, darling, want me to kiss it better?' intrudes a young guy.

'It's all right we're on our way,' I say.

'We must go to find Billy or I will, I worry for him.'

'Have another drink, darling. Get the ladies another drink, Donald!' he commands but we are out the doorway into the light and I know I must go to the nick.

As we get out the door we bump into the Count on his way into town from Basingstoke. He stops dead, looks delighted, puts his hand to his head, knuckle taps, twice: we have only met twice but we hit it off partly because Marmalade and Carlotta were so busy rucking that the poor guy was looking glazed and alone, so we chatted pretty extensively.

'You are friends of Carlotta, no?'

He beams at us. I can't remember if I know his name but it seems not to matter. Angelo has stopped crying but still hiccups small sobs and his face is all blurry with the navy mascara having spread itself about freely. We chatter on and Angelo cheers up while my inside feels like wet cement is hardening and growing to suffocating dimensions.

'Come! We have drink!' Bless him, we follow him back inside and the geezers greet us: a chorus.

'You've perked up, darling!'

'Couldn't tear yourselves away, could you?'

We sit near the door. I tell Angelo his face is a mess and he shoots in the men's bog which nearly causes a riot and comes back looking radiant and alert.

While I tell the Count all about Vic and BB, Angelo goes very quiet, very watchful, sort of pulsates impatience and sips tightly at Coca Cola. Gio nods, shrugs, spreads his hands, puts fingers together like a tent.

'Why you go yourself? To police. Get lawyer, he go for you,' says the Count.

'Don't know any, do I?' I can hear my voice sliding into a blur.

'But Carlotta would know, I will contact her.'

'And you must go home,' says Angelo bossily and he's right because nobody else can do it and even doing a runner is impossible. He pronounces home like hommey and while I'm laughing at him he has us up, out and at the taxi rank. The count gets a taxi for me and pays for it. The two of them stand and wave me farewell and I feel as if I'm off to war, the cement in my gut gives a small bulging tweak.

The house looks just the same from outside – quiet, shabby, safe. When I go upstairs, Vera, the landlady, catches me, tells me we'll have to go.

'I can't have coppers all over the place, dear, looks bad it does and I've always stopped on the right side of the law. My hubby would turn in his grave if he knew.'

'Don't tell him, Vera,' comes to my lips but I don't utter. She comes to a natural break so I hit her with the newspaper. She goggles at it, gets her glasses out of her apron pocket, sits, suddenly, on the stairs.

'Vicky? My Vicky. No, that can't be right, we've got tickets to Southend . . .' she tails off, and weeps great heaving sobs. I knew they'd been mates, drunk barley wine, gone to the pictures together and done the markets on Sunday, but this was pure pain. Poor old thing. It's hard to get to grips with this kind of passionate misery.

'Don't worry, Vera, you've still got us, we'll be here.'

I pat her gently, like she's some old pussy cat.

'No, you bleeding won't, mate. I want you out, the lot of you.'

She snuffles off lighting a damp fag and hiccoughing her grief into her handkerchief.

I take a pillow case and start to fill it with feathers while I try to remember why I'm back here. I don't know. Well, I live here, don't I? I lift the curtain rail and try not to ask myself why the DS pulled it down. This brings Dixie into my mind. She's been suspended and she'll be livid. Why was she suspended? I sit down on the floor and errant feathers fluff out of the pillow case and enjoy their freedom again. I decide I'll chuck all the feathers out the window. And why not? But you can't actually chuck or push feathers, you *can* encourage them, though. I get myself a gin from the bottle that lays on its side among the crap. I whack it down me screech while I ceremonially liberate the feathers.

The door flies open with Vera, brown bear angry, holding on to the handle. The remaining feathers rise up to greet her and she bats them crossly away: 'What's your game, Mary?'

She got my real name from my probation officer and it is typical of her that she has insisted on throwing it at me whenever she's pissed off with me ever since.

'Have you gone bleedin' mad or what? Those feathers are going all over the place.' She stands in front of me, glares.

'Is it because of Vicky? Has it deranged you?' She looks round the room.

'Why did they make this bleeding mess? It don't make no sense.'

She turns round and feathers keep her company, although they begin to sink, miserably, under her horrible onslaught of sanity.

'What's that you got there?' I show her the bottle, it has plenty left. Fortunately the shape of the Burton gin bottle is similar to a demijohn so that even on its side it doesn't empty.

'Get me a glass. We'll drink to Vicky.'

The feathers accompany me into the kitchen and one or two die under the tap as I rinse a glass.

'Got any orange, have you?' But we haven't so she drinks neat gin. Savours it.

'Like the Dutch this is, Geneva, they all drink neat gin.'

Always surprises me when somebody Vera's age speaks of a former life, I shrug it off. She looks lugubrious.

'Vicky used to talk about her kiddies to me a lot. His, I suppose but I always thought of her as a her. It was very sad you know, how she realised she liked men when she was at sea and the wife didn't want to know, did she?'

'You can see that, can't you, Vera? Take a bit of getting used to wouldn't it?'

'Yes, but she took the kiddies away, took the house and everything. Even sent all his presents back, bitch. Never told them he sent them presents. Vic was scared they'd think she just ran away. That's why she hired that lawyer to try to get visiting rights at least. Costing an arm and a leg it was.' Nods gloomily over the gin. We sit and Vera talks about a Victoria I never knew. I try not to listen because it's too sad. She's talking for herself anyway, she drains her glass.

'I'll get my Hoover in here, get this lot out the way.'

'How did they get in this morning?'

'Knocked the front door and one of the lodgers let them in. Come straight up here they did, I come up but they told me to piss off in no uncertain terms. Cheeky buggers. And that young Angelo, he wants to watch it. I seen him going up on the roof.

Lucky for you you was out, isn't it?' I nod agreement, pour
more gin into our glasses, I seem to be past getting any effect
from drink so I toss it down my throat and nearly choke when
Vera says:

'That young Frances was round earlier but I never let her
in. Said she'd got a message for you, told her to come back I
did. Got her foot in the door though she did. I told her: 'If you
don't get your foot out I'll crush it! Little madam! What do
you think that was about?' I shake my head.

'Can't leave it like this, can you?' She's back in moments
with the large menacing Hoover I look at it and it gazes back
at me. I turn it on. Berry comes into my mind, perhaps it's the
motion of the Hoover. I could do with a fix now. I won't
though. All feels like it's the end of something, I'm not sure
what.

18 House Cleaning Blues

The feathers are dead now, and the Hoover eats them up with small punitive sucks of the snaky hose. I get into a rhythm that allows for concentration along with total worry. Over and over, futile: why did I? What did she? Occupation of mind syndrome.

I hear the door open downstairs and Billy comes in. He looks weird in a black alpaca overcoat, baggy pants and white shirt. I only just manage not to laugh. His face is drawn, mouth tucked inwards toward sour misery. Older, more fragile, scrawnier. Something wrong with his mouth. I stop the cleaning. Go over to hug him tight, close. Breathe in stale cell from his clothes, fear from his flesh.

'You look like a pox doctor's clerk, Billy.'

He tries a grin but it doesn't work. 'I was so scared, sweetie.' His voice has lost all its bounce, the 'sweetie' is limp, just hangs there in the air, powerless. I hold his wiry body, push my face into his hair. I lean back.

'I'll run you a bath, put bath oil in it, get the nick off you.'

'They only said they were going to charge me with manslaughter, didn't they?' he says.

'They can't do that. That's stupid.' He breaks away in a strop.

'I don't know if you remember what it's like in there, but they really do seem pretty fucking powerful and stupid or not, I believed them.'

'Oh, BB, I never meant you were stupid. I'm sorry, mate. What's happened to your choppers?' I've got a wail on me now. There's a gap four teeth wide on one side of his mouth. He puts his hand up to cover it.

'Did they belt you, BB?'

'I hit my mouth on the side of the bog when they were stripping me. It's called resisting procedure or something.'

'Is that a new offence like?' I quip, then hush my mouth. He sobs like a kid. I join in for lack of originality and his poor old pots gone. Anyway the day's emotion comes over in a vast, damp wave, grief and fear. I want my mum, but only very briefly, while I'm on automatic.

'Fuck it, BB, reckon we should score?'

'They took your works, anyway I'm sure they'll come back for me. Last thing I need is for you to be gouching out and sitting there drooling with the house full of drugs!' He's getting back to his idea of normal. I feel desperately tired like when you're a kid and you've been to the sea all day, bone weary.

'I'm so sorry about Vic. What happened to her?' I say.

'OD'd they reckon, silly bitch. Hadn't been for Carlotta and the Count I'd have been there forever. You send them did you? Course you did.' Perking up a lot. He squeezes my hand, nearly breaking bones.

'Where'd you get the gear?' I raise one brow, feel the coat. He looks down disdainfully at himself, shudders.

'The Sally Army I think, some old bag got them for me, aren't they ghastly?' He seems to be returning to character. 'They took my gear for evidence. Where were you last night anyway? On the bleeding nest no doubt while I was taking the rap.'

Was that only last night? Feels like about a month. 'Leave it out, BB, we don't do raps, it's a cliché. You took the gear in, nothing to do with me was it?' He gives a half strength glare.

'They were looking for you, all right, darling.' Then he stops, thinks, reaches for a fag, lights up: 'Now there's a funny thing.' He pauses, I don't bite, he looks over at me. Yes he's back on form. I raise him.

'Dixie got suspended.' He looks gratifyingly amazed. I try a trump: 'That's where I was last night.'

'Was that before or after she got suspended?' Cool.

'Before.' He nods.

'Who told you she got suspended?'

'Junkie Tony did. Angelo and me went up the Gate to find out what was happening.'

'He'd know.' BB looks thoughtful.

'Is Angelo over by Carlotta's?' I ask.

'Yes, Gio came in with a brief, there is no charge, so far.

They never mentioned Angelo, I don't think they have any interest in him. He's working tonight then going back to Carlotta's. The brief reckons he can sort out his papers so he should be back soon.'

I put the bath on, the copper geyser whooshes into fearful life round my trembling hand, I chuck the match at it, run. Wait a few moments, go back to look. Triumph, it's alight. Boils fierce hot water into the deep bath. This is usually my excitement for the day, total. I get my Floris bath oil and pour some in, a tiny amount, the scent lifts in the steam. Back in my room BB is in my silk dressing gown in front of the mirror peering at his pots – or where they used to be. He winks at me.

'Bring a whole new concept to the blow job,' I say.

'Dimension, dear, not concept.' He smiles, a small triumph, the first one today.

'Looks quite appealing, BB, like you've been in the wars.'

'That's no lie!'

'Right. Your bath's on. What were you going to say earlier?'

'When's that, sweetie?' The sweetie is recovering its strength.

'When you were talking about the law coming round, and them looking for me.'

'Yeah, it was like they weren't looking for you, more they wanted to turn your gaff over. They seemed quite keen to nick me, but I don't think they expected you to be here.'

'How peculiar,' I muse. BB nods, stretches, shudders.

'Never know what those bastards are up to, even they don't know.'

'So did they know that Vic was dead before they busted us?'

'No, it wasn't until I got to the nick that they told me about Vic popping her clogs.'

'It was a drugs bust then? I wonder if it has anything to do with Dixie getting suspended?'

'Like they thought she was giving you drugs?'

'Or flogging them to you? There have been stories about her selling on confiscated gear.'

'They all do that, it's perks! The reassignment of illegal substances isn't it?' BB says this with total assurance. I'm not so sure.

'But it's definitely not sanctioned, is it?'

'Neither is beating up queers but they do it all the time! I'm off for my bath.'

My mind is in overdrive and I go in my room and poke around in my books, getting worried, hold them by the spines and shake them. 'Think!' I demand of myself, this always stops my brain dead and I know that the memory will surface in its own good time but I need to know if the blank scripts have gone and who had them. Or perhaps they aren't important and they were searching for something else. But Billy's room was hardly touched. I go and have a look at it now, it's scarcely disturbed. I know I've put them somewhere safe. I always hide cheques and stuff in books so where the fuck are they? I go and sit on the bog seat and talk to BB.

'So what happened to your choppers then?' I must find out.

'They told me to strip and I refused. Only had kecks on and a singlet, didn't I? But there were three of them all laughing at me and I couldn't bear it.' He looks at me, shrugs.

'They're such bastards, aren't they? Taking the piss, speculating about my ring, Nasty, so I refused, two of them got hold of me and my face hit the bog. Don't think it was intentional just incidental damage.'

'They get a quack in?'

'No.'

'You ask for one?'

'No. I know what you're going to say; I should get them for assault, but I'm not about to do that. If you remember, they made my life a misery once before and it's never worth it. A shame, unjust, I'm not sufficiently brave, take your pick but I'm simply not up to it, sorry.' His voice has all its old vibrancy back, and then some. Vitriolic as ever, thank God. He has bruises on his arms and shoulders.

'I wasn't going to say that at all, BB, I know what it's like, getting out alive is all!'

'Sweetie, you know what?' he says, and reaches a wet hand to my dry one.

'What's that then?'

'I think my bottle's gone.'

He looks at me to see if I'm responding and I try to suss what he wants me to say. 'So?'

That seems bland enough. He looks up sideways. 'Think I might go and get a straight job, take Angelo away to the seaside, get a B and B.'

'Very appropriate, BB, but we know you're dreaming, you'd be bored shitless if you left London. What's that doctor Johnson said?'

'It's not London I'm tired of, it's all this dodgy life. Now I've got Angelo, I want to settle down. And you should too, I worry about you girl!'

'Bollocks, BB, settle down if you want to baby, but leave me out of it. I've got a job. Anyway, Angelo's got his dancing.'

'He could dance at the seaside.'

'What? On the end of the pier?' I wonder what's behind this new line. Fear I guess.

'Did they ask about me, the bill?'

'Asked where you were, but they didn't seem all that bothered. Which is weird isn't it? Think they knew you were with Dixie?'

'Christ knows.' It suddenly occurs that I've left my room unlocked as I always do but now I'm scared and, as the thought enters my brain, so does Frantic's voice:

'All right, gel? You in there, are yer?' I hear her moving towards my room and I dive out.

'What you bin up to, gel? Poor old Vic's bought it then has she? BB on the missing list, eh? All change the merry-go-round, eh doll?' She laughs gaily as she walks through my room and on into the kitchen.

'Get the kettle on, eh? Tiger was arsting about you. I went down there when I heard about Vic, thought you'd be at work I did.' She pauses to light a fag and fills the kettle.

'So what's the score with Vic then? What's that all about?'

I shrug. 'Who knows, they reckon he topped himself, but they always say that don't they?'

I light the gas. BB comes out, wearing my dressing gown, sees Frantic, his face undergoes a metamorphosis into peevishness via fury and outrage. He makes for his room.

'Hear they had you in as well, Billy. Busy old couple of

days, eh? Perhaps it's purge the pooftahs season? Batter the bum boys, eh?'

She hurrumphs a laugh and BB pushes past her.

'Going to have a lay down, dearie? That's right, gel, get yer feet up, you got that boy of yourn in there keeping the bed warm have yer?' She turns to me, 'What's a matter wiv her? Miserable old cow. What's a matter with her gob? Done a dodgy blow job?'

She is searching cupboards. 'Got any biscuits, dolly? I'm bleeding starving.' She puts cups under the tap. 'There's feathers in this cup.' Her voice is plaintive. 'You discovered some new kinky use for cups have you?' Hurrumphs a laugh; 'Got any sterilised milk, mate?' She waves the bottle at me.

'No? I hate this bleeding pasteurised, got no body, has it?' She opens the drawer in the cabinet looking for spoons and then I remember where I put the blank scripts. I jump up. 'Let me do that, Frannie!'

Her face creases up with shrewdness and suspicion as I shove her out the way and grab spoons and stand with my back hard against the kitchen cabinet. 'Why don't you go and get some milk, I'll give you the money.' Her face is crafty and amused.

'OK, I'll get some biscuits too, shall I?' She stands with her hand out. I'll have to leave the kitchen to get my bag.

'Go and get my bag, Frannie, it's in my room.' She beams at me and is back in seconds;

'Here y'are, gel. What you been doing with the feathers and the Hoover? Can't wait to find out.' She smiles as I give her ten bob.

'Get some fags, Fran,' and off she goes. I shut the door and retrieve the scripts, put them in my pocket, I hear BB shouting from his bedroom and go in.

'Get her out, Shindig, she'll be poking around all over the place. Tell her to fuck off.'

He thumps over in his bed to face the wall. I cover his shoulder with blankets and leave him.

'Sorry mate, can't be done. I want to know what she knows.'

'And she wants to nose into our business!' he says, mumbling into the pillow.

'I'll get her out after we've had our tea, let you get some kip, eh?'

She is back in record time, looking jubilant: 'Hear old Angelo was on the roof then and the two of you crept off like a couple of renegades, wish I'd seen that!'

Laughs a big open-mouthed hoot while she pours the tea. 'There you go, could stand the spoon up in that! So tell me about what happened this morning.' She sits, agog. I drop myself into it straight away.

'Well, when I came home old Vera caught me on the stairs.'

'Where were you all night? Dirty stop-out!' I tell her an amended version of the day's events while she stuffs her face with biscuits and smokes my fags, at the same time as drinking her tea. I don't mention Dixie and neither does she. After the tea she scuttles off at speed.

'I'll find out what the score is, gel and come and wake you up later, eh? You look done in, mate.'

I sleep a sleep of such depth that when I hear her banging on the door it feels as though she's only just left. But it's dark outside. She hovers while I get my body to respond to stimulus and get my arse out. BB is nowhere to be seen and we make for the pub. I am dying for a pint and as we hit the pub I feel almost cheerful. Some of the stuff that has happened in the last few hours hasn't yet risen to the surface of my mind. Rooster is the first person I see, he gives me a blank.

Rooster and me go back a long time, we've operated together for months, amiably, without annoying each other. A partnership. Now, he sucks his teeth and walks off when I greet him. People make room for him to stalk out and even Frantic keeps her mouth shut. Straight away, Sports, one of his cohorts, comes over to me, touches my hand, says:

'Me n'a believe it you see sah, you is fine wit me man. I tell Rooster them 'a lie. But him'a belief all them nonsense, you is all right wit' me.'

But he doesn't hang about, and there is a gap around me like a plague moat. Eyes regard me carefully and bounce off fast if they catch mine. Frantic stares at my face, gives a movement of her shoulders.

'Want a drink, mate?' A rare offer, and sure enough she puts her hand out for money. I ignore it and go to sit by the window, where the strangers sit, and even they shift their arses more than necessary to make room for me. Frantic brings me a pint and sits close to me, she is silent. I wait for her to speak. She drinks her lemonade quietly, looks over at me, winks:

'Well, gel, I fink you've fallen out wiv the world, darling. What's it about, do you reckon?'

'Fucked if I know, mate.' We light up.

I shake my nut sadly; no doubt I will discover soon enough what I've done. And I do; Lickle Miss comes in the pub, all fifteen stone of her. Looks round, spots me, points and laughs.

'What happen, darling?' She laughs again, she is formidable.

'I 'ear you hinform on hevrybody, darling, them all rushing around hiding things, cussing you out to rarse. The games bust up and the ponces? Them running for cover.' She gives out with another loud laugh and people turn to look at us but very briefly.

'You have h'upset the h'apple cart, my dear! And I am glad.'

'But I haven't, I haven't grassed anybody up.'

'That not what I hear at all!' she laughs again. 'Anyway, him gone, bwoy.'

'Them raid t'ree houses this morning, you see. Your own and Harry's and Jimmy place,' she says now.

'But it's got nothing to do with me, Lickle!' She gives a shrug that lifts her breasts and all the flesh around them a good ten inches. A child comes to the pub door and makes signs to her, she sucks her teeth. Lifts her bulk.

'Me soon come y'hear and congratulations, Shindig, you is my kind of 'ooman.' She roars with laughter and is away.

'Well, mate, you got one fan.'

'You better move off, Frannie, you'll get tarred with the same brush, mate.'

'Don't matter, gel, nobody would dare call me a grass wiv my family connections, we're the aristocracy of West London villainy doll. Do you no harm at all being seen wiv me.'

I've always been slightly ashamed of Frantic.

'I'll stick by yer, gel,' she says. And I believe her and feel grateful, momentarily. Then I wonder why. Why is she sticking by me? I feel distinctly uneasy.

Part of my mind deals with the fact that two other gaffs got busted last night. Does this mean it had nothing to do with Dixie and me? The remainder of my brain is supine, playing dead.

'You got the bread for them drinks, darling? I'm strapped.' Frantic back on form. I go to the bar for change and a pint, get the full power pariah treatment from the barmaid, whose face shuts tight. The governor serves me but doesn't indulge in even the tiniest bit of badinage, and I miss it. Won't meet my eye. I give the bread to Frantic and sit beside her, there's lots of room and people are still moving away.

'Look on the bright side, gel, you'll always get a seat.'

She laughs loud and long which bothers the punters because they can't look at us for any length of time and, being a shower of nosey cunts, they want to.

'You know what's happened, mate? Somebody's put the bubble in for you.'

'Fuck, Frannie, that's bleeding perceptive of you.'

''Ere, mate, you can't afford your usual dark sarcasm, I'm the only friend you got.'

She hurrumphs, gurgles, giggles; strikes me she's having a ball.

'What are your plans for this evening, Frannie? You just going to hang with me and take the piss?'

'Yeah, why not? Do you a favour, eh? We could go up to Harry's, get some nignog food, eh?'

And while I'm counting the probable cost of this, Dixie comes in with two drug squad mates.

Everything in the pub stops, including breathing, for moments. Her eyes fix on me and I don't know what to do with my facial expression. A ghastly placating grin threatens and a cringe, but I knock that on the head and settle for a mild truculence allied to slight grievance. Frantic can hardly contain her excitement, even her breath is coming quickly. Nearest I've seen to any kind of arousal in her all the time I've known her. Dixie separates herself while the two geezers go to the bar, where the governor grovels, but abrasively, to prove his independence. I pretend to myself that I can't see her, difficult, because Frantic is nudging and winking like a demented puppet. She goes into action:

'Hello, Sergeant Dixon.'

'Piss off out of it, Frances Philomena.'

'Do what?'

'You heard!' She is loath to leave, her ears go red in frustration at being left out, no doubt.

'She's with me, stay where you are, Frannie.'

'Don't push your luck, Shindig.' Frantic leaves, and the two geezers at the bar stay drinking their pints. They look in the opposite direction. The crowd are torn now, with two directions they can't look in, they mostly examine their hands or feet. Frantic hovers about, then gets herself a bevvy and squats on a bar stool, watching us. She can probably lip read.

'You heard, no doubt, that I got suspended?'

'Yeah, I did hear. But that's got nothing to do with me has it?' She glares like she can't believe what I say.

'Well, my dear,' and the 'dear' sounds like a new form of scabies. 'Somebody told my boss that I was spending time with you and somebody saw you leave my flat while Mr. Connolly was in the cells.' The "mister" blisters.

'You're not suggesting I told them, are you?' I look into her face as I say this and get a vision of her dancing in the buff and can feel a giggle approaching from deep within me, but it's only hysteria, and terror sees it off. Then she looks back into my eyes and her look freezes any likely impulse to laugh.

'You know Tony, don't you? Yes, course you do and he knows you. An old friend of mine you know, and Johnny Mason? Another mutual mate, eh?'

'Was it you put the bubble in for me?' She grins. 'A hint, I think it's time you went on a holiday and I suggest you take Billy along with you or you might just both get an involuntary vacation at her Majesty's pleasure. Know what I mean, do you?' She lifts her luscious arse up off the chair at exactly the same time the two blokes drain their pints. They all leave together. Synchronised terror. The boozer exhales.

Takes all of two seconds for Frantic to get to me.

'So what she say?' I shrug, nonchalant, but can feel my face is still ashen.

She sits herself down and lights one of my fags, drinks:

'You look ever so pale, doll.'

'Told me to get out of town didn't she? Me and BB.'

Frantic proceeds with the third degree: Why? How? When and where? But I manage to keep shtoum.

'So where you going to go then?' She looks at me, levelly, with no humour in her face.

'You reckon I ought to go?' She nods.

'Not forever, like, just get out while things cool off. What she get suspended for? Shagging some old boiler, or dealing in confiscated drugs?'

I feel my cheeks heating up nicely, Frantic looks triumphant.

'You been there, have yer? Dirty little cow! No wonder she wants you out. You oughta know better than that, gel.' She hurrumphs her way into a near hyena job, slaps the table and curls into a veritable ball of mirth.

'What's she like? Bet she goes like a train. No, don't tell me or she'll have me bleeding banished an all. You do believe in

taking your chances don't yer, cock?' And she is overcome with
hilarity. I want to smack her one but satisfy myself with a
sharp ankle kick.

'Oy, there's no need fer that, gel! But you do want to watch
it. I don't know how true it is, but they reckon she knocks out
all the confiscated drugs, and all the geezers are scared shitless
of her. It's even mumbled, on the grapevine, that she's had
geezers topped.'

'Oh cheers, Fran!' She gives a monumental lifting of eyes to
heaven, she is making a meal of this and getting immense
pleasure, so I feel it's time to share the scare with BB. I leave
Frantic grinning at the barman aiming for a free drink, and
making good progress.

When I get home BB's already half packed and he looks better, more organised than I've seen him for weeks.

'You heard then?' I say as I go into the kitchen.

'Heard what?'

'Dixon's warned us off.' He looks blank. 'Told us to leave town or we'll get nicked.'

'You're joking!'

'No, she came in the pub and pulled me. She's put the poison in, spread rumours about me grassing everybody up. Nobody's speaking to me. Even Rooster gave me a blank, the whole pub – weird, like I've got the pox.'

'More fool Rooster for believing it. Are you sure it was her?'

'Good as told me, didn't she? Anyway, whoever it was, the mud's well and truly stuck. She mentioned Tony and Johnny by name.'

'They're slime, you always knew that. Sounds like she's dried up your resources, done you a favour in a way.'

He comes over, gives me a perfunctory hug. Leans back and looks me in the face.

'I've decided to go anyway, sweetie, with or without you. If we don't pay next week's rent we'll have enough to get somewhere out of town. Brighton perhaps? I'll see Angelo later, ask him to come. But I'm definitely off, I never want to be that scared again. I don't want to flog my mutton any more, so why stay? Far too dangerous. It's over sweetie, the London sojourn is over. The bottle's gone.'

He looks at me steadily.

'There will always be a home with me if you want it and I know Angelo will come, when he's ready. This is like a warning, sweetie.' I think about Vic. Then I think about the fact BB hasn't actually got a home, but I'm grateful.

'See, the same thing that happened to Victoria could happen

to me. We're in danger all the time. The law can pick us up and torment us at will. We're known to the law here. I should never have got involved driving Tony about – taking drugs in to Vic! I'm sure she was supposed to take them in to Brixton, so we could all have got busted.'

'Yeah and Tony took no chance at all,' I say.

'Quite! I'm sure he's in with the law.'

'Got to be, hasn't he, been dealing since time began, never gets nicked. And I can't believe Vic took an overdose,' I say. He shrugs and goes on packing.

'No evidence he did. Thing is, they can say what they like, do what they like with the evidence. We don't stand a chance. Anyway I'm too scared. It's over.' I know he's right. I sit on the bed, he pokes about in his case, I watch him. He looks very straight now, hair combed flat.

'You're in disguise.' He pushes me away from his suitcase. Packs more gear. Final stuff.

'I'm going to get a job in a hotel and think things through.'

'What about me? I couldn't work in a hotel, I'd hate it. All those bossy bastards telling me what to do? No chance.'

'I'm sure you could do it if you wanted to. Anyway, we could all share at first, be cheap it would. Oh, come, you're my best friend. You could do anything you want, you know you could.'

'But I don't want to. See, the thing with Tiger is I don't have to do anything much.'

I see his cynical face looking at me.

'It's varied and I can always escape. Imagine working for somebody like his old woman!'

'Imagine being locked up in a cell with somebody like his old woman!' he says shortly. 'Get your head round that one, sweetie.' He bangs a drawer shut.

'What about if Angelo won't come?'

He shrugs. 'He will, I know he will. But it's a matter of survival, Shindig, I can't do another sentence. And now, especially after what Dixon told you, I'm off. Please come, it'll be fun, sweetie.'

It feels as if he's gone already. I mumble something about seeing Berry. I've been dreaming about him a lot, night time and daytime too. Something about him has got me going. I know that it makes no sense to take these guys seriously, they are likely to be whisked away to some war that Uncle Sam is fighting or back to the States at a moment's notice, but he is something exceptional. Not sure I believe in love. But an itch for him drives me up the road in full trot, I have some odd hope he might be there, he's not of course. I think I knew that.

The flat in Pembridge Gardens seems to have got damper in the few days we haven't been there. Grey mould crawls up the walls near the ceiling. There is the rancid smell of ancient dishcloths about the place. A kind of festering stench that reaches into my nose and pulls my brain and all my hopes down. Not a sign of Berry or his gear. Many signs of Colette and Diego having left in a hurry. Broken suitcase open on the floor. Their bed is chaotic, dirty sheets and towels litter the room. A glass, with pink tinged water stands on the sink with two eye droppers erect, the water has a slight crust on it, bloody tissues faded brown. Looks like they've done a runner in a hurry. I search in the room Berry and me shared, the only sign of anybody or anything is an empty Old Spice bottle by the sink. I go upstairs feeling pissed off. In the hall I meet a guy who lives in the next flat.

'What's happening, mate,' I chirp, keeping my end up. He looks shifty. 'Seen Colette at all?'

'No, not for days. Saw her with that Yank in Lyons but that was the last time I seen her.' He looks closely at me:

'I heard you got nicked. That right is it?'

'No, but there's a lot of it about and it can only be a matter of time.' His face creases to concentrate.

'No, that's not what I heard is it?'

'Who knows, mate? Don't worry about it, eh?'

Round the corner past Lyons to the boozer I was last in with Angelo and BB. It feels like years ago. I hate the way the world jerks into motion, everything shatters, fragments, splinters and you're left, naked and scared, holding on to thin strands of brittle sanity, if you're lucky. I sit, alone, and I'm really alone now, and scared, thinking about leaving London. I swift a pint into me without it touching the sides. Better. I feel sentimental over Notting Hill, even Joe Lyons' unique miasma is getting a favourable review in my bonce. All taking on rosy hues it is, but I know it won't last and I need to get my arse out of Notting Hill. Have to go and see Tiger though won't I? And I can't leave without a night of emphatic passion with Berry. I gaze from the window lost in sentimental love for Notting Hill and Soho, then I add Tottenham Court Road, the Roebuck and the Paramount to my compendium of passionate attachments. Bits of Brixton are added and Commercial Road, Aldgate.

Through my misty eyes, I see Berry moving like a bebop king along the road in front of the pub. I bang the window and shoot outside so fast that he's still looking for the sound when I get him in my arms, my face reaching up as far as his neck and his arms round me tight and he bends to kiss me. I'm weeping for joy.

'Hey baby, you ain't supposed to weep when you just found me! You got to save that until I'm gone.' But he's kind of moist eyed too. We are drawing attention to ourselves, not wise for a black guy with a white bird. Everybody loves a lover but they better be the same colour, preferably white. Dirty looks are hitting us from every direction but they bounce off and don't hurt.

Somebody pokes me in the back and when I turn I see some old woman who says 'Sorry!' very loudly and she doesn't move out of the way. 'What's your game, missis?' I say. A couple of young geezers from out of Lyons look at me, waiting.

'More like what's *your* game!' she says and Berry pulls me down the road forcibly. The youngsters mutter and laugh and the woman puffs up with her own importance as defender of the white race. 'Little scrubber! Encouraging them black bastards, shouldn't be allowed.' And murmurs of agreement surround her. I give her the two finger salute behind Berry's back and we hit the stinking flat almost running.

All I smell now is Berry's clean sweet scent and our sex. We are not as violent in sex now, the imperative is still there and every time we meet we fuck, a vigorous hello before we do

drugs or talk. In fact most of our time together we spend in
bed. 'A horizontal trip,' says Colette. Diego and her seem to
have given up sex in favour of drugs and they think we are
base and uncool. Who cares?

'Sheet, man, this place stinks!' he says as he leans over me to
get a cigarette.

'They've gone, Berry, and I've got to leave town.' He looks
at me a shifty kind of look. 'Colette tells me Diego and her are
going to Morocco.' It's an opener but he looks away. 'Why
don't we go with them?' the words hang in the air above the
bed but Berry doesn't go anywhere near them.

'Baby, I got to go stateside.' My stomach falls out of place
and lands somewhere no stomach belongs. 'You hear me?' He
moves my face into range with his two gentle hands, he sees
my tears. 'Hey girl! We always knew this wasn't a forever
thing.' He's crying too now.

'Why?' I bleat and he talks about this man's army or the
service or something, but I am neither listening nor hearing
because I've got this rushing noise in my head. Love's a bastard,
it creeps up on you and puts itself about so you don't have
command of your most basic functions. Now I am weeping
noisily, saying, 'You can't leave me, I love you,' and even when
I hear myself I don't stop. So part of me watches critically and
dies of shame while I perform love's young dream part three:
'lost love'. The Hollywood movies I've been watching since age
eight have had a major impact on me and now Berry brings his
own dramatic input along to share.

'Sheet man, you think I don't love you? I'm crazy for you,
you think I'd be here now if I wasn't? I'm supposed to be on
the base. There's some shit going down with Diego.'

Love exits temporarily, replaced by a panicky feeling of
things moving like tectonic plates, immutable. Like me and
Berry are specks in space. I'm not far wrong either.

I leave him at the tube station full of a feeling of tragic loss,
my gut empty. 'I'll see you again before I go, I swear,' he says.
I write my address on a fag packet. I go to score but Notting

Hill is a desert, in Joe Lyons it's like all the junkies have been
sucked, even Trudy and Freda have disappeared. The only
lowlifes there are a few Teds and some bevvy merchants short
of the price of a pint. I go back to the pub. I know that if I sit
here long enough I will spot somebody I can score off.

I pour Guinness into my empty gut, it disappears without trace
and I feel even more gutted.

Through the window I see Vera crossing the road with a
strange woman and I know this is Victoria's wife. She doesn't
look old exactly, or young and she doesn't look like the same
species as Frantic or me. She is very solid without being fat, as
if every pound of her weighs the full sixteen ounces and
perhaps a bit more. I try to imagine Victoria and her together
but can't. I sit on for a moment or two, resisting the pull of my
nose, but it's no contest and I up and belt out to join them:

'All right, V?' She looks at me then:

'This is Victor's wife, Shindig.' The woman peers at me
close-sightedly as if she's gauging the precise colour of my slap.

'I suppose you're one of his friends are you?' she says.

'What, Vic? Yeah, we all live in the same house don't we?'

'All right for him, wasn't it? Living the high life down here
while I had to struggle to bring up his children.'

Not your normal grieving widow then. Don't waste any
time getting to the point does she?

'I heard you wouldn't let him near them.' Her head goes
down into bull stance, her brows ferment into angry prize
Aberdeen Angus shape and I think she might charge so I step
neatly sideways. Carmen, the film, was not wasted on me.

'Been putting the poison in has he?' she says.

'Perhaps Vic exaggerated,' I reverse.

'I had to work my fingers to the bone.' She repeats my own
and every other mother's mantra – I expect it's universal.

'Victoria wasn't exactly sitting on her arse you know, she
worked hard making money and it was a bleeding sight more
dangerous than housework. And V tells me you wouldn't give
the kids his presents.'

'Don't bring me into it. Let's go and have a cup of tea, eh?'

Mary is doing a feeble woman having the vapours bit, but with an underlying rancour and steel, she perks up and says:

'I'd like a barley wine.' She speaks flatly, like there's no resonance in her at all. I get this vision of the interior of her brain, with tombstone thoughts standing stock still while eddies of aggravation flutter and blow around them. We sit down in the public bar of a boozer towards Holland Park. It's full of old geezers playing cribbage and looking as if they haven't moved since just after the First World War. I look down at their feet expecting puttees. I swear I can suss a faint odour of ancient mud. Expect it's the bog.

'Evening boys!' says old V, the tart. They look up and murmur a conditioned response.

'You're a tart, Vera!' I say and get a glare from Mary and a simper from Vera.

'What you having, V? A port and lemon? And Mary? Barley wine is it? All right, darling, you got that have you?' To the barman, a stripling in his sixties, his face so close shaved his purple blood shows through his skin. He bares his completely white, even dentures at me in what could almost be a smile. Mary and Vera sit at the bare table; they smell of Ashes of Roses and California poppy respectively. My own Tabu, a gift from Berry, outranks both with brassy perfume that clangs in my nostrils and makes the Guinness taste tinny.

We sit and look at one another then we all lift our drinks in unison and imbibe.

'So was it you gave him the idea to sell his body?' She looks straight at me. ''Cause he was never that type when he was up north.' She shuffles her vast handbag about a bit, reaches into it and brings out a packet of Park Drive, she looks at us, hesitates, offers them round. Vera pipes up after a sip or two of port and lemon. I am struck dumb.

'I'm sure Shindig had no influence on Victoria, I expect it was the only way he knew how to make money.'

'He was a trained carpenter.'

'So? He carved out a new career, must have wanted a change,' I say. 'Anyway he was a greedy sod. Couldn't ever get enough money, that's why he got nicked. Turned some geezer over, didn't he?' Vera chucks a venomous glare at me.

'She's going to find out for herself when she goes to the nick,' I say. Vera shifts her false teeth with her tongue which creates a small eruption round her lips, she only does this when she's annoyed, or when she's been at the raspberry jam. I wonder about her age, and Mary's. Nothing like somebody you know croaking it to bring mortality to the front of the mind.

Must be about thirty I suppose, Mary. Berry's twenty one, I saw it in his pay book and now I'm off on one, agonising about love and all that stuff.

Vera and Mary are talking about a Victoria I never knew.

I am thinking about a Berry I probably don't know.

I hear them yatter on without it interfering with my thoughts.

At one point Mary laughs at something Vera says, and she loses several years, but her wobbly chin looks as if it could easily fall into tears and for the first time I feel sorry for her.

'Now, darling, don't you upset yourself,' says Vera, diving on grief like a magpie on a dead rat. And she puts her puffy hands on both our hands on the table, and I worry we might be going to have a Ouija job.

I half listen to the two of them and find myself almost liking Mary. I do notice that after a few pints people tend to become more bearable. Now, suddenly, I feel part of humanity and glad of it. I am sure that Berry will come back and that he loves me. Mary takes out a quid and tells me to get one in. Vera's face has gone lugubrious now in preparation for second-hand suffering. She is enjoying herself.

Berry sometimes talked about me going back to the States with him; most of the guys do, though it doesn't often happen. The whole idea seems idiotic to me, I've read about the racism there and when I went to the base once for a party, it got nasty with the whites, and the blacks weren't too keen on us, so it never seemed like a feasible option to me. This thought triggers me into Berry awareness again, I'm away.

When he's there I am alive and when he's not, I'm waiting for him. He talks in his slow voice which sounds nothing like

New York to me but he tells me about sleeping on the roof and stuff about gangs of kids and his mother whom he loves.

'Yeah man we could go back to the States, no sweat,' he says sometimes. We spend hours speculating about our babies who will take his colour and my blues eyes. All dreams. We play like kids with each other's bodies, discover a thigh and see it a separate entity. Admire it and speculate on alternative uses for a finger, a heel.

'Hey girl, look at this piece of meat I just found in the bed?' Lifting my leg high.

'Yeah, amazing isn't it? What you think it's for?'

'Lookee here baby, I got one too.' We would stagger round the room experimenting with this new discovery. Laughing, falling over on the bed and, finally, fucking. He would cook for us, steaks from the base and greens fried with bacon and eaten with bread rolls. When I talked about race and politics, he would hold me gently, look at my face and shake his head.

'Sheet, man, what do you know about race, girl? I got some dope here.' And we'd smoke and, later we'd shoot up sweet heroin and zonk out. Days we'd spend like this and BB got pissed off because he thought it was all drugs but it wasn't, it was loving, laughing, and drugging all together because we could afford it and it was sweet fun to extend our repertoire of senses into excess.

'I'd love to be black,' I said one day.

'Bullshit! What you want to say a damn fool thing like that for, Miss Limey?'

I saw he was really angry. I shrugged and said something about Billie Holiday and he said; 'Being Billie got nothing to do with being regular black. So if you want to be Billie Holiday say so, but don't talk shit about being black.' He lit a fag and his forehead crease was prominent.

'Hey, hey, lighten up, mate!' I say and he smiles.

'Anyway, you can't be Billie 'cos there ain't but one, now come here and compare.' So we laid bits of ourselves alongside one another and enjoyed the contrast.

'I never liked ofay chicks before I met you. I just fucked them cause they are so damn easy here in Europe.' He smiled to himself. Later he said:

'Don't you never wish being black on yourself, girl.'

Which intrigued me because when I asked him about race in the States he always shrugged it off with a 'What the fuck bullshit you been reading now, Miss Limey. I never came across any of that in New York, you been reading about the south.'

But when he spoke about his mother it was about her shit jobs and him sending her bread home. Sometimes he'd forget and talk about roaches in the building and rats.

Then he'd go back to:

'Sheet, man, our house is better than this.' Which wouldn't take a lot. Vera hardly prioritised modernisation and the house was collapsing while she waits to get re-housed when the area comes down.

'My mother works two damn jobs and still can't hardly survive so don't be telling me I shouldn't be in this man's air force. I can send her more in a month . . .' he looks at me like I can have no understanding and he's right.

And we'd drink some more Southern Comfort and smoke some more dope.

If this is the American way of life I'll take it. I mention Marcus Garvey but he blows a raspberry and pulls me to him.

'Bring your sweet pussy here, girl.'

I tell you, politics was never going to be our thing.

But I found him reading Langston Hughes and shaking his head. 'This is about the south, girl and why he writing so much about women blues. Don't you be thinking stateside like that,' and he chucks the book across the room.

I'm lost in this reverie so I don't notice that we are off, apparently, with all the handbag checking and bog going that this involves. Finally we take our leave of the old men, who seem not to have developed along the road to drunkenness at all, and still sit cribbing away with their big brown pints half drunk. I guess that's the steady trade. We are fairly merry now and we stop at the offy in the Grove to replenish V's stocks.

'You still got some of that gin, have you dear?'

My booze business has gone to buggery of late, and if Rooster has withdrawn his transport and allegiance, then I am truly fucked. And that's another reason to leave town, I think. I nod at Vera.

'We'll get some orange then shall we?' says V and acts the big spender with the geezer in the shop, her voice goes into posh high emphatic while she buys Sherry. Mary and her get into the: 'I'll pay for this,' trip while I cringe by the door. We bundle back to the house and I've forgotten that BB has probably done a moonlight. I remember as we go in and make my face a careful screen. Down in Vera's flat we sit round her table in roughly the same places as in the pub but my mind is on BB and Berry.

Vera and Mary are nattering about children now. Not one of my abiding passions so I slope off up to my room to get the gin. I look into BB's room. His gear has all gone but Angelo's clobber is still in the wardrobe, so at least he is still around. Billy has left the poster of Nasser in my room. I stick it up straight away.

Marmalade and Carlotta arrive with their usual flourish and the initial knock on the front door turns my stomach into a maelstrom and a double declutch takes my bowels into perfidious activity. The sound of whooping cranes issues through the house. I open the door.

'Dear heart, how are you?' says Carlotta while Marmalade envelopes me in delicious rose geranium arms and hugs me. Which makes me want to weep. Clearly, I'm cracking up.

'Here we are, my sweet, a flaunt of fairies to the rescue,' says Carlotta, nosing about the room. Marmalade withdraws, holds me at arms length.

'We've come to help. We heard that you've come unstuck quite badly, they're all saying you've grassed everybody up,' says Marmalade.

'The bold Shindig? Who doesn't know if she's Arthur or Martha?' interjects Carlotta. 'Never! Nevair, nante my dears! What did I parlary, Marmalade? Not on your sweet life!' says Carlotta.

'Plus we want the goss,' adds Marmalade.

'And what about Victoria's funeral? We were in the pub earlier and the landlady said we could have a do there. And she's going to have a collection on Saturday for her funeral. Isn't that bona of her?' says Carlie.

'Especially when she couldn't abide Victoria!' Marmalade laughs. 'Well, who could?'

Vera's voice comes up at us 'You got lost with that gin, dear? And who was that at the door?'

Marmalade flutes down the stairs:

'Only us, my petal! Shall we come down and bring the mother's ruin with us?'

'That you, Marmalade? Come on down then, darling. Got Carlie with you have you?' I whisper the news that Victoria's wife is down there.

'I've got a friend here,' says V.

'Can't wait to vadar what the bold Victoria wedded, too camp for words!' And he takes the gin from my nerveless hand and trolls downstairs like a rather spectacular galleon in full sail. We follow in his wake.

'Aren't you looking bona, Vera?' and Marmalade smiles at Mary. 'And who's this?' Mary has a slightly stunned look on her face, normal enough for a first encounter with Marmalade. Carlotta fluffs in and shakes hands with Mary.

'Not sisters, are you?' he says.

'No, I'm Mrs Connolly,' Mary pauses to let the title sink in. 'Victor's wife.' She looks Carlotta in the eye, waiting. They seem to be staring each other out and I can't bear it.

'We were all mates of Vic's, Mary. This is Carlotta and this is Marmalade,' I say.

Marmalade shakes Mary's hand and tells her how sorry he is.

Vera opens the gin and I pull up chairs.

'I don't know, Vera. What are you going to do about Victoria?'

Everybody stops, and looks at me. Then at Mary.

'Victor? When the police release his body, I'll take him home.'

We all gawp at her.

'Aye, he's a place in his mum's grave waiting for him.'

'Because we were thinking of having a party,' says Marmalade.

'Sort of a wake . . .' adds Carlie. 'For all her friends to remember her, in the pub.'

'Oh, that would be nice, Mary,' says V the conciliator.

'I think, if any of you ever bothered looking, that she was a he and we've two kiddies to prove it. One of each.'

'You could have a party anyway,' I say, and I've no idea why I'm creased with embarrassment when I should be enjoying the spectacle.

'We will!' says Carlie.

'And we'll send flowers,' I say.

'Why don't we all go?' says Marmalade, and the idea of a cavalcade of queens and their acolytes travelling in convoy up north is so marvellous that I start laughing. Must be the trauma of the day, I can't stop. Carlie thuds my back with his fist: 'To stop me going into hysteria.' Meanwhile, Mary and Vera are soaking up the sherry and gin respectively and looking solemn.

'Strikes me,' says Vera, with great pomp. 'We haven't given nearly enough attention to Victoria's death.'

Mary murmurs; 'Victor.'

'Sorry, dear,' says V and pats her hand. I wonder if hand patting takes over from sex when you're old? I do hope not. 'What did the police say, Mary? Do you want to tell us? It's your place as his wife.'

'They said he died of heart failure.'

'Well, everybody dies of heart failure, don't they?' says Carlotta nastily. 'What caused it? Do they know? I heard he was beaten to a pulp.'

'I went to see him and there were no signs of beating on his body. A bit blue round the gills but apart from that he looked normal,' says Mary, loudly.

'They are having a coroner's report because they aren't sure what caused it, but there was no sign of beating on him.'

'Well, you and BB went to see him the day before didn't you? How was he then?' Vera again, to me.

'Oh, did you? I didn't know that,' says Carlotta.

'Yes you did, I told you!' protests Marmalade.

It occurs to me that the drugs that BB and myself took in to Victoria might have killed him but the bill seem not to know or care. But once the coroner does his stuff . . . I feel icy terror wending its slinky way up my back.

The others are talking about the funeral. They ask what I think but I'm in a world of my own.

'I think we should have a big do down here at the boozer, and couldn't we bring him back here?' I say.

'That's a bit macabre isn't it?' from Carlie.

'I don't want any bodies back here, thank you very much.' But you can see Vera is thinking about it and that the idea is appealing:

'Well, I'll take him back to Burnley anyway but if you want to have a wake down here . . .'

We all look at each other. I feel woozy and just make it upstairs before I collapse.

22 Travelling All Alone

It's that kind of stupor that allows no dreams and is a rehearsal for death. I wake up and know it's the middle of the night. I can see a light under my door which makes the darkness as thick as oxtail soup. First second, I feel great, then all the grief siphons up into my brain and I stiffen into a rigor of fear and misery.

I hear a buzzing noise and go to BB's room. From the landing light I see a body in the bed and for a moment I think he's come back. Then I smell the Ashes of Roses and see Mary's neat little shoes, straight from her trotters, standing close together, entirely erect. Her breath gurgles in and out of her. I'm tempted to hold her nostrils closed out of pique that she's not BB. She does one of those snorts, and for a second I think she might be going to oblige me by snuffing it, then she does a complicated and ghastly gobble and turns over, sighs, resumes her gurgle breath.

I leave her snuffling and blowing in hideous regularity and I go back to my room, I take a slug of Bourbon that hits my gut with the velocity of a small bomb and I feel stunned enough to kip. I get under the eiderdown. So where the fuck is Angelo? Perhaps BB found him and they've gone. Some of my internal organs sink a few inches in despair. Must have dozed. Then I hear the scream. The scream is followed by a lot of verbals in Mary's voice, loud, alarmed. Angelo's high Latino outrage joins her northern diatribe so I get in there fast. The main light is on and Mary is bolt upright in bed defending her virtue with blankets drawn to her chin.

'Who you are? Why you are here in our bed?'

Simultaneously Mary makes with her own queries: 'Who the bloody hell are you? Get out of it.'

Angelo's wiry little body with it's dancer's muscles is shaping up to the supine Mary. He turns as I come into the room:

'Who this old bag is, Shindig?'

'Who you calling an old bag? Cheeky little black bastard.'
'It's his lattie, Mary, him and his bloke. You're in his bed.'
'Yes, my bed! The bed of my lover and me!'
'All I know is Vera said I could sleep here.' Her face is a picture of obstinacy, jaw set, eyes gimlet bright. She should have a beard. It would suit her.
'Why aren't you in Victoria's room?'
'I couldn't sleep in there, much too upsetting!'
'Kip in my room, Angelo,' I say.
'Is my bed this! I hope you pay me.' He flounces elegantly out.

In my room Angelo tells me that Billy came to his work at the interval to say he'd meet him in the all night café after the show but he didn't turn up.

Poor little fucker, been waiting until he was asked to leave because they thought he was grafting.

'That doesn't make sense, if you just sat there for hours.'
'Geezers keep approach me talk to me, I say no but they chat me so. Buy me coffee.' He shrugs a graceful move, smiles.
'Then I worry. I ask the goovenor where is Billy, you know him BB where he?'
'Then he chucked you out? Yeah, BB got a bit of a reputation.'
'A reputation?'
'Yeah, Angelo, he's not universally loved.' He looks blank.
'So where he is?' He ruminates while I roll a joint using my last fag. He takes it from me and improves on the structure, hands it back to light. We are sitting on the floor by the gas fire, leaning against the bed. I've put on some Bessie Smith, but quietly.
'He tell me we must go, you must go too, he say we go to the sea, yes? I think perhaps he has gone, he was very scared.' He gives a small shrug. 'He will be waiting for me.'
My own thoughts are more on the lines of him getting nicked again but I say nothing.
He takes a draw, coughs one of those neat little, 'preliminary to smoking' coughs, takes a next toke. Draws in slow, he smokes through his hands like an Arab.
'I say I must stay until the end of show then I come. Perhaps

two weeks or three, I must stay, or no more work.' He passes the joint to me. So BB had gone off on his Jack.

'What did he say when you told him you must stay?'

'OK, he say OK, is fine see ya later, I stay here pay rent.'

I kip in the chair and wake stiff as a truncheon.

I make my way to Notting Hill on automatic; if Dixie wants me she'll find me. I hit a café, consume a greasy breakfast quickly and feel neither fuller nor emptier. It just disappears inside me to no effect. Paranoia joins terror misery, grief and sadness to make a royal flush. On my fourth cup of tea it occurs to me that if Dixon is suspended she can't nick me, but then she was with two cops in the pub. At this point I decide to stop thinking.

I have *The Member of the Wedding* and I immerse myself totally in it but the words pour through my mind like an enema, not touching the cortex. My brain is taking independent action and insists on functioning brightly, showing up vivid options that make it worse. I'm afraid to go to Tiger's and I emerge from the café about eleven and slippy tit past Joe Lyons, peering in through the window as I go. Trudy looks straight out at me and her mouth falls open as she looks. She rustles herself into motion like a stick insect and shambles out the door. I put my finger to my lips and shoot round the corner to the flat. It is locked up from the outside with a heavy padlock. So that's over.

We stand together and her dry stench comes at me.

'Hear you're in deep shit, mate. Want a jack? Can use my works.'

'No, Trudy, ta.' I feel all warm and grateful and want to cry.

'What's the word, Trudy?' She laughs and the greenish teeth are evident:

'Which one do you want, man? There's as many words as a Chambers dictionary.'

She laughs and for some extraordinary reason I choose now to become hysterical. I find myself sobbing and hooting with high pitched shrieks and can't stop.

'Hey man, cool it!' She grabs hold of me and I shrink back fast, causing us both to tumble and stagger. We almost crash to the ground, my body in close proximity to hers and that unique junkie odour works like unsavoury smelling salts. I straighten up. She pulls away and I sit on the doorstep, she joins me.

'You all right, man?' she says. Nods her head a yes. She pats me down like she's doing a search. Continues,

'Well, like I say, man, what word do you want? The creative gifts of the whole West End are involved in shaping your life. Or death.' She laughs, gives me a fag, sits on the steps of the house, looks up at me.

'The word is that you ripped off Dixon for drugs and now she's after you, but seriously. Or that you have already decamped to Morocco or India or any other places you care to mention. Or that you are involved in big time gangsterism and have been topped. Probably in the foundations of a motorway already.' She looks up and grins.

'Take yer pick, man.' Don't know if I should laugh or cry.

'That Yank being sent back and them chasing Diego gave some ammunition to the rumour mongers, not that they need it. Those guys can make bricks without a wisp of straw.'

'Who? What Yank?'

'The Puerto Rican geezer with Colette. Been nicking stuff from the PX and he's done a runner with her. Plus the black geezer you was with is being sent home.'

'You sure?'

'Course I'm not sure. A Yank called Frankie told us, he came in looking for you in Lyons. But these facts have the same mythical status as the stuff going round about you. The law were in looking for Colette and her bloke. Yesterday I think it was.'

Poor bloody Berry is my first thought. Poor fucker just wanted to be a serviceman, which is a crap ambition but his own. I must see him.

'I wouldn't try to see him if I was you, Shindig. I don't know, or want to know, what you've done, but if I was you I'd take to me toes for a while.'

'I've done fuckall, Trudy.' My voice has a bleat in it.

'I believe you, thousands wouldn't. But I don't think you'll find that has a lot to do with anything. We've all seen people go down for things they haven't done, haven't we, man? And watched the guilty thrive, so what's new?' She is looking cold in that way junkies do, hunching her shoulders, scraping her feet. Like the flesh is not sufficient to keep the internal organs warm.

'You sound straight, Trudy.'

'Yeah, just caught me didn't you? I'm off for a cure later on today.'

'Why's that then?'

'Family pressure man. Every now and then they reckon it's black sheep week. Remember they've got an errant daughter and book me in for a rebore, don't they?' Laughs, pushes past me.

'Got to get back, seeing Tone for some more gear. Can't go in empty-handed can I?'

'Shit man, do you want to go?' I say. She screws up her eyes, laughs derisive.

'Course I don't fucking want to go. I wanted to last week and told my mother. Changed my mind now, haven't I, but the family process has begun, what can I do? Won't recognise me when I come back will you?'

'Where you going, Epsom?'

'Nah, man. Off to the sanatorium I am, no messing with my mother. Nothing but the best. All private ponces in there, none of yer hoi polloi. Love me, won't they?' She laughs raucously. 'It's a career move, man. Come back fresh as a daisy and start all over again.' She laughs.

'Put some pounds on, eh?' I say.

'Get out of town, Shindig, on your toes man!' She stands up, grins and shakes my hand.

'You're a junk tourist anyway, man. Get out while you're ahead. You don't have the commitment to be a real junkie, Shindig. Takes a kind of insane dedication. You lack the balls, you're kind of a dilettante, man.'

I look at her, don't know if I should be insulted or what. Never occurred to me until now that I might get hooked. See myself as a recreational junkie.

'You're too squeamish, girl.'

I don't know what to think about this. She continues:

'Good luck, man. By the way, some quack that Johnny was
into up west . . .' I stiffen.

'I see you knew him, got busted didn't he? Never got
charged but they'll be going through his papers, won't they?
All his patients' names, eh?'

Of course I gave a phoney name, still I am shaken.

'Be cool, baby.' She rackets off in the direction of Lyons,
cackling. I look at my hand, it can still feel her scaly, dry claw.
I need to sit down and discuss this with myself but Lyons is
out of the question.

This has been one of the longest days of my life and I've drunk
more tea than enough, now I am full of tea and misery, the tea
washes back and forth as I walk. The misery is stationary, a
lump. I'm afraid to meet anyone I know and afraid to be alone.
Early evening, I know I've got to go to Uxbridge to see if I can
find Berry. I can't just let him be sent back without talking to
him. Now we've declared our love, I joke to myself but I don't
feel like laughing.

Uxbridge is one of mine and Rooster's regular trips. Now
I've got to go back, alone. I give myself a tug out of gloom into
something more sensible. I arrive in Uxbridge and hit the first
boozer. Open the door. The whole company turns its bodies to
stare at me, once, then back to their drink.

'I think you want the lounge.' A snotty barmaid looks as if
she might well be wearing starched drawers. I smile and the
gruesome lot ignore me.

'Sorry, I wanted the ladies.'

'Well, you won't find it in here, this is the public bar.'

I go into the lounge bar where identical punters huddle
round the same barmaid, who's moved her scrawny arse round
the corner. She hasn't changed her demeanour and is still
misery incarnate. I smile a big cheesy and pretend I don't notice
the icy crack.

'Nice night isn't it?' I say. She delivers my beer, arm straight
ahead, face pinched up tight. I don't know where the pub that
the coloured guys use is, and I'd like to find it quickish then
either snatch Berry or find out where he is. Normally, I'd drop
a question, casual like, into the conversation, but there is no

conversation so I drink up and look round for a face half open, but they're all shut tight as drums.

'Excuse me!' I say. And hear my voice quaver out of control. 'Could anybody tell me where the coloured Americans drink round here?'

'No, and you'd better get out if that's what you're looking for. We don't want no bleeding nigger lovers in here.' From the barmaid. Time to go.

In cowboy films when the good guy goes into a bar and they all blank him, a kid or an old man comes out afterwards and whispers the info in his ear, sotto voce. So I wait outside for a moment or two. Doesn't work for me, probably an American thing. I go in the direction that looks liveliest and it pays off.

23   He Sho' Don't Mean No Harm

The singing is exquisite harmony and it comes out into the grey street and astonishes the walls. As I open the door the sound swells over me and saturates me in mellow noise. The whole pub is a sea of dark faces, sitting, standing, singing or not. Nobody sees me as I stand there, bewitched.

> Annie had a baby can't work no more. Annie had a baby
>   can't work no more.
> Annie had a baby can't work no more, no more no more
>   no more.

But it is embellished and worked around and voices of every shade and substance weave around and return to:

> Work with me Annie mnn mnn
> Work with me Annie, work with me Annie, let's get it
>   while the getting is good
> So good, so good, so motherloving good,
> Work with me Annie. Let's get it while the getting is
>   good.'

And so it continues for five minutes or so, endless repetitions, never quite the same. I begin to suss out who the main voices are, also my shortest route to the bar. Then I spot Lefty, the evil dwarf from the Mapleton. He detaches himself from his beer, approaches like a bantam cock on an errand of great importance, straight for me.

'Hi there, baby! You look like a lady on a mission, couldn't keep your sweet self away from me, huh?'

'That's right, Lefty. Got it in one, you're one clever little motherfucker, aren't you?'

'Certainly am, baby girl.' His eyes are hard and sour like last time. The singing has stopped and some old guy with stripes right up his arm comes over, his gut is vast and it makes a separate pilgrimage of its own ahead of the rest of his bulk.

'Hey, Lefty, my man, so this is what you studs do in London, huh?' He takes my hand in his.

'I'm going to have to be more venturesome if this is the kind of thing you come up with. You going to get the lady a drink, boy?' It sounds like a command. Lefty's whole attitude has changed. He scuttles to the bar. The big man finds me a seat and I sit obediently by his side. He asks my name and I tell him 'Shindig' and he leans away from me, opens his eyes until they are round as golf balls.

'That's some name, honey! What in the world was your mummy thinking of?'

'It's a nickname,' I had been reduced to monosyllables, rare for me.

'That right is it? You know I kind of guessed that. Do you want to know what they call me?'

'Yes, why not?'

'Well, little lady, they call me Denver.'

'That where you're from is it?' I want to get back into this conversation.

'Nope. It's where I joined the service.'

Leftie comes back with a beer for me, then he disappears. I want to ask Denver about Berry and I am preparing my mouth for action, but now, a man with straightened hair with half a pound of pomade on it, glistening under the lights, has got up and is singing a Billy Eckstein number. 'My Foolish Heart' quivers and quavers and I am absorbed in watching his throat and imagining the state of his pillows with all the grease on his hair. Denver, and the whole room is singing around his solo, and they add beautiful twists and gorgeous notes that don't occur on the records. Denver has this high sweet voice. I'm trapped with him.

When the music has ended I put my hand on the stripes.

'You got a lot of these, haven't you?'

'I surely have, I'm a master sergeant.' He sounds proud and tired as he says it, like he remembers how old he is. I smile at him.

'Are you flirting with me, girl?'

He looks at me cynically. I shrug.

'Now, what are you here for, little lady?'

'I'm looking for a guy.'

'Well honey, you're surely in the right place . . .'

'Not just any guy – Berry – that's his name.'

'Friend of yours?'

'Certainly is.'

His face gives nothing away. His jowls are full of old scars from ingrown whiskers, his eyes are settled in comfy beds of fat, and his hair so short his head gleams darkly through.

'Do you know him?'

'I believe I might.' His big old eyes look sideways at me from among a mass of red veins.

I wait for him to enlarge. He doesn't.

A guy begins to sing 'Old Man River' and there is only a low humming to accompany him and it comes from a dozen throats in perfect harmony. I have this big lump in my throat and couldn't speak if I wanted to. My mind is full of Paul Robeson going to Wales for the miners' strike, sentiment boils over into maudlin. Rudimentary sobs threaten, I swallow them. I look around the room, furtive grins keep me company. The singing fills the bar. There is not a single woman in the place, even the bar has a man behind it.

After the singing ends, Denver turns to me. His face is tough like tanned leather.

'Your friend; he shipped out yesterday.'

He watches me, carefully, to see my reaction. I keep my face as still as possible, while my entire interior clasps itself tight and screams. My main thought is that the last time I saw him getting on the tube was the last time I'll ever see him. And I didn't know. Now, I know that I never believed he'd go. That I always expected I'd see him again, expected to spot him, duffel bag on his shoulder, coming round the corner. But I won't, ever.

Must have sat there a while because a brandy is in my hand.

'Listen honey, what were you expecting? You surely didn't expect he'd marry you did you?'

'Hadn't thought about it. He was over here for another year, wasn't he?'

'Way I understand it he was mixing with a crowd of drug fiends and breaking the law. That's why he got sent Stateside.' Heavy face looks solemn, accusing too.

'Swing Low Sweet Chariot' has begun but it's sweet Cadillac

like Dizzy. Denver joins in but his eye is still on me. He stops singing, speaks;

'See, you little ofay chicks think you could go back Stateside, and it would be like some giant PX, with a great house and better life. Well, baby girl, it ain't never gonna be like that; to the whites you'd be some nigger lover and to the coloureds you'd be grey meat. So you see, honey, it was never a real good idea.'

'Grey meat' hangs, like some obscene pall, in my mind. I never heard the expression before, wish I hadn't now. I know I won't forget this one. So nasty but I won't ask him about it. No need. His eyes are tight on my face, watching me.

'See girl, when our innocent coloured boys come here, they are knocked over by the fact there's so much white pussy putting out, but it don't never work.'

I feel my mind tighten back into shape, and anger gets my thoughts organised.

'It works perfectly well here, and in France. Perhaps we Europeans handle things better, perhaps we aren't eaten up with prejudice.'

He opens his eyes wide again but no indication of what he's thinking. Just surprise.

'Perhaps you could be right, Shindig, perhaps you could be right. But your friend Berry has long gone.'

'I want to see his CO, I want his address.'

'OK, you leave it with me. Give me your address and I'll see he gets it. Now, little lady, can I buy you another drink?'

I realise the brandy has gone and I have no memory of drinking it.

Lefty materialises.

'Get me a brandy please, Lefty and whatever Denver is drinking. And have one yourself.' I hand him money,

'No, actually Lefty, I'll go myself,' I stand. Look over to the bar and there is Rooster coming in the door and after him comes Frantic, making jagged disturbances in the atmosphere, displacing more air than anyone else in the world. They don't see me and I want to sit down again. In fact, Denver gently pulls me back down and Lefty makes for the bar while Denver pushes my money away. I don't know if there's anything I can say to Denver. Nothing seems appropriate.

He offers me a cigarette and I refuse it, light one of my own.

'Hey there, girl! I didn't mean to cause you no grief, just putting you straight.'

Lefty has arrived at the bar and Rooster is greeting him like some long lost comrade. Frantic looks scared and Rooster looks foreign. His clothes, hair, out of place and his eyes dart nervously. I enjoy his discomfort for a few moments, then I realise that I must either go and speak to him or stay where I am. I know I have a need to grind Denver's fat self-satisfied face into the ground.

'Well, big man, thanks so much for your views on race, sex and grey meat, it's been good to hear the honest ideas of a bigot. No wonder all those coloured intellectuals came to live in Europe if your ideas are typical. Just because you got all those stripes you got some power in the service, but you have no power over me, mate!'

My voice has got higher.

'From where I'm standing you're just a stooge, fighting for Mr Whitey!'

Shit. Where did that come from. Sometimes my ideas appear on the hoof.

His face starts off passive, but boils halfway through my dissertation, he breaths in a great breath and looks like he might whack me one when I get to the end. The pub goes silent half way through and I think there's a chance I might get lynched so after that, I have no choice. I march to the bar, can hardly see with rage, knock some furniture sideways on the way.

'I won't be staying for that drink, Lefty. Get back to that fat cocksucker you hear!'

Rooster laughs, and Frantic shrieks.

'See yer doing yer stuff, gel.' She turns to Rooster; 'Could start a fight in an empty church, this one!'

'Come now.' Rooster kind of guides me out the door and into the dark.

The singing has begun again. And it's just as beautiful. This big sound follows us into the street, assails the air, keeps us company for a while. Lost its magic for me. Soured.

We hurry to the motor.

'What was that about then, gel?'

'Wish you'd keep your fucking hooter out of my business, Frannie. And what you doing out here with Rooster, anyway?'

'You jealous are yer? 'Ere Rooster, she's only bleeding jealous of you, darling.'

We've been walking along the pavement with the hard sky above and the music just gone from our ears.

'Don't be so stupid, Frannie,' I say. 'Where we going, Rooster?'

'Make I take you home now?'

I am grateful and I collapse between him and Frantic, she is rabbiting away but I am not receiving. I am stuck with the fact I'll never feel Berry again or smell him. Or touch him. Me and Rooster haven't talked since the law put the bubble in and it feels good to sit beside his solid body, giving off a slight pleasant feral scent each time he lifts his arm.

Back into town through dead streets enlivened by crowds leaving cinemas. Out they come doing their John Wayne strut before they remember who they are and scuttle back to safety behind closed doors. As we get into London the pubs are turning out, the merry and not so merry lurch home.

We drop off Frantic. She wants to know where we're going and why, nosy cow.

24 Cryin' Woman Blues

I never credited old Rooster with a lot of sensitivity.

Now, after he decants Frantic, we zoom up to north London.

The Suez crisis has had a distressing effect on the petrol pumps of Britain and we have resorted to the jerry can and rubber hose method. We are compelled to make ingenious forays to find well filled motors and redress the balance. I like to think I am supporting Nasser in my efforts. Tonight we hit Hampstead and I slip back into my role of Rooster's little helper, it feels safe. We find a couple of tanks to siphon, I wipe my mouth carefully. I have no desire to go up with my next fag, suttee doesn't appeal. I insert a chiclet of gum. Rooster had hardly spoken since we left Uxbridge.

'How come we own a canal in somebody else's country half way across the world, Rooster?'

Rooster laughs 'How come you own we, man? T'rartit. How come the British carry them nastiness over the entire world and them call it civilisation?'

He goes into a kind of laugh fest. I join in but hiccup so it's a near thing to weeping.

'Come now, we travel a lickle. You must drive.' Moves his arse over to the right. So I go round the outside. I don't even want to drive I feel so low, but I can't resist.

We leave town. To the café by the airport.

'You don't know you must practise for when you have your test?' We giggle. We know I'll get a bent licence. We arrive and sit in the motor. We talk about Berry's exodus and I find myself grizzling like some sad old thing in purgatory.

'Is not big time love you know,' he says. I'm not sure if he means all love, or this love.

'I know. It's the snatching away. Like some big bastard

hand moving the pieces of my life around some weird board. Fucks up my head.'

Rooster sucks his teeth.

'Man, you don't know them do that to we all ways? All the bloodclot time? Them have us in them hand and if them choose to squeeze.'

He holds up his hand and demonstrates. Tight crushing.

'Is the wuckhouse for we, man. You think them don't know all we business? You is wrong boy!'

Shakes his head and laughs.

I snuggle into his long body and he holds me.

'You is my lickle fren, man. I don't belief them when them say you is grass you know.'

'No?'

I'd like to ask why he blanked me. But I watch instead as he builds a joint with his arms around me. His big hands move tenderly, adroit, neat. He hardly looks as he builds, like he's on automatic. My own spliffs look like unmade beds, his are like a Saville Row pair of trousers, with a neat turn-up.

'Work of art, Rooster.'

He sighs.

'Move now! You don't know I lose money tonight.' He shakes his head.

'Sorry, Rooster,' he shrugs.

'Friends come fust, Shindig.' He looks at me. 'You must stay by me tonight, Bernice arks about you this long time.' He must be feeling really guilty, he gets uneasy when I get together with his missis. We get along far too well for his liking.

I move along the bench seat, sit behind the steering wheel. The camber on the road makes me sink down and I look over at his big dark face in the light of the glowing joint he lights from the lighter in the dash. Rooster takes enormous pride in his fat American car. With its polished chrome gleaming and its silver grin, it is like a small ice cream parlour on the move.

'No man, me must h'ignore you cause Jack tell me so. You don't know that?'

'How the fuck would I know? You think I'm psychic?'

'What happen with Dixon?' he asks.

'She got suspended. Told me to get out of town or else. So why must you ignore me?

'I don't arks man, come take a draw. Him say that you is dangerous.'

'And you, naturally, believed him?' He shrugs, I leave it.

'I better not do any deals for the time being, eh Rooster.' His relief is evident.

I crash at Rooster's pad in one of his kids' bunk beds. His wife is glad to see me and I give her all the scandal about the Grove.

Next day after a good night's kip I wake up to the fact that Berry is really gone. And the news is full of invasion talk. But like he said; what would a guy from the motor pool do in a war? I'm sure they'd think of something. On the bus I look at the paper over some woman's shoulder. The papers are full of Nasser now, my hero. I spend the day at Tiger's, not talking a lot. Tiger says, 'Never talk about politics, do I?' but all his mates are ready to invade tomorrow or today. Of course they are all far too old but the spirit is more than willing, in theory. I bring out my own opinion on the subject and Tiger takes me aside and gives me a résumé of my duties and they don't include political analysis. Then they all go into what we did in the war stuff which I neither believe nor enjoy. In fact, it is a deeply frustrating day. I amble into the pub under the Dilly and flirt with the barman. I can't face home or the Roebuck, both of them remind me of Berry and both of them are places that Dixon knows where to find me. I feel in limbo and am happy to stay there, my mind is turned off for the moment and the drink is working well tonight. I walk towards Oxford Street, I'm feeling almost happy as I hear the car draw up beside me, I turn and see Jack from the drug squad.

'Been looking for you, darling, going to get in and keep us company, are you?'

'Always a pleasure, Jack!' I say and my belly sinks fast.

'What can I do for you?'

He grins at me.

'Get in here, for a start, Shindig.' He shoves over to make room for me beside him in the back. The driver is some leery looking young git who looks me over like I'm a piece of mutton he's happened upon. Just the two of them in the squad car by the looks of it.

'Yeah, just the two of us, your mate Dixon's off on her hols, lucky girl.' The driver sniggers.

'Yes, doll, been round your drum and everything, we have. We met Vera and Vic's missis and none of them knew where you were. We even ran into your mate Rooster, he wasn't pleased to see us at all, didn't know your whereabouts either. Were beginning to get worried about your welfare we were, weren't we John?'

He sniggers again, the driver.

Jack looks at me shrewdly. I look back, gormless.

'Never thought we'd come across you by chance like this. Must be fate, eh?'

The truly diabolical thing with the law is that it's never, ever, an even match. You, or in this case me, always get the fish on hook role while the law get to play the angler with a nice pliable rod. So they can reel you in, let you off the hook or just play silly buggers, let you swim away then pull you back in. I've had a busy day, now I'm tired.

'Yes, touch and go if Dixon comes back to us, it is.' Looks at me to see what effect his words are having.

I keep my face as still as possible but can feel it swarming all over the place with mixed terror, relief, anxiety. A lot of stuff to hold down. I actually feel my eyes scurrying hither and yon. I keep them still by effort of will and can feel myself looking constipated.

'Why's that then?' I say to stop the mind motion.

'Could be promotion or could be a transfer, who knows? But she's on her holidays anyway,' he says. I say nothing. 'Yes, seems like she blotted her copy book and got kicked upstairs. 'Playing around with young birds so they say.' He takes out his fags, offers me one, I take it.

'Can't be bad, eh John?' John makes a non committal sound.

'That's nice,' I say. 'I mean being on holiday.' Getting back control of my bowels, been bucketing around since I got in the motor.

'You could say that,' he says and gives me a light.

'Dropped you in it darling, now why would she have done that do you think?' I look at him through the smoke and think of Joan Crawford, draw strength from the image. Use a bit of Crawford.

'Damned if I know, Jack. Thought we were friends, didn't I?'

John sniggers and I glare at his back.

'So, what do you want, Jack?'

'Oh, a little chat,' said in such a light tone of voice that I'm scared.

'That all?'

'Might be, that's up to you darling.'

Don't like the sound of that, it could mean anything. I move away from him a bit.

'Oh, don't worry sweetheart, I'm not after your body, I leave that to Dixon.' John sniggers again.

'And John here is a newly wed, so you're safe from us.'

He smiles at me, like I should say thanks or something.

'Oh ta, mate!' I say with moderate sarcasm that's lost on them.

'So what do you want to chat about then?'

'People, mutual friends. Want to go for a drink do you?'

I am torn between my need for a drink and the possibility of being seen with the law.

'Where?'

'Little place I know. Don't worry darling, I don't want to be seen with you either.'

The car turns swiftly and whisks up the road at well above the speed limit. He knocks the door of a pub that opens up for us. We leave John outside. We sit in the private bar and I can hear the sounds of clearing up while Jack goes for the drinks.

If he was going to nick me surely he would have taken me in, I think. But I'm not sure. The thing you learn about the law is the fact that there are no certainties. This might be some complex game to get information out of me, then take me in. What possible information have I got anyway?

He didn't ask what I wanted and comes back with two beers.

'So what's this about, Jack?'

'I'll tell you.' And he lifts the glass to me and looks so sincere that I am terrified all over again.

'Don't worry, Shindig, I'm not going to nick you, not if you co-operate.' Oh shit.

'Don't worry, I'm not asking you to grass anybody up, not exactly, I want you to do something for me, as a personal favour.'

'Why?' I thought I'd thought it, but I must have said it aloud.

His face goes dead hard, then he thinks better of it and a horrible creepy look comes over his eek, and I realise that I am going to be subject to gentle persuasion. I have experienced this form of torture before and don't rate it.

'Because I need your help.'

'Right!' I say smartly. He looks well startled but recovers his sang froid, if that can apply to the bloodless creep. I watch his face but remember that he is watching mine, too. So I beam at him, covering all my hostility with consummate ingratiating love. Can see he doesn't trust it. He's right.

'Well, darling, first thing you got to understand is that we don't want you. You are irrelevant, the boys we are after are the geezers that make money out of drugs. Not the little people that choose to mess up their lives fixing up, smoking a bit of charge, all small beer.'

We both drink at this mention of beer.

'Cheers!' I say.

'Cheers!' says he.

'Johnny Mason,' he says.

'Yes,' I say.

'Mate of yours?'

'Kind of.'

I'm waiting for him to get on with it, what ever it is.

'Tell me what you want and I'll tell you if I can help,' I say.

'Mason uses several quacks, gets birds to go and get scripts for coke, barbs, heroin. But coke is favourite. Sells better to more savoury people. But you know all this, don't you?'

I remember the blank scripts lurking in my gaff. The bowel twists again.

'Yes.'

'So it's no surprise to you. Course it wouldn't be, would it?

Little bird told me you've helped Mason on at least one
occasion.'

'The little birds of this world have a lot to answer for,
Jack.'

'Ain't that the truth, gel?' he smiles. 'You're a proper little
helper aren't you, dolly? What with Rooster and Johnny
Mason and old Tiger, too.'

He gives me a look so meaningful that it is very nearly
constitutes GBH. I choke on my beer.'

'Look darling, I don't give a flying fuck if you been there or
not.'

'Right,' I say. And wait for him to come out with what he
wants.

'Now, there is one particular quack that we'd like to pull.
He's been taking liberties all over the place. Bastard thinks he's
above the law.'

His face is getting all bunchy, muscles riveting into anger.

'We'll get him, with or without your help.' He relaxes a bit.
Looks at me speculatively, summing up how much use I can be
to him.

Gives me a crap feeling. I'm out of control, and while my
entire life is pretty much out of control, I don't usually have to
recognise it. I wonder what this is really about. Has the quack
ripped him off personally?

'So? You on are you?'

'Do what?' I say with not a spark of intelligence presenting
itself to either one of us.

'Come on, Shindig, you're a bright bird, will you go and get
a script from him?'

'Do I have to?'

'You do if you don't want me turning your gaff over and
finding a weight, yes!' He laughs and finishes his beer.

'Have another beer, help you decide.' He's gone.

I don't really have a choice. Have a dreadful feeling that it
won't end there.

He approaches with two beers.

'OK.'

'There's a good girl. Now, I'll give you a lift home and I'll
be in touch. Don't tell anybody about seeing me and you can
tell BB that he's safe if he wants to come back.'

We drink our beer in silence except for us drawing on our fags. Then he speaks,

'You're doing yourself a favour, doll.' I want to ask how he makes that out but I don't.

John is parked near the door, we get in and he drives to Notting Hill without asking. When we get to the Gate he turns and Jack directs him. He stops round the corner from the house, I get up and out, Jack touches my arm.

'Be in touch I will, Shindig, soon.'

'Good night, John,' I say. He sniggers, I think I knew he would.

The house is alight when I get home, soon as I get in the front
door, Vera attacks me with affectionate worry.

'Darling, they've only bin round looking for yer, haven't
they, the law.'

'Yes, you better get going, dear,' adds Mary.

'It's sorted, don't worry. I've seen them and it's OK.'

'When?'

'Just now, Vera, get off my back, please.'

'What you bin up to, girl? No, I don't want to know. The
wake's on Monday, darling!' Vera says, well perky.

Mary puffs up like a pouter pigeon, it gives her a beady
look.

'Yes, the body's coming here in the morning and it will be
here all day and night then I'm taking him back home on
Tuesday.'

Vera smiles at me. It almost instils confidence in me but not
quite.

With Jack lurking about and the quack imminent. I need to
watch points.

'I'm fucked, Vera. Must get to kip.'

'All right, want a cup of tea, my sweet?' says V.

'No, ta, darling.'

I do wonder about the unnatural amount of affection
coming from Vera but it feels like my legs will hardly carry
me up the stairs. I sleep so soundly that when Vera brings me
a cup of tea at eleven thirty in the morning I have no sense of
the intervening hours. Then all the stuff comes sliding up from
my unconscious with unnecessary speed. Jack arrives first in my
mind and the fact that he could turn up any time, he is followed
by Dixon and Victoria, the wake and then, finally, a great
sadness that Berry has gone. Meanwhile, Vera has made a place
for herself on my bed.

'Getting on my tits she is, darling.'

'Who's that then, V?' Like I don't know.

'Mary, I think she wants to move in.'

'Thought she had. Tell her to fuck off, Vera. Soon as Vic's funeral is over. What's happened to her kids, anyway?'

'Yeah, she'll see them when she goes up won't she?'

'Wouldn't put it past her to bring the buggers back down here. Then you'll have the whole family taking over your life.'

'Don't!'

'Yeah V, you got to get shot of her, mate.'

'I can't just tell her to go. I feel sorry for her.'

'Feel a bleeding sight more sorry for you if she stays, darling. She's a nosy cunt. Wants us all out doesn't she?'

'Yes.' She gives me a lit fag and I draw long and hard on it. She looks defeated but underneath her chin is firming up nicely, Vera's made up her mind, just wants somebody to blame if it goes wrong.

Vera doesn't stay long.

Angelo's voice comes up at me as I get halfway down the stairs.

'The old bag, she tell me I must go!'

'Oh dear!' says Vera, inadequately I feel.

'Old bag she is, old bag puta!'

'So what happened?' I hear Vera ask and I look at the three of them, all comical figures. Angelo thrusting his head forward at Mary, who retreats into furious indignation – she seems to have a great well of indignation that she dips into frequently. Poor old V just looks tired, but still interested and still with a look of humour on her eek. Like she's enjoying the fun of it, in spite of herself. She looks over at me, raises her eyebrows, laughs.

'What you got to laugh about, Vera?' says Mary. 'This little bugger was rude to me.'

'So what?' says Vera. 'You're rude to everybody.'

She kind of expands into her indignation, I can see the emotion, like yeast, working through her entire being. Now she rises visibly, almost a tiny levitation.

'I'll thank you to mind your own business, you little tart.'

'Listen you fucking lumpy old pudding, watch it, you hear me?' I say.

Angelo leans forward to push her or whack her one, I hold him but not too tightly.

I have visions of it getting really interesting but Vera comes in like a damp cloth, spreading itself on the flames, removing the ignition.

'Now, girls, we're all upset, aren't we?'

'Come on, Angelo, come upstairs with me.' I say and he swears and comes, looking over his shoulder.

I tell him that the law told me BB can come back but even as I say it, I'm not sure if he should. Angelo tells me he'll bell him but he doesn't exactly look overjoyed.

'I will tell, see if he wants to come back.' Shrugs eloquently but no idea what it means, the shrug.

It's too early for business at the club but Tiger is poncing about behind the bar. He's definitely lost his bounce and I wonder why. 'You all right are you?' I ask and he says he is and I leave it at that. There's only so much worry a girl can cope with, Tiger has always been one of the certainties in my life, I want to keep it that way, he says he will try to get along without me on Monday and if he gets time he'll pop into the wake. 'Be nice to see old Vera again.'

'I never knew you knew Vera,' I say and Tiger winks and says; 'There's a lot you don't know, darling. Now off you go, mate, I'm expecting Sid and it's private.' His face shuts down then, like there's no way in and I realise again that I only know a small part of Tiger.

Back home it's all go and I get engrossed in talk of flowers, then Frantic shows. She kisses Vera hello which causes V to look both gratified and terrified at once.

'All right, my darling?' to me. 'You might have told me you was going down Tiger's, missed you by minutes, I did.'

'What do you want, Frannie? Anything special or just general aggravation purposes?'

'What you have for yer dinner, gel, vinegar on a fork?'

She looks round the room. Takes a fag from my packet, lights up with one of V's matches.

'Thought you was going to have a party, didn't I? Thought old Vic was being brought back here for a laying in – or is that when you're born?'

She laughs a small giggle.

'So is he coming back or not?'

'Yes, on Monday,' says V with due solemnity.

'Right, show me respects like, eh? What I wanted to know was, do you want some nice smoked salmon, for the do, like?'

'Do what?'

'Lovely load of smoked salmon, also some sorbets, water ices, lovely they are. I can store them for you until the last minute. Make a fantastic buffet. Better than ham, get yer some lemons from me auntie and rolls from a mate of mine. All at a lot less than cost price.'

Vera looks as if she's just fallen in to the fact of the requirements for a funeral tea. Looks well interested. Mary looks resistant.

'Bit of class. Victoria would love it.'

'That's right, don't be a pleb all your life, eh?' I chip in, I love smoked salmon. Must have knocked over a Jewish deli. I think.

'What do you think, Mary?'

Mary says nothing.

'Half cost. Get an estimate and I'll match it and halve it. Can't say fairer than that can I?'

Vera and Mary are in a huddle now, Frantic points upstairs.

'Leave you two ladies to think about it, eh?'

'Think she'll go for it do you?' she asks as we get inside my room.

'You can get the bevvy from the base can't you? All right with Rooster now aren't yer? Better start girding yer loins like, gel, or somebody else will take over.'

She collapses on my bed.

I pour myself a drop of Philadelphia in a cup.

'Want some?

'Nah, you know me mate, got all the virtues haven't I?'

She looks at me with her cynical, ancient eyes.

'Give us a fag, mate.'

Takes a deep drag on her fag. She's the only person I know who visibly inhales with their entire body.

'Seen Jack have you?' I am startled out of any cool.

'Thought so.' She gives one of her nods, leaves it at that, which is worse than an interrogation.

'Right, I'll go and see if they've made up their minds about that salmon. Coming with?'

'It's OK though,' I say.

'What is?'

'Jack is.'

'Good, so that's you off the hook then? You can start operating again, can't you?'

It occurs to me that she might be right, Jack isn't going to nick me for anything else while I'm working for him. I hope.

But what about Dixon?

I wasn't home when they brought the casket back and planted it in the scullery on trestles. The coffin had arrived with the lid on and they waited until I came back to lift it and look at him. We did it with due ceremony and all peered in at the late Victoria.

I've seen livelier mackerel on the fishmonger's slab last thing on a Friday afternoon. Any vestige of character has been eliminated. Pale, bland, deader than anybody I ever saw. I've seen a few corpses. And I know it's perfectly possible for them to look rather gorgeous. In some cases they've looked better in death than they have in the last few years of life. But in Vic's case they seem to have made no effort at all.

Mary has gone off to have the vapours and V and me look sadly at the poor old bugger, with all his personality removed by death and slack undertaking, we shake our heads over him. Not what he would have wanted is it? A person for whom making a stir was first nature and now, this. As I say, sad.

So I suggest I get lippy and eye make up on him, pronto. Vera is all for it and gets a big bag of slap from upstairs and I'm just about to begin when Mary pops into sight and goes imperious.

'I'm not having him painted like some poof,' she declares. The fact that it is exactly what he would have wanted doesn't impress her a bit. V's mouth takes a distinct downturn.

'Don't have a lot to do with you, Mary. We're his mates and we know what he would have wanted,' I say. V agrees.

'Yes,' says V. 'He never went out without his face on, did he, Shindig?'

'Certainly not! wouldn't even open the front door without his lippy and eye make up. Anyway, he doesn't look anything like himself now.'

'He looks less, less of a person,' says V.

'He'd even check his eek before he got on the blower. I've watched him in phone boxes, slapping up,' I say. V nods, we both smile tenderly at this eccentricity.

'He looks like a man,' Mary declares. But, he doesn't, he doesn't look like anybody or anything much and I must say he always had a strong presence. Not necessarily of any particular gender but still distinctly sexual in its ambiguity. So I carry on dabbing at his cheeks, cold as charity they are and the powder lays on top of the flesh, doesn't look good at all. Have to put some foundation on I suppose, but the feel of his skin is kind of tacky and I'm not at all sure if it will work.

'We could always shut the lid, couldn't we?' says V and though Mary obviously wants to disagree for the sake of disagreement, she says that's probably the best thing. So that's what we do, although I am miffed at not getting to stretch my artistic talents. Now it's like an armed truce in the house with the two of them sniping at each other. By the look of Vera's face I can't see Mary lasting five minutes after Vic's been shipped out.

I leave the two of them having a ruck about the location of a collection tin by the coffin. I go upstairs to find myself some suitable funereal gear to wear. Got this black suit with the tightest skirt ever, had it tapered by the tailor up west who does all the working girl's gear. I look great, though I'm almost completely immobilised. I add scarlet stiletto shoes for a touch of colour and feel very pleased with the effect. I tie the riah back tight, aiming for a severe effect of deep seriousness. Contrast this with extra long spiky lashes that remind me of spiders, but nice.

They begin to arrive just after midday. People L haven't seen for years. People I hoped never to see again. And some I thought were dead. The early ones are quiet to start with and Frantic and myself help them off with their coats and give them drinks. V and Mary sit, more queenly than the queens, a pair of duchesses against the wall, overseeing the event, hoping for tributes. Unfortunately, the effect is lost to a great degree because nobody knows who Mary is. Most don't even know of her existence but we make it our business to tell them, so they go into a peering examination of her. In minute detail in some cases. Mary takes this as a manifestation of respect I think.

I had a draw before it began and I take it easy on the drink. I'm keeping permanently on my toes in case Jack arrives and I need all my wits about me.

I told Frantic about it, at some moment of indiscretion. She was remarkably sanguine. Said it happens all the time. 'It's not like grassing one of yer own is it? Bleeding quacks? Fucking loaded, aren't they? Shouldn't be fiddling, should they? Don't worry about it, gel, not going to send a team round is he?' She finished her homily with a gust of laughter. Good old Frantic I think. Then I think about her having it away with Nifty and trying on my job for size with Rooster, so I don't get too carried away.

After about an hour things begin to hot up. The respectful first intake have either gone or are talking quietly among themselves. Not many console Mary but she seems not to notice. Sitting with her trotters together in a foul dark dress that crosses over her bosom and is pinned with a big, ugly brooch, topped with a woollen garment, she looks lumpy and dull beside V, who looks pretty damn good. Her titfer is rakish over one eye and is getting closer to her eye as the day wears on. She has been liberal with the slap and a Margaret Lockwood beauty spot has joined her Joan Crawford lipstick to create a fetchingly colourful ensemble.

'Bona capella, darling!' I tell her and she beams at me.

We put most of the furniture out in the back yard and the bog in the yard has come into its own; some people have set up outside in the sun. A young couple with a small baby sit out there along with a contingent from the club in Westbourne Grove.

'Who are they, then? That couple, they look too normal for any of your mates,' says Frantic.

'I don't know but they obviously liked her, they brought a big bunch of flowers.' We have both deserted our posts and sit in the sun eyeballing the crowd.

Queenly screeches and low, bellicose laughter come out to us with every now and then a hush to show respect. Arch, high camp along with ruffians straight from the boozer, here for the party. Among these are several straight looking geezers and a few diesel dykes, I think I spotted Gerry among them.

I came across Gerry a few weeks ago when I was in the pub that Carly performs in. I had been bored. A group of dykes are playing pool in the back bar. I amble to the ladies' bog, past them. The only male accoutrement they lack is whiskers and some of them are making an effort in that direction. One, with a magnificent DA, Brylcreemed into stiff place catches me on the way back.

'Want a drink, darling?' and she smiles. The others look away carefully.

'I'm with some friends,' I begin.

She interrupts:

'They're busy, mate, come and have a bevvy with us.'

'You on a bet are you?' I ask, and she laughs, so I sit down to watch the pool. She has ginger hair and green eyes that glitter evilly and is far younger than her initial appearance. She brings my beer and gives the cue to one of her mates, sits.

'Don't remember me, do yer?'

'No, should I?'

'Up to you mate, think about it. Last time you saw me I was wearing a skirt.'

'Gerry? St Helena's academy.'

'Right!'

One of my brief sojourns had been in a remand home in Ealing where I learned a couple of vital skills. One was to fight; another was how to swear. The other main skill I learned about was sex. Gerry had assisted in my thirst for knowledge and now, here she is again.

V and Mary have left their podium and mingle now. The gaff is packed. Marmalade and Carlotta have put in a glamorous appearance and seem to be wafting near the kitchen door. They wave and throw kisses. Vera is making signals at us both. We go over to her. Amazing the number of people can fit in here. There is a small ruckus in the front area, by the bins. But you expect that. I cop a deaf 'un.

'What is it, darling?' I ask V.

'The nosh, bring it down now and put it on the table.'

We had forgotten this part of our duties. I shoot upstairs and carry down plates of sandwiches and stuff to the table that V has cleared ready. The noise from the front area has risen to a wailing crescendo. Vera makes signs at me to get outside and sort it.

First thing I see is the weeping boy. He is supported on either side by a boy and a girl, all are excessively young, all have tragic faces. They look up reproachfully at me, like I should know what it's all about. I ask.

'You all right?'

The central boy goes into paroxysms of grief.

'This is Bob,' says the girl. Like that explains anything.

'Hello Bob, do you want to come in and have a drink?'

This causes more paroxysms. The girl pulls me down to whisper in my earhole.

'Vic's lover.'

'Do what?' I say. The second boy takes over and wheezes into my earhole.

'His paramour.'

Frantic has slipped up behind me, now she giggles, a snuffling noise.

'Victoria? Had a lover?' My voice sounds stupefied, and so it should. I want to tell them not to be stupid. What time did he have for a lover? He was either out flogging his mutton or out with Vera, far as I knew.

'He was my boyfriend, for ages.' Adds an emotional hiccup to prove the veracity.

'Better get in and get yerselves a drink, mate,' says Frantic. I'm not so sure. They go into the room and make no impression in the mêlée. But the weeping will seep into the awareness of the mob soon I'm afraid. It does too.

Mary is doing a sort of tour of the joint. Barley wine in one hand, Park Drive in the other, she proceeds, in an orderly fashion. She gives small regal nods as she goes and I notice her ankles have swollen so they bulge slightly over her shoes, like milk boiling up in a pan. I wonder what she's saying and look at the weeping Bob on the other side of the room. Frantic winks at me from near Bob and his mates. Marmalade and Carlotta seem to be apart from the rest of the crowd, they smile over at me and I beckon them. Can't wait to tell them about Bob.

Mary is moving diagonally across the room to the point where Bob and his crew are even now making their weepy presence felt. She approaches them, all benign solicitude.

'You all right, son?' she says. He looks up and sees some sympathy going begging, aims for it;

'I've lost my lover, what else can I say?' V has materialised and pats his shoulder.

Mary clearly didn't hear what Bob said. She turns to speak to V.

'He's lost his lover, poor boy,' says V and Mary, sensing a bit of competition in the sympathy stakes says;

'Well, I've lost my husband!' with an unsaid 'so there' at the end.

'Sad though isn't it for the poor boy?' says V.

'So how did you lose your girlfriend, dear?' asks Vera.

'What girlfriend? He never had no girlfriend.' From the girl with him. With more strop than necessary.

'Oh sorry, dear, a boyfriend then?' says V liberally.

'My lover,' says Bob with full on doleful expression and sorrowful voice.

'Never mind that now dear, we're here to say goodbye to Victor. This lady's husband.'

'Not Victoria?' says the girl with Bob in a breathless little voice which is pure Marilyn. She looks from face to face, mouth ajar.

'That's what he called himself, yes,' Mary's voice both sharpens and quivers, it has taken on some ice but is not quite so assured as it was, like she senses danger. Bob has revved up to full strength howl now, and people are looking over and most are then looking away swiftly.

'He was my lover.' That's what Bob is saying, but it doesn't come out all of piece. In dreadful noisy jerks of sound, it emerges. Mary's face is rigid now.

I want to look away but I can't, I look from face to face. Bob's young, bland, fairly empty, Mary's startled and quite furious. Can see pulses in her temples. I know what she means too. Even after death Victoria won't just lie down and leave it at that, he has to bring his perversions into this, his final event. I can almost hear him laugh.

Mary opens her mouth and nothing comes out, except air. Vera dives in:

'I think we should all go upstairs to talk quietly about this.'

'Oh, no! For a start I don't believe a word of it,' says Mary, unwisely I feel. 'And I think you should leave, now!'

'Oh no!' howls Bob, a right little attention seeker I reckon.

'I must see his lovely face once more.' Born drama queen.

Well, beauty is in the eye of the beholder I know, but I swear a look of disbelief travels round the whole room. One to the other we consult with our faces and all agree that Victoria was certainly not lovely.

'Well, you can't. The lid of the coffin is down and it's staying down.'

The girl with Bob gets two small red blotches on her cheeks and pipes up;

'I think that Bob should be allowed to spend some time alone with the casket.'

I get one of those flashes and a clear vision of Victoria, being in love, with a bunch of flowers in his hand and a dopey look on his eek, plighting his troth to Bob. One knee job and everything. Then Rooster and Lickle Miss come through the door and I wave across, so I miss the first blow, now it's all go.

Mary, it seems, throws a punch at Bob or one of his entourage. He is rearing up and has his hands up like an old time boxer, making tiny ineffectual jabs at the air. At about the same time, two coppers in civvies, who must have known and nicked Vic, come in with a massive bunch of flowers; courtesy of the vice squad. Touching really, but lousy timing.

The barney continues.

Mary hits like a street fighter, with her right she whacks him one in the snout, with her left she grabs his jacket and the noise of it tearing sounds strangely loud over the drinkers and talkers. She draws his head down and nuts him neatly and accurately. I've never had the confidence to do that and am

filled with envy. Same time her knee comes up into his groin
and he gives this squeaky scream. Bob is totalled.

On the deck. Even in the midst of this drama I am keenly
aware that I'm very grateful that I never hit her a poke.

Then Rooster has hold of Mary. Vera is faffing like her
hands are full of flour and she's shaking it off. Mary looks
extremely happy and I guess she's wanted to fill somebody in
for days, probably me, now she has the look of a fulfilled lady.

Bob is trashed and weeping, Frantic brings a glass of brandy
for him, Mary cops it and gulls it in one. Frantic goes back for
another one, and I get a tea towel for the blood from his nose.

Seems like Mary is a kind of heroine. Could have gone
either way. Fights are weird and the allegiance of a crowd has
nothing to do with justice. Now, Mary is given a chair, fussed
over. I look over and she preens at me.

Might wins out over right again.

Typical.

I pick Bob up, his two mates seem singularly incompetent.
His nose will never be the same again, but it was nothing
special to start with and as a woman whose nose has got in the
firing line several times, I haven't much sympathy. His jacket is
something else. Torn from stem to stern but mostly at the
seams, although one pocket is destroyed.

'You can get that fixed easy!' I say, helpfully I thought.

'I want to get the police. That woman . . .'

'That old boiler assaulted him,' says the girl.

'Yes!' says boy number two.

Then one of the vice squad is there and I scoot. Next thing
you know, the boy and his team slither off, giving out glares
and a foot stamp or two. Bob turns at the door, hankie
muffling his words, still they manage to ring out.

'I don't think any of you knew the real Victoria, no wonder
she had to turn to me for love.'

They do a joint flounce as they leave.

Mary is now holding court at the table, stubbing her Park
Drive out on a plate, trotters together again, barley wine in

hand, talking to one copper and Lickle Miss, who is another woman knows how to fight. I am exhausted and wonder about the ascendancy of Mary in the scheme of things. Hope it doesn't mean she's got her feet back under the table permanently.

'Must have a bit of a history, fighting like that. I'd match her against any of my aunties I would. Not against me mum though,' says Frantic.

'I'm going to shoot soon mate, got to see somebody.' She takes a fag.

'We going to get paid are we?'

'We are, but I don't think now is the time to ask do you?'

'Well, I need the bread now.'

I finish up lending her two quid on account of her being boracic. I wave it goodbye for permanent.

The diesel one returns and Frantic introduces herself on her way out. Looks like instant friendship and the thought travels across my mind that Frantic must have a use for Gerry. She is lurking now by the door. Gerry comes over to me.

'Clever gel! You handled that like a pro, mate,' she says and laughs, I don't know what she means. I choose not to investigate.

'How you doing, Gerry? You knew Vic did you?'

'Yeah, knew her well, we both lived in a gaff in Victoria a while ago now but I'd see her up west sometimes. Used to go out with a mate of mine, geezer works in the garage with me.'

'That what you doing now? No more driving and taking away?'

'Even more taking and driving away but it's all legit now. Got a bird I been with two years, she's a nurse. Right respectable old cunt I am now.'

'That her over there is it '

'Leave it out, gel, haven't given up all me vices, she's on duty, the bird.' Finger to nose, crafty style.

'I'm impressed, Gerry. So what's this about Vic?'

'Well, he had this boyfriend, on and off when we was living there. But what I come over to tell you was that he left a pile of gear at my house, suitcase full. Do you want it? Or should I give it to his missis? The bird's been on at me to get shot of it for months, and now he's snuffed it like, no point in hanging on to it, so it's you or the bint or the bin. Give you me number if you like.'

She writes it down for me.

'That's the work number. Let's say a week, eh? If you don't get back to me I'll chuck the lot, eh?'

'What's in it?'

'Papers and stuff. I wouldn't have looked but you know how nosy birds are, don't you?'

'Course I do, I am one, aren't I?'

'You? No mate you're one of us, just haven't recognised it yet.'

I'm not wearing that but I don't say, instead:

'We got to meet up, talk about the bad old days,' she says, and we must.

'Got to shoot mate! Don't forget, a week, bell me. And I still fancy you, gel.'

Her mates are all saying goodbye to Vera and Mary and they exit on a wave of testosterone. Their birds trotting along beside and slightly behind. Chattering among themselves like sparrows.

'Aren't they lovely. If I was only younger . . .'

'Vera, behave!' I say.

'You could do a lot worse, dear.'

I'm afraid she might be going to get into her homespun philosophy stage of drunkenness so I split upstairs to change my skirt and for a draw of weed. Frantic has disappeared.

When I come back down Angelo has appeared with the Count and the atmosphere has changed. By this time most of the strangers have gone and somebody puts on some Sonny Boy Williams, 'Don't start me Talking' and we kind of get cool.

'Victoria would have loved this,' says V and we all agree and even Marmalade and Carlotta say some nice things about Vic. Mary talks about him when he was young.

The mood changes again when Mary starts talking about a will.

'A will?'

Seems like we all say the same thing simultaneously, and those that don't voice it are thinking it.

'Oh no, dear,' says Vera. 'He never believed in any of that, said the more trouble he left behind him the better.' We all nod, that sounds like the Vic we all knew and loved, or hated as the case may be.

'I'm sure he didn't mean it,' says Mary, with total certainty. She looks round all our faces, challenging anybody to deny it. Nobody cares enough to argue the toss,

'So where are his papers?'

'Don't think he ever had any, dear,' says V; 'Did he, Shindig?'

I don't want to know about this, but now everyone is looking at me. The memory of Gerry and the suitcase of papers occurs to me but I'm not inclined to share the thought, certainly not with Mary.

'Shouldn't think so, you looked in his room have you?'

I think we've all been through Vic's room. I know I had a poke about up there, in case there was any stuff he borrowed over the months he's been here. Found a silk scarf of mine and a nice mauve pair of kid gloves that are Vic incarnate and I took as a memento. No papers as far as I could see.

'Surely it all goes to you dear, you were married to him,' says V.

'What? All his debts? I couldn't even find his seaman's book, he always kept stuff like that when I knew him. He had a collection of all sorts of papers. Insurance, I'm sure he had insurance. Everybody has insurance.' Said with such emphasis that I'm sure she believes it.

She looks at us all as if we've nicked it. Vera turns away from her.

'Get us a drink, darling,' she says to me. 'We'll all have a drink and toast Vic. I think we can leave all this for another day, can't we?'

Mary stalks upstairs and we all settle down.

Rooster gets out his dope and we both skin up.

Then we remember the funny things that we shared with Victoria.

And we love her briefly, but fervently. And Mary is not here to say she was a he.

About four in the morning we are falling by the wayside when Marmalade comes up with some lovely methedrine. Vera argues the toss about taking drugs but I whack half an amp in her glass. I go upstairs to the bog and in mid stream I remember the collection tin. It's gone. I check when I come back down. Yes, it's away all right.

'Mary took it upstairs with her, didn't she?' says Carlotta. 'I'm sure she had it in her hot little hand when she went upstairs.'

'Cheeky mare,' says Vera.

'Why you don't arks her gie it back man?' says Rooster, and Marmalade and Carlotta do high pitched giggles that tear into my newly aware sped up ears. We all look at Vera.

'You ought to pull her,' I say. Suddenly, no doubt due to the speed, I want justice. Marmalade and Carlie want entertainment as I'm sure we all do. Rooster busies himself with an old glass yoghurt pot and some white rum that I found for him. He sucks his teeth, fills the pipe with grass and passes it to me to light. The bubbles sound fierce, the blow tastes warm and smooth and mellows in with the methedrine that is rising itself into my awareness. I watch them combining beautifully together. Be nice to give Mary a pull, question her fully. Interesting, but not essential.

Vera won't smoke a pipe so the speed is working well on her. Starts clearing up.

Angelo has been asleep and now he opens an eye and takes a toke on the pipe, coughs and laughs. I help V tidy up and we talk about Victoria. It's as if we finally say goodbye to her as we zip round removing the evidence of the wake. Appropriate when you think about it, all speeding, all blocked up, good way to say goodbye to a speed queen.

I thought I felt her leave just after Marmalade came up with the Methedrine but I could have been wrong and none of us are likely to forget her in a hurry. Bob will remain for me a mystery of the mid twentieth century but I can't even think about that now. At some time Vera tells me she's going north with Mary but it doesn't sink in until I go to bed and do a resumé of the day. She gave no reason.

As soon as Vera and Mary have exited on their trail up north, Jack arrives on the doorstep. I kiss Vera goodbye and give her a hug. She doesn't travel well, except locally. I think Shepherds Bush is her limit westward and Oxford Street in the other direction.

I sympathise fully with her, the countryside is a kind of death and it begins as soon as the fields start.

'Don't worry V, it's a town you're going to.' I pat her hair, which still has the marks of her metal curlers on it. She has sworn she won't let Mary come back with her but I don't trust her resolve. Today, she looks old and quivery. I slip her a large gin from stock and she perks up a bit, but foreign territory will terrify her.

'Got your curlers have you, darling?' Vera nods.

'Stop fussing, Shindig,' says Mary.

'How much did you say was in that tin, Mary?' I snap. Revenge.

'Fourteen pound and some change. And I'm spending it on flowers,' said Mary, terse like.

At last the hearse and the black car drive off and it's as I come back indoors that Jack puts in his appearance.

'All right, doll? Better come inside, hadn't I? So to speak.' Rude git. He chortles at his wit and takes my arm like he knows me well and we both go inside the house.

'I hear a couple of the boys from Vice came and showed their respects.'

'Pity they never showed any respect when he was alive really, isn't it?'

Jack steps back like I've dropped a bad fart. Shakes his nut in admonishment. 'See, my dear, that's where you go wrong. We do something kind, something humane, and still you've got

to be nasty about it.' Shakes his head some more, sadly, at my
lack of gratitude. I stifle my mouth which is both painful and
foreign to me. He perks up immeasurably as he gets in the car.

'So, off we go, to our esteemed friend, the doctor.'

I'll just drop you off, you go and see him and I'll catch you
in the boozer, eh? I'll show you where on the way there. Can't
be implicated can I, my dear? You heard of entrapment I'm
sure.' Gives this light little laugh.

'That all, is it?' I say. He nods.

'And after that you can do what you like. Contract over, as
they say. I always know where to find you don't I, darling?' He
leers at me. Which makes my heart do a small, frightened leap,
then sink to my lower intestine.

Going back to the quack isn't even slightly like the first time.
For a start I'm not doing it for myself, Jack's hot breath is on
my neck. Metaphorically and literally.

This geezer is really pushing his luck. They busted him and
went through his paperwork before, he wasn't charged because
they could find nothing to pin on him, but does he take this as
a warning? Certainly not. He uses the experience to reaffirm
his extreme cleverness. Thus he has pissed off and invoked the
ire of some of the most unpleasant, vengeful and malignant
motherfuckers in the universe, namely the DS. The thought
that I should warn him about this, slides through my mind, it
doesn't touch the sides.

He is delighted to see me but I know it is nothing personal, any
reasonably tasty bird would do. Guilt threatens to overcome
me for a second there. Then he oozes out self confidence that
washes all over me a sort of tidal wave of lust and this renews
a nice vigorous disdain in my heart.

'Hi, there! Good to see you.' He fumbles for my name, and
my body at the same time. I give him a shove that comes off
rather too well and I turn it into a joke.

'Hey, man, don't take that as a rejection will you?'

He does one of the rich chuckles that are so much part of
his repertoire.

'And what can I do for you, my dear?' Looks at me quizzical like, it occurs to me that he must have quite a turnover in importunate birds.

'Jane, wasn't it?' He can scarcely catch his breath and his hot little minces are all over the place. I beckon him to me and the game begins.

Doesn't take long and he gives me a big script of both charlie and H. He seems to have wised up with the script pad, locks it in a drawer as soon as he finishes writing.

Cracks me up having to hand it over to Jack, can feel part of me die as he takes it. We meet in the same pub that BB and me went to last time. No sign of Renee, but it's early in the day and I don't hang about. Don't even investigate the pink interior; I try to forget my last event here. I feel contaminated by the deal with Jack. Have no sympathy with the quack but it leaves a foul taste, helping the enemy.

'I'll get back to you, Shindig, if we need you.'

He looks at me with a sort of half smile, so I don't know if it's a wind up or not.

'Probably won't.' I say nothing. 'Then again, you might have to give evidence.'

He looks at me to gauge my reaction. I try to remain in stone face style but I can feel terror and alarm swarming over my face. He had promised me, by implication at least, that I would not be involved in any court procedure. What did I tell you? The law can't be trusted at all. I can feel my gut going into unbidden spasm now. I turn away, worn out by all the involuntary internal organ movement.

'Don't worry,' were Jack's last words, and they are words that have always called me to a vigorous state of concern.

I walk abstracted to Tiger's.

'See Jack did you?' He nods before I answer. 'Was in earlier wasn't he?'

I don't mention that I hit his old woman's pub. Expect that if he doesn't know now, he soon will. I've got Tiger placed at the very top of the jungle telegraph stakes. It's Tuesday and Tiger disappears every Tuesday on some mysterious mission so I'll have the gaff to myself as soon as he shoots off. Usually I enjoy this, today I feel trapped. Tiger is not on the best of form, we rattle around together, separately. I'm glad when he finally pisses off.

Now, much later, in the club, alone, I worry. The usual geezers come in between three and four, I'm unnaturally matey with them but they seem not to notice. Then a couple of musos go through to rehearse so I spend some time shooting the breeze with them. They say that Nifty is missing me and we use this as launch pad to discuss love in all its guises. Mostly, we speak of our own unusual and vast capacity for love and of the fickleness of the hearts of our lovers. All the time, the thought of Jack coming back demanding more favours with menaces lurks and impinges into my mind. About five, I allow myself a light ale and start to feel that everything will be fine; I get a surge of energy and sort out the mixers, fill some crates with empties and generally busy myself about the place. I have Berry on my mind now and I fantasise about him coming through the door and us both going to Morocco. Sometimes I do such a job on myself that I really believe in my fantasy and then I'm gutted when he doesn't show. It's worse than usual this time.

I put on some Elvis and the old boys whinge and expose their limitations in taste.

I ignore them and jerk about to the music while I extend my repertoire of graft behind the bar. I astound myself when I remove an entire shelf of glasses, lifting them, sticky, from the shelf. I wash them dreamily and clean beneath them.

Billy must have crept in, because as I stand up and face the room there he is, grinning broadly with half his teeth gone. My jaw drops.

'Well, sweetie, vada the eek on you?'

'BB, where did you come from?'

'Well, I came for the funeral but I gather I very cleverly missed it.'

'How did that happen?'

'Angelo belled me at work and I got the date wrong. Thought I'd come and see you anyway. Plus visit the other light of my life, of course.'

'So how long you here for, BB?'

'Got a couple of days off so here I am, you lucky palone you!'

'Fuck, you missed a brilliant day, mate.'

I go round the bar and hug him. He hugs me back and I'm engulfed in affection. I feel my eyes filling up.

'Never give none of us a cuddle do yer?' says one of the punters,

'I couldn't trust myself not to be overcome with desire could I?' I say.

He claims my attention as barmaid and BB shoots behind the bar and begins to wash glasses, gathering betting slips, tidying up.

'Don't know how you work in this chaos, sweetie,' he chides me gently and I realise how much I've missed him. He bustles and fusses.

'Seen much of Angelo have you?' he asks from among the debris.

'Course I have, we still live in the same lattie don't we?'

I have heard Angelo has been playing away but I don't believe it or want to. Besides, I want BB to talk about me, I long to share all my traumas; I have them ready lined up to tell him.

'You heard anything dodgy about him, have you?' he asks.

'No, darling, and I wouldn't believe it if I did. People always want to put the mix in, don't they?'

'You seen him since you been up, have you?'

'No, we're meeting later at the Harmony. Come if you like.'

'When Tiger comes back I will. You sure you want me to?'

He lights up a fag, sits himself on a stool. He nods.

'Know what?' he says. 'I don't think I'll bother investigating what he's been up to, Angelo,' he smiles at me, shrugs.

'Wise girl,' I say. 'Know when to leave things alone mate.'

The crew are moving off and I realise it's after seven.

'Go if you want to, BB. Tiger will be back soon and I'll join you, go ahead man.'

'No, sweetie, I need to talk to you.' He gives a gusty sigh, puts his fag out. The rest of the regulars are making their weary way back to a boozer, neither drunk nor sober, they meander off on their vital male business.

'Goodnight, gel, tell old Tiger we waited as long as we could.'

'Must have found himself a bit on the side. See, Shindig, you missed your chance there, darling.' They both laugh fatly. As ever, they are delighted with their wit.

'Want a beer, BB?' He nods and I open two light ales.

He tells me Brighton is good. He also says that he has a chance of buying in to a business. Then I tell him about the wake and we're laughing so loudly that when Tiger appears like some genie, we don't hear him.

'All right, mate? I'll lock up, eh?' he says.

'You back in town then are you, Billy?'

'Only here for a couple of days, Tiger.'

'Yeah mate. I can see your effect on the gaff. Want to get off do you? He looks benignly on the gleaming ashtrays. I realise I won't get any credit for my own efforts. Tiger has taken his jacket off and hung it carefully in the cupboard. It looks like he's settling in for the night. Usually he leaves when I do and I imagine him rushing home to Renee and her sparkling gaff and the Blue Grass. I realise I know fuckall about Tiger's private life.

'Anybody bring anything in for us did they, Shindig?' He looks anxiously round.

'No, Tiger, you expecting something are you?'

'I was, but don't worry, gel.'

He sits down and looks prepared to engage in conversation.

'What happened to that black geezer of yourn, Shindig?'

'Who? Rooster?'

'No, mate, the Yank.'

'Never knew you met him, Tiger.'

'Seen you down the Harmony, didn't I? Remember?' But I don't, and this is the first time Tiger has ever taken any interest in my personal life, apart from trying to get into my knickers. It is oddly worrying. I almost say I was in his old woman's pub earlier but I don't. He pours himself a beer and whisky chaser and his spiv moustache looks droopy rather than perky and I notice how ancient he is. Before it hasn't mattered, now, in the overhead lights that he turns on as he ambles about checking tables and putting chairs straight, I can see that he is as old as Vera, who is my benchmark of old age.

'Went back to the States, didn't he? Think he got sent back. You all right are you, Tiger? You don't look your usual perky self, sweetheart.'

He looks up and grins.

'Nothing wrong with me, gel, I'm fighting fit, mate.' He gives a little laugh that doesn't quite come off, 'Fuck off out of it then you two, go and have fun!' he says, and laughs again. But he still looks fucked to me.

BB and me walk through the court, out into Dean Street and we amble down towards Shaftesbury Avenue.

'What did you want to talk about?' I ask BB.

'Oh, that.' He gives a small movement of his shoulders, not quite a shrug.

Now he's got me intrigued. My mind runs over all the possibilities. Two only really, he's found a new boyfriend or he hasn't. Such are the limitations of my imagination.

'I've been working at this café.'

'Thought it was a hotel?'

'I began at a hotel but this is better, more scope. Lovely feely owns it. She's asked me if I want to go into partnership with her.'

'And do you?'

'Oh yes. It's a brilliant idea. We have local artists exhibiting and poetry readings, and we want music too.'

'And frothy coffee?' I ask.

'And gorgeous food. It's a lovely atmosphere and I do, of course, want to be a partner. Just one tiny problem. Money.'

'Can't you just work your way in? Do you have to invest?'

'Yes, sweetie, I do. She needs money to buy out her ghastly husband. And we want to tart it up on a massive scale.'

'So, what do you think?' I don't really have any opinion on the matter. I want BB to come back to London.

'I think it's a good idea.'

'Are you interested though?'

He looks at me like I'm being especially dim. He gives another big gusty sigh. He'll blow me away if this goes on.

'Do you want to invest in it?'

'Me?'

'Well, yes, you.'

'I've never got any bread have I?'

'We could both get some bread, couldn't we? I was thinking of coming up and working Piccadilly two nights a week and you could work like stink with the booze and perhaps do some cheques and stuff and we could raise the breeze like that.'

Can't think why I should consider this at all.

'Why me, BB?'

'You're my friend and I'd like you to be part of it. It would be fun, we could nurture local talent. Supply a need. Be a cultural centre of excellence.'

'Don't let anybody else do the adverts, BB, you got a gift for it, darling. So what's in it for me?' I consider, carefully, the fact that I live in London, have no aptitude for the catering industry and am boracic lint. That apart, it's a great idea.

'I'm boracic, aren't I?'

'Think about it, just think about it, Shindig.' I nod.

Then I tell him about Jack. He resists the impulse to say I told you so but the words are very nearly visible in the vicinity of his mouth. I come back with;

'So, mate, I'd give the notion of doing Piccadilly a miss. He's well on the alert for all our activities.'

'Mine too?' he asks, and I tell him that Jack mentioned his name. I was going to tell him that Jack said he could come back, but I don't. I move the subject along.

'What you going to do about your choppers, BB?'

His hand goes to his mouth. 'I don't know, could get some false choppers but then I'd be like Vera, pots slipping all over the place.' He shudders.

'Don't be silly, BB. You won't turn into an old bird just because you get dentures.' He shudders again. We are outside the Harmony now. He comes back to the subject of money.

'Couldn't you hit Tiger for a few bob?'

'How much of a few bob we talking here?'

'Couple of grand,' he says it quietly, it comes out like aggravated assault on my earholes.

I don't even think in anything over a hundred quid, it's beyond my comprehension. My philosophy is simple: keep out of the nick with a fiver in my bin and I'm laughing. A score, I'm in ecstasy.

'Well, it wouldn't have to be all at once. And we'd do it all legit; you'd be a full partner.'

'You are joking, let's get this straight: You want me to borrow bread for a deal I know nothing about, in another part of the country . . .'

He interrupts. 'Oh forget I asked, sweetie!' in full moody mode.

'You are fucking joking aren't you? You got to be, BB. I'd have to be . . .'

He flounces into the Harmony and I feel guilt nip at my insides, always eager to surface. I think about letting him go, but I lost too many people just recently.

I come from behind him, grab his shoulder and I tell him I'll think about his proposition. It don't sound like a goer to me though.

Angelo who is bouncing and prancing with good health meets us as we go inside. I have BB's idea simmering in the bottom of my mind. My brain picks at it like an old chicken carcass. Seeing it from different sides. Chewing at the meaty bits. It would be good to be part of something 'respectable' without having to sell my soul to convention. Get these visions of BB and me enjoying the high life, famed for our establishment. Both of us queening it behind the bar giving out our invaluable opinions on the artwork of delicious, available young things. The present owner has mysteriously disappeared; it's just BB and me. Then I get a vision of Berry being part of it, looking gorgeous. Get these visions of a gaff of quite unbelievable couth, subtle, rich, lavish with no hint of vulgarity. Or perhaps something extremely vulgar could set it off. A pianola for instance, what a gas. In half an hour I have myself convinced that it's a brilliant idea.

I feel strangely unsettled. I can't get into dancing and I have this longing for Berry, which is just plain silly. I want to get home and have an early night.

I leave the two of them dancing together affectionately.

I feel bereft.

By the time I get home I am sure the investment is not only out of my league but also a really lousy idea.

I sink into unhappy kip. The chasing dream starts straight away, the one where your legs are in concrete and demons pursue, in this case it's Tiger's old woman, Renee, who is pursuing me with Max Factor pancake makeup at the ready and a powder puff the size of a large sanitary towel. I run and she trips me and sprays me with Blue Grass toilet water then carries through with tacky hair lacquer that freezes me into total immobility. 'That's the one, that's the guilty girl!' Then a cast of thousands joins in chasing and yelling. A normal kind of dream. I wake in a cold sweat.

In the morning I meet BB and we don't speak about the café, but the idea has taken root in my mind.

28   Grieving and Worryin' Blues

Then things go sort of quiet. Like I'm waiting. Waiting for Jack to get back to me or for Dixie to pounce. Rock and hard place don't begin to describe it.

The funeral had taken over my life, and the fuss with Vera and Mary. Now, it is quiet, too quiet. Rooster and me recommence our business but it's not the same. We go up country to a base that's hungry for dope and I buy enough booze to feed me for weeks. Store it away from home because since the bust I don't trust home and the truth is I don't trust Rooster either and he sees me as a liability. The spectre of the nick looms, I think I'm reconciled to it but don't entirely believe in it so I carry on as normal.

I've found that the fixing up is a no no, the squalor of it all gets to me. Colette was entertaining but now, I can hardly bear to look at the characters in Joe Lyons. It's all linked with getting nicked, Berry, and fear.

BB talking about Brighton seems to have shoved the pieces in my mind round a bit. The idea of escape has highlighted the fact that I am trapped. I'm in neutral waiting for the next event. I try not to think about that. My mental processes go on without me and focus on Berry most of the time. I read Zola, again. I even give Ulysses a whirl. Which sends me back to Steinbeck for comfort and safety. I read with such intensity that it blocks my fears out. Everything else is blocked out too. Nobody and nothing is getting in any more. I look at some magnificent stud or glorious girl and recognise the beauty, but only aesthetically, the lust is not engaged. The loins are left lonely, the vitals do not attach. I think it might be for ever and I don't care.

Even Frantic has eased off me. Perversely, I miss her and don't know if it's a good or bad miss. The whole world appears to be moving away from me, indifferent to me. My life is like potatoes without salt, tasteless, bland. This must be what limbo is like.

Anyway, I work, in the loosest possible interpretation of that word, at Tiger's.

Now, I'm even boring Tiger.

'Know what you need, gel,' he says.

'Leave it out, Tiger!'

'Wasn't thinking of that. What you need is a chutzpah insert, darling. Lost the old panache haven't yer? The old pizzazz has fucked off out of it, mate.' He chuckles and pats me on my shoulder. I bristle, but I think he's right.

'If you was a geezer I'd say the lead in your pencil has had a retraction. The old tackle's not up to scratch.' He laughs and looks choked when I don't laugh back.

He tries to cheer me up, shuts up the club, takes me to the races. He has me putting bets on for him all over the track. Like a blue arsed fly scooting around. Ten bob here five quid there. Must be method in it but it's beyond me.

We drive back to London in near silence and he drops me off home squeezing my hand.

'Chin up, mate.' He bungs me a couple of quid as I get out. I nearly give it back to him, a first this. I think he might need it. But I know he'd be mortally offended, so would I, so I stick it in my bras as usual.

'Thanks, cocker,' I say and give him a peck on his cheek. I get out the car. He leans out and calls me back.

'Why don't you get stuck into one of your bleeding shwartzers, gel? Do yerself a favour! I'm sick of you mooning about like a wet tit. Get the smile back on yer face.' See how he cares about me? He's away before I have a chance to comment. He's right, I've lost it.

Instead of sex I sit and play cards with Vera in her kitchen. She came back without Mary, but Mary is still hanging on in there, with letters full of threats and promises. She will come down and help V with all kinds of things that Vera had never thought of and I can feel her hot, interfering breath on my neck all the

way from the north and our cosy evenings are shot through
with insecurity.

Angelo is buzzing around merry as ever. I hate that, wish he'd
share in my gloom. But failing that, I go to the club with him.
We dance and until 'Heartbreak Hotel' comes on the Juke, I'm
fine. Then I go into meltdown. Angelo comes and sits with me,
licks his hanky and cleans my face which bounces me out of
my mood long enough to dance a slow one with a very straight
looking girl. My bare inside arm on the flatness of her long
hair, and the bones in her shoulders remind me of love, they
send twinges of something interesting through me but I can't
be bothered. I'm in a decline for sure.

'You is a big woman,' says Rooster. His way of saying 'get
a grip'.

'Is romance, is beautiful, you must cry, weep!' says Angelo.
He doesn't specify how long.

'Oh, don't think I don't know what you're going through,
darling,' says Vera. And proceeds to tell me in detail of her
own broken heart. This seems to be an ongoing process that
continued throughout the war and for several years after, and
covered a multitude of men of all natures and types. I am
spending a fair bit of time with Vera. I kind of fall into her
kitchen if it's not too late. Our conversations continue over
several days sometimes. This evening we are still talking about
my broken heart, in theory. In fact, we talk, yet again about
Vera and her interesting love life.

'Yeah, mate, during the war we was all at it like knives. Get
some gin down here, dolly and I'll make us egg and chips.'

When I come back she carries on like I never left.

She's taken on this déjà vu look, her spine straightens
and you can see the right little goer she used to be, still
alive and well inside.

In the morning I gravitate to the kitchen.

'Piss the bed did you, darling?'

She's reading my paper, which involves a lot of finger and

thumb licking, turning pages and a good deal of sighing. Time I get it, it's like chip paper. She looks up now.

'Marylin Monroe has married that Arthur Miller, dear. You'd think she'd find somebody a bit more handsome wouldn't you? Beautiful girl like that.'

'He's brilliant,' I say. 'Anyway, that's old news.'

Then I hear the post man. I belt up the stairs and lift three letters. One for me and I rip it apart standing in the hall. It's from Celeste, the big woman I met at the art show. She must have got my address from Billy. I don't even read it, I'm so gutted. I take the two letters down to Vera. She is making tea and looks at me.

'Sit down, gel.'

'Has he got your address, mate?'

'Course he has, I wrote it down for him, didn't I?'

She opens a packet of Garibaldis.

'What? On a fag packet?' I nod.

'Because this waiting for the postman every day is changing your sleep pattern. Which don't necessarily matter, apart from the fact I'll have to start charging you for B and B.' She gives a dry chuckle. Comes behind me and gives a sort of twist to my shoulder, meant to reassure, and it works enough so that my eyes fill with tears.

'At least you got something.' Like I should be grateful. She looks at a letter. 'Rates!' Chucks it on the table. She settles in to read the second one. I pour the tea.

'Let it draw, mate, be like cat's piss it will.' Without looking up, she goes back to the letter. 'Mary wants to come down to see me.'

'Why?'

'Don't ask, gel.' She puts the letter aside. Pours tea carefully, half a cup in each cup then back again to fill them. Parity in strength.

'How did you get shot of her anyway, Vera?' She looks over at me.

'Read yer post first.'

I look at it. Inside the envelope is a printed card. It's an invitation to a gallery. I turn the card over and see Celeste has scrawled something on the back; 'Hi! Remember me? Do come along to this, I know you'll enjoy it.'

Vera is watching me.

'See! Somebody loves yer!' Said with maximum good cheer, like I've won the bleeding pools.

'Wouldn't say that.' I sound about ten years old and in a sulk.

'Have a Garibaldi and get yer face in order.' A command.

'Hang on V, my mouth's as dry as a nun's cunt,' I say.

I put three spoons of sugar in my tea, stir it and drink.

'Who's it from? Your letter?'

'Celeste. Some woman who paints.'

'Get her round, darling, she could do the bathroom where you and Billy blew up the boiler and destroyed the paint work.'

'Not that sort of painter is she?'

'Knew she wouldn't be. You never have it off with the artisan class do you? Now that would be well handy. But oh no, it's always bleeding artists with you and Billy.'

'Oh, sorry Vera. I'll lower me sights, darling.'

'Raise your sights more like. Respectable decorator or plumber never comes amiss. So what's she like, this bird? Any good is she?'

'I hardly know her Vera.' And Vera goes on to advise me that I'd be better off with a woman.

'Much more reliable, dear.' And goes straight on to talk about Mary, there's got to be an irony there somewhere.

'So how did you get shot of her?'

'I tricked her, didn't I?'

'How come?'

'Well, when we got up there she changed into this important woman. Kept on about they couldn't manage without her. Never mind she'd just been down here and they never noticed.' She slurps more tea.

'Anyway, I went along with this and she was hoist by her own whatsit like. When I was coming back she obviously wanted to come back with me but I kept saying how she couldn't leave her kiddies so soon again and she couldn't disagree.'

'What are the kids like?

'Like Victoria, wiry, bold, bit feral. Wouldn't want them down here, darling.'

'That what she's suggesting, is it?'

'Don't worry, mate, I'll tell her she can't come.'

I get this feeling that just telling her might not be enough.

Meanwhile, Frantic turns up at work in unnaturally friendly form.

'Here Tiger, I bought a beer for yer.' She approaches him where he sits among the cohorts and acolytes, carefully carrying a glass of beer. She deposits it with ceremony.

'Well, fuck me gently! Frannie buying beer?' he says.

He leans back round her and yells at me: 'Whatever it is, don't buy it, Shindig. Don't care how good it sounds, or reasonable, don't buy it.'

All the men laugh and Frantic joins in. I can see she's nettled, but she doesn't let it faze her.

She has brought the suitcase that Gerry was talking about, dumps it on the floor.

'You had a look through it, have you?'

'Course not, but Gerry said it's only old papers and stuff.'

She gives me a fag and has her own light, which sets off all kinds of alarm bells. I feel I should tell her that a personality transplant is no way to influence people.

'Whatever she's flogging you, don't you touch it with a barge pole!' Tiger yells across the room.

'And get us some drinks in, dolly.'

She gives a shrug and flounces out, she could learn a thing or two about flouncing from the gay boys.

I get back to reading *Keep the Aspidistra Flying* and Tiger carries on sitting with the boys. He seems to be back on form after the day at the races. I'm feeling better myself. I push all my worries away with the assistance of a sneaky brandy or two.

Tiger does one of his glass clearing pilgrimages then sits by the bar.

'How is Vera?' he asks.

'She's fine. Missing Vic.'

'You miss a dose of the clap when it's gone, don't you?' he says. 'Give her my regards.

'What did Frannie want?' he asks. 'Because if it's some new deal of hers I wouldn't touch it. I know you won't anyway, but she's got herself involved with some heavyweights, I hear. And you know Frannie; she'll slip out from under same as always, come out smelling of roses and everybody else is likely to have egg on their faces.'

I nod. 'No chance. Don't trust her a bleeding inch, Tiger.'

'That's wise, gel. Get yer stuff home will you, Shindig, seems to be a lot of it about and I want it out. OK?' He grins at me. 'They're coming in to do a stock take, darling. Bunce problems, gel.'

'What other problems are there, mate?'

'You ask me? You, with your tragically broken heart, ask me? Like you don't know? What's that they say; money can't buy you love.'

He looks ancient again. Expect he always did, just with somebody as rare as Tiger it didn't figure.

'Listen, gel. I'll take you home, and bring your gear.'

'That's uncommonly civil of you, cock,' I say. 'Frantic brought Victoria's suitcase too.'

'Watch she hasn't planted anything in it, dolly.' He laughs but I'm not so sure.

'I'll get shot of this lot and we'll fuck off, eh?'

And this is a first. He asks the cohorts to leave.

The gang go resentfully.

'You're losing your touch, Tiger. Closing early? Not getting past it are you?'

And all four of them laugh. One looks guilty and one looks away.

Tiger drives me home with the suitcase and all kinds of gear that has accumulated in my name behind the bar and also some bags from the cellar. He helps me with the plastic bags and a couple of paper ones that I have no memory of.

He drops me home and doesn't come in.

I don't pull him for using me to clean up his premises, I haven't the heart.

'Buy you a pint?' I say. He looks like a beaten docket but dredges me up a grin. Squeezes my leg.

'You're a good gel, Shindig. No, mate. I got things to do haven't I?

'What's going on, Tiger?'

'What makes you think anything's wrong?' I hadn't said

wrong. 'Something of nothing, mate, don't worry, it'll be good as gold, darling, don't worry.'

He lights a fag for both of us.

'Renee's gone offside.' I take this in best I can.

'How do you mean, Tiger?'

'Done a runner hasn't she.' I must say my heart lifts slightly at the thought she won't be round the club any more. This good thought is followed with the speed of light by the second thought that the rate things are going, none of us will be round the club any more. No club.

'How come?'

'Run off with some young geezer, hasn't she?' I giggle. He joins in.

'It's not bleeding funny, mate, we are talking of the woman I love.' He laughs and his ochre teeth look horse like in the street light.

'Sorry, Tiger it's just the idea of anybody running off with Renee, bizarre isn't it?'

'What's shaken me is she's demonstrating all the symptoms of love. Sickening it is. Worst part is she's shafted me for the pub.'

'Fuck!' I'm not sure what this means in the terms of commerce but I do know that Tiger has been shafting Renee, or rather shafting everything female in sight except Renee. And this is not without a weird kind of justice.

'Don't worry, dolly, I'll get it sorted, we'll be all right,' says Tiger.

But he looks none too sure to me.

29 What Makes These Things Happen To Me?

In fact, far from getting sorted, things proceed to go down the pan at an alarming speed.

All signs and portents are best seen in retrospect. Then you get the full significance of them.

The boys in Tiger's were harbingers of things to come, but as they all looked their normal unsavoury selves I never sussed it. A little less respect for Tiger, his jokes not going down quite so well. The piss taken a little more, a tiny bit more savagely. Jackal type action was well clear in retrospect. A shift of power. A sliding away of the old order into new chaos.

Then on the next, and final evening, only I didn't know it was the final evening at the time; after the boys have gone on their way and the two of us are sitting there together chucking words at each other in a desultory manner as is, or was, our wont, Big Sid comes in. We both grin at him, frantically.

'Evening all,' says Sid and looks round the gaff like he's a carpet fitter giving a rough estimate.

'Have a beer, Sid,' from Tiger. And Sid looks at us both in turn. There is a silence there, and it yawns loud and long. I can't believe I ever thought that Sid was harmless. 'No thanks. I need to have a word with you. In private, Tiger.' Looks at me like I'm a spent condom. So I slink off, don't I?

'I'll tidy up a bit shall I, Tiger?' He says nothing. But his poor old eek looks the grisly grey colour again and his skin seems to have grown outsize and it hangs in puckers from his bones. I shift my arse over to the tables and rub them over and clean the ashtrays, vigorously. I don't want to hear what they say, and this is a first for me. When Sid leaves, after a few minutes, Tiger looks destroyed.

I shut the door after Sid and turn round to Tiger. I wait for him to speak. He doesn't. He gives himself a large brandy. I get behind the bar, wash glasses under the tap. Stand around. Don't know what to do with myself.

'Better find yerself a new job, darling. I won't be here no more after today.'

I want to ask him why, or hug him or something, but his face is one big negative. So I keep it light.

'What do you reckon I'm suited to then? And don't be crude!'

'Well, gel, you're the barmaid to end all barmaids aren't you?'

'Course I am.'

'I'll give you a reference: Polite and moderate in her language. Gracious in adversity. Hard grafter. Customer relations expert. Charming to a fault.' And his voice kind of breaks about then. I hold him and feel how skinny he is, I inhale the Lifebuoy soap scent and want to cry. He pushes me away gently. 'Well, darling, this won't buy the baby no new shoes, will it? Come on, gel, let's be having you, we're off out for some nosh. A celebration.'

We go to a posh Italian place in Old Compton Street and the staff make a great deal of fuss of Tiger.

'Make the most of it, darling, they haven't heard about my fall from grace yet have they?'

'What's it about, Tiger?'

'Changes at the top, gel. A management reshuffle, like a cabinet reshuffle only more serious.'

I know there's no point asking him for details and I'm not sure I want to know, anyway. So we live it up and accept champagne on the house.

'Come on, darling, drink up and be merry for tomorrow we die.' He lifts his glass, we clink and he puts his hand over mine. But I can hardly stop myself from crying. At the end of the evening, Tiger pays for a taxi for me. He bungs me a few quid as I get in,

'That'll cover your wages, darling.' He gives a crooked grin.

I reach up and kiss him on the cheek.

'Be careful, dolly, you know how shit sticks,' are his final words of the evening. I find myself weeping my way home.

With no Tiger's to go to, I spend even more time in Vera's kitchen.

'Your mate Jackson Pollock died, I see.' She amazes me. 'He was the one Billy was always on about, wasn't he?'

'Yes, we both like him.' She makes a noise that probably means she doesn't agree.

'Well, he's dead now; don't like the look of that.' She whacks the paper down; there is a black and white reproduction of a painting.

'Don't do him justice, does it?' I say. 'Need the colour, don't you?' she snorts.

'What you doing today?' she asks. It's like she feels I should be getting busy. She's right. But it's none of her business. I can see us falling out if I don't get a job soon.

Within a couple of days of Tiger's nemesis, Frantic comes round for a nice gloat. She looks smarter these days. Matching gear, anyway. She comes into the kitchen.

'Any chance of a cuppa, V? Makes the best cup of tea in west London, don't yer darling?'

'Bollocks!' retorts V.

'That's nice, isn't it? That's fucking charming, that is!'

She helps herself to one of my fags and a light.

'Got any bickies, have yer?' V smacks her hand away from the biscuit barrel.

'Get an ash tray, Frannie.' Frantic laughs.

'So what's all this about Tiger then? Been a very naughty boy, I hear. Been thieving, little bit of the light fingers. Come unstuck.'

'Really? What have you heard?' I say, hedging.

'He's fucked. A write-off. That's what I heard, but I thought you'd know the facts.'

'If that's what you heard then it must be true, mustn't it?'

She looks at me, hard.

'So that's you out of work then, is it?

'Looks like it.'

'You know, I can always get you a job, Shindig.'

Vera blows a raspberry. Frantic turns on her.

'You want to fucking watch it, Vera.'

'Don't speak to her like that. You're taking a right fucking liberty, Fran.' I say. First she looks surprised; then I can actually see her brain working out if it's worth a full scale ruck. Or might we be useful.

'Where do you get off, Frannie? Using my bleeding drum as a snack bar anyway? Not as if you contribute anything is it?' says V

'Sorry, V!' She has made up her mind and smarms up to Vera. 'Forgive us, darling?' She kisses V on the cheek and I think V might whack her one but she doesn't and it's cool. But Frantic has changed her place in the pecking order, or thinks she has.

'I'm all right thanks, Frannie I've got work with Celeste whenever I want it. Not short of a couple of bob darling, thanks.'

'We're off out now, Frannie, me and Shindig,' says Vera and she stands by the table, quietly, waiting. Frantic goes to the door, stops, turns.

'There's a chance you could have your old job back, Shindig. I've got a bit of pull in that direction,' she winks. 'If you fancy it? Don't say nothing now. Think about it.' Swells with her own importance.

'Time Tiger went, dolly, getting too old, face don't fit no more. Know what I mean? Anyway, you heard him, he cheeked me more than enough over the years.' She gleams jubilant joy at me, I want to smash her face in. During this conversation I have achieved a total poker face. I say nothing.

'Yeah, mate, time he went.'

They hang there, her final few words.

Seeing her got me off my arse where I'd been cogitating. Spurred me into thought, anyway and I hoped that activity would follow without me having to make any decisions. Time is still off-key. Hadn't got back into synch. Or it might be the routine of Tiger I miss.

I begin by searching the suitcase and find Victoria's personal life documented quite thoroughly, Mary had been right; his seaman's book is there and his passport. His birth certificate and marriage certificate too. It occurs to me that when I die

the only record of my life will be my police record and that
feels so cool and romantic to me that I grin and roll a joint.
The only person who would appreciate this fact is BB. I need
to see him, for the sake of my sanity if nothing else. I think
I'll send this stuff to Mary. Then I find the insurance policy
that has no name of a beneficiary on it and that I will ask
BB about, there must be some way we can get our hot little
hands on it, so I put the whole lot back in the suitcase. Then
I turn my attention to Tiger's paperwork. This came to light
when I sorted the bags from the club and I'm not sure he
knows what he was giving me to take home. It doesn't make
a lot of sense to me and I'm not even sure if it is Tiger's, but
among receipts for beer and old rate demands are some documents that look interesting. And BB is just the person to suss
them.

I guess that's when I decide that I must go to Brighton. But for
now I stuff all the papers into the case and, mainly because I
don't want Vera poking about in it, I climb to the top of the
house, get a table and chair and just reach the loft space and
shove the case in there. I go back downstairs and talk to Vera
but I say nothing about going to Brighton, in fact I say I might
try for a job at Fullers chocolate factory. Her eyebrows rise so
high as to threaten the top of her head with assault and she
gives out with an incredulous laugh.

So she doesn't believe it any more than I do.

I go to the Roebuck early evening and it's almost the same as
before. I see Rooster and we spar around. Good to be there
again. See all the faces. Rooster tells me about some big deal
coming up. I hear his words.

'Listen man, me have a nice lickle ting come up soon,
y'hear. You can advance me some loot now? You can't arks
Tiger?'

I tell him about Tiger. His face is between disbelief and low
scale panic.

I warn Rooster that things are getting dangerous and that
Jack has pulled me, but he dismisses it with a tooth suck and:

'Your business that man! See if you can't find some loot for me now!'

'I'll see what's happening up the road.' In the past I have occasionally been called upon to put some bread up front for one of Rooster's escapades and he's always straightened me out, eventually.

'Soon come!' One of Rooster's own sayings, with its 'could be a day or a week implications'. I hijack it now.

'I'll go over the Paramount eh, might see somebody handy.'

Not very likely, with that busted flush of characters ligging and hoping to score pussy. A Yank comes up to me; 'Hey there babee, what's happening with you, girl? You want to . . .' And I burst into tears and run. Get control of myself by the time I get over the road and I look in Maples, hoping to bore myself back into restraint. I stand there peering into the window at expensive furniture, seeing myself reflected in the window looking large as life and twice as skinny. I pose and try to align my reflection with a particularly fine table. I realise I can't face the dance hall and stand looking at myself, preparing to give myself a talking to, when I see a group of Teds reflected, walking behind me. They enter my sight from the right and exit left, quietly strutting their stuff, as if they don't see me. I turn, feeling spooked. Something about the atmosphere gets me going. There are more Teds around than usual, but that's not what starts me worrying. I'm used to them strutting round by the Grove. It's the fact they are quiet. Not so leery. Black geezers go past and the Teds don't do their usual racist abuse routine. By the dance hall, where seldom is heard an encouraging word and practically never is seen a white face of the male gender, there is a quiet huddle. Their bright gear and fancy hair marks them out. They send a chill through me. For the first time they are not just a joke. Feels like all kinds of changes are happening. The world moving along without me.

I go down the tube. Make my way to Notting Hill and scoot home full of misery for Tiger, for myself, for Berry.

Vera is not back and I wonder where she is. But I'm fucked, I fall into bed and cry myself to sleep.

The big hand that Rooster talked about in the car that

night, picked the next morning as its time and tightened in the very early hours just before the sun put in an early, dazzling appearance. About the same time Britain was strangling the Suez and shafting a few nations round the world, the hand took time off for light relief and it came and marmalised me. There was no connection. Just big hands, inexplicable power, the shit hitting the fan with vigour.

When the noise came I was asleep. The crump of a door being bashed in with unnecessary force and the voices of ironic coppers prevailed on my dreams. A strange guy stood at the end of my bed, grinning happily. Proving again that one woman's disaster is another geezer's joy.

'Look what we found, Shindig'. Holding up a bag of weed the like of which me and Rooster could only dream of.

30   Cell Bound Blues

The opening in the door produces a plate with baked beans and a piece of bread and marge and cup of tea, cold.

'How long am I going to be here?'

She either doesn't hear, or doesn't want to.

The joint is silent and I think they have forgotten me. No idea what time it is.

Every now and again a door opens or closes and I hear movement. I tense up, ready.

Then nothing.

I want a light, shout out loud.

'Can I have a light, please?' I shout, several times and can hear my voice losing confidence. I want to cry but I won't.

Minutes after I stop yelling, a hand appears with a lighter.

I rush to the door.

'When am I getting out?'

Quiet, it's just me and the old bird jailer who seems to have taken a vow of silence.

The hours creak along, I could have been here for days.

There is movement now. A man is brought in by a male jailer and I realise that the shift has changed. I listen to their voices.

I yell out again for a light.

No reply.

When they finally come for me it is a relief.

A female copper opens the cell door and tells me to follow her. We go upstairs and she knocks on a door. An extremely smooth copper looks up from his paperwork and smiles.

'Won't keep you long, Shindig, just got to clear up a couple of things. Do sit down.'

It had been hours since they left me on my own, I'd done desperation, panic and terror. At one point a vast wave of confessional zeal had overcome me and if only somebody had asked, I would have confessed to anything they suggested, I wanted out so much.

The copper seems to look down at me from a great height.

I sit. He looks over at me, beams out confidence and well being. Reminds me of the quack.

'You can go now.' To the uniform female. She leaves.

'Now, Shindig, you don't mind if I call you Shindig do you?'

I shake my head vigorously, seriously alarmed that the amount of charm being oozed in my direction might wash me away. Have an idea the amount of fanny sent out is in direct proportion to the sentence they hope to chuck my way.

'Course not.' My voice is brisk as counterbalance, or it might have seized up with lack of use.

'Good,' he says, giving the word full value. He pauses. Takes out a cigarette case.

'Expect you'd like one of these, eh?'

I'd love to say 'no' but I grab, a greedy toddler going for a dummy. He looks even sleeker as he breaths out self satisfaction and puts the case away without taking one himself.

'Now, my dear.'

I had bets on with myself that he'd call me 'my dear'.

'I'm sure that the drugs we found in your flat weren't yours, were they?' He looks benignly at me, a half smile on his eek. An invitation.

'No, they weren't. Never seen them before in my life.'

'If you only knew how very often I hear that phrase.' It occurs to me to tell him that is because his team never leave anything to chance and bring their own. But he knows that. He looks rueful, suave.

'It's true.' I say. He gives the impression of being several feet above me, looking down from a great height.

'If that's so then we must ascertain who put them there. Mustn't we?'

This is his first venture into pig speak. He smiles warmly, looks tenderly at the photographs of a healthy looking woman and two brats that have no obvious signs of pig. He leans forward at me over the desk. He is very different from Jack. For a second I think of asking him about Jack. Feel it would muddy the water.

'Do you want to know what I think?'

No, but you're going to tell me. I just want out of here. I don't voice this. He looks cute in an enquiring way, like a small dog with its head slightly on one side. A malignant terrier.

'I think you have been mixing with some very dangerous people. This darkie, for instance.'

You can tell by the way he says it that he thinks he's being moderate in not using 'nigger'. He looks at the desk as if he needs to remind himself of Rooster's name.

'Mmn, yes, this darkie.' I say nothing and hate myself for it. You racist cunt, are the words that leap to mind, so it's probably just as well I stay quiet. The idea of Rooster as dangerous is ludicrous.

'You're smiling I see.' I hadn't noticed. I wipe the smile off my face before he tells me to. Think I'll play it safe.

'Did you know that in Jamaica he was charged with murdering a policeman?'

This is an old story, and if it's true, I am full of admiration.

'I never believed him,' I say.

He looks at me with dangerous reproach. I move delicately back into good girl mode. I slip him my sweetest, most demure smile. It works, the piranha disappears but my fear comes roaring up to make me dizzy when I think about the gear they planted in my gaff.

'So, it doesn't scare you at all that you are with a potential killer?'

I want to tell him my theory that we are all potential killers and that the inclination is encouraged in war time but perhaps not now, eh? I say:

'I'm not with him, he's my mate.'

'You expect us to believe this do you?'

'Yes, it's the truth. He's got a wife and a bunch of kids. Anyway we don't fancy each other.'

'We'll leave it at that, shall we?' I know he'll believe just what he wants to believe and now, my main concern is to get out of this joint.

'Know what I think, do you?' Doesn't wait to hear. 'I think you are in the power of this evil man.'

I laugh, an involuntary hoot of sheer incredulity. 'Bollocks!' my first honest word to date.

'I think you should consider this, carefully.' He pushes himself up with his hands on his desk.

The uniformed female returns as if by magic.

'Take her down again, officer. She wants to have some time on her own. She needs to give her situation some thought.' She takes me by the arm.

'Before you go, there's something else.' She lets go of my arm.

'Seen these before, have you?' He passes me the two prescription forms that I'd nicked from the quack weeks ago.

My face felt as if it blanched but I can't be sure. Made a superhuman effort to keep it under control. I hear my voice is squeaky now. 'No.'

He shakes his head gently. 'There seem to be a lot of things with no explanation in your life, don't there?'

As I go out the door he says:

'Your black friend says the drugs are yours, you know. Is that right?'

'Certainly not, and I don't believe you.'

He shrugs. 'See how you feel in a few hours.'

'What are you charging me with?' I ask.

'Remains to be seen, my dear.' And he gives this urbane smile that makes me think: come back Jack, all is forgiven.

'If you find you have anything to tell me, let the jailer know. I or one of my colleagues will be here. Any time at all.'

He beams at me with an unhealthy confidence that reached to his toes.

It looks like mid morning in his office. Back in the cells it could be any time. I think of 'Darkness at Noon,' but I drive the thought away quickly. Concern about Rooster is high too. Would he drop me in it? Worse still, would I drop him in it?

The jailer is now an elderly bloke and all the cells are empty, except mine. I persuade the jailer to part with an ancient dog-eared *Woman's Own* which I read avidly. All the time I read the feeble stuff, my brain is on a separate mission of worry. All I've got to do is drop Rooster in it and there's a fair chance I'll be out. But I can't. For a start I don't trust the bill, they are just as likely to come up with something new to lay on me when they've got Rooster. Plus he would get a long sentence. Can see the headlines in the *Express* now: 'White girl forced to run drugs for one of our colonial cousins.' A wily foreigners rule again, headline in the *Daily Mail*. And I'd come out sounding like a right idiot and Rooster would get twenty years and deportation. I have, apparently, a conscience. I am surprised at the vigour of this organ. Then my thoughts turn to reasons not to grass. On principle, first. Then the force of pure common sense kicks in. I'd hate myself.

How the fuck did I get to work with Rooster anyway? I think back and remember a conversation I had with Marmalade after Rooster first proposed we should work together. I wasn't keen to start with.

'Too butch for you, dear?' Marmalade asked.

'Too bleeding domineering. Spent half an hour with the geezer and he's telling me how to organise my life. Including telling me I'm sitting on a goldmine.'

'But you could work with him?' I shrugged and Marmalade shrugged and said,

'That's all it takes, darling.' And that's how it happened. He wanted a bird to work with and he'd picked me. We had been moving in the same circles.

'Flattering, really,' I'd said to Marmalade.

'Not exactly, darling, he wanted a girl who hasn't got a bloke in tow and there aren't that many around. You don't have to be bosom friends just get on with each other.'

I'd been getting booze off the base for months but it was a bit desultory to say the least. I was reliant on various iffy characters to take me and to bring the bottles in. So I was paying out right, left and centre for a service that was unreliable. In theory, Rooster and I should team up. He takes dope there and could bring back the booze. Marmalade continues to set me straight:

'Yes, there is really only you. And you've done all the spadework. So to speak.' He snuffles a laugh.

I'd been in Nell's in Berwick Street at the time of our second conversation, when all the decisions had been made already. I could hear the stall holders shouting out their wares, softly, beneath the sounds of dryers and chat, as I sat. One of those days when your whole body is on alert, twanging away in response to things it usually ignores. Nerves tweak, hormones hassle into life. Each pore open to stimulus, every body hair seeking out a friend to whistle against. I slither, move my arse lower into the soggy seat squashed by years of heavy and light female bottoms making their peace with the nasty green Rexene. Into reverie. Got Nifty's cock on my mind. Not the best or the largest but an interesting shape, more personality somehow. When it's hard it kind of hangs out away from his belly, too long to assume that rather featureless rigidity of most cocks. Never entirely hard but a good filler. It has a long foreskin that gives it an unusual lemon shape and has large purple veins running along its grey black matt length to the surprising pink exclamation at its end. Pull the skin sideways and it becomes shiny and sleek and the colour changes to a dark glossy plum brown like a horse chestnut. A cock of great character I'd say. I shift in my seat. My mind frantic for amusement. I am having my hair bleached as my mind travels forward and back on Niftys cock. Bleach festers on my head with its pissy smell making my eyes water. Anybody would think of cock. Or food.

Winkles curled on white, crisp bread. Butter with very little salt laying on the surface of the bread, pale, creamy. Dowsed in wine vinegar with black pepper piebald, the vinegar forming pools like oil, floating on the butter, winkles all collected together, piled high, a luscious, chewy mouthful.

Marmalade's here. 'Hello, treasure, sweet thing!' His lovely willowy person is leaning over me and he breathes Pastis in my face. 'You want to see your ecaf darling, what in the world are you thinking about? Or need I ask?'

'Who's been at the Absinthe, you sinful old tart!'

'Ricard for breakfast, my sweet! What *are* you doing with the riah?' He prods at the plastic sack containing my nut.

'Ugh, nasty, *do* hope it doesn't all fall out . . . just when auntie's found a nice new opening for you.' He sits back like a Cheshire cat, waiting for applause.

'Wheee!' I oblige with enthusiasm, disturbing the whole hairdressing emporium.

'Just what I need, a new opening, where is it? I'm sure there must be a market.' We laugh rudely. The crew of birds glare. He explains Rooster had decided to make me an offer after our first conversation. Knew he would. Sounds good to me. See him this evening in the Harmony.

'You going to thank me then? Ungrateful girl!'

I give him a big hug which involves adjusting my head sideways, almost falling out the chair. Nell comes over and asks him if he wants a haircut. He touches her hand delicately, taking her small finger in his hand: 'No thank you, my love, you only do ladies don't you? Mind you,' archly. 'Shindig's no lady, are you, treasure? Oh, isn't that just too divine.' He touches a rather nasty plastic slide in her hair and Nell almost simpers.

'How long will she be?'

And they chat about my hair together, Nell takes the plastic sack off and Marmalade rummages about a bit making oohing and ahing noises and intelligent little sounds. They go off together towards the teapot making conversation.

Outside, Soho crosses her legs in her daytime sleep, trumps a fart that consists of sweet sex, good food and hand made shoes. Turns over and sleeps the sleep of the just.

The noise of the barrow boys outside in the street is a murmur that rises and falls, their movements a dance in the bright light. Look at those spring greens! The brightness of them: 'Full of iron' said my nan and even this didn't put me off. Just barely cooked at all, water boiled fast then out with them, so the bitter taste is still there, then thrown in a frying pan with four rashers of fat streaky bacon, whip out the bacon fast, under the grill with it, turn the pan up high high high so it catches light, a half minute or so then out and on to a hot plate. Butter and herbs are optional. Some of the greens brown with the fire and all chewy but insubstantial, could eat pounds of them, as many as you can get in a pan, and perhaps soft calves' liver – carefully cooked so it still has some give in the meat, not dry, dry liver is hell – succulent and sweet with the underlying taste of offal, or kidney with the bubble of blood in the centre and the very faintest aroma of piss . . . mnn . . . Hungry!

'How much longer, Nell?' My plaintive little voice doesn't even reach them. There is something totally enfeebling about having your head in a sack of bleach. I try again:

'For fuck's sake, Nell!' Overkill, all heads turn, even the ones under dryers, Nell is affronted. Bustles her nice bottom down the shop bristling with outrage.

'This is not a knocking shop, Shindig!' And I grin my finest 'Sorry darling'. Marmalade glares disapproval. I am chastened.

This salon is used almost exclusively by working girls who languish with their faces in a state of disrepair, looking bored out of their skulls. I wonder what they think about. Are their minds full of money and rampant men? There are no indications at all. Do they contemplate sex with their lovers with joy or is it all down to shopping lists and mundanities? That one there, pursing her lips as her eyebrows are diminished, twenty and world weary to fuck. Does she enjoy sweet fantasies of food as she humps her punters? I look at her arm with its nice pale brown moles and light fair hair fur. She moves her arm to lift her fag and at her elbow her skin folds into enchanting tiny creases. I want to lean across and touch her. She looks up at me, my heart leaps joyfully. 'Pass us that ashtray, dolly.' I try to interpret this as some convoluted flirt but it's impossible. I pass the ash tray.

Nell comes and rinses off the bleach, washes my hair, covers it in gunk and rinses off gunk with a lot of muscular movement and faint whiffs of delicious sweat. Why am I so randy? Perhaps the bleach has uncovered a new deep wellspring of rampancy. Don't know whether to be pleased, I think I will. I'll enjoy my new-found extra lust, the scent of Nell is fresh and sour and completely erotic, and I draw in her scent. Nell has been talking to me, I haven't heard a word. 'What's that, Nell?'

'You getting a cold are you? Sniffing away?'

'No, Nell, thought I smelled something I recognised.'

'Probably somebody's scent.'

'Yeah, I reckon.'

'Your friend, got beautiful hair hasn't he?'

'Marmalade? Yeah, gorgeous.'

'That what he's called is it?'

'What else? Beats the hell out of Ginger.'

I look at myself in the mirror.

'Fuck me gently, Nell, I look like a baboon's arse!' My face is bright red and my hair is invisible. Nell laughs.

'Wait 'til it's dried and combed out, then see.' And she commences to put it on horrible rollers with furry spike inserts, torturing my nut every time she puts another one in. My head throbs sore.

'What's that they say? Gentlemen prefer blondes?' says Nell as she pops on a bright blue hairnet and pink plastic ear protectors and pushes the great hairdryer up behind me and over my head. I'm in a black nightmare with roaring hot air in my mind, my brain lobes twitch their protest at this nonsense. My head feels sore, the skin on my face is burning, my mind has jettisoned any lucidity. Goes into stasis. Finally Nell lifts the drier off my head takes one roller out and tests the hair for curl. This skimpy bit of flaxen hair boings back obediently. I am ready. Now Nell goes to it with brio and I look extraordinary, like Brunhilde, sort of a herrenvolk job. When my face loses its hairdryer radiance and calms into morning pallor I expect it will look better, she combs and loops, pins and backcombs. Gets higher and higher.

'Gorgeous, darling! Look like the principal boy sweetie, how very clever you are Nell. How do you *do* that with the loops?' Marmalade puts down his gondola shopping basket full of veggies, that he buys for their colour and arranges exquisitely, like still lifes in his kitchen. He peers intently at Nell's hands. They discuss Marmalade's innate artistic talents that are considerable.

I get out the slap and put on some long spiky nylon lashes, amazing the improvement a pair of lashes can make. The ecaf is almost restored to humanity. I apply liberal quantities of spitty mascara over grey eye shadow. Scarlet lipstick cheers me and takes away from my rosy chops. Looks pretty good really . . . yes, think I'm glad to be blonde. Marmalade stands behind me, lowers himself until his head is on a level with mine and smiles over my shoulder into the mirror, our faces together, laughing.

'Bona, darling, absolutely bona.'

'You start working with Rooster this very evening, sweetie. I'm sure he'll appreciate the riah.'

Not sure if he did, Rooster proved to be remarkably tight with praise for my accomplishments. Generous with criticism though.

I am so deep in reverie that it comes as a shock when there is a bang on the cell door. The food aperture opens and a lighted cigarette comes through. 'The inspector thought you might like a ciggy.'

A female jailer has appeared, half her face anyway. 'Thanks,' I say and feel this enormous gratitude well up, so I almost weep with joy.

'I'll get you out for a wash later, eh? Want a cup of tea, do you?' Seems like a change in policy has occurred. A change for the better. I haven't heard any sound from the other cells for hours.

She's back with a cup of tea within minutes. This time she opens the door and I see she is young and chubby faced with an eager to please expression. Must be new. She leans against the edge of the door.

'Quiet here isn't it?' I say. 'Always like this, is it?'

'Not usually, no,' she says. Looks as if she might say more but doesn't. Instead, she looks round the cell, nods, shuts the door with a cheery smile. I flop back on the wooden shelf with its smelly rubber mattress and coagulated blankets, filth frozen into a stiff solid mass.

Why the fuck didn't I dump those bleeding scripts weeks ago, that or flog them? Should have known it would all end in tears. Then I wonder if they carried on reefing my gaff after I was pulled and what else they might have found. On to heavy duty worry about my future, do I have one?

Don't know what time it is. Don't matter a lot. I try to kip but the blanket stinks and I get the horrors thinking about what I might catch from it. I get obsessed about time, must know what the time is. I ring the bell and chubby chops appears magically fast.

'You want to talk to the inspector, do you?' She has opened the door and stands looking at me.

'No. I wanted to know what the time is.' Her face falls a bit and I feel sorry for her. 'It's five o'clock.' And she just stands there looking at me. I've only been here eleven hours. It feels like a week.

She smiles at me.

'You can go home, Miss Green.'

'Home?'

She laughs at me. 'Yes, home. And if I was you I'd go before they change their minds. She hands me over to the desk sergeant on the way out and signs something.

'The inspector says there's no point keeping you in; we know where you are, don't we, darling? You're not thinking of moving house are you? And you must come in and sign here every day to prove you haven't left the country.' He winks at me. I take my property that consists of a purse and box of matches. I count the money for him. I sign the form and scuttle out into the evening where rush hour is just beginning to shift a million people sideways and north and south to parts of London that I don't want to think about.

I get a bus to the Grove and as I pass the greasy spoon on the corner of Lancaster Road I see Henry, he yells across to me, something about Rooster so I go over to him. He walks towards me, though walk is never accurate when you speak of Henry, he cavorts, dances, grimaces in a fair imitation of a minstrel in the Black and White minstrel show. He Uncle Toms it up, skinning his teeth, jive talking. High giggling. He moves to silent music, an invisible audience. He is the exception that proves the rule and the whites all love him. His is the acceptable face of the immigrant. This is the guy they are thinking of when they say:

'Some of my best friends are black you know.' He's crazy but I'm not sure how crazy. He's also a grass.

'Hear your good fren him was arrested.' And he sort of sniggers.

'Them have warrant for him in Jamaica you know, them remove him already.' He makes like a plane taking off with his hand and laughs.

'I haven't got any friends, me. Or none that you'd know

anyway.' I sweep past him into the café. I don't believe that Rooster has been sent back, I don't want to believe it. But I want to know the word on the street, I also want twenty fags and this is the place for both. It has its normal complement of layabouts and taxi drivers along with the boss, who is here at four in the morning and here he is again, perhaps he never sleeps?

They are slurping their thick tea from even thicker white cups. I chirp a greeting and am greeted in turn by the governor who leers at me.

'What you doing out, gel? We heard you got nicked along with that goolie who drives the big Yankee motor.'

'Just let me out, didn't they.'

The bunch of them seem inclined to stare at me in a witless way and I'm getting the dead needle. Two or three cab drivers who use this café regularly look at me, like I'm the floor show. The law also use this place so a lot of cross fertilisation in the way of information happens.

'Cup of tea, like? Any chance of a cup of tea?' Peevishly.

'Sorry, gel, one tea coming up.' From the governor. I wonder what they've been saying about me, paranoia strikes.

I want to be invisible but I always forget that there are characters like this, watching from their dreary lives as I cavort. So really I shouldn't be dismayed that they think they know me, but I am. One taxi driver is very familiar like he's a mate or something. 'Remember? I drove you and your mates to the Green Door many a time and the Maribu with all those queers, I know Marmalade well. And Frances, of course. And I've driven you home with any amount of goolies.'

'And there was me thinking you taxi drivers were like priests, with a vow of silence.'

'Yes, we was having bets on how long you'd get.' From some rascally git who I wouldn't usually speak to. I get my tea and mount one of the nasty high stools that are the only concession to customer care in the joint. In fact they have been used as weapons of assault so often that they all creak and wobble under anybody brave enough to sit on one.

'So what's happening then?' I ask.

The governor looks out from behind his large glass case full of curling sarnies and London cheese cakes with grubby coconut on top. He shrugs. I drink my tea which is so strong as to coat an entire gullet with tannin in the time it takes to get it down you.

I get off the stool, ready to go.

'So, you out on bail are you?'

I nod and get my purse out.

'No, mate, on the house, intit?' says the governor.

Before I can get out the door the taxi driver tells me he's glad I'm not his daughter and I say that I'm extremely glad about that too. Then they all gang up to tell me the error of my ways.

'Yes, don't know what you young girls see in them bleeding niggers.'

'I think they hypnotise them. It's like witch doctors,' says the governor.

'No, it's the fact they're so fucking good looking, mate. And their natural rhythm of course,' I say.

I take my melancholy home through the traffic. A car slows down as it passes. For a moment my heart lifts, thinking it's Rooster in his bulbous old motor, then reality asserts itself and. I turn to see the sharp, brittle lines of the Wolsey with the small light on the bonnet. It slows to a crawl beside me, I see their pale copper faces looking at me, then it takes off swiftly, after they make sure I know they've seen me. I crash my heels on the ground and the steel blakies ring against the pavement. This does not cheer me as much as it usually does. The sound is limp, no power. Perhaps it only works at night or when I'm stoned.

There is no sign of Vera and my room has the smell of hot bedroom so I open the window. I tidy up a bit. The destruction is nothing like the last law invasion. Weren't concentrating, were they? No feathers this time. I pick up books, dump the ones soaked in whisky in the bin. A lot of my stuff has been ruined by over vigorous efforts of the bill, but you expect that. Old photographs crumble and I chuck them in the bin. I know I must go but instead I lay down on the bed. I have this dreadful feeling everything is beyond my doing. Out of my control and I can only wait. Waiting is the worst. I read and I'm on my way to California in an ancient jalopy. Can nearly smell the sweat and filth, the fruit rotting on the trees, the fear and dying pride.

I hear Vera coughing her lungs into purgatory on her way upstairs. I jump off the bed and pretend to be tidying up. She bowls in and her face goes blank.

'You all right, darling?' she starts off with. 'How long you been back?'

I tell her half an hour.

'Good thing I wasn't in last night, isn't it? They might have lifted me for keeping a disorderly house.'

'Where were you?'

'On the nest, where do you think? Met up with this geezer I see from time to time, when he can escape his missis.'

'Oh, right,' I say. I want to know where and who with and all that stuff but haven't quite got the bottle to ask. So much for lonely fucking V, that's my sympathy on hold.

'You never told me you had a bloke.'

'You never asked, I've got a few blokes as it happens.' I'm choked, like she's been lying to me. She laughs.

'You been underestimating me haven't you, darling? So what was it for this time?'

I tell her. 'Possession as far as I know. They had a fucking great bag of weed that Rooster and me could never bleeding aspire to in a million years. Plus they found a couple of scripts nicked from a quack.'

'Oh, dear. You're for it, darling. Sounds like they're determined to send you down don't it, mate? Come and have a cup of tea, darling.'

I follow her to the kitchen. We sit with the teapot as we have so many times before, and I keep thinking about good times we've had here.

'You had a chat with Jack? Or Dixon?' V asks.

'They aren't around any more, darling. All gone.'

'Omygawd! That's well out of order, isn't it? Must have had a shake up, eh? Means they'll be out to prove points.' She shakes her nut. 'New brooms and all that old fanny.'

She sighs, shakes her nut again, prepared for a tragedy. I notice she looks different.

'You dyed your riah?'

She smirks. 'A tint. Cover the grey. What do you reckon?'

'It's nice, I think,' I say. She smiles brightly at me.

'Seen Rooster have you? Cause he'll be the one they want to stitch up. You know what the bill are like with coloureds.'

'Yes, they said I should drop him in it.'

'You're not going to though, are you?' Her face conveys no doubt at all that I'll do the right thing. 'Course not.' She continues: 'Cause it never ends there, darling, it's never just one time, finish. The bill get a hold of you.'

She pours tea in her equal parity way.

'I've known people who got involved with those bastards, they're a slippery lot. Think they own you. Worse than any gangsters they are. More bleeding pull too.'

Gives me my cup and saucer, pushes the sugar my way.

'They do bleeding own you once you do them any favours,' I say. She shakes her nut. Looks at me, anxious face.

'No, mate, I won't drop him in it.'

'He'd cut your earholes off if you did anyway, gel,' she laughs. I carry on:

'I went to the café when I came back, they all seemed to know more about me than I do.'

'I've told you before to keep out of there, they're a nosy lot of cunts hang around in there. Nothing better to do than sit around scandalising people, don't miss a thing they don't. All local inbreds from Notting Dale they are, half of them related to Frannie. Bet she never got done.'

'Think she had something to do with it, do you?'

'No, course not, but if there's been a change in the law there's going to be a change in who gets the bungs. And there's been a change in personnel at the top, up west.'

She nods in the direction that she imagines to be west.

'All linked, darling. One hand washes the other, know what I mean?' I'm not entirely sure I do but I nod wisely.

We sit, a couple of sad sacks. Fags in our hands, grief in our hearts.

''Cos one of Tiger's mates turned up to see me, was arsting about you. Told me that Tiger blotted his copy book with the new geezers.'

'Say how, did he? '

'No. just said he's out, Tiger. So either Frantic's done somebody a big favour or she's having it off with some geezer.'

'Won't last will it?' I say but I don't believe my own words.

'Wouldn't bet on it, cocker. Got staying power that bird.'

I can't see it myself but what do I know?

'So, you want to pack yer gear up? Cos you're going to go down, mate.' She puts her fag out, pours another dark brown cup of tea. Gets out the brandy bottle.

'Want a drop? Best thing you can do, darling, get in touch with a brief I know, see what he says. Won't cost you, he owes me. I'll hang on to your gear and you can come back here when you get out. Can't say fairer than that, can I?'

And she can't.

But I don't hang about. I make my bid for freedom don't I?

I pack some of my stuff up and leave it at that.

'They'll be back, darling,' says Vera.

'What you want me to do, fucking surrender? '

'No need to get nasty with me, gel! You can save that for Holloway, see how far it gets you in there!'

I think these were the words that impelled my flight. They chilled me something rotten.

'I'm shooting down the road, got to see somebody, V.'

She looks at me like some old lizard with a dry cynical eye. Says nothing verbally. The eyes have it.

I get outside the house. Flounce in my full skirt, sandals and my duster coat.

And where do you go in sandals? The seaside. If I shoot down to Brighton, I'll find BB, get out the way for a few days, they'll forget about me won't they?

They don't, do they? I must be one of the pieces that are intrinsic to the pattern the bill have decided on for the shape of things to come.

They nick me at Victoria station. They wait until I've bought my ticket and am joining the merry throng on their way home from work, home to the sea, my mind is full of buckets and spades. Then whoosh!

'Mary Green?' I hear the voice and feel the collar.

'This girl had the benefit of approved school training,'

Damned if I know who said that. Was it the beak? Or the clerk of court? I laugh. But it's ironic, I think. A wry giggle. The magistrate doesn't understand and warns me that I'll get more time if I disrespect the court. I keep quiet as he sentences me to six months. I do instant counting and know I'll be inside for Christmas. Why this seems of primary importance is not clear to me.

The beak looks at his watch as he sends me down. Is it time for lunch yet?

Possession of illegal substances. That was it. The scripts seem to have disappeared off the charge sheet. He looks over his bins at me like I'm a specimen of roach. Reiterates my vast list of sins that sound like the sensible option to me. I smile, winsome. He is not impressed 'She absconded from approved school after having run away from home at the age of fifteen.' He pauses, 'When she was recaptured the approved school refused to accept her.' He looks beakily at me. Shakes his nut a fraction. The court is bored and I regret my lack of glamour in sin. They pick their nails and he looks at the list. I hope something more fascinating turns up for them.

In the wagon, in a tiny cage with a shelf. It stinks of bodies, piss, vomit. There is also the inexplicable sharp stink of methylated spirit and disinfectant – which is the worst of the lot. The noise is deafening. The entire thing rattles at each bump we go over, every corner makes metal scrape against metal. A vast tea trolley with one dodgy wheel and an attitude would describe our progress. The driver is hell bent on using the full facility of his brakes, dramatically. Probably a renegade from the flying squad.

I perch my arse on the shelf, but this gives me less stability, more leeway for fatal falls. I stand again with arms wedged against either side, my legs braced.

A mixed bunch are picked up as we travel from court to court, the old hands join us as if it's a merry trip. The disconsolate bring their sorry minds and carcasses to the operation in a state of terror. I am somewhere in between. A couple of particularly vivid females arrive, with strop to spare.

'All right, gorgeous? How you doing, long time no see.'

'In for another clutch reline, darling!'

'Yeah, off on me holidays.'

'Miserable lot in here aren't they?'

'Cheer up, you wankers!' bawled at double strength. Can feel the revulsion from the quiet types. There is a shrinking away.

'Wait till you girls get to Holloway, mate, there'll be some noise then all right.' Followed by a gust of filthy laughter. I wonder is she related to Frantic. Her mate joins the mirth and I can see six months of inescapable noise.

'Yeah, mate, wailing and gnashing of teeth then, girls.'

'That you, Dora?' A voice from the other end of the van.

'Who's that?'

'Me, isn't it?'

They play a three way guessing game for some time while I attempt to acquire the skill of closing my ears. The men assert their right to dominate the van now. We have stopped at a court and several geezers pile in. From their fulsome throats, noisy banter issues. They keep up verbals with the loud women, with the screws, but mainly with each other through the lurching, stopping, starting promenade from court to court all over London. I get engaged in a dialogue with my mother, this happens only when I am truly fucked. She emerges to gloat in my mind and I can't shake her. We argue about my life.

In the next cage I feel a feathery movement like breath but pushing through the wire insistent. A choking sound, I realise that the geezer in there is having a fit, a dry throaty sound turns liquid, bubbly. I start to yell but the bird on the other side gets in first.

'Here, mister, this bloke's having a fit!'

He takes his time, the screw. Sanguine to a fault, he unlocks the one cage. He wears an air of seen it all before, while several people advise him to put something in the man's mouth. The man is removed and his feet drum a merry tattoo on the metal floor as he's bundled out the back door into the yard. It is near impossible to see from inside this thick mesh. The door closes again and we are off. Holloway must be the last prison we visit. Some of the regulars announce the stops.

'And here we are at Brixton, folks, anybody for Brixton?' A male voice.

'Ooh, yes, not half, I'll have some of that!' A female voice. Followed by guffaws all round. Somebody female starts to weep, and scream, rhythmically. I join her, silently.

Reception is hell. A stripping, internal searching place of total humiliation. It sets the mood for the entire sentence.

'Get your clothes off, Green.'

She watches me and calls her mate in to look at my posh knickers and bras.

'Look at the state of these, Mavis. How much they rush you for these then? Can't wait till you get into your uniform. Wait there.'

I am naked. Her mate laughs, looking me up, then down. Then laughs again. Both leave me in a cell with wire over the top. They chat about this and that as they go to the next cell.

'Hello, Jill, you back with us are you? Get yer drawers off then. Hold the pad between yer legs until he searches you, eh? Good girl.'

'Wish they were all like Jill, don't you?'

'Yes I do. Some of these snooty cows could learn a lot from Jill. Where's Mayer? She's supposed to be working collecting their clothes. Giving out gowns.'

They move out of earshot. I cringe. The door opens and a tall scrawny bird with a big hooter hands me a grey cotton wrap. She takes the opportunity to snigger at the body.

'Shindig. Well, that's nice intit, remember me, do you?'

Know the face, can't remember the context and it feels important that I do.

'No, I thought not. Too fucking high and mighty, aren't you.'

She closes the door and I hear her murmuring to the screws.

The quack here could hardly be more different from the one I hustled. Small careworn guy. I want to ask him how it affects his sex life; reaming women's apertures all day. But one of the screws is there in her supervisory capacity. She stands and gazes at my genitals, dead casual like. I'm not sure if it would have been better if she'd taken an interest. I suck my teeth and say I don't relish her peering up my crack. She gets the hump.

'I'm here for your protection, who do you think you are?'

Who indeed.

Night time on the wings women call out to each other and it is sad and funny: 'They'll never keep us apart, see you in church on Sunday!' From one wing to another a great caterwauling love cry, and back again with messages of fidelity and fags: 'You'd better get that half ounce to me by Friday or I'll cut your bleeding earholes off!' and 'I still love you darling, don't forget.'

The eternal prying screws with their eyes to the holes in the doors of the cells and their minds away with the fairies. C wing, the vale of tears with weeping and howling, banging on door with desperate head, feet rattling along the wing, fast. Door open, vigorously, sound of loud screw voices, muffled protesting woman dragging feet, door slammed shut. Finality. Yelling misery is broken off for a few minutes. The padded cell with its own stench that rises so high in the sinus, up into the brain a confusion of pain plummets back into the base gut and reverberates a vomit through mind. The strips, rubber mattress, plastic potty, canvas jacket with metal lock at the neck, chafing – hard times on soft flesh – arse high. No lavatory paper, no sanitary protection, no privacy.

Doctor wafts in on a cloud of Je Reviens with wrinkled nose and hand stitching on her jacket. 'Oh yes you're doing fine, she's doing fine isn't she nurse? Yes, I thought so.'

Degradation. The wing. 'I found my thrill on Blueberry Hill'

a fair imitation of Fats Domino flying across the air, by the
time 'When I found you' is reached for the second or third time
a discordant chorus is taking part and screws march up and
down hitting doors and yelling.

'Quiet, you girls!' We are all girls in here, even the sixty-
year-old preventive detention girls and the corrective training
lasses of seventy or more who live in their neat cells with
curtains, carpets and radios – and what more could a girl
want?

Daytime on the wing and buckets feature large. The sound of
zinc being dragged across stone floors, a jarring brain squealing
sound. The smell of wet stone and soap, the feeling of mind-
numbing boredom, soaking in so deep that any thought process
drowns in the soapy water. The slop buckets that we bring out
in the morning to share as we tip them down the landing bog.
Metal squeal is a perpetual threat, an intermittent reality. My
ears cringe as they wait.

My new home, B wing. With the cell in the corner where
women had waited to be hanged by the neck until they were
dead. In the bogs to fight and I don't have any inclination to
fight. Know I've got to put up a show if I don't want to get
done over on a regular basis. Cold stone logical, not an angry
cell in me, just fear of fighting, I whack my chief tormentor
hard as I can and get knocked flat onto the piss-soaked floor.

'Let her get up.' They walk away from me. I dry myself on
hard bog roll.

I meet Nickie on the landing on the way back to my cell.

'Want to work in the kitchen, do you? Best job in the nick.'

'I'll think about it.'

Rooster has gone to crown court. The inspector sent in a young
police woman with the cradle marks still on her arse in a final
bid to get me to give evidence against him.

'Didn't have time to come in himself, Shindig, you'll have to
make do with me.'

'He's given up has he? Anyway, I'd prefer you, you're better
looking.' She smiles. Gives me a packet of fags.

'You could be out in a week you know.' She strikes a match. 'Sooner.'

My face lights up at the thought, I can't help it.

'Don't let on you're a shit and shave sentence merchant, 'cos we all know you're just a kid at heart. How old are you? Nineteen?'

Appealing to my vulnerability. Don't work, do it? Though I detect a slight sniffle of self pity making its way up from somewhere way down deep inside, up to behind my schnozz. She proceeds to explain the delights of a straight life to me, with its babies and attendant hubby. This serves to save me from temptation.

'You going to do that are you?'

'What, get married? I expect so. When I meet mister right.'

'Not going to meet him in the bill, are you?'

'There are some good men in the police force, Shindig. Just you haven't seen them at their best,' she laughs. 'You're in a good place to meet miss right here aren't you? Or miss wrong, anyway.'

She smiles and stands up. One of the screws over the other side of the room stands too, to show her out I guess. And she leans over and lifts my chin in her palm. Looks into my eyes.

'You'll be all right, darling, don't you worry.' And that makes me bawl my eyes out, once I reach the safety of my cell.

32 Oh Me Oh My What Will Become of Poor Me?

Everybody lives for visits in here. It's the thing that keeps us sane. Also the one thing that drives us crazy. Our hopes and fears are all tied up with the outside and the strings are twanged with letters and the visits, or lack of visits, cause insane passions to fly through the wing and shake it to its foundations. Infectious drama is the stuff of life in here and it can rush along the landings, insert itself into every cell and cranny and cause mayhem. A rumour, carefully nurtured, can kill. The screws, when bored, can light a fire of anger, can mix a girl's brain into a merry furore. They read our letters and know just what will aggravate.

'Hear your Freddy's got a new girlfriend. That right is it?' says one screw and the wing boredom and the rumour mongers will do the rest. Next thing you know, every aggravation has been dredged up and there's full scale war.

By the time a visit happens, it is almost certain to be an anti-climax. But it's the anticipation that keeps us all going through the dreary days and lonely nights of this parallel universe that is the nick. When I was called to the visitors room I had no idea what to expect.

This time I was snatched off the wing by a screw. At first I thought I was being taken to the governor and had reached a level of high terror before she told me I had a visitor. By then we were half way out the door and through the yard. A brilliant autumn day with the sun splitting the trees – although there aren't a lot of trees to be split, the light startles me and the screw has us moving so fast that I forget to scan the ground for butts. Visitors in the know will light a fag as they come in the gate and stub it out before they get to the visiting room, leaving nearly entire fags on the ground to be lifted by us inmates. I arrive in the visiting room unprepared. I drag a comb through the riah and place my feet, in their beetle crushers, well under the table. My hairy, bone white legs poking into the world from beneath my lavender cotton frock are my special bane. The huge Minnie Mouse boots with white ankle socks my particular mortification. I sit, tense as a wire, and wait. I had sent out visiting orders but had heard nothing. I twitch and look at the other visitors. Clinging to their loved ones with their eyes, bodily contact is not allowed. All the intensity and frustration flies from the prisoner to the visitor. The visitor, not knowing what to do with this level of passion chucks it back for the prisoner to bring home to the wing as anger or sadness. These ordinary people made crazy.

I light a fag and feel a surge of energy in the room. Sort of fizz twitches the air, makes me look up and there is Marmalade in all his glory. He trolls in with a single rose in his left hand. He bends over to kiss me on my eek. His eyes settle on the cotton dress momentarily, his lips twitch into preparation for a smile.

'How are you dear heart sweet thing? Don't you look camp?'

Then he giggles a trumpet of sound.

'Have you put on weight, girl? Suits you. But I wouldn't put on any more if I was you.'

He arranges himself on the hard chair, to best advantage, looks round imperiously, gives a big smile to the public, who have problems keeping their eyes off him, takes my hand in his two hands and smiles into my eyes.

'How are you, darling? Are you bearing up?'

'I'm fine, Marmalade.' He puts the flower behind my ear and I laugh, then find I'm crying and don't know why.

Since I came here I have kept weeping down to a minimum and never in public. The first days on B wing were the worst but I still find great gouts of profound misery invade, and now, I'm gasping and wheezing at poor Marmalade and can feel my eyes getting red, my nose leaking. He just looks at me with huge sympathy which makes me weep more. His eyes fill and cause me to indulge in a paroxysm of sobbing. He puts his hands in his lap, leans back.

'We all miss you, sweetheart. Vera is distracted, got a new lodger in Victoria's room but she's got your room as a sort of shrine. She's going to have it decorated for when you come out. We were surprised I must say. Carlie thought you were just a lodger, didn't she? But I always said no, Vera adores you. Won't have a word against you. She's adopted you.'

'How is Carlotta?' I snuffle.

'Driving me mad, as usual. Gio is taking her to Italy in the spring.' He bungs me a hankie.

'Do you know, they confiscated my gondola when I arrived here? Outrageous! What did they think I was bringing you? A dildo?' He raises his brows and looks archly round the room.

'Any half decent palones in here, are there? Must be some old diesels.'

He gives the room a comprehensive sweep with his eyes. Disappointed, they return to me.

'There must *be* some bona feelys in here, it's a tradition, darling.' He sounds peevish, like he thinks I haven't been looking. 'Have you had it off with any screws? Do tell.'

'I've met a nice diesel dyke.' I sound defensive.

'That's no good, bread and bread, darling. What you need is something nice and femme.'

He sounds very sure about this. Wish I had his certainty.

'Someone to watch over me?'

'Exactly!'

'Tell me what's happening outside.'

'They seem to be charging Rooster with everything they can think of, keep away from that one my sweet.' He nods. 'Supplying drugs. You name it, they're sticking it on Rooster. Poor bastard. Been round his house searching several times and every time they come up with something new. Possession of property from the American base. Theft of prescriptions. Receiving.'

'Prescriptions? He has nothing to do with prescription drugs.'

Marmalade moves his shoulders, a rudimentary shrug. What's that got to do with it?

'I brought some tobacco for you but they said you can't have it.'

'Get it up to Rooster, he's on remand. Who's visiting him?'

'No idea, his wife I suppose. Nobody wants to get involved,

do they? Shit sticking and all that.' Gives the room a once-over, brows raised. He gives me a fag, we light up. The entire visiting room is blue with smoke. A fug hangs like cloud cover two feet from the ceiling. Must be the blank scripts I lifted from the quack they're sticking on Rooster. I open my mouth to tell Marmalade but he speaks first.

'Celeste thinks it's well camp of you, being in here. Remember Celeste, darling? She's taken two of my pictures to put in her gallery. She says she'll come and see you if you send a VO.'

He smiles and I get the impression I should be grateful.

I think about the level of detachment that would find it camp to be in nick.

'Tell her don't bother, I want to see BB or Vera.'

'Oh, Angelo has gone. Or is going, when we went to see to Vera, she told us. BB wrote to V and will come with her next time. You'll like that won't you?' He wears the face of distaste he always puts on when talking about BB.

'Do hope you don't mind Vera giving *me* a VO! I thought you'd be glad to see me!'

'Course not, I'm delighted as ever to vada your bona old eek! What's happened to Tiger? Anybody seen him?'

'No, not as far as I know. Everything seems to have changed up west. A lot of the old boys have gone. Funny it is, you go somewhere familiar and there are new faces. Odd. But it doesn't make any difference to us, does it? Except Frantic's involved in Tiger's old place, screwing the governor or something I suppose. Who knows with that one?'

He puts out his fag, looks round the room again, sighs. I wonder what he's after, so I say nothing

'Lot of gossip up west about paintings I heard, or Celeste told me. Lot of nicked pictures gone missing. I wondered if Tiger might have been involved – had his fingers in everything, didn't he?' He looks at me archly, but shrewd. I think about the paintings in the cellar. I shake my head solemnly.

'Wouldn't know a Breugel from a bog roll, would he?' I say.

We witter on and from about ten minutes into the half hour visit I can think of nothing except the fact that he'll be going out into the sunlit world of pubs. That wonderful, special darkness of a bar when you leave sunlight behind you but know it's there, waiting for you after your cool pint. This wrecks the visit for me.

'It's not for long, is it? You'll be out in three months or so.'

Marmalade sounds quite manic with good cheer as he says goodbye and I want to whack him one. He flounces off with the virtue of his visit shining from every orifice. Bows to his public, which consists of every other inmate and most of their visitors, and swirls off into real life taking his hanky with him. The screw takes my rose away as we leave the visiting room. Back on the wing we queue for tea and I decide that, yes, I will go for the job in the kitchen. That evening I get talking to a girl called May. She sings with a band when she's not in here and I know her from the Harmony. We talk about Jazz. She talks, I bluff. After lock up she sings 'My kitchen man'. I know it's for me. The sound of her voice cheers me up and makes me sad.

Time extends and shrinks in the nick. A day can do a fair imitation of a week while sleep shrinks into moments. I read my Dostoyevsky until lights out then it's open season for the night terrors.

I sleep until the dreams come and terrorise me. Usual chasing one has been joined by a particularly bleak burying number that has me in a cold sweat, nightly. Takes weeks to get used the constant noise. About the time I transfer to Zola.

33   Saturday Night Fish Fry

'You know what day this is, do you?'

Greta's voice fills my ears as she looks up from the spuds.

'Yeah, Friday we're doing fish.'

'Aye but it's no' just any Friday, it's my anniversary, hen.'

'What of, Greta? Your wedding?'

'Not at all! It's the anniversary of when I finally left Dougie.'

'How long ago was that then, Greta?'

'Five years two weeks and a day!'

She hoots with laughter and I find myself infected and cackling along with her. 'So why is this an anniversary?'

'Every day's a pigging anniversary without that bastard!' We both laugh at the pure sense of it.

'All right, girls, keep it down, you're here to work not to lark about,' Miss Ivans yells across the kitchen and Greta blows a raspberry. 'Watch it there, McDonald, it's no problem to send you back to the wing you know. And you Green, have you got your batter mixed?' Miss Ivans doesn't miss much.

'I'm terribly sorry Miss Ivans, but you've got to have a laugh haven't you?' says Greta with mock piety.

'No, all you have to do is get on with those spuds, look at poor Ruby working away there while you're larking about.'

We both look round at Ruby who is bent over the sink intent on the taters. Ruby is ancient and has always been here, grovelling away like a good'un, now she smiles up at Miss Ivans. 'Thank you, Miss Ivans!' In fact good old Ruby works so slowly and methodically that the spuds are reduced to a quarter of their former selves and all in slow motion. Greta is a spud barber par excellence, bringing to the job an expertise and speed that would make you gasp. She barges back to the sink and inadvertently nearly flattens Ruby, she makes a face at me and winks lewdly.

'Thank you, Miss Ivans,' she parrots.

Miss Ivans looks suspicious: 'The batter, Green!'

I giggle, snuffling over the mixer bowl and realise that I have forgotten how much flour I've put in. I guess and hope for the best. Greta goes into full speed graft mode and sings 'Your Cheating Heart' in her big strong confident voice. I join in and incorporate some arm waving mime into my preliminary batter mixing, I lift the vast metal bowl over to the machine. Nickie meets me at the centre table

'She's a nuisance that one.' She nods towards Greta. 'How long is she in for this time?'

'Ten days I think, a fine as usual. She's a great grafter, that's why Ivans has her here, plus she's a laugh.' I start the motor and the mixture churns away.

Nickie is my best mate and she is a snob. She has red hair, cut very short and her face is more freckle than not. Her eyes are orange brown and she is in love with Sylvia who also works in the kitchen. Nickie got me into the kitchen. She flirts outrageously with all the screws who adore her, Sylv does not adore her and is deeply worried that the rest of the female members of her family will find out about Nickie and herself.

Nickie has firm ideas about class, she believes in it. She is in for taking and driving away which is classy. I am in for drugs which is not classy but she treats me as an equal. Nickie says that we are the intellectuals, because we read books. I accept this as part of my persona, gladly. Everybody needs a persona in here. So I schlep my Dostoyevsky around with me at all times. It is getting increasingly weighed down with grease. I am the queen of the deep fryer, the chip maker, the roast spud operative and the fish crisper for four hundred and twenty hungry souls. There is only room to fry either fish or chips. On Friday we have boiled spuds and fried fish. Another day we will have chips and sausages. Sundays I come into my own frying roasties – my! But we know how to keep a girl's body in close contact with her soul. I take my responsibilities dead seriously lest I get lynched.

Nickie and Sylv and me are all on B wing which we feel is a better class of wing altogether, partly because it is well away from the nutters on C1, partly because we are doing between six and eighteen months so we feel infinitely superior to the lesser mortals like Greta who are only in for an overnight stop – under six months – but mostly a few days for fines.

Greta perambulates back and forth between King's Cross where she drinks and Holloway where she rests up until her debt to society is paid in time or in money. She is large, raffish, noisy and has a great line in filthy jokes that I try to remember and take back, along with the stolen food, to May on the wing. I always forget the cogent bit and now May has told me not to bother with the jokes, she'll make do with the nosh! I have gained two stone in the six weeks I've been here while May is still as thin as a rail in spite of my heavy nickage of food for her. She sings lovely blues to me in her cell and enjoys my Thelonius Monk records that I got sent in as an affectation. She is due out soon and I try not to think about that.

I regard the batter, it is like wallpaper paste and has a terrible grey sheen to it. I poke at it nervously then remember that it always looks like wallpaper paste, I leave it to fester and I hope. Nickie and me are sorting out the special diets and we sing as we stand. This has been a passion for weeks here. Every time more than two girls are gathered together we sing Elvis. Entire queues can be seen and heard rendering versions of 'Blue Suede Shoes' counterpointed by 'I want you I need you I love you'. As they await their delicious lumpy grey porridge, their slopping out, their bread and margarine, their baths. All these events are enlivened by singing girls. This drives some of the screws quite mad; they jump up and down in overactive fury. As they stop the front of the queue from singing the back resumes and one particular screw is rumoured to have divided herself entirely in half in an excess of zeal and neurosis.

Now I contribute my own tuneless warble while Nickie does a very fair Elvis impersonation. Greta joins in with 'Blue Suede Shoes'. We have one eye on Miss Ivans but she is a sensible old stick and ignores the wind-up, she is not like your average screw. I busily nick bits and pieces of food for May and worry about her release date and the batter. I find I work better with a good worry or two to feed on, I go into auto drive. Nickie is amusing herself by sharing her worries about Sylv – does she, doesn't she love her – so I join her worries to my own and I do a joint worry job. But I find it difficult to worry about Sylv. Her entire mind is locked into her black roots; she measures them daily, hourly even. 'What d'you reckon, Shindig, they getting worse are they?'

She obtains safety razor blades and spends long hours shaving her legs by bevelling the blade and drawing it over the hairs. 'Have a look for us, Shindig, I missed any have I? Just do that bit for us, gel, I can't reach it. Can't let yerself go, can you?'

She gives me an old fashioned look and peers into her two inch square of mirror. 'Look at me teeth! You got any of that tooth paste May bought you? Lucky May don't smoke, intit? My mum sent me a note after church last week, she reckons I ain't half putting it on.' She stands and tightens her belt. 'You reckon I'm getting fat do you? Our Rene and Joan are losing weight, it's that bleeding kitchen that does it.'

She can fret for an hour without ever getting or feeling the need for an answer. Her complete extended family were lifted heisting and now all the little ones are being looked after by the satellites that send frequent missives in about their welfare. I imagine them all in a sort of Fagin's set-up but all dressed extremely smartly with plucked eyebrows. 'In for a clutch re-line aren't I? Read this for us, Shindig, I can't make out our Doreen's writing.' Neither can I but I make out a list of names that I imagine are the kids. I read it out slowly; they are all doing all right apparently.

'What do you reckon to this colour lipstick, doll, do it suit me? I don't half miss my little ones you know.' She gives an emotional sigh. I go back to my book; she is in my cell because I have a radiator which she leans over as she plucks her eyebrows. ''Ere, you don't reckon my mum knows about me and Nickie do you? It would kill her, the shame! Never been none of 'them' in our family.'

With impeccable good sense the prison authorities have put the Sylv family all on different wings, thus half the entire prison population finds itself kept busy smuggling notes from mother to daughter, sister to aunt, niece to . . . and on to infinity. A further industry is involved with getting notes from the male relatives via the men from the Ville who work here in Hollo-way. There are ten of these heart stopping specimens at any one time and a terrible flutter they cause when they come to the kitchen. So, as I say, I don't worry about Sylv.

Tea break and Miss Ivans lets us go out in the yard and

here come the boys. These elegant chaps in their grey dungarees are the reason for most of the primping in the wing. See them as they shuffle along with their ghastly haircuts and prison pallor. Look at the intelligence radiating from their eyes. Hear their charm and wit as they make obscene comments from the sides of their gobs. I'm always overjoyed to see them. Watch Sylv as she lifts her uniform skirt to exhibit her newly shaven legs, see all the girls simper and giggle. Hear big Greta whistle at them and comment on their anatomy.

'Look at the state of that, will ye!' We guffaw and bend over in mirth. 'Would you ever give that houseroom?'

They respond badly to Greta's barracking and the other women come out to be coy, look reproachful. And will you look at us? Here we are in our uniform cotton dresses and big black shoes, some of us with newly won spots on our pallid faces from the unaccustomed amount of starch that we are whacking into ourselves. Hair stringy, greasy from lack of washing yet still all the old hormones are apparently at work, lust lit large in eyes, bodies squirm and contort ... Greta, Nickie and me watch as the bold Sylv simpers her hello wave. But then when did profound repellence ever stop the desire to copulate? Humanity would stop, wouldn't it? Frissons of desire float vibrant in the air. The boys are shepherded away by their own glum screw. And back with us to the kitchen and me to my nice grey batter. Peeling pieces of fish from a mass of lately frozen, Grimsby-boxed cod I am immersed in deepest thought as Miss Ivans comes up behind me; first thing I know is her hand on my shoulder and voice in my earhole:

'That batter doesn't look too good, Green.'

'You nearly give me a heart attack there, Miss! I thought that was you feeling my collar.'

'And you were right.' She pokes at the batter, lifts some with a wooden spoon and lets it drop, desolate, back into the bowl. You sure you did the measurements right, are you?'

'Just like you told me, Miss Ivans, you know me, obedient to a fault.'

She looks at me with her cynical old eye and gives me a tiny shove. 'Get off with you, Green.'

We both know that a horrible revenge will be wreaked by

B wing if I make a fuck-up so I give it a good worry for the next half hour while I prepare the fish and consequently I work with a ferocious speed.

'Here, Shindig! Cop this for us will yer? I've got to go and see the governor.' My hand feels the note and I stuff it in my bra as Miss Ivans calls me. 'Here Green, you can help me with the dry goods for the Christmas cake.' I scuttle over fast with the taste of raisins already in my mouth. I stuff myself with dried fruit and wonder how soon I can escape to the bog to read Sylv's note. I am torn by curiosity, greed and the sight of half a bottle of brandy on the table. The entire kitchen is centred on this, I can feel Greta pulling it magnet-like toward her as I vacillate.

'What size were you thinking of getting before you stop stuffing yourself or haven't you thought about it? Because the rate you're going, you've no chance of getting into your gear when you leave.'

I hadn't even been thinking as I noshed the dried fruit, I'd been in automatic while I watched Greta doing a slippy – tits up to the table, stout red arm outstretched, hand bent to the shape of a half bottle – eyes on Miss Ivans – at least six women staring transfixed, willing her onward ... 'Don't even think about it, McDonald!' Miss Ivan's voice stentorian as she snatches the brandy, walks to the cupboard and locks it away.

She shakes her head sadly. 'Sorry, Miss, I didn't realise I was doing it, can I go to the lav?'

'Yes, go on, McDonald.' She sounds resigned.

'Can I go for a smoke, miss?'

'Yes, Green and when you get back you'd better put the fryer on and give that batter another stir.'

The note, which is from Sylv's husband, is a nasty, greasy, mis-spelled mess, a declaration of love and an appeal for money, so dirty it is barely legible and I could swear it smells of shit – and how else do I think it got out? I almost drop it in an outbreak of fastidiousness and decide I don't want to know any more details of the family Sylv. I wrap the letter in more hard bog roll scrub my hands and Nickie has come up and I see her shadow before she arrives.

'That a letter from her old man?'

I am stuffing it back in my bras, reluctant now I've seen the state of it. 'Yeah, Nickie, you want to see it?'

'No thanks, darling, you seen one you seen them all!' Pulls a face and looks sad. 'What the fuck did Greta think she was up to? She'd have got a sentence out of that if it come off, silly cow.'

'Don't make for serious circumspection, being in here.'

'That's what I tell you, they're idiots those C wingers.' She hands me a roll-up and I bring out my halved matches and we light up.

Back in the kitchen I slurp the fish in the batter and chuck it into the fat with a show of confidence. The first few pieces look like cardboard but after that it fluffs and bubbles and I nick crumbs off it and eat them and it is the best batter I ever made. I put the first few bits into C wing's tray and sort out the biggest for good old B wing and I am filled with relief and joy.

The next time the screw comes for me for a visit I leave the kitchen in high good humour. I got a lot of kudos from Marmalade coming to see me and I sit with a grin welling up on my face. When I see Sid, the grin aborts. I am both confused and disappointed. How did he get a VO for a start? And why is he visiting me? I am full of uneasy fear mixed with curiosity. He approaches the table and smiles one of those smiles that crinkle round the eyes but don't actually involve them; they remain shrewd and piercing even as his voice takes on the oily sound of reassurance. He calls me 'my dear' and my mind goes back to the smooth copper and the quack.

I don't know what to say and busk it with: 'All right, Sid? Nice to see you, how you doing?' He eases himself down onto the chair puffing and blowing like a grampus. I want to make a joke about him losing some weight but I don't. I am waiting for him to tell me what he wants. He must want something or he wouldn't be here.

When Marmalade had visited me everybody looked at him, both surreptitiously and blatantly; with Sid, even the screws look once and then away, fast. I reckon he's dead sinister.

He wants to know about Billy.

'You was off to Brighton were you when you got nicked I hear? Going to see Billy, eh? I got something for him so if you got his address, be handy it would . . .' The end of the sentence gapes a question. I tell him I don't have an address and don't mention the phone number. He eases himself on the chair, puts his elbows on the table then reaches in his pocket and pushes a packet of snout towards me. I remember he doesn't smoke but he brings out a very fancy lighter and lights me up.

'Now, Shindig, I want you to have a good think, see if you can't remember anything Tiger said to you or gave to you to keep for him. He emptied out the cellar recently, didn't he? What happened to the gear? Vera tells me you brought a load of stuff back to the house, is that right?' His eyes are very steady and I don't know what to do with mine, I can feel them tending to slither away from him.

I think of him as somebody I am flogging a couple of bottles of dodgy liquor to and feel my face take on its frank and honest look. 'Yes, that's right. But I dumped most of the stuff.' Said thoughtfully while my mind asks itself how he knows these facts. How close is he to Vera, what's their connection?

'Where did you dump it, Shindig?'

'In the bin, where else?'

He looks at me shrewdly. 'See, old Tiger's left a lot of unfinished business, and somebody's got to clear it up.' He starts to move his bulk into the vertical and tells me that he will get somebody to meet me when I get out and that he'll drive me down to Brighton himself and we can find Billy together. 'Least I can do, eh? Got to help mates when they're in shtouk. Oh and I brought you in a newspaper, the screw said you'll get it this evening, I know how you like to keep in touch, you and Billy.'

He gives a wink that doesn't reassure me. I feel paranoia twitch and spasm into active life as I watch him leave the visiting room well before the end of visiting time.

The screw purloins the packet of fags as she takes me back to the kitchen.

The paper, a *Daily Mirror*, arrives on the wing when I come back from the cocoa round. I look through it with a serious lack of interest – being in here seems to have divorced me from the real world. Behind the world news, towards the back of the paper there is a report that Sid has marked. 'Musician dies in suspicious circumstances', is the header. I read on and Johnny Mason is named, he was found dead in his flat and it is perfectly clear to me that he has been topped. His family declare that he was a good son and that his career was about to take off with him getting a job in the dance band on the Queen Mary. A wife had come forth and spoken highly of his accomplishments and of the loss that his two sons will suffer. I am shocked and scared rigid. Way down in the paper is a report of a certain doctor being struck off the register by the

BMA. This is my first real inkling that whatever I am involved in is heavy duty stuff and that when I get out I must get as far away from London as I possibly can. I can't quite see Sid traipsing up to the nick to give me this for the good of my health and am afraid it is a warning. And why is he so keen to see Billy and how did he know I was on my way to Brighton when I got nicked?

A couple of days after Sid's visit, Vera turns up. She arrives looking gorgeous. I hardly recognise her. She's done something spectacular to her hair and has a full set of slap on. She looks like one of the old French tarts that I drool over in Curzon Street. High heels, straight skirt and fitted jacket.

'Look at you, mate!' I say, so she poses in that daft way, turning one leg outwards one knee in. 'Aren't you the bona palone, darling?' She curtsies then sits on the straight chair. 'Where have you been? Or are you going?'

'Got a lift, didn't I? Old boyfriend of mine just showed up and been pursuing me like the randy old goat he is.' She laughs. 'So how are you, Shindig? Found yerself a bird have you? Bet you're at it like knives in here.'

'Not that bleeding easy is it, V? You can find somebody but having it away is a work of art. Got to be timed like a military operation, hasn't it?'

We natter on in our comfortable way about nothing in particular then I can't resist a small interrogation.

'I want to know about this new geezer. Who? How? When did you meet him?'

She looks a bit evasive. 'Been buzzing around for bleeding donkey's years, hasn't he?'

She takes out a snout, passes me one.

'Sounds like a bluebottle on a dung heap.'

'Charming!' I'm being nasty and I know it.

'Sorry, mate.'

But I'm well annoyed. I definitely don't want anybody in Vera's knickers. And certainly not in the house.

'That's all right, cock, I can afford to be magnanimous can't I? Make allowances for prison neuroses. I see it hasn't affected your appetite anyway.' Archly. She leans over the table, pokes

me with her hand where my waist was until I got into the
kitchen to work. I see a new ring on her finger

'Soon lose that when I get out, no bother.'

'If you say so.'

'So this serious is it, the geezer and you?'

'At my age? Don't be silly. Just an old bleeding mate, intit?
Expect you met him, mate of Tiger's he is.'

She puts her wrinkly hand over mine and I know it's going
to be fine. The brown spots grin up at me reassuring.

'Ted, it is. He knows you from the club. You know him, do
you?'

I can place him but don't let on.

'Expect so, all those white guys look the same to me, mate.
All old, all randy, all repulsive. How is Tiger?'

'Don't know, darling, nobody's seen him have they?'

'Still? That's months, what about Renee? She still off, is
she?'

'Yes, peculiar isn't it? People go missing but they always
turn up, don't they? See if I can't find out, darling.'

'Do you think he's been topped?' I look at her face, it goes
into a wobble.

'Course he hasn't. Why would he be topped? Don't be silly,
Shindig. The nick's getting to you, mate, morbid you're getting.
Expect he's just gone to another town and set up there.'

'At his age? With all his contacts? I doubt that.'

And I do.

'You knew him, didn't you?' I say.

'Yes, course I did, but you knew that, didn't you? Same as
Sid, known him since he was a nipper, haven't I? He wants to
help you, darling, let him.' I want to know how well she knows
him but her face shuts up tight. She's getting fed up with this
line of questioning.

'Did you know Johnny Mason, Vera?' She looks up sharp
as a ferret. 'Because Sid left me a paper when he came in and
apparently Johnny died in mysterious circumstances. That's
usually code for murdered, isn't it? I thought you might have
known him?'

'No, I never knew him and that's for definite.'

Gives an abrupt little motion of her head, terminating.

She lights us both up and changes the subject with a lurch.

'What you going to do about gear when you come out? None of it's going to fit you, is it? Unless you go on a diet, fast.' She chortles, but it sounds false. 'Yes, that's what you need, a fast, fast!' I am diverted.

'I've got some loose stuff, haven't I? And I've got that big coat of Carlotta's, and some shoes. Fuck's sake get me some shoes in, I've got those pink sandals in here.'

'You got a million pair of shoes haven't you, gel. Black patent be nice. And that big skirt and the coat. I'll get them in, dolly.'

'Don't send them in until the last week, they lose them. Heard from Mary, have you?'

'Oh yes, she's delighted with your fall from grace, always knew you'd come to a sticky end, didn't she?'

'Well, it wasn't hard to guess was it? I sometimes think my whole life has been aimed at ending up here.'

Her face changes radically. One of the things I love Vera for is her total spontaneity. Like a kid she is.

'You shouldn't be in here at all if you ask me. Lot of old bollocks this whole case. They're persecuting you to get at that Rooster, I reckon. They ought to go after the real bleeding villains, mate!' Her hands have come over the table to meet mine and now they pat and fondle my hands. Her face is full of affection, her eyes melting with emotion. Is she talking about me? Is she feeling guilty or something?

'I never meant it, V. Just joking, gel.' Now I'm patting her hands and the screw comes up and tells us to keep our hands to ourselves. I make a mock lunge for the screw's arse and she terminates my visit. It was over anyway and well worth the laugh.

After lights out my mind starts to unravel Vera's visit. Why did she look so glamorous? I want my old Vera back, the one with the loose dentures and carpet slippers. It's all unsettling. I know Ted, one of Tiger's least desirable cohorts, a slimeball. I find it hard to think about sex and Vera; bring Ted into the equation and the idea is too repulsive to contemplate. So I don't.

Three days before my release and I am wound up to a tight ball of terror mixed with excitement. Nicky and me have discussed, at length, the first pint, the first taste of freedom, being able to decide when to get up, when to eat. I know I don't want to be met by Sid, and I get a letter from Marmalade telling me that Celeste wants to come along with him to meet me. I still don't know why he's pushing me at Celeste but that kiss was phenomenal and the idea seems agreeable to me.

So, I'm in the kitchen, poncing about with the spud machine when a bird called Edna takes the piss and I chuck a knife at her. To be fair, it could have been a spoon or a fork, or even a potato, it just happens to be a knife because that's what is in my hand at the time. It has no point or blade to speak of and I don't aim it for her heart, I just chuck it at her and it only hits her arm, but all hell breaks loose.

I am up before the governor with Miss Ivans and Edna giving evidence against me and the governor saying that I have an exemplary record in Holloway and that she is disappointed in me, but she docks me three days anyway.

I am accompanied to my cell to fester in solitary gloom. Of course, three days is nothing in the scheme of things, I've had hangovers that have lasted longer. But it feels like an eternity and I'm banned from the kitchen. I wring my withers and even weep until I realise that Sid will not be able to meet me and that is a huge relief.

35 God Bless the Child That's Got Her Own

Coming out the gate at eight twenty in the morning, the speed is what hits me first. Cars appear to threaten me personally. Then there is the cacophony. Both shatter my brain. I know I can't cross the road and I stand paralysed. I am used to the squealing buckets on stone floor, hollow voices of girls at night. Outside, different, faster noises spread sharp glitters in my ears. The everywhere hum of traffic in the background. There is the noise of a zillion human beings just being and moving. The size and the redness of buses lit up like warships, appals me. Taxis, malignant black corvettes dashing fast, jagged, venomous. Discordant colours cut my eyes. Pedestrians scuttling black beetles moving at a canter. I want to dive back inside but it would be strictly against the law, and fatal for paperwork.

Five other women have made their re-emergence into society today and we all stand, like so many spare pricks for a minute or two, then a couple of them join together to walk away. A car takes one and the final one is met by a man who kisses her affectionately and the two of them exit, a single unit along the road.

I had expected the gang to be here, waiting for me. There is no sense to this expectation, I am clear in my mind that Sid won't know what day I am coming out yet I expect in some feeble-minded way that Marmalade and Celeste will be here. They are not and I have twelve and six between me and destitution. I feel tears of self pity prick my lids, I have no provisional plans for my thoughts. All directed toward the ebullience of being released into joy. I feel filleted, empty, sick. Had been elated, had my speech ready in my mouth, my bold swagger ready in my back. I swallow the speech and it chokes me and leaves me emptier than before. My shoulders collapse.

I wait, a few minutes I guess, my sense of time has gone,

along with all my other faculties. I have no watch, I swapped it for tobacco during my last week, who needs a bleeding watch? I'll be out and get another one, won't I? The screws open the gate for the dustbins.

'You still here, Green? Thought you were having a reception committee, way you told it!' She laughs, relishing it.

'Get done for loitering if you don't get off out of it, mate.' The bin men laugh along with her.

'You must be treating them too well!' says one of the men, they all laugh.

'Ain't you got no home to go to?' More loud laughter.

I take my sad carcass down the hill, but smartly, following the way the other two women went. Peeled, all my skin has been folded back and every sound and motion of the air is burning me. My clothes are too tight round my waist and the buttons bulge out. The new gear either didn't arrived or the bastard screws have kept it for badness. I expect it is sitting in a cubbyhole somewhere. My flimsy coat flutters out and silly summer sandals, pale on wet grey pavement, are idiotic. I can smell fear on myself when I pull my coat tight, and sweat, my deodorant ran out three days ago.

I realise that it was all lies; Marmalade had no intention of coming to meet me. Self-pity washes them away with a river of maudlin grief. I bite my lip.

The black taxi lumbers along beside me and I am terrified it might be Sid.

I hear Frantic before I see her: 'Fuck me gently, gel, you ain't alf put it on!' She follows this up with a shriek of laughter. I have stopped and am standing, gormless, when she leaps out and grabs me. 'Wake up, sunshine! I come to meet yer! You going to get in or what?'

I am delighted in a shocked sort of way and I give her a hug, she tenses up and I let go fast and get in the taxi. 'All right, Stan, take us up west then.'

'Welcome out, mate!' says Stan and he turns round to look at me and give me a wink.

'Meet Uncle Stan,' says Frantic,

'Glad to meet you, Stan!' I say and am horribly aware of my unsuitable gear.

'He's donating his services this morning 'cos he owes me

one, and now you owe me one.' She gives a slow wink. 'A big one.' And I remember how dangerous she is.

'I must go home and change, have a bath, see Vera.'

'Hang about, mate, we got some talking to do. I thought a nice big fry-up would be in order. The Archer Street café do yer?' She bungs me a fag and we light up.

London presses outside the window, full tilt it swaggers by, all movement, all noise. I lean back in the seat and take a lungful of smoke and think I am getting back to reality.

Inside, the last few days, I'd planned it all pretty comprehensively. I'd spend some time with V, drink tea, have several baths, three at least, retire to my own room, play records and spread all my books open around me. I would soak myself in isolation and words. Blitz my soul in Bessie, soak my mind in Steinbeck. Zonk out with Zola. Just be me, with nobody telling me or asking me or being with me. I'd work through my clothes seeing what fits, try on all eighteen pairs of shoes one after the other. I'd stalk in my highest heels and prance in my mules. All alone. The noise my own noise, the scent my own scent. My own sheets, my own bath oil, mostly though, my own books and my own space. Alone. Evening time, I'd get V to do a comb up for me, backcomb and loop my hair into a rough approximation of a Grecian. I'd spend at least an hour on my slap, it would be a confection of Lancome and Arden topped off with the longest lashes and blackest kohl I can find in my box of tricks. The palest lipstick and no powder, just basic sheen. Then, out, all alone with the world all around me, air on my skin, sounds buffeting my ears but none of it anything to do with me, alone to watch and listen and be. I'd shoot up west to the pub for my first pint of Guinness. Paddy would put the shamrock on it and I'd look at the beauty of it, carry it, carefully, like a new born child, to a table by myself. I'd insert my tongue into it just to appreciate the flavour, the texture, the substance of it. I'd dip and diddle then drink it so slowly I'd hardly know if it was out or in. It would flow into my throat and coat the sides and sink down slow and easy and rest in my belly gentle and strong. The thought would make me gasp with pleasure every time I got to this particular part of my scenario. The second pint I'd use a different method, drinking half of it in one mouthful, savouring its slither down, the weight of it bulging inside. The second half, I would hold up to appraise the white foam on the sides of the glass, hardly moving on its way down to the remaining black beauty, then: every last molecule, each bubble would get my personal attention. I could taste it as I thought about it. Then I'd gull it like there's no tomorrow – and there might not be, as far as I'm concerned. Just let it get that far and I'd be a happy woman. But no, not enough. I'd shoot up to the nosh bar and get me a salt beef sandwich with a pickled cucumber. I'd ask for extra fat, not enough people appreciate beef fat – I'd kill for it. The guy would feed it to me, watch me eat it, delighted. Make his day it would. Then I'd go and capture Nifty or Slim, a safe cock. I'd like to find something new but there's always the danger of it not coming up to par, so I'll stick with a dick I know for tonight. Thank god I've got a few bob stashed in the house.

What's that they say about the best laid plans? Now Frantic tells me that Vera doesn't want me back there.

'State of your boat race, darling!' I can feel my face rigid with shock. I can't believe this.

'Vera was great last visit.'

'There's been a lot of changes since you were last at her'n. I'm not welcome no more.'

I remember that she was never all that welcome but Vera must have said something radical to bring it to Frantic's awareness.

'I went round to say I was going to pick you up and bring you home and she said she don't want you there no more, but she's hanging on to your gear and we can go and get it.'

'Marmalade and Celeste were supposed to be meeting me and big Sid.'

Frantic looks alarmed for a moment but Stan says something about a short cut and the moment passes.

'That Celeste was after me, mate. I told her straight: I don't sip from the furry cup, missis!' I try to imagine Celeste's face and laugh for the first time since I came out. Frantic joins in and we arrive at one of the best greasy spoons in London giggling.

'Thanks, Stan! Much appreciated,' I say.

'How did you know I was coming out today?' is the first thing I ask when we sit down and have our lovely orange tea in front of us, I put three spoons of sugar into it, in the nick you can choose either to have your mean ration of sugar on the porridge or in the tea. I had always chosen the porridge option, now the syrupy tea delights my taste buds and they near drown in bliss.

'And what's in it for you?' she laughs. 'O ye of little faith, gel! Me auntie went to visit our Margie and she told me your new release date. They all liked you, my family – even Auntie Rose.' I am pleased about this though I can't think why.

'So you'll be all right on your next sentence.' I look up, shocked and she laughs.

'We've always got somebody in Holloway, and if we haven't we got more than enough influence with a couple of screws.' She fills her fork, carries it to her mouth and talks through it, she doesn't look at me as she speaks.

'Did you say Sid was going to meet you?'

'Yes, he came and visited me. He said he'd drive me to Brighton to see BB. Don't reckon BB would be too keen on that. He brought a newspaper for me, a report of Johnny Mason being found dead under suspicious circumstances.'

'I wasn't going to tell you about that, not straight away. Tell you what, mate, I reckon you better keep out of Sid's way.' She looks seriously shifty.

She takes my hand and pushes a couple of quid in it.

'There yer go, dolly.' I feel my gob, hanging, amazed, so startled out of place I can't close it to speak.

'That's all right, gel.' She answers before I can thank her. Her eyes are sharp, like a fast rat on coke.

'Meet old Greta did yer?'

'Greta the spud barber?'

'That's the one, darling. Fucking amazing, isn't she? Heard you got in the kitchen, who was that down to?'

'Nickie.'

'She back in is she? Was Johnnie in?'

'Which Johnnie? Skinny little Johnnie or big Johnnie?'

'Johnnie the knife.'

'Johnnie the knife? No, never met her. Blonde Johnnie was

in when I got there but she got out after a couple of weeks, I got her place in the kitchen, didn't I?'

'Miss Ivans still in there, is she?'

'Yeah, she's all right isn't she?' Frantic does one of those hand moves that means yes and no. I look over at her and she looks away.

'You heard anything about Tiger, Fran?'

'Not a dickey, mate. Weird, intit? And your vile mate, Renee hasn't been seen at all. I know she's done a runner, like but they always come back, don't they? Even if they're doing well.'

'Specially if they're doing well, they come back to gloat,' I say, and Frantic adds;

'And if they're doing badly they creep back and you hear about it on the grapevine, weeks later.'

'Yeah, seen shopping in East Ham, former godfather with a shopping bag full of bacon bits and reject veggies,' I say. 'And where would she go to get all that diabolical schmutter if not the East End?' I add.

'True.'

'Still working down Tiger's club are you, Fran?' Her face shuts down.

'Never worked down there did I, except the odd day. But if you want your old job back it could be arranged.' She puffs up a bit with the importance of being a minor star in the firmament of the criminal classes.

'So who you shagging then, Fran?'

'Nose ointment,' is all she says and makes the gesture of fuck off and mind your own business, to which there is no known answer.

'What's all this about Sid?' I ask.

She looks at me as if she's deciding whether or not and how much to tell me. Like she's tailoring it in her mind.

'Well, Shindig, the first thing you got to know is it's bleeding war up west now. The old bosses have been made redundant like.' She gives a sharp grunt of laughter. 'There's been a takeover by new, younger and much harder people. You don't even want to know about them, darling. Tiger was big mates with the old lot but he let them down too. He got away with a lot of liberties because they all went back years. He robbed them, see. He was given things to look after and he flogged them, he was supposed to be collecting money and keeping it for them, in the bank, but he was spending it, on the horses mostly. So Sid, who is well in there with the new lot, must suspect that Tiger give you something to keep for him. Something valuable.' Her eyes probe my face and I try to keep it blank.

'So do you think Tiger's dead?' I can hardly get the final word out.

'I don't know, mate, but Renee took off with one of the new lot. And most of his mates are well in with them too. Or Sid might think you got a record of what Tiger was up to and that might drop him in it.' The implications of all this are worse than alarming, they terrify me.

'So I'm in a lose lose situation then?'

'You could say that, yes,' she laughs a short bark. 'Never mind, gel you got me to help and advise you haven't you?'

'Yes, aren't I the lucky girl.'

My brain scuttles through all the permutations and comes up with nothing useful.

I might as well hear it all, though I can guess.

'So what about Johnny Mason?' Frantic shrugs.

'He was on the fiddle too and he got on the wrong side of somebody or other. I reckon he was topped as an example.'

'And what about you, Frannie?'

'I'm all right, mate, I'm well in there. And Jimmy's in with the new lot, he won't let anything happen to me.'

'He still in the frame, is he?' She winks and smirks.

'He is but I wouldn't mind some back up info from you like, can never be too careful can you?'

'And Sid? What position has he got in the new order?'

'Very close to the top, gel, so I reckon best thing you can do is disappear, for now anyway. I'll sort it for you if you like.' She lights a fag.

'Oh and Dixon has retired on full pension and Jack's on leave. In fact the law seems to have had a big clear out too, enema time at the old corral, eh?'

'Is there a connection, Frannie?' She shrugs and gives a guileless smile.

It has only taken a few minutes for her to give me her take

on the changes but it feels like a tectonic plate job to me and I am definitely running scared.

Plus I don't know how much truth there is in any of this.

'Not to worry eh, gel?' she says and we both laugh though mine is near hysteria.

I feel filthy dirty and just want a bath, a change of kit and my own drum back. I need some peace to think. I am convinced that if I go back to Vera's on my own she will let me stay. I also realise that I have to retrieve the suitcase that I put up in the loft, fast.

'Want me to come with yer to Vera's put in a good word like?' says Frantic when I tell her.

'No thanks, mate.' Her eek drops a bit but she hasn't given up.

'Got a lot of stuff there, have yer?'

'Quite a bit, yeah?'

'You want to get it out quick, wouldn't trust that fucking Ted a bleeding inch, you can drive can't you?'

'Yeah course I can, all those months with Rooster. Expert, aren't I?'

'Could get a motor, go and get it. All in one go like.'

'And where the fuck would I take it?'

Soon as the words hit the air I realise it's an error. Her evil eye gleams out, busy with ideas, schemes and dreadful plans.

'Haven't you got a gaff to go to then?' Three seconds top whack it takes. 'I know just the place, cheap, cheerful and charming, just off Latimer Road. One of my aunties just happens to have a spare room.'

'No ta, Fran. Might be going to Brighton, mightn't I. Or Morocco.'

'Get you! Bleeding foreign parts, eh?'

'Never know do you?'

'Your mate Colette was back, she was asking about you. She give me a phone number for you. Looked brilliant she did. Clean and lively, looked like she's off that muck to me.'

I am feeling better now I've decided that Vera will have me back, everything seems possible, except, of course, living with Frantic's auntie. That will always be a no, no and now I begin to remember the disadvantages of Frantic's friendship.

Frantic pays the bill and we stand outside

I look around and just breathe in the fumes.

Warms my heart.

Soho hasn't missed me, still the same raucous old baggage as ever.

She throbs away, we both do.

I want to get some decent clobber on and get myself a nice shlong. If I'm about to be topped by Sid I might as well fit in as much joy as possible.

Vera is home when I hit the house. Seems shocked to see me rather than pleased. She drops her mug of tea when I walk into the kitchen.

'How'd you get in, darling?'

'Got my keys, haven't I? I knocked but you didn't answer.' I give her a hug but instead of her eyes tearing up, she looks at me, hard. I try a look of reproach, deep sadness in my eyes. Should work, but she turns away.

I bend to pick up the broken china. 'I'm sorry, darling, your room's just as you left it but you can't stay no more. It's Ted, he don't want you here, do he?' says Vera.

'Why's that then? And since when do you do what some bloke tells you?'

'It's not a matter of doing what some bloke tells me. I got lonely after you and Victoria went, didn't I? Then Ted come round to do some work in the kitchen, and . . .'

'And got his feet under the table.'

'Yes, mate, you got it in one, and it's dead handy, pays rent, buys nosh. Farts in bed, usual man stuff.'

'Christ, Vera, you're a little bit shallow aren't you?'

'Hope so, gel, my age you can't afford depth and constancy, no time, darling.'

'I very nearly fancied you, mate,' I say, pushing it.

'I'm not surprised, darling, I'm having me third shot at temptress.' Then she laughs, mouth wide revealing more pink plastic than enough.

'Glad you never let my room, V, but why?'

'Oh, Ted wouldn't let me, said leave it as it was until you come back.'

I take this in and digest it. It swells like a malignant lump. Festers in my bonce.

'How long has he been here, V?'

'Just after you went down, gel. I never told you because you never needed to know. Hadn't seen him for years and he turns up at the pub, sniffing round. Likes you he does, wanted to go in and clean your room up but I says no, let her do that for herself, she's lazy enough without you encouraging her.'

'So nobody's been in there then?'

'Except me.'

Then I fall in.

'Why was he going to clean it up if I wasn't coming back anyway?'

Vera looks irritated.

'You was, wasn't you? Then we talked it over and decided we'd do up the house and get different people in. I told you months ago and this last little set-to decided me. Scared me something rotten it did, bleeding drug squad all over the place. Getting too old for all that nonsense with the law.'

'Why'd you keep the room for me then?' I'm starting to get windy. Sounds to me like good old Ted has been pulling her strings something rotten. I get this nasty insight that he moved in just to get at my room. But that makes no sense, all he had to do was break in and with the kind of mates he's got he'd have had no bother. My gut gets this nasty significant feeling, all by itself it starts making shit links.

She looks at me sideways on, a look of total disparagement, continues: 'Sweetheart, I don't care about his bleeding motives, do I? If he fucks off tomorrow I'll be no worse off than before. Mary would have come down otherwise.'

She laughs at me.

'He takes me out, he's company.'

'We used to go out, didn't we?' Her face finally takes on the desired sentimental look, but she scrubs it in seconds.

'And we will again, sweetheart. He's not here all the time and just because you don't live here no more don't mean we can't be mates' do it?' She stands up.

'I changed the lock on your door, darling, put a padlock and hasp on the outside. No telling who might want to get in there. Frannie was round once or twice, and you know her.'

'Seen her today, didn't I? Gave me two quid.'

Vera looks more surprised then I've ever seen her, including all the business with Victoria.

'You want to watch that, mate!'

'I was touched.'

'And you can bet your balls you will be again, darling, touched for two hundred per cent whatever she give you.' She nods with great assurance and I'm sure she's right.

'Come on then, gel, we'll go and have a look at yer room.' She trundles up the stairs, wheezing a bit.

Inside, the room smells weird. It's cleaner than I remember but it smells stale. Vera goes over to the window, opens it, several ancient feathers flake off, stiff. Stuck to the bottom of the sash window. I go over and pick them off. Looks unbelievably shabby. Stains of all kinds on the carpet.

'Want to sort it out on yer own, do you?'

'Please, darling. Is Ted around, V?'

'No, he never come back last night, did he?'

'That normal for him, is it?'

'Yeah, got into a game or something I expect.' She looks round the room. 'I'll leave you to it then, dolly. Come down when you're ready. Got a gaff yet, have yer? Can leave your books and gear until the end of the week, but I'd sort your papers and stuff out now.'

'Might take longer than a week, mate.'

'Won't have to, dolly. No use you thinking I'll weaken 'cos I bleeding won't!' She laughs. Which I take to mean I'm in with a chance, the insane optimist is back in my mind, living alongside a very scared bird. Normal.

'Can I have a bath, Vera? And change my clobber?'

'Go on then but don't take too long, Ted will be back.'

Now, back in my old room alone at last as they say, I look for my bread, three stashes, all present and correct. I get a small lump of dope from inside the back of the alarm clock. I roll a tiny joint, breathe it in gently, sweetly. It has lost a lot of its potency but it's still nice charge. Cheered by this, I realise I don't need anybody. I'll sling my hook, get a new drum. Won't tell anybody where I am. Begin again.

I get the suitcase down first. Have a shufti in it and get my passport from the kitchen cabinet and shove it down the side.

The geyser worked first time but though I have the door

bolted the thought of Ted coming back has me in and out the bath in record time, but it's still bliss to be clean. I dress carefully. I run my hands over my nylon legs, sniff the leather of a handbag, spray myself with toilet water by Jean Patou and want to collapse.

Instead, I stuff most of my gear in a big trunk that Berry and me bought in Shepherds Bush. The thought of Ted the Ferret poking about in my gear feels well intrusive. I might see if I can't go down and stay with BB but I need a few days rest and recuperation first. Yeah man, good to be back. I'll have a look in the tobacconist's window today. Work my way through the 'No Coloureds no Irish no dogs' adverts for rooms. Find one that takes anybody, absentee landlord preferred, pay a bit extra. Yeah. Feeling chuffed now. Get a totally new pad see how long it takes Frantic to find me. I smile to myself. My mind is busy with all this while I pack papers into the suitcase, photos and treasures. Stuff I forgot I had all goes in with a couple of books. I lock it. Yes, getting out of Vera's is favourite; the law won't know where I am, either.

When the knock on the door comes I think it's Vera although knocking is hardly her style. Ted the Ferret moves swiftly and furtively in before I get to the door.

'All right, darling?' He grins, a mixture of slyness and subtle threat. He stands and looks at me as I go back to stuffing shoes down the side of the trunk His eyes are all over the place and his body is never still. Always a nervous jerk here, a twitch there. I never noticed any of this when he was down Tiger's, the geezers all blurred into one undesirable nuisance when I was behind the bar. Now, alone, he seems distinctly twitchy.

'What do you want, Ted?'

'See I got Vera to keep yer room for yer?'

'Yeah, so you did.'

'Well, I know what it's like when you come out to nothing and all yer gear's gone.'

He'll get to the point soon. I stand and look at him. He offers me a fag. I light up.

'Heard anything from Tiger have you, dolly?' Looks at me

and I know that Tiger is dead. Something about the way he looks and speaks. I'm certain.

'Thought he'd done a runner. That right, is it?' My voice is shaky. It feels as if somebody is squeezing my windpipe from way down low in my solar plexus.

'That's what I heard dear, but you never know, do you? Very fond of you was Tiger, thought he might of bin in touch. Written to you?'

He looks profoundly uncomfortable now. I don't help him.

'Never told you nothing like? Cos he left a lot of unfinished business behind him.'

'What sort of unfinished business?' He shrugs. He looks harder now, more fly. Dreadful shrewdness gleams in his eyes, also impatience.

'You know better than to ask that, sweetheart.' I look at him steadily.

'Listen, darling, you don't want to know.' Holds his finger up beside his nose.

'Have a little think, darling, did he give you any papers, anything like that?'

Now he's downright menacing, he's moved into my space. Looks at the suitcase. Breathes into my face.

I step back. He follows so his breath is still in my face.

'Don't know what you're on about, Ted.' I try to push past him and get at the suitcase.

'Think we better have a shufti round the gaff, don't you, gel?' Vera says from close behind me, I never heard her come in the room. My jaw feels like it's got a stone weight hanging on it pulling my face out of shape.

'You look like you lost a dollar found a sixpence. That's life, gel,' says Vera. 'Better have a look round for ourselves, see if you overlooked anything, Shindig. See, what we need is a guided tour, we need you to point out the significance of what we're looking for.' She barges past me aiming for the case. Looks me in the face.

'See, Tiger owed a lot of money out. Ted and me thought he might have sent you something. A left luggage ticket, pawn tickets, something like that.'

'What do you mean "Owed"?'

'What?' says V.

'You said owed, like he's dead or something.

'Not as far as I know he's not dead,' says Ted. And now he's steady as a rock.

'And why would he send me his stuff?'

'Because you're the only cunt dozy enough not to realise he's using you,' says Ted. He's really getting on my tits now.

'What do you think he was doing when he got you putting on all those bets for him?' He moves in on me. 'Paying money over to half the West End, trotting about with envelopes all over the place, what the fuck do you think you was doing?'

I have no idea what they're on about. Half the time with Tiger I never knew and I'm no wiser now.

'She don't know what she knows, Ted. She needs to sit down and work it out,' says Vera and she moves towards me, dead sinister. A new and nasty Vera pushes me down in the chair. I stand up again.

'Look, I'm off, I don't know what you're talking about, too naïve no doubt and I'm not staying here for the third degree.'

I lift the suitcase but Vera holds on to it.

'Can't let you do that, sweetheart,' she says. She gets hold of the handle and so do I. Our hands touch.

'Look, Vera I don't know what this is all about, if I did I'd tell you. I got fuckall from Tiger in the way of papers, you been here while I was in the nick so I'm sure you got all my mail. Lets just stop all this nonsense and I'll leave, eh? Thanks for visiting me in Holloway, Vera.' I pull at the handle. She doesn't let go and her chin goes into determination. Ted now enters the fray.

'Sit down, darling.' He shoves me and I fall into the chair again. The two of them stand over me looking menacing.

It's like being threatened by your grandparents. I look at them and laugh.

'You got to be joking. What you going to do? Keep me here against my will?' I laugh hysterically and Vera whacks me one in the mush.

'You cheeky little cunt, I been dying to do that for months.'

Ted laughs. 'Well, if she don't behave herself you might be called upon to do a lot more of that, Vera.'

This is a fucking nightmare. My lip is bleeding, I can feel blood trickling down my chin.

'Better go and get on the blower, V. I told you this wouldn't work. Tell him it's not working, he can get over here himself. I told you we should have got a phone put in.'

'Don't start, Teddys. She just needs a bit of inducement. I'll go down the phone and he'll be up here in minutes. I'm sure she'll respond well to a bit of encouragement.' She gives me this really nasty smile and looks more pleased with herself than I've ever seen her.

Now I'm scared. Icy nastiness seeps up from my gut, grabs my heart and squeezes, hard.

I got to get out before anybody else turns up. Vera goes downstairs and I hear Frantic's voice calling up.

'You up there, gel? I got the car. Thanks, Vera.'

She comes through the door like a train, I grab the suitcase and before Ted can move we are out the door, down the stairs. We charge past Vera and into a Morris van before she can stop us. Frantic has us away in seconds, clunking in first gear all the way to the Grove. Vera stands in the roadway waving her arms about, and then Ted joins her.

'Never knew I could drive did you, mate? What happened to the gob, darling?'

I've blotted my mouth but can feel it's bleeding. She stops the car by whacking her foot on the brake, clutch control doesn't figure so we shudder to a halt like a camel on heat.

'Vera only belted me one, didn't she?'

'You're joking. What she do? Hit you with her handbag?' She hoots a long, convoluted giggle that becomes a cough as she lights up.

'You'd better drive, mate.' Slithers out from under the wheel. 'Soon get the hang of it I will. You can show me one afternoon; can't be hard, all the coons can do it. Got the van off of Gerry, told her I was moving you.'

All the whys and wherefores come into my mind, but my relief to be away is so profound that I don't say a dickey. Frantic looks sidelong at me.

'I got you that gaff with me auntie, darling, knew you wouldn't be able to stay in Vera's with Ted. What happened, did he grope yer and Vera caught him? Can't keep his hands to himself can he? Dirty old git.' She nods to herself like I've confirmed what she said.

'Yes, one day down Tiger's he got me in a corner, I kneed him didn't I?' she says.

'Never tried it on with me down there, did he?' I say.

'You complaining, gel?' She laughs. 'You was under Tiger's wing, wasn't you? All scared of him, wasn't they? Din't you know that? 'Til the last couple months before he went. He had a lot of pull, old Tiger, until he lost it.'

'I never realised.'

'Don't bleeding believe you, mate. You got to be the most naïve cunt in the world. Couldn't make you up, nobody would believe you. Anyway, you're better off out of it. Right, gel, to Latimer Road. Don't spare the horses,' she chortles, drags comprehensively on her fag and slides down the seat

'Fucking bow and arrow country down there, Frannie. The heart of Teddy Boy land.'

'You'll be all right long as you don't bring none of yer nig nog mates home, gel,' she laughs.

Don't fancy staying down there one bit but right now I'm glad to be on the move, anywhere. Don't begin to understand why she's so keen to get me out of Vera's way. Questions fester deep in my mind, sending up querulous spurts that have no answers. I am knackered, I didn't sleep at all last night, pre-release nerves had me excited and worried to the extent that kip was out of the question.

When we get to Auntie's and she shows me a bed, I can hardly restrain myself from instant sleep and I am pleased to crash immediately. The chasing dream has now elevated Vera to chief pursuer assisted by Ted who has several pairs of hands – all grasping towards me, all clasping and reaching damply while I run away with Frantic transformed into a huge baby that weighs a ton, in a bassinet. I wake up to find myself wound tight inside a blanket roll with the case in the bed with me. Auntie is by the bed with a cup of tea.

'Want a cuppa, mate? You always take your luggage to bed? Our Frances tells me you been having a rough time of it.

Don't expect this as a regular part of the service will you?' She exits briskly and I look round the room. There are teddy bears on the cupboard door and toys on the top of the wardrobe. The house is buzzing. Radio, television and records all play their part in the cacophony, along with loud voices arguing. I lie there contemplating my future. Takes all of five seconds so I start on the recent past. Look for indications of Vera's treachery earlier in our friendship. Which wasn't a friendship at all. And what about bleeding Frantic? Now she's got me in her home territory I'm trapped. And what about Tiger? Earlier on I was sure he was dead, now I don't know.

The door flies open and Auntie is back. 'Want some dinner, do yer? On the table in five minutes.'

She's gone again, a scrawny woman with a face like a humorous bloodhound. No argument. I get up and look for my shoes which are all I removed before I went to bed. Not a sign of them. I poke under the bed, not a shoe in sight. Paranoia has been lurking since I opened my eyes and now it is rampant. Obviously Frantic has nicked my shoes so I can't escape. I also realise that I have lost all my shoes along with all my other gear at Vera's in my trunk.

There is a bang on the door: 'Dinner's up!'

I mutter my OK and stuff the suitcase under the bed.

There are six of us round the table, all faces to the trough, all quiet. The food is excellent. Shepherds pie of rare quality. I am surprised at how hungry I am. Either nobody notices my stockinged feet or they don't care. It's got to be a Frantic confiscation job. The conversation gradually builds up, a mixture of banter and serious dissent but all good humoured stuff. I sink into myself, ignore it all. I wonder where Frantic is but don't put too much energy into it, I am happy to stuff my face and be cool. Someone asks, your name really Shindig and how did you get it? They are all looking at me, expectantly.

Trapped, I tell them about the geezer in the club which brings the conversation round to Tiger. Auntie knew him well when she was young. Used to work the markets, he did, with one of her aunts. Was a good looking man when he was young they say, the older ones. Like Max Miller, fast on the uptake.

Too fly for his own good, says the man of the house. And round it goes while we eat spotted Dick with custard and have large cups of brown tea. It feels as if a person could be absorbed into this crowd, no trouble at all. Get lost in it, sink into the family and become part of the organism.

Then a youth comes in with full Ted regalia, shuffles his shoulders sideways, then lifts each one in turn. He does a twirl and they all cheer. Looking good, Vince, they say and laugh when he tells them he's going to give the coons what for tonight. He relates how he chased a couple of them last night. 'Yeah, we'll get them out, those bastards.' He looks round the admiring faces.

'Nobody asked them to come down here did they? Dirty bastards,' says a young boy. Auntie hushes them up, looking at me.

'We got a mate of Frances staying a few days,' she says brightly and Vince looks keenly at me. I feel queasy. I know the face, he's one of the geezers took the piss out of me and Berry on our way to the Mapleton one night and I am sure he must remember me. I smile at him but my heart's not in it.

'All right, Vince,' I say. Look him straight in the eye, not a glimmer. Expect we all look the same to him, us nigger lovers. Teds all look similar to me, but then they wear a kind of uniform for that purpose I guess. Don't often find myself this close to a Ted and now I look at the velvet collar and cuffs; he preens, does that thing where he grins at his public, head to one side then up straight, looks me in the eye:

'You'll have to come out with us one night, darling.' The family all grin, that's our boy, said without words.

'Yeah, you never know your luck, Vince,' I say. Auntie laughs. And I ask if I can wash up. The young boy, the cheeky one, says he'll dry and the family tell me I got a friend for life in Auntie. Lots of raucous stuff about the boy offering to help me and telling Vince he'll have to watch it. It's like I have been here for weeks.

We chat in the scullery with the copper and mangle, he gets me a pair of slippers. When the phone rings I am startled. Not the sort of gaff to have a blower. The boy answers it, calls the older man who speaks into the receiver like a B movie actor, scarcely moves his lips. Tells somebody that it's all right, rings off. Looks well dodgy but smiles at me and leaves.

'Think I could use the phone do you, Terry?' I ask the youngster, he flushes up, looks swiftly over his shoulder.

'If you're quick.'

I get BB's work number and ring it fast before anybody comes in the room. It rings several times, I pray to God he's there. At last his voice sings out across the miles:

'Bona days and happy nights café. Bonita Barbarossa polariing!'

'That you BB?'

'Course it is.' His voice goes shrill. 'Shindig, is that you sweetie? Where are you? Angelo is here, he says that they're after you, who ever they are. Get out *now*. Come here immediately, you are in danger, sweetie. Angelo is terrified, apparently. That Ted cut up rough with him, got really heavy and Vera's in with him so do be careful, sweetie.' I want to explain about my shoes but he talks over me.

He gives me the address carefully and I hope it sticks in my slippery brain.

'Get down here, girl.' I put the phone down as Auntie comes into the room.

'That Frances was it?' I say it was and she nods. 'Loves the blower does Frances. Got it put in for us, din't she. On her way back is she?'

'I think so, yes. I'm off to see her now.' I pick up my bag and make for the door.

You're not going with those things on your feet are you? Get the lady her shoes, Tel,' she orders the young boy. 'Did you clean them like I told you; he does all the shoes, our Tel. See you later will we, darling?'

He gets my freshly polished shoes, gives them to me.

'Yes, I'll catch up with Franny. And thanks for the dinner.'

The boy walks out with me. He must know it wasn't Frantic on the blower but all he says is, 'I'll walk you to the station, mate, can be a bit dodgy round here fer strangers.' He takes the case from my hand and carries it.

On the corner by the station, several Teds are preening and stretching like so many deformed swans. Vince is among them, he separates himself from the rest, pushing himself away from the wall until he stands in front of me.

'Changed yer mind have yer, gal? Going to come out with me are yer?' He puts his fag out and flicks it past me with his thumb to the kerb.

'In a hurry, in't she? Got to meet our Frances, hasn't she?' Tel ushers me into the station.

He's gone before I can say goodbye, leaving the case beside me.

On the tube I write BB's address on a fag packet along with Colette's phone number.

37 Done Changed My Way of Living

This time I make it through Victoria and on to the Brighton train. I watch London mutate and deteriorate from city into suburbs, from pebbledash houses that remind me of home, into scruffy countryside and finally into fields. I retreat to the bar. The entire joint seems to be full of bookies clerks, spivs and undesirables. Like Tiger's it is. I create a small stir and feel at home until I think of my precarious position at the moment. Secrecy and 'Brighton Rock' and Pinkie are in the front of my mind as I order a beer. I slither back to the carriage keeping my head down. I can feel myself getting excited at the thought of the sea. Like when I was a little kid. I know it's not cool but I am filled with idiotic joy at the thought of that mass of water moving itself about. I fancy I can smell salt.

When the train slides in I wait until most of the passengers have gone before I get off. I have no idea where to go. I look to see if BB is around but as he didn't know what train I was on, I'm not optimistic. I rummage in my handbag for the address. Past the ticket man looking for a taxi sign. BB is skulking by the door, he gestures for me to join him.

One finger on his lips, a shushing.

'Sweetie!' a sibilant hiss. Angelo has manifested in an ancient van. He snatches the suitcase. 'Get in!' and I do, followed by BB. He seems to be making the very most of the drama. I giggle hysterically and BB pinches me. We are off. Angelo is driving and the three of us squeeze into the front.

Angelo had caught Ted the Ferret going through his gear and when he complained, Ted had threatened him. He had collected all his gear while the two of them were out and got on a train down here. I told them about Vera whacking me one.

'You want to be more careful who you mix with, sweetie,' says BB.

'I never suspected old V of violent tendencies. Can we go and look at the sea, BB?'

'You are joking!'

'No, I haven't seen the sea for years. I need something to perk me up.'

'Oh, if you say so.' He sounds petulant and more shrill than he was in London.

Angelo drives to the sea. We stop and look at the phosphorescence and listen to the pebbles on the beach dragging back and forth. We are all quiet for a few minutes. BB speaks:

'What about your books, Shindig? Have you left them behind? And the poster of Nasser?' I tell him about the trunk that I left in the middle of my room. But most of my books were still on the shelves with my records and some pictures. It hadn't occurred to me that I wouldn't be able to go back and get them any time. Not until Ted came in.

'I brought all the photographs though and loads of papers. That's what Ted and Vera seemed to be after so we must go through them. All my clothes and shoes are in the trunk.'

'You can replace them, sweetie, nothing could replace you.' He touches me and I squeeze his hand.

We are on the prom while Angelo is throwing pebbles into the sea.

'Wonder why they wanted Angelo's gear?'

'Obviously they have no idea what they're looking for and are just casting around for anything that looks like it has a connection, but a connection with what?'

'Tiger, he's the connection. I think he's dead, you know, BB.' My voice is leaden.

'Why do you say that?'

I shrug. He turns abruptly. In the dark his face looks white and gallant and fine. Angelo comes back to us.

'I am very glad you have come here, Sheendeeg. You will be safe with us.' He grins. 'We will go home, yes?' He still says the word 'Home' like homme but he does it on purpose now. I laugh and we all get in the van.

'Didn't know you could drive, Angelo.' He shrugs elegantly like driving is a natural accomplishment.

The flat is bare and elegant. I have a room with a mattress and a chair. The main room is heated by a coal fire that is alight and we huddle round it. We have emptied the contents of the suitcase on the floor in the centre and now we all seem to have drawn back, appalled by the prospect. Angelo dives in first and looks at the photos one by one, making small noises of appreciation or disparagement. 'Oh no, no, no. The riah is terrible!' or 'This is bona, darling!' Good fun but BB gets into serious appraisal straight away.

'Pawn tickets or left luggage tickets is what Ted was after,' I say and BB nods. 'Clues.'

'But it's not going to be in my gear, is it? We need to look through Tiger's stuff. I put a lot of his papers from the club in here, the ones that looked important. But they just look like receipts and records now.'

'They must think he bunged you something before he went, and you, being less astute than the average bird didn't notice.'

I collapse back and look at the photos. I have no idea where most of them came from. Occurs to me that some of these must come from Victoria's stuff. I poke in deeper and realise that the vast majority of bits and pieces have nothing to do with me.

'Why didn't they just dive in and search the gaff while I was inside?'

'Been wondering about that, sweetie. Must be something only you would recognise. Do you think?'

'I haven't a clue, darling. Unless they think I know something significant.'

'What, and they're prepared to get it out of you by any means?' His voice sinks on the last few words.

I try to remember if Tiger gave me anything significant but I can't. Not that he never gave me anything, more that he often shoved things my way, bits and pieces that I dumped as soon as possible mostly.

'I think this is a dead loss, BB,' I say. Angelo nods, stands, stretches. Does a few steps. High kicks.

'Have you got work down here, Angelo?'

'Nante, but I'm helping in the café, I'm learning polari and flirting with all the customers.'

'Using his natural talents.'

'Sounds fun. Can I work there too?'

'Oh yes that will be bona. Is it possible?'

BB is engrossed in reading letters. He looks up, shakes his nut.

'Not a good idea, sweetie. They'll know about me being here and might come down looking for you. You seem to be a hot number, darling. What's the score with Frantic?'

'No idea. Got to be after something but fucked if I know what. She gave me two quid when I came out.'

'Now that's sinister. I expect she knows about the Tiger thing and hopes to get it out of you too. All too ghastly to contemplate, sweetie.' He shudders with great finesse.

'Isn't it though, we going to the pub are we?'

BB looks wary. 'Just go somewhere local, eh? I don't want you to be seen, sweetie. I think it all sounds hideously dangerous. Just because you're paranoid doesn't mean they aren't after you!' He laughs but it's a hollow one. I don't tell him how keen Sid was to have his address, there's no point in alarming him. We go for a pint and talk about other things, gossip for the most part. I'd forgotten how much I enjoyed being with BB.

Now, I take over the role of housewife while the boys go off to work. Mornings, we spend together talking and it's like the old days before Vic got nicked. I am supposed to stay in the house all the time, according to BB. Nobody must see me, but after a week I begin to explore, second hand bookshops are my new vice, and the Lanes. I wear a headscarf and a big coat, my regular clobber now. Fortunately BB's clothes fit me, but I can spend hours mourning the loss of my clothes, and I do. Any money I have, I hang on to for emergencies. The boys are great but I hate not being able to spend money. When I bring it up with BB he tells me not to worry, as I don't get out I don't need money.

'How long do I have to stay in fucking purdah then, BB?'

'Until all this Tiger stuff blows over, I suppose. Nobody has come looking for us as far as I know.'

'How will we know? I mean, is it a five year sentence or what? You can't afford to keep me indefinitely can you? Couldn't I get a little job?'

'Sacrilege, sweetie! Never thought I'd hear those words emitting. Hey, Angelo, Shindig wants to work.'

'Cheque books be OK, yes?'

'No, she means real work. Chambermaid or something.'

'Oh yes! With uniform, bona!' says Angelo.

'I could,' I say. They both crease up and I take offence.

'I haven't even seen the café yet. And you wanted me to invest in it.'

'Listen sweetie, this is temporary. You'll be back on form soon and have money, pay us back. Help us all out, I have confidence in your talents. Can't keep a good palone down, eh?' I wish I had his confidence. For me, it feels as if this is it, my life, for ever. I chafe.

'How come Angelo can work? They were looking for him too?'

'I'm sure you're the one they've got their eyes on. They believe you have a key to something with Tiger. Are you sure you don't, sweetie? Think. No, don't think, then it might come to you.'

'I wish I knew what I was trying to remember, BB, how will I recognise it?'

I'm getting bored and long for Soho and a bit of action. I wander down to the beach, empty because it's cold and windy. Stand still; look at the sea shifting itself in chunks that look near solid. I stand until the water comes close to my feet then I step back. I'm down to my last fiver and reckon it's now or never. I look at the number for Colette again. I've been looking at it for days, this time I decide I'll ring it. What have I got to lose?

I gather my change together and go into a pub just off the front. Have a pint, first one since my first night here. The geezer behind the bar comes on with the usual patter and I respond with the usual answers. We establish that he's never seen me before because I've never been in here before and work from there out. It's agreeable just sitting at the bar gently shooting the breeze. I think about the Roebuck and wonder about Rooster, and Frantic. I think about trying to get her

auntie's number and belling her but knock the idea back. My
second pint slips down well and I ask where the phone is.
Outside in the hallway. I put the paper with the number on it
against the wall, get a mass of change and get the operator to
get the number. International exchange fires my imagination;
I get the operator and tell her the number.

'Just a moment, madam.' And then I go through at least
three operators each one sounding more foreign than the last.
The final one tells me she will ring me back when she has a
connection and is gone before I can ask how long that will
take. I move from leg to leg in the gravy-brown pub hallway.
I visualise myself in Casablana doing a Humphrey Bogart, so
into the idea that I speak out of the side of my mouth when
the operator gets back to me, tells me to put in the money. Her
voice sounds close.

'Hello.'

'Hello, Colette, that you?'

'Aye.'

'It's Shindig.'

'Oh, right, how ya doing hen? You coming out here then,
are you? Diego's doing great, he heard from Berry in the States,
he got out of the service. Why don't you come and stay? It
will . . .' Then all the words crumble into bits and I can't make
out anything she's saying. The operator comes back into my
ear with apologies. And advice to try later. But Colette's there,
out there in the world. Part of me doesn't believe in abroad
and now I feel like an international traveller by proxy.

'You look pleased with yourself,' says the barman.

'Just spoke to somebody in Morocco, didn't I?'

'Hope you paid for the call,' he jokes, one of those not quite
a jokes. Grins at me. Pulls me another pint. I look at the clock.

'On the house, Jane. To welcome you.' I always go back to
Jane. Saves confusion.

'Is it half two or three closing?'

'Half past two, darling. Down from the smoke are you,
Jane? Yeah never understand closing times, but don't worry, I
always have friends who stay on. Take their time to finish their
drinks.'

'Thanks, but I've got an appointment.' I can't wait to be
gone now.

I feel lifted by hope and excitement into a realm of anything is possible. I want to relish this feeling, hug it tight. I also want to tell BB. He has strictly forbidden me to go to the café, but I know where it is. The few pints have helped my resolve and I say affectionate farewells to the guy at the pub. Promise I'll be back, but I know I won't. I am also sure that BB will be glad to see me, after all, I'll be on my way soon so what does it matter? It's been over two weeks and nobody's come looking for me so it must be safe. I step out into the grey rain and think of the colours of Morocco, what a gas? Gauguin colours, browns and golds, oranges and yellows. The rain feels good on my face and I laugh out loud. Salt is high in my nose, I lick my lips and grin.

The café is dark enough inside so the people are hard to make out. It is very orange with nice gleams of brightness shining out. The coffee machine reflects the light above the counter and I can see BB being camp, lit as if he's on a stage. I stand at the door before I make my entrance. An old guy sits close to BB, I recognise the type from his back, as sharp as a fast ferret, sleek as a wet toad. When he turns to light his fag I see Ted, his baggy old face lit from above then below from a match. He is in animated conversation with BB. Lifts BB's two hands with his own to take a light, his face bends to the light. As I watch they both laugh together. Danger buzzes in my brain and drives it away from sanity into fear. The rain gets to me now; it runs in my eyes and down my neck.

That afternoon time does a fair imitation of eternity. I fret and fidget in my mind while I sit frozen into terror. I realise I have nowhere to go. I don't have the bread to get to Morocco. What was I thinking about? Morocco? How the fuck would I get there? Simple answers come at me and I reject them all. Part of me says: 'Wait and see what BB has to say.' But that part is outvoted by the paranoia that rips in full flood and washes all sense, common or rare, into the gully of panic. Even while I indulge in this, small outcrops of logic stick their heads up. I shoot them down.

Good thing Tiger got me a passport when he was trying to tempt me to Le Mans.

'Always come in handy, gel, never know when you might have to do a runner.' And he'd revealed the ochre teeth and the tache had turned up at the ends and he looked the nearest he ever got to attractive. As I remember him I have a sort of itch in my mind, like something trying to get in, or out. I scratch it with a part of my brain and it goes running off screaming and I am back in the flat scared into rigidity again. But there is something there; this is the first time I know it. I get the passport ready anyway and pack odds and sods in the suitcase. Fret from thought to thought. Wish I had some dope. Empty the case again. And wait. Is BB involved with Ted? Who sent Ted? Is it coincidence that he's in Brighton? No. He must be looking for me. How did he find BB? All kinds of pointless questions that have no answers rush into and vacate my mind so that it feels as if it's had an enema and is laying on its back exhausted when I hear the key in the door. I turn and see BB's face and feel relief first. He looks frantic with worry, so least he hasn't sold me out.

'Sweetie! Oh there you are, thank God you're safe.' He comes and squashes me close. He leans away and looks me in the face.

'Sit down now. Have a ciggy. Stay calm, sweetie.' He pats me gently, lights us both up, and puts his hands on my shoulders looks me straight in the eye.

'Ted the Ferret showed this afternoon in the café. Let on it was all casual like, was down here on business, just happened along. But he asked me about you. Had we seen you. Poor Angelo hid in the kitchen when he came in, but he seemed to know we were together.'

'What did he say?'

'That you'd gone missing, he had some bread for you, if I saw you I must tell you. Is that possible?'

'What, that he's got bread for me? No, all cash up front with that mob isn't it? Cash up front and knives in the back, mate.'

'Who sent him? That's what I wonder.' He gets a bottle of gin out of the wardrobe, pours us a slug each.

'Big Sid, he came to visit me in the nick and he tried to get me to tell him where you lived.'

'You didn't tell me that.'

'I know. I didn't want to worry you. What does he want with you, BB?'

'Sid? He's been besotted with me since the first time he saw me with you in the club, or so he says. Mind you I don't think that would stop him from maiming me in the interests of business or if I got in his way.'

Sid in love is a bizarre idea, my mind scrabbles with the thought and puts it away for later consideration.

'You're going to have to go, you know.' BB looks thoroughly miserable as he says it.

'Do you think Ted knows where you live?'

'No, why should he? He reckons he came to Brighton and just dropped in, but that's pure bollocks isn't it? And I'm pretty sure that if he could find the café, it's not going to be beyond him to find our lattie.'

'Did he expect you to believe that?' I say. BB shrugs.

'Didn't argue the toss did I? No, sweetie. You'll have to go, but where? I don't think London's on, do you?' He looks at me.

'I came to the café today Billy. I just looked in. I saw Ted. I was about to come in, and I saw him.'

His face tightens up, as if he's going to get mad, then changes his mind mid stream.

'Thank Christ you didn't just bowl in. I'm surprised you haven't been before, knowing you. We've both been expecting you for days, sweetie. Had no idea you had all that self control. What brought that on today then?'

'I contacted Colette. In Morocco. Went to a pub and phoned her. They got back to me in five minutes and I spoke to her. She said go and join her. Diego's heard from Berry. I was so excited I had to tell you.' All the excitement has gone now.

'You must go, sweetie, immediately. You've got a passport haven't you? Then go and get a ferry as soon as Angelo gets off, he can take you in the van. How much money have you got? I'll lend you as much as I can. You can speak French, can't you?' I am terrified at the thought of going, I drink my gin, fast.

'Okay, BB, just give me a little time to get my head round this, eh?'

'Sorry, Shindig. Take your time but I do think you need to be off soon.'

We both sit facing each other, not stirring an iota. How could I have thought he was in cahoots with Ted? He takes my hands in his, looks into my eyes. I want to weep.

'I'm so scared for you, sweetie. My fave palone off to North Africa all on her own.'

'Come with me, Billy. I don't think I can do it on my own. I'm scared.'

'Trouble is, I think I'm more scared of what will happen to you if you stay here. These bastards are serious, girl.'

He lifts his gin to his mouth, drinks. Shakes his head.

'I can't come with you, Shindig. I haven't even got a passport and Angelo and me want to make a go of this café business. The owner is leaving it all to us now, all the decisions about the décor . . .' He shrugs an elegant movement then reaches for me and we both weep into each other's necks, but not for long.

'What do you reckon to the café then?' He is back on form.

'I like it, Billy. I have a couple of style suggestions, naturally.' And we both hiccup laughs and tears, all mixed up damply.

'Hey, girl! You didn't think I was selling you out when you saw Ted with me did you?'

His face is a waterlogged mess and he looks terribly young and vulnerable. Somehow the fact of his missing teeth makes him younger.

'Not for a moment, Billy,' I lie.

'Because I'd trust you with my life, sweetie.'

I hope I'm up to it.

38 All By Myself

The ferry is half empty and I take on a refugee rôle. I've been watching war films since I was a kid. I skulk on deck and watch the sea as it moves under us. I imagine I'm on the run from the Nazis.

The boys said their goodbyes and we all got tearful again. I waved to them weepily, I have no idea when I'll see them again. There was much talk about coming for holidays once I'm settled but I feel that's a bit previous, given the fact that I don't even know how I'm getting there. Angelo has given me a rosary and a few quid. BB has contributed a new watch and a bag of toiletries including half a gross of condoms, I fear for the customs search. I also have a long list of addresses that seems to cover every omiepalone in North Africa.

'When we get some money we'll send it to you.'

'No, my darling Sheendeeg, we bring it to you in Tangier in the sun with all the warm boys,' says Angelo. They are holding hands on the quay and look at each other and laugh. I feel lonely as fuck.

'Yeah, get a bar in Tangier, eh?'

Dream on baby, says the part of my brain that thinks of itself as sensible. I look at the list of addresses that BB gave me. Then Tiger's voice joins in: 'Just wave yer legs about, gel, you'll be laughing. Don't let the bastards grind you down mate,' seems to involve a lot of laughing in there and now I want to weep. I'm scared. People understand my schoolgirl French but I don't understand a bleeding word they say. And I'm not even in France yet. I've never been in this much lumber before, I ponder as the water gallops under me.

My affinity with the sea deserts me about half way across the channel. And it's while I'm settled over a bog, spewing up my ring that it comes to me. The itch that's been trying to get through my mind, clinks into place. I dropped my keys in the last frantic rush to the bog and as they hit the metal deck, I fell in; an affinity of the rings perhaps. When nine tenths of my gut is safely down the bog and the remaining tenth in crisis, my mind has space to function and I remember; I had a key of Tiger's. He'd bunged it to me on one of our final evenings together, when we'd gone to the boozer. He'd reached across, lifted my key ring from the table where I'd put it down to light a fag. I fiddle a lot with my key ring, it's not healthy.

'There you go, gel, don't tell nobody I never give you nothing.' Three negatives, does that make a positive? I thought. And he'd lifted my keys and bunged a small key on to the ring.

'That's worth money, gel. A lot of money.' And he'd looked ultra solemn with his bloodshot eyes. 'Hang on to it for us.' I'd opened my mouth to ask him about the key but he'd started to bustle just then so I drank up and we left.

But it isn't on the key ring now, I know because I had pruned a lot of the old keys when I was going to Brighton. I remember looking at it and putting it somewhere safe. Trouble with Tiger is you never know when to take him seriously, trouble with my safe places I can never remember them. The bucketing boat seems to have got in a rhythm that agrees with my own particular digestive system. I look at my green face and decide a bit of slap won't come amiss. I am pulling those strange faces that seem obligatory when I powder my nose. That's it. My loose powder. I never use it but schlep it around like a talisman because it's Chanel and the box is gorgeous. I open it and remove the filter thing on the top; it feels like water round my finger when I poke into the bottom of the box. I had shoved the key deep in the powder. I push into it and there it is. A left luggage locker key.

I go straight to the café when I get back to Brighton. BB looks over at me and dives out from behind the counter. His face is extreme worry incarnate.

'You're taking your chances aren't you, girl?' But he grabs me into a tight, sinewy hug and Angelo comes out from the back to kiss me hello. BB looks round the café nervously.

'What are you doing here, sweetie? Ted the Ferret was down

again, we spotted him peering in at us, and so they're all looking for you. Why aren't you in France?' He bustles me into the back of the café a bit like a hen shaping up to her chicks. His arms flurry round me until I sit on a stool.

'Hang on, BB, get out of my face for fuck's sake.' And then I burst into tears. He holds me gently but I can feel the tension of his body, actively waiting.

'How'd you get back anyway?'

'I let on I hadn't got a passport so they sent me back.' I hiccup and Angelo has a brandy in his hand. I guzzle it down.

'But why?' He sounds exasperated. Angelo pushes him out the way.

'She look ill, do leave her, Billy.' BB flounces off to serve somebody and I lighten up and relax. I realise my entire body is knotted around my empty gut.

'Soup, you need soup.' And over the soup and bread I begin to feel almost human again, I explain to BB and Angelo that I found the key and that I almost chucked it over the side.

BB holds out his hand and I give him the key. He peers at it.

'Waterloo,' he says. 'Waterloo left luggage.' He looks excited now. 'You must go and get it.' He says this with complete certainty and firmness. I gulp. I have no idea what is likely to be in the left luggage and I have no intention of going on my Jack. I feel my head shaking itself in negative motion of its own velocity. His entire person is concentrated now and he has a little frown between his eyes. He appears to have forgotten me.

'What is in there?' Angelo has come into the kitchen. 'Do you know what is there?'

'No, but it's got to be valuable.'

Then BB comes out of his trance and says: 'But we don't know do we? Not for sure. Do you think Ted and co know what they're looking for? '

'No, BB, I think it's hunt the thimble time. Okay. I'll go but I'm not going alone. You'll have to come with me. We could go up now.' Angelo is happy to look after the café and we decide to take the van.

I've never driven anything like the van, its hard work and illuminates all my limitations as a driver. So I give most of my attention to driving while BB gets thoroughly paranoid, vocally. He runs through all the people who are likely to grass us up if they spot us and it includes almost everybody we know.

'See, sweetie, we don't even know who it is that's after us, do we?' He puts his fag in my gob for me to draw on; this van needs at least three hands to drive it.

'Probably all the low life in London. But we don't know that, do we?'

'No we don't, but that day with Vera and Ted they were belling some geezer to come and sort me out.' We hit a particularly nasty bit of road with cars rushing at us and this thing has no speed. I can feel sweat on my forehead and I want to cry.

'Look, BB, I'm not up to driving this thing in London, we'll have to stop outside and get a tube in.'

'Oh, dear heart, I'm sorry and I've just been rabbiting on haven't I. What can I do?' He flaps his hands about as if he might lend me one to help me.

'Fuckall, BB, you can do sweet fuckall, this thing's got no poke and I'm scared we'll get marmalised by oncoming traffic.'

I've driven down to Brighton loads of times with Rooster but it's mostly been at about four in the morning in a decent motor. Now, people are getting frantic trying to get round us and we are stuck at twenty miles an hour on the flat bits. Down to under ten on hills.

'If we hit another hill like that big one we'll be fucked!' I say and I can feel my arms shaking and my shoulders rigid, locked up to my head as I try to keep the steering wheel steady. Then people start flashing us and I think it's venom until I realise that the left headlight is not working so we can't even see the verge. We stop and the engine boils away with the shock of the trip, and the carcass of the van trembles like some old greyhound on its last run. BB stands looking like a spare prick, moving from foot to foot.

'Aren't you going to turn it off?' He looks quizzical and nervous.

'Listen, sweetheart, if I turn this cunt off that will be it, finito. A dead motor!'

'Oops, sorry I asked.' He turns away in a flamboyant gesture just as the police motorbike draws up.

'Got a problem, sir?' says this young copper. But he doesn't turn his engine off. BB looks as butch as possible.

'My wife got tired so we thought we'd stop for a moment, officer.' He puts his hand on my shoulder.

'Good idea. Did you know that one of your headlamps is not working?'

'No, officer, we didn't, did we, darling?' And he turns to me. I give a winsome smile and approach him.

'No,' I coo and look him in the eye. 'What do you suggest we do, officer?' Letting the air out of my lungs in breathless desire, I put my hand on his handlebar. I lean forward in my best vamp style while BB brings up the rear in supportive hubby fashion. The cop reddens a bit but his eyes are slithering down over me.

'Well, my advice is to get up to Banstead and see if you can't find somebody to look at those lights.' His eyes are on my tits as he says this. He lets the bike into gear.

'Don't suppose you're in the AA, are you? No,' and he puts his foot on the throttle. 'Take care sir, madam.' And he's away. My legs are soft rubber and I don't think I can drive any more.

'Christ,' says BB. 'I was so scared I nearly had a bowel movement. Nice arse though!' He leans against the motor. 'Get it in to the side and dump it,' he says.

'Where did you get it?'

'One of Angelo's friends flogged it to us for a fiver.'

'So it's probably nicked and I've got no licence or insurance, Jesus, BB. Let's get shot of the bleeder before that copper changes his mind.' I let in the clutch and it rolls to the side, I put my foot down and it mounts the grass verge.

'Bye-bye, little van,' says BB. 'That's any chance of getting back tonight fucked.' He laughs and I join in but it goes dangerously hysterical so I stop.

I stand at the side of the road and put my thumb out. BB stands back in the darkness not quite out of sight. The third motor stops. A jolly, half drunk commercial traveller is delighted to have our company and regales us with tales of great feats of salesmanship, his line is carpets and the car smells pleasantly of woollen samples. His hand strays towards my leg as he drives and he grins when he makes contact. I wait a second or two then withdraw to the corner. While he explains to us the merits of the Axminster over the Wilton, BB manages to get his thieving mitts on a nice leather briefcase. When we say goodbye in Balham I entrance the geezer with my lallies, make a huge show of pulling my skirt down while I tug it up to my arse as BB snaffles the briefcase.

'What's that for then, the loot?'

'It's leather, sweetie, get a couple of quid for this at Uncle's.' He hefts it and admires the leather surface as we go into yet more comprehensive speculation about what's in the locker. We sit on top of the bus at the front and view the evening from above while we have a look in the briefcase. 'Razor is the only thing any use to us,' he says.

'Yeah, we can cut our throats if we get caught,' I say. He rustles papers about.

'We'll dump these in a bin, eh?' He looks over at me, waves the briefcase and giggles. 'Ought to have a bag with swag written on it, didn't we?'

We light up and our state of exaggerated paranoia transmits into hysteria. People on the bus laugh along with us and it's all very merry for a few minutes. BB stops laughing first and then I wind down to a halt and we look seriously at each other. We grab each other's hands.

'Ain't love grand,' says one old girl to another, which starts us off giggling again.

'Have you ever got it wrong, missis,' I murmur. But BB gives me a peck on my cheek to please them and they smile indulgently. The heterosexual world are such optimists.

'So, who is likely to grass us up if they see us?' I say. Wish I hadn't asked really. As we approach Waterloo we are into our second score of likely informants and that's just the ones we know the names of. We reckon it's got to be jewels or passports, or money. BB suggests drugs but I don't think Tiger wouldn't involve himself in drugs. As Johnny Mason had said, Tiger is one of the old school, not agin a bit of violence and robbery but pimping or drugs would be anathema to him.

We walk the last few hundred yards into the station in a whirl of excitement and terror. I want BB to go alone to the locker in case it's a trap. I share the idea with BB but he's not keen.

'Be better if you go, girls are less suspicious looking. Anyway they get less time if they get caught.'

'No they don't, they penalise girls for going against the so-called norm,' I say.

'And what would you know about norms?' says he and we are so busy squabbling that we are there now anyway and BB goes up to the locker dead casual like, while I hover in what I imagine is wifely concern behind him but close enough to see into the locker. It looks empty at first, then we see on the floor bits of what looks like old lino. We snaffle them into the briefcase and scuttle off to the pub under the arches. BB speaks from the side of his mouth and our fast ferret speed must look well suspicious.

'Painting,' I breathe. He nods.

'More than one, sweetie, two. Did I lock it up again, the locker?'

'Yes,' I say. 'Why?' He shrugs and we bustle into the pub under the arches and go right to the back. He shoves the case at me and I sit down while he goes to the bar. I peer inside and put my hand in slyly. I slither off to the bog with the case in hand. I sit down on the closed seat and take out two tiny paintings. They don't look much, just ancient. A name in the corner of one is Van something so I am convinced they are Dutch masters. Back in the bar I see BB, drinks in hand looking round frantic and pale. I hiss at him softly and his face clears, relief soaks from the inside out. I laugh.

'You thought I'd done a runner didn't you, BB?'

'I didn't believe it, sweetie, but the thought slid across my mind there for a moment, whisked away by reason of course.'

'Of course!' We both laugh and sit so close together I can feel warmth from his leg.

'They're Dutch miniatures, BB. Old masters. Must be or why would they have been nicked?' He grins and takes the case to the men's bog. I gull my Guinness fast, look round and notice some geezer clocking me. He looks up and away as soon as I look at him but it's enough for me. When BB comes back I say we must move. He is looking very clever with himself practically hugging himself with delight.

'Listen BB, we better get out of here, it's a place they all use and that geezer was clocking me.'

'Yes, sweetie, as fast as possible I would have thought.' He whacks his drink down him and we make for the door at speed. Outside, we take a breather as we walk down the hill.

Like all main line stations, Waterloo is a congregation point for hustlers of all kinds, the pickings are rich with full pockets, lovely luggage to reassign, kids on the run ready for a bit of career redirection. So we don't want to hang about too long. We walk towards the river and find a seat. We light up and BB chucks the empty fag packet away.

'Last two fags, sweetie, have to get some or we'll have brain failure.'

'What do you reckon they are then, BB?'

He shrugs, laughs; 'Old. They are very old and I think you're right, they are Dutch. But they must be worth a bomb.' Obviously he has no more idea about them than I do, which I find both reassuring and alarming at the same time. He grabs my hand and we do a jubilation job of squeaks and giggles.

'We're rich, BB, or we will be. Think of the gear we can buy? Shoes, cashmere coats gorgeous luggage. Books!'

'I can get the café for me and Angelo.'

'Or we can all go to Tangier, BB. Colette loves it and she was a right no-hoper and I might see Berry again.' We laugh.

'Import him, sweetie, and we could get a bona club with drag acts. And we could employ the foul Carlotta and really pull rank on her, tell her what to wear and put her really low down on the bill.' We chortle together and fly high on fantastic schemes. The need for another fag jettisons us back into reality.

'We need somewhere to stay for the night.' I state the obvious. 'Or, you could go up west and see if you can find a contact.' I break off as I think that I am not about to let the paintings far away from my hot little hands.

'See, they're not looking for you, BB, only me.'

'Far as we know, sweetie, but I don't think I'm about to trot round the West End trying the idea out for size, thank you!' He has been hugging the case and now he puts it down as we do a money check. We root around his pockets and my bag and have enough to get a bed and breakfast for the night while we think. We go back towards the station to find a fleapit.

'Perhaps they'll let us in without paying as we got luggage. Then we can do a runner. And tomorrow I'm sure we can come up with brilliant wheezes.'

'Don't think one briefcase will convince them do you?'

'We could say we're travelling light.'

39 Don't Trust Nobody Blues

The voice, when it comes, pinions me into terror, galvanises my bowels into uproar and my bladder into instant fierce action.

'Shindig! Hey darling! What's a matter, gel, you got cloth ears?' Gerry has her head stuck out of a car window. She stops. 'Want a lift, gel? Hi, BB, how you doing mate? Taken up rent collecting have you? No wonder you haven't shown yer face.'

BB still has a white knuckle grip on the briefcase while Gerry hoots at her joke. He lifts it up and looks at it, tries a smile; 'I'm trying to flog it, aren't I?' The smile doesn't really come off.

'Got a fag, Gerry?' I say. She bungs us one each takes a draw, leans back to look at us. 'So what you two doing down here? You're West End types. I've got to pick the bird up in an hour, just dropped one of me mates off at the station, want to go for a pint?' We both hesitate then I say no and BB says why not.

'We're boracic, Gerry,' I say. She laughs.

'Don't worry about that, mate, I'm loaded. Want to go to the Tavern?'

'No thanks, I don't want to see any of that mob,' I say.

'Oh! Right, say no more.' And Gerry puts her finger beside her nose. 'Keep it dark, eh?' I grin.

'Right, I'll park here.' And she gets out smartly, locks the car and we walk to the nearest pub. She goes to the bar and BB and me go into a huddle. One of the only disadvantages of knocking about with poofs is that you can't do the swift conversations in the ladies' bog that are so essential for strategy decisions. So we turn to each other.

'She's okay isn't she, Shindig?'

'Good as gold,' I say.

'Ask her not to tell anybody she's seen us?'

Gerry comes back to ask us what we want.

'Ordered you a pint of the black stuff, what do you want, BB?'

'Can I have a gin and tonic, please?'

'Course you can my flower, fuck the expense!' And both of them laugh.

We sit at a table.

'Frannie's well worried about you, gel,' says Gerry, and I feel BB stiffen beside me. We have all lit up and now BB goes to get some fags. Gerry turns to me.

'You all right, mate? I heard some dodgy geezers were seeking you out like. That right, is it?' My face must have undergone a bit of a twist, terror or something showing through. She puts her arm round me, gives me a squeeze and I can feel tears welling up and confession imminent.

'Don't worry, mate, I won't tell nobody I seen you. What's the score with BB?'

'Will you tell her or will I?' says BB who has arrived to hear the last few words.

'You do it, BB, but before he starts, Gerry, whatever you do, don't tell Frantic.'

She looks at me and BB, spits on her hand and shakes both our hands.

'Promise,' she says.

'Hope you haven't flogged us some old nag, Gerry,' BB quips.

'No mate, I'd never sell her, might trade her in but I'd never flog her.'

I listen to BB's amended version of our position in which he leaves out everything but the fact that we've got paintings to flog and we're skint. A work of artistic narrative. I squeeze his leg to congratulate him.

Gerry looks at us both seriously.

'I think you need a professional,' she states.

'Quite,' says BB, 'but a professional what? I mean it's not like unloading a few thousand smokes or getting shot of gold bars, is it?'

'No, and that's why you need a professional to value them for you. What were you thinking of doing? Going up Bond Street and asking if anybody wants a dodgy couple of paintings?'

I had been thinking along those lines and now I feel a right mug.

'First place you go, darling, they'll be on the blower saying a bird and a poof are trying to flog something of incredible value – always supposing that what you got is, in fact, valuable.' BB looks quite cast down now, we both pride ourselves on what clever bastards we are but we hadn't thought this one through at all.

'You got to find out what you got before you can flog it.' We both sit like the wise monkeys, not a dickey emits from either of us.

'Do that sum it up or do that sum it up?' We both nod solemnly. 'So, who do you know?'

I think Celeste, but we really want somebody who has no connection with us.

'Who did it belong to, before it belonged to you like?' We look at each other, I give a tiny head shake.

'Look, darling, I don't want to know no more than necessary. But I know a guy in the East End, a nice old Yiddish geezer, knows about pictures and antiques. Look, I'll go and give him a bell now, I could shoot down there and see him. Let him have a look at what you got like. Okay?'

I feel myself nod and so does BB but we have both starched up into rigid terror at the thought of letting the paintings out of our sight.

'She's a bit eager isn't she, sweetie?' says BB when Gerry has gone to the phone. I shrug.

'We need somebody who knows what they're on about, don't we?' I say. 'But we'll have to go with her.'

'Definitely,' says BB and then it occurs to me that Gerry might be selling us out on the blower.

Then we realise that the briefcase has gone. BB reaches for it and it is gone!

I feel my entire face fall, literally, the skin and bones and all the internal bits of my ecaf do a southward shift. I feel my tongue retreating down my throat, which in turn seems to sink towards my gut. I look at BB and open the gob but no sound emits, I produce a couple of gasping noiseless gapes. BB is looking under seats in that futile panic that overcomes you at these times, his movements getting faster and faster, more and more jagged so that people are getting the dead needle with him.

Gerry comes back from the blower and stands looking at him.

'He's only fucking lost the bleeding briefcase, hasn't he?' and my voice comes out dead loud so that people glare at us intently.

'I lost it? I like that!' and BB's voice is a hoot of outrage so the pub governor comes over with his 'Is there something wrong, sir, madam?' eyeballing the three of us in a sarky manner. Like he wouldn't know what to call us.

Gerry looks at me and I say, 'No, we lost a case but it didn't have anything in it. If it turns up, let us know, eh?'

'You sure, madam?' he says and we all nod, fiercely, so that he is convinced that we are all up to no good.

'Sure you don't want me to call the police, sir?' Looking at Gerry. He gives a dreadful knowing look at us all. We shift ourselves, fast.

Outside, BB asks Gerry if she's arranged a meet with the guy in the East End.

'Yes, course I have, bit bleeding pointless now though, isn't it?'

Then BB has his finest hour though it only takes a few seconds. 'Well, sweetie, you don't think I'd be stupid enough to leave them in the bloody briefcase for somebody to nick, do you?' Looking significantly at me, he taps his chest, pulls apart his jacket and the two oblong shapes are clearly visible under his shirt.

'You clever little cunt!' I throw myself at him and deliver a smacker on his face somewhere, but he moves too quickly for any accuracy.

'What about the bird?' I ask as we drive through the city.

Gerry shrugs. 'She won't mind, she's used to my comings and goings isn't she?'

I had to fight BB for the front seat and now he sits in the back in full preen. We have decided that BB should go in with Gerry to see the man. We are both terrified to let Gerry out of our sight and I'm none too pleased to see the two of them scuttling into the greasy night. It takes three fags lit one from the other before they come back with the news that our pictures are genuine. Genuine what is not certain; but even the generic Dutch miniature of this age is going to be valuable. The geezer has told BB that he can organise a buyer for us. He was appalled to see the pictures naked with no protection and has now wrapped them in cloth for us and BB carries a paper carrier bag with 'Blooms Salt Beef' written on the side, which sets off hunger bells. I dowse them. The guy has given BB a tenner on the strength of the deal, and down to the fact that he knows Gerry. He is talking five grand.

We all flop into the motor exhausted.

We finish up staying near Gerry in Victoria in a sleazy dump that BB used when he was working. The companionable sound of girls going in and out all night is reassuring. We share a room and alternate between high excitement and blind panic. We talk all night until it's starting to get light, then sleep takes over. I dream about Arabs and sandstorms along with the usual chasing, this time by camels. We jerk into life again when the cleaner bangs on the door at ten to tell us we've just missed breakfast. We are going to meet Gerry at midday. As soon as we see her, things take on an alarming dynamic of their own.

The whole deal is done with a speed to make you gasp. By early afternoon, Gerry has the money and has relieved us of the paintings and a ton, which is all she will take. BB is convinced that we are being robbed and that the paintings are worth millions. I point out that if we'd been offered five hundred we would have taken it and this shuts him up. We book ourselves into a posh hotel in Kensington for the night. We spread the money on the bed and count it several times. It makes us gasp, the speed it all happens, the amount of the money. We agree that I will take three and BB will get two grand. I buy three pairs of shoes within the hour. We open bank accounts and are peeved to find that we don't get a cheque book the same day. They will send them to BB's address. We keep a few hundred back to get me to Tangier, go

to Harrods to buy luggage and finish up buying a load of gear
for us both and presents for Angelo.

Back at the hotel in Kensington I put on my new suit and
brandish my soft leather bag. I want to go to Soho, just once. I
look at BB, I don't need to voice my desire, he shakes his head,
'Too dangerous, sweetie.' But he's preening in a gorgeous velvet
jacket and we both look at each other. 'Just for a quickie?' I
say. He turns and looks over his shoulder into the mirror, 'You
look gorgeous, Billy, it's wasted on me.'

'Suppose somebody like the evil Ted sees us?'

'He never goes to the Harmony,' I say and now, with the
money and the new gear it is hard to take the threats seriously.
They reckon money can't buy you love but it can certainly buy
you a lot of confidence. BB shrugs and we leave our keys at the
desk, the porter gets us a taxi and I give him half a dollar which
BB says is far too much and we squabble about the amount a
tip should be, which, considering the times we've done runners
from all kinds of establishments, is a new experience for us and
it keeps us absorbed until we get to Old Compton Street.

It is warm and fragrant in the street and Soho is at her best,
rascals and renegades are legion in the early evening air,
anything could happen and I get that coming home feeling that
fills me with excitement and delicious dread. We go to a pub
first and we both drink faster than usual, then we hit the
Harmony. It is its lovely self with all kinds and types of
characters enjoying the scene. We look at each other and smile.
I lean over to squeeze BB's hand at the same time that I see Sid
with a small contingent of Tiger's mates eyeing us up and
sliding in our direction. I am so scared that I have none of the
usual bucketing gut terror syndrome, it's as if the terror goes
straight to my legs. BB has seen them as well and we both run
and don't stop until we get a taxi which we get to drop us at
Gloucester Road tube, far enough away from the hotel to fool
the cab driver. When we get back to the hotel we are in a cold
sweat in spite of the warmth. We get a Green Line coach back
to Brighton and Angelo.

We have another look through the old suitcase and BB takes charge of the insurance document. I think we should burn the case with all of Tiger's stuff in it, but BB wants to keep it. He reckons it will be some kind of guarantee. Personally, I think it's a liability and should be dumped forthwith. Angelo agrees with me and I hope he will burn the wretched thing after I go. I can't believe that Sid and co will just let it all go because I am gone, but BB says that the way Sid feels about him he is in no danger. I argue the toss about this and BB takes no notice of my warnings.

Then I get this feeling of release, it's nothing to do with me any more. This time I have got a ticket to Tangier from Thomas Cook. First thing in the morning I am away on the ferry from Dover.

When I say goodbye to BB and Angelo I almost pity them for being stuck in boring old Britain. I cling to them while they say goodbye but the frantic terror of the last time is gone. I have been reading up on Tangier and it sounds wonderful. I keep telling myself that I'll love it; even as Soho impinges on my mind and my dreams. I am assured there will be no Guinness for a start, and no bars to speak of, except one called Dean's bar. It all sounds very male, though I have lots of addresses of poofs and BB says they'll love me, I doubt it.

This time, going on to the ferry, with my new leather luggage and nice subtle, expensive gear, I feel in charge. I have the regulation fifty quid – or forty eight – that is all that can be taken out of the country at any one time. I also have two hundred concealed about my person. I am excited at the thought of travelling across France and Spain to Algeciras and on a ferry to Tangier. It makes me feel like a world traveller; a frightened world traveller but I could get used to this, I reckon. I reckon without the sea and my natural terror of the new.

40 A New Leaf Blues

From the ferry I catch my first glimpse of Tangier. It looks like all the shoeboxes in New Oxford Street have gathered themselves together in roughly perpendicular glory to greet me.

The first thing that hits me is the heat and the second is the lack of green. These two facts are knocked for six by the fact that there are three million people in my immediate vicinity and they are all rushing at me and I can't understand a dickey bird. My suitcase slithers in my sweaty hand and a gaggle of small boys surround me and try to take it from me. I bat them away, not sure if they are offering help or intent on skulduggery. Without language it's impossible to know and the first taxi I see, I leap inside. I tell the man the name of the bar and he speaks some curious English which joins with my curious French to baffle us both. We look at each other blankly; 'All right, Tommy,' he says and he drives off.

'White slavery!' A *News of the World* headline enters my mind but I don't care. I want a cool beer above all. The smell is fascinating, spicy, sexy. The scent of kif is everywhere, it seems to hang in the air along with drains and people. A good smell. I lean back in the seat while the driver jerks the gear lever and we stop outside a café. I give him a couple of quid in English change and he is delighted. I feel like some kind of colonial twat but I haven't got to grips with the duerra yet. He hands me out my case and says something about bints that I don't understand.

I am to meet a friend of BB's in the cafe. He is called Lavish and I expect an exotic omiepalone. Once I am in the cool I drink a pallid beer then some mint tea, and I wait. I have a fag and wait some more. Go through the scenario where I reckon I got the wrong place, wrong day, wrong country. I haven't got Colette's address but if the worst comes to the worst I can bell her. I don't altogether trust her and Diego with a load of bunce, anyway. Don't trust myself come to that, think I might panic and fritter it on a North African wardrobe plus gold. This geezer is supposed to be one hundred per cent but his time-keeping isn't up to much.

The black guy slides over to my table and asks me if I'm waiting for somebody. His voice is East Coast American and his suit is sharp. He smiles and sits beside me.

'You don't want to sit here all alone, girl, there are preda-tors everywhere in this town.' He snaps his fingers and orders arak and the waiter brings it with a thick glass jug of icy water. He pours water into the two glasses of liquor and as I put it to my lips and tongue the ice I hear a very familiar voice:

'See you brought yer own, gel. Like there aren't enough shwartzers here already?'

And there's Tiger in a white suit with a dodgy Panama hat and his usual grin moving his tache up his face and revealing the ochre choppers.

'So what you bin up to, my gel?'

I have never been more pleased to see another human being in my life. For a start, I am delighted he's alive. Then it occurs to me that I've got his bread stashed about my person.

'What you doing, gel? The world tour is it?' Viewing me critically. Shakes his nut.

'Friend of yourn?' He nods at the Yank, who I'd forgotten.

'No, mate, we only just met.' The guy eases away.

'So what brought you here then, gel? Right, Ali, get us a couple of bevvies over here, mate!' Lifts two fingers and the waiter nods.

'Does he understand English, Tiger?'

'Understands two drinks don't he?' Grins a piratical one at me and if he's surprised to see me it doesn't show. And I am overwhelmed with emotion and can feel a need to con-fess all just to make it up to him that I thought he was dead and I robbed his stash. My brain gets into gear and it tells me there is nothing to be gained by being skint and that BB is relying on me. One of my roles is advance party of one to find a gaff that is suitable for an emporium of some kind for us all.

Still, and perhaps because of all this hectic mind activity, I shout at him.

'I thought you was fucking dead, Tiger!' It belts out into the room, loud, like an accusation and along with it tears.

He winks, the rest of his face remains still and the open eye looks like it belongs to a basilisk. He grins again. 'Don't know why you thought that, mate. I'm fit as a flea. Suits me here it does.'

But it doesn't. As soon as he says it I can see he's a fish out of water here. Dislocated. But he is a lively fish, a jolly old mackerel in a white suit with no club, no bookies' runners, no shifty cohorts, and no West End to know like the back of his hand. But it's a fuck of a sight better than the death I had consigned him to.

The drinks come. Beers this time.

'You won't find no Guinness over here, darling,' he says and he sits down. 'So what brings you here?'

'I came to see Colette and Diego, didn't I?'

'I don't know, did you? You tell me,' he says with the reptile eye cold on me.

'Renee over here is she?' I ask.

'No mate, I think she's living in Chingford which is something she always lusted after. Only tried to get me topped, didn't she? Cunt.'

'She was always a first rate cunt, wasn't she?' I say and I feel the familiar unease that I always did feel around her. Like her nastiness reaches all the way out here. I shiver.

'Too right,' he says. 'Even when we got married she showed cuntish tendencies you know.' He shakes his nut and it feels like one of our ongoing conversations in the club and I relax.

'We went on honeymoon to Southend and she only cleaned the fucking bedroom out before she'd give me a bit. And it weren't worth the effort anyway.' He shudders and I almost imagine Tiger and Renee at it, but abort the thought as too nasty to contemplate. He leans over towards me and lights a Gauloise.

'Only thing that's better here, gel, the snout.' He hands me one lit and it feels fat and foreign and tastes exotic; yes, I'm going to like it here. Part of my mind is concerned about Lavish and where he is, another part is waiting for Tiger to accuse me of theft and yet another is concerned with the bread in my bras and knickers.

'And the weather,' continues Tiger. 'The weather here is brilliant. Yes, brilliant all the fucking time, I long for rain and fog and I haven't bin here five minutes.' He looks gloomy.

'Miss London do you?'

'Fucking right, gel. So what you bin up to then? Cause I heard you was in a bit of bother . . .'

No idea what he's heard. Doesn't occur to me to ask how he heard.

'I done six months, didn't I? Only I only did four and a bit, lost a few days' remission.'

'Naughty, gel. What was that for then, drugs?' He nods before I answer and I think about the fact that it's all down to him that I had to leave London and I still don't and probably won't ever, know why.

And it doesn't matter. But I can't leave it, can I?

We both draw on our fags and sip the pale beer

'Tiger, what were all those paintings about? Down in the cellar?' He looks like he's going to deny knowledge of them at first, then decides he might as well tell me.

'I was keeping them for somebody. You know me, wouldn't know a Vermeer from a vagina, me,' he says terse as fuck and his trap shuts tight.

'Word is that you owe a lot of money up west.'

'That right is it? Then it must be true, eh gel?'

He looks through me rather than at me, with a chilly glint that I've seen before in his eye, mostly when he was looking at Frantic. I realise that we are not going to be mates any more and that we might not have ever been mates and this realisation makes me sad, as much for my own lack of judgement as anything else and I think that Tiger is probably right. Contract over as they say. But I don't want to believe this.

'Ted started chasing me soon as I got out the nick, him and Vera, my landlady,' I say.

'No? That right is it?' His face is both blank and devious. 'So that why you come out here is it?'

'What are they after you for, Tiger?'

'Nosy little cunt aren't you?' He shrugs, takes a mouthful of beer, pulls a face. Shrugs.

'I owe a lot of money, gel, which wouldn't matter if old Jackie was still around, or Billy. But they got a new team in and my face don't fit no more. Plus fucking Renee put the bubble in, didn't she? Cunt.'

'Cunt!' I reiterate. With fervour.

'Like a lot of bleeding rats they was, couldn't get out fast enough most of them. So I pulled a bit of a stroke like.' He grins. 'Left with the money I got for the club, and it definitely wasn't mine, gel. Pension money.'

My brain creaks into gear. 'But Tiger, if you got all this bread for the paintings, can't you just pay it back?'

His cynical old eyes make me feel like a naïve twat again. 'Not that simple, is it? Lost a lot on the gee-gees. Anyway, I can't go back no more so it's all a bit fucking academic.' He's clearly forgotten he put the locker key my way, which is handy and I'm not going to tell him

There is still no sign of Lavish and the bar is almost empty now.

'What time are you supposed to see this geezer? You sure this is the right place, are you?'

'Central Café, isn't it?'

'No, mate.'

'That's what I told the taxi.'

Tiger shrugs his shoulders, they hunch up and I never noticed before how skinny he is and how bleeding ancient. His tan seems to make him look older and there's something shifty about him that I never saw before or never minded before, because really Tiger has always been shiftiness incarnate, but it used to be stylish, now it's not.

He walks me round the corner, leaves me at the door of a very different café. I clock what can only be Lavish as soon as I get to the door. He turns and spots me.

'You must be Billy's mate, Shindig?' He holds me at arm's length.

'Well, vada you, dolly, just what I expected, Billy described you to a tee. And who's your friend?'

I turn round to introduce Tiger but he's gone.

I only ever see Tiger on the horizon after this first time and as soon as he sees me he scuttles off in the opposite direction

Colette looks like a different bird. She has lost her gaunt junkie appearance, and has a fantastic tan, but it's more than that. Not only is she clean but she has acquired a kind of respectability in a dope dealer kind of way and refuses to talk about the old hustling days. She feels a cut above all that and, I suspect, a cut above me. Diego looks about the same but Colette is clearly in charge of that team. Their flat is near the Petit Socco and seems to be a stopping off point for every itinerant traveller from the States and Britain, so although they say they are happy to have me stay, I begin looking for my own gaff from day one. After I get my money banked, of course.

I am watched all the time in Tangier. Everywhere I go and whatever I do is followed with varying degrees of interest by a million eyes – at least. I find this disturbing and I long for the anonymity of London. I love to walk alone but here that is impossible. I find myself with a team of small boys in pursuit blagging fags, or undesirable men creeping up on me and any privacy is gone. I also long for Berry and BB. I haven't fixed up since Berry went and now I am smoking a lot of decent blow with Colette and various Yanks. She is of the opinion that I should shack up with one of these guys and I am sure she has offered me to them. I have no moral objection, it's a good idea. But I don't and Colette takes to calling me Miss Lovelorn. I get a flat over a shop in the Ville Nouveau and I hang out in the Hotel El Minzah in the afternoon so I can drink tea and talk to English people, and I even go to the Anglican church once or twice. I am in danger of becoming an ex pat.

I am obviously not living up to my potential as a free spirit. I am afraid I am a parochial type. I even seek out Tiger on several occasions in an unfocused way, trying to get into his psyche and looking in likely spots. I once catch sight of him at a fried fish stall but he clears off a bit sharpish. I haunt it for

days but I always have my entourage of followers so am at a
disadvantage, though the fish is delicious and the owner makes
me welcome. But I never catch up with Tiger. Then I hear from
Colette that he has moved on to South America or somewhere
but I have no evidence for this. In fact, I am sure she is lying
but he might as well be in Rio as far as I am concerned.

My twentieth birthday is coming up and it doesn't seem so old
now, I've no intention of dying until I'm thirty at least. Tangier
doesn't seem so bad. Besides, I met this old American queer in
a weird restaurant that does Sunday lunches, he's a writer and
he's so cool he's practically desiccated. He calls this the Inter-
zone. He's a weird geezer and he fascinates me. Only shot his
bleeding wife, didn't he and how's that for cool? We turn on
to mescaline, which kind of opens up parts of my mind that I
never knew were there and it becomes clear to me that I should
be writing, too. So I start writing this down.

No point rushing things though, is there?

I miss Soho more than anybody or anything and dream frequently of the Sunset club and Jack Isows, the hairdressers and,
and everything. Especially when it's dusk, I remember Soho
tarted up and ready for all comers with a grin on her eek and
a concealed weapon about her person. Of course, Tangier is a
woman too, but if she speaks to me it's in Arabic. As far as I'm
concerned they can keep their bleeding medina and the Kasbah.
Give me Berwick Street market any day.